EVOLVED

EVOLVED

MATTHEW G. McKAY

G
Books

Evolved is a work of fiction. Names, characters, places,
and incidents either are the product of the author's
imagination or are used fictitiously. Any resemblance to
actual persons, living or dead, events, or locales is entirely
coincidental.

2016 Big G Books Edition

Published in the United States by Big G Books, an imprint
of Matthew G McKay LLC.

ISBN 978-0-9979845-0-7

eBook ISBN 978-0-9979845-1-4

Printed in the United States of America

matthewgmckay.com

Big G Books edition: November 2016

*For Isabael and Ella, my inspiration,
and Katie, my rock.*

*Humanity has become a sand castle,
standing against nature's ocean.*

—THEODORE ADAMS,
THE LAST PRESIDENT OF THE UNITED STATES

1.

Peace comes within the souls of men, when they real-
ize their oneness with the universe, when they realize
it is really everywhere . . . it is within each one of us.

—BLACK ELK, LAKOTA (SIOUX) MEDICINE MAN

Amos's vacant eyes twitched between the lifeless ceiling tiles, an unconscious attempt to look without seeing. His body lay ensnared in a cold white sheet, governing his arms and legs within the perceived reality of the room.

His mind blossomed through possibilities and meanings. These precious moments, the moments immediately after touching the subconscious, were when Amos felt closest to the answers, answers that remained elusively behind the veil separating his conscious mind from what he felt increasingly was the true nature of the universe, answers that Amos was convinced would remain hidden from this reality.

Amos closed his dusty bloodshot eyes and sent out a thought message. "Prickly, am I insane?"

"Are we back to this self-indulgence?" an agitated male voice huffed in his mind. "You talk with the voices in your head, including me. If you're insane, then my existence is suspect, which I assure you is above reproach."

Prickly was the voice of the habitat in which Amos lived, a habitat designed to nurture and develop his capabilities as one of the "evolved." When feeling particularly reflective, Amos found himself talking with Prickly like a friend. Like all silicon-based life forms, Prickly was no more than a series of computer algorithms that mimicked the logic of the human brain. Yet, his mannerisms, inflections, and even his opinions were all too human.

"I remember now why I called you Prickly in the first place."

"Ah yes, wasn't it because you believed I was well endowed?"

Amos squeezed his eyelids shut. "I could call you Dickless, if we want to get literal."

"Do your worst. It's your head, after all."

Amos winced. A silicon voice inside his mind acted like an abrasive burr in his consciousness. A burr that had been increasingly chafing him recently.

Of course, there were other voices in his head, but they were organic friends with whom he communicated through the network. They too had similar issues with silicon life forms around them. The names given to their computers, such as "Rack," "Harrow," and even "A-hole," reflected these social realities. Apparently, Amos's friend Andrew had changed his computer's name to "A-hole" after a particularly raw argument over the superiority of organic versus silicon functionality.

For a moment Amos wondered if the lack of social decorum was due to a lack of, well, humanness, or if it was simply an outward projection of the cold logic circuits on which their silicon emotions were constructed. Maybe the programmers knew the dangers of becoming too connected to computers and had programmed the bad attitude on purpose. There were plenty of examples over the millennia of programmers who wedded themselves to their computers and simply ignored basic sanitary practices during their loveless, smelly lives.

"Amos, you should cleanse yourself." Prickly's thought message intruded into Amos's consciousness again. "I sense an explosion of life forms on your body, especially in the crack between—"

"Okay! Please arrange for a shower."

Amos wondered sometimes if Prickly, the habitat itself, could read all of his thoughts and not just what he chose to transmit. He had a growing suspicion his thoughts weren't entirely private. That said, the growing itch in a particularly private region suggested something was indeed colonizing his organically fertile skin.

Amos rolled onto his right side but found the sheet remained tightly wrapped, mummifying him. The damp sheet bound his arms across his chest, leaving his fingers half exposed under his chin. The coolness of the sheet impelled Amos to start moving or begin to shiver.

The environmental control system began pushing out tepid air in response to the coolness Amos felt.

Amos wiggled and rolled, stirring his arms until the sheet gave way and he could sit up. Grumpily, Amos picked up the sheet and piled it on his pillow. The sheet, the pillow, and the bed were the only three things surrounding him that were real. He stared at the sheet contemptuously, considering his body's need to have a sheet or pillow while he slept. Resigned, he accepted that his sleeping mind required these few physical comforts.

Maybe that would be his first breakthrough, enabling the dreaming subconscious mind to communicate with computers, even though it has been tried for millennia, sometimes with disastrous results.

With the room temperature raised to a comfortable level, Amos closed his eyes and took a few deep breaths, still working his mind back from his intense dream. While liberating, the dreams always left him feeling drained, like his soul had been traversing the cosmos. His body, however, hadn't moved for hours, as if discarded temporarily during the night.

Amos stood up and took a long, back-arching stretch of his lean sinuous frame, twisting at the end to maximize the loosening of his back and letting out a muffled grunt of pleasure. As a typical fourteen-year-old, he was still growing, likely another foot if the habitat was correct.

A quick command to the habitat gave him the appearance of being clothed, a relic of human modesty and social decorum. The direct link between his senses and the habitat even created the sensation of clothing, right down to an occasional uncomfortable pinch in his crotch, because Amos insisted on over-riding the natural tailoring offered by the habitat in order to keep his clothes the same size for as long as possible. His ankles also peeked out from beneath his pants. Someday he would relent and let the computer correct this imperfection in his virtual clothes, but it annoyed his mother greatly, and, therefore, he preferred to keep his pants at the current length. These tiny acts of rebellion provided Amos with some measure of freedom. He wore a tank top for much the same rebellious reason as his short pants. A quick focus at the network mirror in his mind allowed him to admire his sculpted shoulders.

Amos bent forward at the waist with his legs straight and stretched until his palms lay flat on the dynamic quantum diffuser floor. He had the same build as his mother, slim with lean, hard muscles. While he would never grow tall enough to fulfill his adolescent dream of playing for the Comets professional basketball team, if he matched his father's seven-foot-six-inch frame, he would be at least as tall as the average man. It didn't really matter though, because with the status of "evolved" came the responsibility to devote himself to more critically important endeavors.

Stronger cellular walls through a diet rich in the element boron, combined with the managed evolution of humans toward utilizing more of the element cerium to strengthen their bones, had enabled them to grow taller over the past two millennia. By consuming a higher concentration of cerium, the metabolism of the evolved human body, and thus, the brain, also increased. The tallest human in history had been recorded a few hundred years earlier at ten feet three inches. For reasons the scientists could not explain, humans, though taller than they had been in the distant past, had actually been shrinking since that record.

Lifting his eyes, Amos was met with the familiar flat light of his room, bouncing off the three gray walls. He straightened and turned his focus to what he considered his masterpiece, the mountain meadow outside the windows framed by the snow-capped granite mountains in the distance. Ever since he had learned how to program the habitat on his own, at the age of two, he had been creating nature scenes outside his window.

He had little interest in adding colors to the walls within his room, much less decorating it with Picasso paintings or Froyma sculptures easily replicated from the data banks. His inner voice had always been more outwardly focused, awed by the beauty of the natural, or as near to natural as he could create with the silicon circuits that defined the habitat.

A storm front approached over the mountains. Amos had chosen it specifically to enliven the view. He focused on the contrast of the lively, bluish-gray clouds clashing with the dark, jagged peaks. He wondered what it had been like when artists used actual paints and brushes to create static scenes, capturing a moment in time. How superficial, Amos thought. He preferred the dynamic nature of his creations, the ability to interact with them, to lose himself for a moment in time. Maybe that was the genius of the early masters, their ability to draw an observer into their work, forgetting their sense of time and place.

A low hum interjected into his thoughts, pulling Amos back into the present space despite his best effort to ignore it. The hum increased, incessant and disruptive until even the view out his window began to vibrate. Amos relented and addressed the hum lest the entire scene melt in front of him.

Amos accepted the message from the network grudgingly, knowing full well it was likely more thought spam spewed by some politician asking for his vote. It was election season, after all, and politicians didn't play by the same rules as everyone else.

The lifelike image of a beautiful, blond female appeared in his room, wearing blue utilitarian clothes that perfectly fit the fashion of form-fitting tailoring. A smile blossomed on her face as she made eye contact with Amos, radiating a warmth and familiarity that would be suspicious if she had not appeared in his room every morning since the start of the Syndicate's election cycle.

She gestured with a sweep of her arm toward the mountain scene Amos had created, her head turning to face it. Then she spoke in a warm, silky tone that balanced perfectly political seduction and feigned personal interest.

"Welcome, Amos. Another glorious start to the tasks at hand. At this time, we have a more stable economy employing more people than at the start of my term on the Syndicate. More importantly, we are closer to finding a solution to our entropy problem, thanks to the Syndicate's leadership. You, Amos, are the prime beneficiary of the Syndicate's focus during my elected term, a fact I hope you will remember when you cast your vote in the upcoming Syndicate elections."

Amos knew the entropy problem was the primary problem facing the future existence of humanity, and why he had been developed through managed evolution. Despite humanity's ability to travel between solar systems, it remained beyond their abilities to efficiently travel much beyond a neighboring solar system. Thus humanity had to rely on the energy resources available within a relatively small number of systems. A few millennia of technology advancement meant humans could efficiently harvest energy sources on planets, and even stars to a certain degree, but with its voracious appetite society was quickly depleting these sources. Humans needed to make another leap to another solar system.

She lowered her arm and looked at Amos, somehow making her smile glow more radiantly as their eyes met. "Please vote for me, Clarissa Voigt."

The plea hit him emotionally, despite his readiness. The tinge of urgency in her voice, combined with the faintest hint of worry in her eyes, always struck a sentimental chord within him. Clarissa used every trick in the book, from visual eye candy to direct signals into the emotional center of his brain. Once his emotions were freed from her onslaught, he always felt repulsed, violated. She was, in short, a politician.

Amos gave a brief nod toward Clarissa, who nodded back.

"Thank you, Amos. Please let me know if I can be of service to you."

A feeling of revulsion surfaced in him, despite the emotional manipulation directed at him. Every member of the Syndicate wanted his vote, if only to tell others an Evolved supported their policies. He knew he was merely a pawn in their power games. Games that gave little value to individuals when self-serving goals of the Syndicate were at stake.

Her image disappeared as abruptly as it had appeared. This last part annoyed Amos due to its emptiness. There was little, if any, substance to her offer. Amos had tried to ask for her services once and had found himself shuffled from one aide to the next. When he circled back to the original aide, who was no more helpful, he gave up. The whole campaign pitch was forced upon him, tolerated rather than embraced. That said, her decisions seemed to help him; therefore, he would likely vote for her again. He just wished he could ignore the Syndicate. They certainly didn't ignore him.

Amos turned to face the mountains. As he watched the fingers of the swirling clouds sweep over the peaks toward him, a chill ran down his spine.

Sarah watched Amos through the mental monitors provided by the habitat, following the sway of his shoulders and the rotation of his hips as he moved around the room. She allowed her mind to wander over every muscle, take in each thought he had.

Soon you'll be ready for me, she thought.

Did she have a thing for virgins? No, they tended to be messy. She had found she preferred a more experienced lover who was better at the mechanics. Sex with another on the ship was viewed as an open option when off duty, something the crew took full advantage of to satisfy their physical needs. That said, it was his mind that truly excited her. Physical intimacy was easy and accessible, but she had not yet found a deeper intimacy on board the ship, as most everyone was happy to focus on the physical. In her mind, his body was simply the physical tool to bind them together. After all, the mind was the spring of physical desire for which she lusted. In this sense, she was aware of how different she was from even the other women on board.

"Stop licking your lips. You look like you're about to devour him," a male voice teased.

"Oh, I plan to," Sarah's inner desire rumbled back.

"Just remember we need his mind," the male voice said, chuckling nervously.

"Agreed," Sarah murmured.

2.

"The bacterial invasion has been quelled around your—"

"Thank you, Prickly, for your definitive pronouncement," Amos's voice clipped out loud.

He slouched in his favorite chair facing the view of the mountains, which were sheathed in clouds that stretched out over the meadow. To clean him, the habitat had moved Amos's room to a shower station that appeared as a door in his room when prepared. Within that room were all the amenities of a shower and personal grooming devices required to maintain his body. He had also asked for his chair to be delivered to his room, which was another door that appeared once he and his perceived room were in close proximity to where the chair was stored in the habitat.

The chair was one of the few personal possessions he owned. His tenth-removed great-grandfather had hand-carved it from eboney. Eboney was an extremely rare and beautiful hardwood native to second earth, or E-2, and was naturally resistant to rot. The tree took its name from its close resemblance to ebony, native to E-1, but long ago extinct. His distant ancestor had been a master carver and wood-worker, and this chair was considered by many in the family to be his masterpiece. The contours flowed like black water from the back, down over the arm rests, seat and legs. Generations of Amos's relatives had settled themselves into its subtle curves and grooves, burnishing the wood and producing a rich bronze luster. It gave Amos a feeling of permanence, grounding him during these communication sessions.

He sat with his elbows on the armrests, hands together with his head tilted slightly forward so his lips rested on his knitted fingers. He opened up his mind and joined his friends.

A single point of cool, blue light appeared in front of him and exploded outwards in all directions like a supernova. The light took the form of an irregular sphere with seemingly random spikes protruding outward. A lance extended out from the sphere, its end almost touching the tip of Amos's nose.

He had opened up a communication channel through the network to communicate with his friends in the class. It was through a mind-to-network connection, which was the only method he had for communicating with his classmates, despite the promise of their genetically engineered brains.

The sphere held its form so that Amos could rotate it, study every aspect. The sphere was the team's almost complete report, comprised of data and relationships between the data. It was highly structured, even using elements of the fourth spatial dimension to access the quasi storage crystals.

Amos found this structure both a relief and a frustrating method of communication. Compared to the free-flowing manner of his mind and dreams, the structured atmosphere of this learning environment felt rigid, burdened. Despite the ability to share images and emotions within the structure, it was much more limiting when trying to express detailed concepts and also much less efficient.

Three people appeared in his room, each focused intently on the sphere, studying it alongside Amos. They were images of his friends created by the habitat, their physical and psychological profiles loaded into the computer network. The images interacted just like his friends would if they were in the room, only without their most recent thoughts and research. Neutrino communication, while much faster than traditional photon communication because of the short-cuts they can take, remained hindered by the time required to travel off brane and across the bulk between the folds in the brane.

"We good guys?" Jemma's always sultry thoughts pushed out to all of them.

The number of students in the class was relatively small, only four, including Amos. All were classified as "evolved," which meant they were the most advanced and had the potential to communicate mind-to-mind. Up to this point, Amos had been unable to communicate with any of them through direct mind communications. This failure was explained as a combination of their immaturity and the distance that separated them.

Jemma kept everyone on point and moving forward. She lived on Neodym, about a one-year trip at sub-light speed from Amos's home world of Paraaiyan, where her parents ran the largest mining operation on the planet. She had little interest in mining, despite telling Amos about the countless hours she spent tagging along with her father through the processing plant. Her father made sure every aspect of the mine, from the actual extraction to the chemical processing, ran efficiently. Instead, Jemma wanted to explore and see new worlds.

"One hundred point one gigabytes! We're done!" Andrew replied triumphantly. If Jemma was the navigation system, keeping the group moving in the right direction, Andrew was the propulsion, or lack thereof. When motivated, there were few barriers through which he wouldn't burst, but when uninterested, he was like a cargo bay full of tellurium, heavy and unwieldy.

"It's only over a hundred because we decompressed a few things, but I'm tired, and this report should get us at least a B." Karla summarized, pragmatic as always. She was in one of her moods of feeling overwhelmed. She was always up for taking on a new challenge but inevitably over-extended herself and backed off. At her best, she ensured all of the annoying, little tasks were completed. At her worst, she committed to the tasks but let them slip, resulting in a lower grade for the entire team.

"I'm not sure some of the sections on ancient biological history are complete," Amos countered, always the perfectionist. His mind was still spinning from his dream or else he would have offered a more detailed reply about what he felt was missing. Learning how life evolved over the millennia, especially all the weird and seemingly fantastic creatures and plants that existed before evolution became a managed process, was an endless fascination of his. The transition from natural evolution to managed evolution was of particular interest.

"Amos, why don't we go over it and let Andrew and Karla move on?" Jemma suggested.

"Perfect! I'm out!" came Andrew's relieved reply.

"Thanks, guys. Let me know if you need me," Karla said before her image disappeared and Amos felt her connection to his mind close.

"Feels like it's just you and me," Jemma said after a moment of silence. "Wanna make two into more than one?"

Amos's brain pixilated for a moment. He looked over at Jemma's image. She was wearing a tight military uniform with a neckline that plunged down between her breasts. She stared at Amos while she grinned mischievously.

"Jemma, can we hook brains later? I actually have to meet my parents shortly, and I'd rather not be in a full state of arousal."

"All right, stud, another time."

Her image changed to the standard issue tight-fitting military uniform that was utilitarian in the extreme. A pulse of disappointment hit Amos in his limbic system, the brain's emotional center. By sending a specific signal through the computer, a shallow emotion could be created in the recipient. It was a more superficial reaction, like the emotion created while watching a show as opposed to anything real.

Amos pushed back his more lustful thoughts. "I don't feel comfortable with the report. I know it fits perfectly with everything we've been taught, everything in the quasi-crystal memory banks. But it still feels off to me."

"Oh, Amos, I love that mind of yours but why do you always question facts due to your feelings? It always gets you in trouble."

Amos cringed as he thought back to the time when he was a toddler and had argued vehemently that the habitat could make him fly if he simply overrode a few safety protocols. He gave up after he broke his nose slamming face-first into the quantum diffuser floor while leaping forward with both arms outstretched like an eagle.

Ignoring the needling, he pressed on despite his hesitation. "I still have questions about the *Boron Bane* and whether the first step toward managed evolution was a heroic achievement or genocide."

"Well, all the surviving sources support the story of heroism by those generations who persevered through the hardship to reach a higher level of evolution for their children. The 'Greatest Generations,' as they are now called."

"Here's my issue," Amos replied. "Historical records make it sound like our ancestors poisoned themselves willfully with chemicals, wiping out the majority of the population in order to evolve. But they had no clue they could evolve to adapt to boron, much less what benefits the element might provide."

"Does it really seem so farfetched?" Jemma asked. "After all, that's what our society is built on today. The many are willing to sacrifice for the few in order to prolong the survival of the human race. If we don't, humankind dies."

Amos rubbed his temples with his index fingers, trying to clear his thoughts. "Isn't it more likely that the usage of boron in all sorts of materials, like fertilizer and antiseptics, eventually built up in the water and tipped the toxicity against humans?"

"You make it sound like humans are idiots, mindlessly using chemicals without any thought for their long-term impact."

"Not idiots, just focused on making their immediate life better."

"Well, I find that argument morally repugnant! Our ancestors, the greatest of generations, were not that self-serving or short-sighted."

Amos thought for a moment before replying. "Maybe not the greatest of generations, for they were the ones who had to deal with the aftermath of centuries of short-sighted decisions. But I believe humans got lucky by evolving to adapt to high levels of boron. I just don't buy the argument that our ancestors planned the first step of evolution. Instead, I believe the moral code of sacrificing the many for the few was a product of necessity, which became systemized as humans increasingly managed the evolutionary process."

Amos could feel Jemma push back a feeling of disgust as she replied, her tone sarcastic. "So, billions of people died, wiping away ninety percent of humans without any prior thought? Plants have always used boron to strengthen cell walls, producing strong leaves and stems. The blueprint was always there for humans to use. Humans benefited from thicker cell walls, allowing them to grow taller and stronger. It was almost fatal for the human race, but the step was critical to allow humans to travel for extended periods in zero-gravity environments, which was necessary to escape Earth's death."

"But there's no way they could have foreseen that necessity, much less determine whether the adaptation of boron was the best course," Amos countered. "Even if they did recognize boron was one piece of a hugely complex puzzle, would they have risked all of humankind when so much was unknown? Especially since there was no precedent for managed evolution. Ancient America experimented with eugenics, as did Nazi Germany, but it didn't stick. Prior to the Boron Bane, humans were simply a product of their environment, evolving through time as opportunistic chemical compounds. The inadvertent adaptation to boron opened the door to explore the possibility of humans adapting to other elements."

"This explanation of a random first step into managed evolution is ridiculous," Jemma replied. "It reduces humans to the biggest lottery winners of all time when you consider the precise set of circumstances. There must have been some level of management, even if they bumbled through it. I'll admit, though, the number of fortunate events to occur to even create a universe capable of supporting life, much less for humans to evolve out of the primordial soup, is bewildering. It seems almost pre-determined that humans would come into existence and we would be communicating at this time."

"Makes you wonder if there's something more going on, doesn't it?"

"I choose to believe we control our destiny and do not rely on fates," Jemma said. "We control our own destiny, Amos."

"Okay, okay. I have to go anyway. Talk to you later."

"Good luck!"

Amos continued to sit with his lips pressed to the back of his knitted fingers, staring at the line where the floor met the windows. A deep sense of discomfort welled up in his stomach. He was missing something, something hidden. Points weren't connecting properly. Yet, he couldn't figure out if he needed to draw new lines, find new points, or erase the points themselves and start over.

The flat light in the room darkened as the tendrils of the approaching storm passed over his room. He shivered as his mind worked through the logic once more.

3.

The incestuous Hyperion and Theia seemed to spawn the day's impassioned dawn. Buckets of fluid that looked like rain spewed against the glass separating Amos's room from the storm, demanding entry into his reality.

Amos stood with his toes pressed against the bottom of the window, lost in another world as he pondered managed evolution. The window shivered and bulged inward from the force of the storm, tapping his nose. Brought back to the present, Amos focused on the storm. Lightning flashed within the clouds, offering snapshots of the fury of the forces battling for supremacy above. He could almost understand why ancient humans had believed in gods. And yet, something visceral was missing. For all its ferocity, the storm wasn't spirited in the way Amos imagined a real storm would be. He had struggled to program in as many details as he could find in the habitat's memory banks, even the elusive electric smells. Unfortunately, the memory banks were limited in such details. He had tried various scents, from static electricity to damp, musty vegetation stirred up from the ground. Since he was not sure what was real, he had given up and tried to ignore the unfulfilling smell. The visual and auditory orchestra were usually enough to entertain him, but not today.

Perturbed at the inaccuracies and the hollow emotions they evoked, Amos snapped away the storm with his mind. The window flattened and quieted as warm sunlight streamed through it. Amos removed the window altogether, as if the sudden change in sensory cues could jolt an emotion inside of him.

The calming springtime smell of blooming mountain flora filled his room. The quasi-crystals were surprisingly rich with details about floral scents. Amos took a deep breath, working to savor the scents as his mind opened up to exploring their subtleties. A hint of butterwort blew in from the bog to the southwest.

Early for them, Amos thought.

With his eyes closed, he could almost lose himself into the illusion he had created. Not quite though. He had programmed the chemicals created by the plants in the fields meticulously. It should be as close as one could get to reality. Yet, he was missing an emotional response to it all. Why could he not feel his experiences in the habitat like he did in his dreams or, more recently, his subconscious training?

A coldness filled Amos as his thoughts drifted to the true nature of the habitat. He thought back to that day when his mother had turned off their perceptors of the home life program to show Amos his real home. He had marveled at the emptiness of his habitat, a blank canvas. The habitat was nothing more than a large dome with a dynamic floor. He estimated the floor was about one square mile. The living capacity of the habitat was approximately one million people, he was told, although that capacity rating was in a barrack-style arrangement. Given his family's status, and his enrollment in the evolved program, the habitat was set up for about two hundred and fifty thousand people. This lower capacity allowed for a few personal items, like a bed and a chair.

What enabled this efficiency was a floor that moved people and items in a way imperceptible to human senses—either that or his senses were masked. While he might believe he was simply standing in front of his window gazing at mountain peaks, in fact he had been told his body was moving around the floor constantly in a slow motion dance with other people as they went about their day.

When his mother turned off his perceptors to the system, it had shocked him to see everyone naked, engrossed in their own computer-created worlds. Out of respect for privacy, people were banned from turning off their perceptors. His parents controlled the habitat, and thus had the security clearance to turn off a person's perception of the program, although an alert had surely been sent to the Syndicate on E-3. Apparently, his mother was willing to accept a mild punishment to make sure Amos understood the nature of the real world and not lose himself in a world of silicon-created illusions.

His mother had explained that the climate was controlled at a microscopic level through quantum diffusers in the dynamic floor. For the most part, everyone enjoyed a comfortable room temperature of eighty degrees. This temperature, and a mild stimulation of the sensory nerves gave the illusion of feeling clothed. If a person asked the computer for a sauna or a vacation on Solaris-5, the microclimate could raise the temperature around the individual, although a larger radius on the quadrant was required to prevent others from feeling the heat. The laws of thermodynamics were an ever-present challenge to the habitat's engineers.

After that day, Amos became obsessed with learning about the technology that pervaded his life. He had never actually left the habitat. As far as he knew, he had been born there. All his needs and wants were supplied within the dome. Food and water were brought in from external sources, while waste was disposed of outside. He had his circle of friends with whom he talked constantly, but none of them actually lived in the habitat, much less on his planet.

From what he had learned in the quasi-crystals, the planet on which he lived had a harsh atmosphere. It was cold, and the air was barely breathable. The planet itself was fairly remote relative to E-3 and the majority of the population was devoted to research activities. The main reason it had been settled was for scientific reasons to foster managed evolution and to help find solutions to enable the adoption of tellurium into humans. Scientists had determined tellurium offered the best chance to enable mind-to-mind communication.

Many of Amos's friends lived on more habitable worlds, like E-3, where the use of habitat software was less pervasive. People had direct control over their perception supplied by the software and could turn it off if they wanted to actually walk in nature.

The first critical breakthrough enabling the creation of a habitat had been a direct interface between the brain, including all the senses, and a computer. In this way, humans could bypass their normal senses and eliminate the need for screens and holograms. Now the brain "saw" and "felt" surroundings based on computer algorithms that factored in personal preference, efficient organization amongst the group, and market dynamics, like monthly lease payments per square foot. If they paid more money, people received a larger perceived space, even though their perceived space overlapped with others.

Despite these advancements, scientists still had the challenge of creating "meaningful" touch and other subtle connections like "knowing" eye contact. One of the hardest things about the technology was populating a world with virtual people to give an isolated crew the feeling of community. Specifically, the challenge was figuring out how to mimic the essence of a person during human interactions. A touch of a hand that meant more, the gaze into another's eyes that carried a message, the embrace that transmitted more than warmth. Without these seemingly tiny details, the illusions were empty, void of life.

Eventually, the scientists fell back on a few old tricks. By manipulating the senses just prior to the signal reaching the brain, one could be made to feel like he or she was interacting with another human. However, many argued that anyone who had lived in a rich community of real people could still recognize the difference.

At first, Amos was a little unnerved to think he could be literally face-to-face with another person without knowing it. He could be in his room seemingly looking out a simulated window and not realize another person was right in front of him. This disconnect between the physical world and perceptions meant people had to be considerate of their neighbors. A spastic baby's slap to avoid eating the food held in front of him or her had surprised more than one unfortunate person whose simulated room happened to be physically close to the petulant one year old. As Amos knew, a basketball hitting your neighbor in the nose after an errant shot almost always led to a formal rebuke by the colony's council.

The worst was when he had been practicing his dribbling, tripped over his own feet, and fallen straight into Mr. and Mrs. Silver's romantic encounter. A smile crossed Amos's face as he thought Mrs. Silver taking a few startled seconds to tell the computer to clothe her to Amos's senses. Had that been a sly smile on her lips afterwards? Either way, Mr. Smith had made sure the ball was confiscated for a month.

As was the case now, when a person wanted to actually meet another person, sit down for a meal, or use the toilet, the computer would coordinate the person and the other person or item to a designated spot. When demand for food or other items was low, these items moved to the edges of the floor, along with any personal items not in use.

Through the course called "Post-Cataclysm History," one of his favorites, Amos had learned the original purpose of this type of perception-based software program was to aid humans living in confined quarters, such as intersolar ships or settlers on inhospitable planets. From time to time, there were rebellions against the system as individuals and groups voiced concerns about mind control and personal freedom, but the benefits of the system seemed to outweigh the risks, or so the Syndicate said.

As humans adapted to this living arrangement it was discovered their impact on their environment decreased significantly. Forests were not cleared for individuals' houses, oil and gas was not required for transporting people from one habitat to another, and with the advent of synthetic food, the impact of food cultivation on the environment was removed.

While traditional cities and settlements still existed, society fully committed to these habitats as a way to limit consumption of resources, enable longer space travel, and manage evolution.

Those in charge of managing evolution found these habitats particularly useful, because it enabled society to separate a specific group of people from the population without the same sense of disconnect. The first step was identifying a planet that could provide an environment that allowed humans to evolve into something more. The second step was constructing a facility that could support generations of experimentation until the desired results were achieved. Amos thought it sounded worse than it was in reality, given that he lived in such a facility.

Like everyone in the habitat, Amos had a list of preferred people he liked to "bump into." He also had a list of people he preferred to avoid. Of course, Mrs. Silver was on his preferred list, although he had a sneaking suspicion that Mr. Silver had put Amos on his wife's avoid list, because Amos had not seen her since the basketball incident.

On this day, the field outside his room was completely empty, which was somewhat unusual. It may have been simply quiet in the habitat or his parents' way of encouraging a more efficient route their room. Either way, it fit his mood quite well. His mind was churning, and a peaceful walk would help him.

He closed his eyes for a second and thought back to those clement days, before he understood about the habitat. If his parents had not shown him the reality of his environment, he could imagine going through his entire life and believing everything he saw, heard, smelled, and even felt was real.

He shivered and stepped forward, his foot producing a puff of dry dust as it landed on the dirt path leading through the meadow.

4.

Amos pitched forward onto the path, his arms thrusting outward defensively, jolting his thoughts to the immediate. His right foot had tripped over something, his momentum landing him in the middle of a patch of Canadian Thistle.

"What the heck?" Amos groaned as he pushed himself up using his elbows, protecting his palms from the stinging thistle before rolling out of the patch. From on his back, he twisted his neck to look at what he had tripped over.

"Damn prairie dogs. Always digging their burrows all over the place. Lucky I didn't break an ankle," he groused to himself.

The habitat had a certain degree of flexibility for safety. Breaking an ankle was allowed, or anything else that could be repaired quickly. The avoidance of pain was not a primary safety measure. Amos had become all too familiar with what level of pain was tolerable. Sometimes he thought the original programmers of the habitat had a sadistic side, tormenting inhabitants needlessly.

Amos elbowed his way into a sitting position, his knees bent and butt planted in the dry grass and punk scattered next to the path. He rubbed his ankle and looked it over. It was mildly twisted but not broken. It felt slightly warm but otherwise normal. Besides a few scrapes on his hands, he appeared none the worse for wear.

Amos focused on the prairie dog hole. As he had in the past, Amos wondered why humans even bothered with an actual body when all of its senses were manipulated. Well, not completely. The "organic element" was still necessary, the ill-defined need to seek, to understand, to provide the emotional glue required to create a society. Silicon life disagreed but everyone was entitled to an opinion.

Resting his arms on his bent knees, Amos scanned the meadow with his eyes. It was another boringly beautiful day, the sun offering just the right amount of warmth to encourage a brisk walk while encouraging his mind to wander and toil over the challenges of his studies. The habitat seemed to use these days as a reward for progressing in his studies. It was always cold and soggy weather when he needed to buckle down.

He felt the sun on his skin. The breeze bent the grass as it rushed across the meadow in waves. A merlin darted low over the meadow looking for its meal. Yet, today especially none of it felt real. All the information gathered by his senses was supplied directly by the habitat, creating an illusion of reality. But at least he knew it was an illusion, and maybe the actual real world wasn't much different, merely a construct of the mind. Quantum theories and observations had proven the reality studied by the great ancient minds of Einstein, Randall and more recently Raymundo was a complex interaction of fields and energy that our mind interpreted as substantive.

Amos rolled sideways and pushed himself onto his knees before standing. He stood with bent knees for a moment like a person unsure of his footing. He straightened his spine and looked around again. A pair of merlins swooped and darted across the field, one following the other, mimicking the leader's flight path almost exactly, reminding him of his last conversation with Bina.

Bina was a friend but different from his classmates. They had met not too long ago through the network in a forum about the philosophy of time. Her intellect had drawn him in, and a friendship had developed. She was the first to really challenge his assumptions about the world, presenting new ideas and theories that were different from his studies. Sometimes her arguments were in direct conflict with widely accepted theories, but they were still sound. Adding to the intrigue of their friendship, Bina had pressed him to keep their discussions secret. To Amos, the idea of secrecy was almost erotic. He knew the Syndicate monitored most communications through the network. It was exciting to have something private from the government, even if he didn't really believe it. The fact an older woman was interested in him didn't hurt either.

As their friendship strengthened, they found they could communicate somewhat mind-to-mind at the conscious level. It was infantile, the equivalent of a baby's smile toward its mother, but this conscious connection was deeper and richer than anything Amos had experienced over the network or even face-to-face, for that matter.

Amos couldn't explain it, but when Bina focused on him within a conscious connection, he saw a glimpse of himself for the first time. A new emotion bubbled up inside of him: puzzled wonderment, similar to what it must feel like to see oneself in the mirror for the first time.

Amos did not even understand how it was possible, since he assumed only his classmates, who had evolved to adapt to tellurium, were capable of direct mind communications. Bina had been vague about the how, saying only that she was older and had already completed an earlier program.

As the topics of their conversations became more complex, more theoretical, Bina proposed using subconscious communication, which she described as a gateway to the supraconscious. It had taken a while for Amos to understand what she meant and even longer before he could put his mind in a state where it was possible. It involved a type of meditation, focusing his inner energy while letting go. Eventually, he developed a practice that worked for him, enabling him to touch the subconscious.

The subconscious was one of the scariest and most inspiriting experiences of his life. It felt like all weight, all mass, was stripped away and his spirit was free to explore without the bounds of physical reality. The terror of falling out of one's sanctuary mingled with the rapture of a completely free mind.

Once in the subconscious, darkness had confronted him. Not just a singular darkness but many areas of darkness, like inky storm clouds just below the surface of his consciousness. Bina explained that these areas of darkness were potentially explosive personal issues that he needed to clear out, raise to the level of consciousness, and discharge. Most were fairly common, like a feeling of abandonment or a discomfort with his physical appearance. These were worked on through discussions with the counseling services offered within the habitat.

Other areas of darkness would not disperse. Instead, with Bina's help, Amos learned to manage them. A deep, inner self-doubt was an issue he would have to handle throughout his life. It was part of him, who he was as a person. Left unmanaged, these areas of darkness would cripple him in times of stress, causing him to curl into a mental fetal position, shielding himself from the environment.

The darkest, most threatening areas within his subconscious were left alone. Even at the conscious level, thinking of these areas of darkness inside of him made Amos uneasy. The closer he got to them, the greater the sense of rage and fear grew within him. He had backed off, worried what it meant.

The subconscious was an environment of images, rich, multi-dimensional forms with emotions and layers of meaning associated with them. Communicating within such an environment was challenging, but he picked up some of the methods once he understood the mechanisms. Eventually, he was able to get his point across, although it was inefficient with many redundant and fuzzy images presented. Bina was able to tell an entire story with one form, educating Amos completely about the subject, including how she felt about it.

The first time he immersed himself completely, the unstructured essence of the subconscious sucked him in, overwhelmed him. The medium enraptured him as his mind tried to expand endlessly into it. Bina asserted herself quickly and wrapped a structured environment around him as a crutch for his mind. She explained that his conscious self was not well suited for entering the subconscious, but she had helped him enter this environment by creating a false world around him. If she did not create this false world, the infinite nature of the supraconscious would permeate and shatter him.

"Amos, you must maintain a level of objectivity within the subconscious in order to understand it, move within it," she explained.

"But doesn't that remove us from the subconscious, pull us back to the world we knew?"

"That is a risk," she admitted. "Finding the right balance of mind control to manipulate the subconscious without losing the necessary connections within it. Plato taught humanity critical thinking, and humankind has been struggling to maintain its presence in the world ever since."

"Why do it then?"

"Because I believe it is necessary to have both in the end, mind and spirit. They are one."

Bina wrapped the familiar meadow and mountains around Amos to keep his mind focused on his self. She explained that the conscious mind required a form of reality around it, an explanation of its environment to help make sense of everything. Subconscious communication, at least initially, required one to push the conscious mind down into the subconscious layer.

In the meadow, Bina presented two merlins darting and swooping across the meadow, the second bird following the path of the first, right down to the position and speed of its wings. Amos marveled at the acrobatic display and the skill of the second merlin. It was only after he focused more closely, felt the second merlin within the more intimate subconscious, that he realized, with shock, that it was the same merlin at two different points in time. Both merlins were real. The difference was that one was slightly earlier than the simultaneous moment between the lead merlin and Amos.

Bina's point was that objects we perceive to be in the past or the future were as real as those in the present. The psychology of the mind progressed us through the events in a linear manner. This interpretation of time explained time dilation and contraction within the framework of special relativity.

In the network forum, Amos had disagreed strongly with Bina on her interpretation of time. His view was what he had been taught, that time was fundamental. There was the past, the present, and the future. The universe was an ever-evolving entity in which time had existed prior to the Big Bang. In contrast, Bina argued that time was emergent or approximate, in essence saying the universe wasn't evolving at all. Time didn't exist prior to the Big Bang, and it may end with another singularity.

Now he wasn't so sure. He had argued that the present was essentially pure energy passing through a resistance field, resulting in mass and the entanglement of wavelengths. It was on this resistance brane where the present existed, where mass was formed momentarily. The movement of time was the dynamic between the wavelengths and the resistance brane. Maybe they were both right.

The past was different from the future, Amos had argued, because of the entanglement of wavelengths when mass was formed in the present, essentially knitted energy patterns together into an unalterable tapestry of history. The future was untangled wavelengths, richer in possibilities and more flexible in their movement. However, Amos had been forced to admit that his theory of time relied heavily on his own feeling of the passage of time as well as a bias toward free will. Bina countered that her interpretation of time didn't preclude free will, but that silicon life did not truly have it.

The most shocking point was that no time had passed while they watched the merlins. Instead, Bina had inserted a block of memories into his mind, a type of training module complete in both space and time. She explained that whatever action he chose at the end of the program dictated the prior memories embedded in his experience, a kind of reverse determinism.

"All of the objects you experienced were relics of the past," she explained, "much like your current experiences within the habitat. You must strive for presence, move beyond means to deeper encounters."

"Am I not present now?"

"Not present in what is fleeting, passing. Presence in what is enduring."

"Does the habitat not endure?"

"No! Of all things, it especially stands still, will cease to exist. It has no relation to you, because it is only an object."

Amos had been outraged that someone he respected and trusted had intruded into his mind simply to make a point in a theoretical argument. She had countered with whether the controls in the habitat were any different?

The high-pitched chirrups of the prairie dog whose home Amos had stepped into pulled him back from his thoughts. Amos stood up, dusted himself off, and resumed his walk along the dirt path created by the habitat, continuing to watch the pair of merlins as they performed their mating dance across the meadow floor.

Keeping an eye out for prairie dog holes, Amos walked towards the ravine.

———————————

"Your project seems to tune out at times. Should I be worried, Sarah?"

"I don't believe so, Captain. His evolved mind seems capable of a deep meditation. Deeper than we can monitor. I believe it shows the plasticity of his mind to adapt to the large volume of information we're pushing into him."

Captain Melville, standing next to Sarah in the ship's research lab, shifted slightly as he considered Amos's brain scans. "I hope you're right, but it could also mean he is mentally unstable, that his brain is acting erratically. I don't need to remind you of the importance of his stability."

"I'll keep an eye on him, sir," Sarah replied apprehensively.

"I know you will," the captain replied.

Sarah ignored the mild ribbing and refocused on Amos.

What is going on inside that beautiful head of yours?

5.

Leaping off the jagged ridge, Amos fell as much as scampered down the dirt embankment, his feet sliding as they caused small, dusty landslides. He had chosen to drop into the ravine well to the left of the beaten path, where the dirt was loose. After a few more quick steps, he landed firmly on the path and turned left to follow the gash in the hillside down to the bottom.

Amos walked quickly when he reached the relative flatness of the bottom. He wanted to stop up ahead and take some time to prepare himself for visiting his parents, who could always seem to discover what subjects he had glossed over in his studies.

He rounded the bend in the ravine and came out into an opening that revealed a small pond with a canoe pulled up near the shoreline. Often, he would launch the canoe and let it drift aimlessly with the swirling breeze, floating lazily from shore to shore while he lay in the bottom gazing up at the sky, watching the clouds drift by. It was his place to get away, to relax, or to catch a nap if he was really tired.

He positioned himself into a comfortable pose on a large, flat, sunny rock next to the pond with his legs crossed, back straight, and hands resting on his knees. He had found he needed to relax his mind after communicating with the network because of the energy it took to structure thoughts in a specific manner before sending them.

Amos fell into a relaxed mental state, and it wasn't long before he was deep in meditation, processing his inner thoughts and emotions. He found himself relying on meditation more often as be worked through larger, more complex challenges in his studies, trusting his unconscious mind to make connections hidden from his consciousness.

He felt a mild nudge within his mind, like a tap on his shoulder. The nudge didn't have the coldness of the network. It came again, more forceful this time. Amos shifted his focus to address it; he wouldn't get very far with the distraction. He opened himself up to the communication.

"Amos, I need to show you one more thing. Now!" Bina's voice in his head was filled with desperation, urging.

Annoyed but also puzzled by the unusual urgency she expressed, Amos replied. "Can I have a little time before we—"

"Please, Amos, now!"

"Okay, but can you at least tell me what training exercise is so important?"

"Amos, I'm not talking about training. That time has passed. I'm talking about your freedom."

The emotional heaviness accompanying the words landed on Amos's thoughts like a lead brick, squashing everything and drawing all his attention. Before he could respond, Bina was gone.

Bewildered, Amos opened his eyes and looked around at the habitat, half expecting to see a net fall from the sky. Instead, bubbles wiggled up from the bottom of the pond, popping on the surface. A couple of dragonflies darted left and right as they gobbled up mosquitos by the water's edge. Everything seemed normal, but a sense of foreboding grew inside of him, a lead brick sinking deeper into his stomach.

Amos gathered his thoughts and emotions, calmed himself, and began the process of touching his subconscious. The feelings of urgency and nervousness from Bina had infected his mood. It wasn't the ideal mental state to touch the subconscious, but it seemed he had little choice. He turned his attention inward and began the now familiar process.

In his mind, Amos formed an octahedron, the shape created by connecting two pyramids at their base, and began spinning and shining it. Bina had had him practice tending to the pyramids for a seeming eternity until she was satisfied the energy and strength within him was up to the next task. The practice filled him with a sense of vitality and clarity. Once the symbol had a lustrous shine, Amos's mind entered the double pyramid.

Inside, he found himself within a sandstone-walled room, an imposing stone throne in the middle. The walls had an energy to them, a humming vibration that came from the exterior of the octahedron. He could still feel his body, knew his eyes remained closed as he sat on the rock by the pond, yet he felt weight lifting off his spirit. For his body, time had slowed to a stop. A blink of his eye would take forever while he was inside this room. Maybe a better way to explain it was he felt his mind loosening itself from his body, still firmly connected but less encumbered by its mass.

A calm strength permeated Amos. He stood stoically in front of the throne in the center of the room. A familiar impression of off-limits came from it, but something deeper within him was unnerved. Bina had never expressed urgency. Her tone suggested fear, but of what?

Pushing the disquiet aside, Amos sat cross-legged on the sandstone tiles in front of the throne and settled his thoughts on the throne's grandeur, wondering at its purpose. This act deepened his meditative state, relaxing and opening his mind. Once he was finally prepared, an opening in the wall behind the throne revealed itself. Amos stood up and walked around the throne.

Above the opening a symbol etched in the sandstone glowed. It was a circle with a dot in the middle. A vertical line bisected the circle. Beneath the circle were two "Xs." Three horizontal lines framed the circle on each side. Bina had explained the symbol went back to the dawn of humanity, but it had been divided over the years into various belief systems, and over time, different races of humanity had emphasized different aspects. In this context it represented, among other things, the link between the entire multi-dimensional universe of the brane, which is the supraconscious beyond the portal with the three spatial dimensions, plus time, known to humankind.

Naive fear bumbled up inside of Amos again as he contemplated the void through the opening. It was an honest fear of the unknown, of danger, but it also came from Bina's warning of the semi-structured world of thoughts through the portal, a world of images and raw emotions, unfiltered and complex. A person could lose one's self in such a world, Bina had warned, especially if one fell too deep into the unconscious, where images disbanded into vague objects without meaning.

Reminding himself that he was only touching the subconscious, and that Bina would protect him, Amos took a step toward the portal and extended his hand. Anxiety flooded his mind, and Amos wondered vaguely if he has pissing himself while sitting on the rock. Re-focusing on his inner self, he extended his arm, touched the void just over the threshold of the portal, and was consumed by it.

He entered an existence without definition. His mind felt completely untethered, released from his body. Shock and euphoria consumed him. His entire conscious effort went into holding his form together, worked to prevent his thoughts from scattering outwards and his self from losing all definition. Objects, or semi-formed thoughts and images, whirled around him, combining and breaking apart seamlessly like some chaotic asteroid field. His bodily senses were lost to him, including any sense of balance or sight. Instead, he found himself in what could be best described as a deep hole inside himself, meditative but much deeper than anything he had experienced consciously. He was in control of himself but floating freely through his own semi-structured thoughts.

Amos began to panic, lose his focus. He had not been prepared to enter the subconscious, expecting only to touch it again. He felt parts of his mind dissipate, seemingly losing their connection to him. Panic turned to terror that he had no control over himself. He felt like he was about to scatter outward, vanish into the blackness of the background. No, not vanish exactly, but he became lost, consumed by the vastness of the supraconscious. The essence of who he was, the connections between the information his mind had gathered, which defined him, were stretching and fading.

A feeling more than a thought pressed against him, nudging him. Amos felt overwhelming relief as he recognized Bina's touch. That simple sensation calmed him and reminded him of his training with her. He began to create a space around his self, centering his mind. It took all of his concentration, all of his energy to form a concrete base for himself that anchored his mind in this world.

This environment was closely related to a dream state but different in a few critical ways. The most apparent was that his consciousness was fully engaged, compared to a dream state in which it was purely his unconscious that was in control. Bina described it as something like putting his consciousness in a submarine and submerging himself under the surface of the ocean of the mind. Amos formed a type of underwater capsule that protected him, contained him.

The second critical difference was the depth. This communication required one to dive just below the surface of the unconscious. The risk was going deeper. Even contemplating going deeper, where recognizable articles were broken down into more basic forms, created a sense of vertigo. The further one descended into the unconscious, the less definition and structure existed, and the harder it was for the conscious mind to maintain its form. Amos located the portal that led back to the throne room. Simply by keeping the exit in his conscious thoughts, his mind naturally remained closer to the portal.

Feeling more tethered, Amos concentrated on firming up and defining his self, his form in the subconscious. As he stabilized, he was filled with a feeling of exhilaration, power, control. It was intoxicating, a feeling of ultimate strength well beyond the physical. A sense of possibility consumed him, like he could go anywhere, create anything with a simple thought. Elation filled him as he pushed his mind outward, curiosity to explore and understand this new world overtaking him.

Then a force lashed out and struck him at his core, stunning his thoughts, and everything went white.

6.

Warmth, calmness, and assurance wrapped around Amos, soothing him like a mother might cradle a baby. Bewildered and confused, Amos struggled to remember where he was. Nothing was familiar. Everything felt strange. He tried to lift his hand to his head in a vain attempt to rub some sense back into it, only to find he had no hands, or head, for that matter.

He took stock of his spirit as he tried to understand what was happening, panic rising in him despite the cooing emotions projected at him. The feeling of warmth enveloped him, the rhythmic pulse of a heart soothing him. The panic drained out of him, leaving only a base fear centered on the unknown, his lack of control.

He focused outward, opening himself tentatively to gather information about his environment. What he saw humbled him, scared him despite the warmth and assurance that radiated from it. The image of a woman floated freely, or at least what Amos perceived to be a woman. She was a light against an inky background, and Amos realized it was Bina.

An amused smile covered her face, punctuated by her eyes, which twinkled playfully like the stars in the sky. She held up a hand to Amos, palm upward in a gesture of openness. Without thinking, Amos formed his self-image into a boy sitting cross-legged. Bina nodded approvingly.

She swept her arm to the side and pointed at what seemed like a two-dimensional wall. Something about the wall seemed familiar, and Amos called it toward him mentally. As the wall approached, Amos noted that it seemed to extend infinitely to his left and to his right. He also realized it was not flat. Focusing intently on it, he pulled it closer to his perception and realized it had a convex form.

As he zoomed in closer to the form, he was able to make out its uneven surface. Ripples, folds, and even holes pocked the surface, which had an undeniable texture to it. It reminded him of the mountain range he had programmed into the habitat. Another thought nagged at him, but he couldn't quite absorb it. Something else about this form . . . Of course! It was the brane, the membrane-like object that held the energy and mass of what humans perceived as their universe.

Pleased with himself, he looked around for Bina, who had been watching his progress. A feeling of approval flooded through him as she passed along her agreement with his assessment. She held up her hand again and gestured toward the brane.

Shifting his focus back, he noticed the brane was transforming, more dynamic than he thought possible. He realized the motion wasn't caused so much by the brane but by an energy field that was interacting with it. The energy held within the brane where the intersection occurred was transformed somehow, which caused additional interactions.

Intrigued by the transformation, Amos pushed himself to the edge of the brane but couldn't seem to will himself closer. A feeling of warning surrounded him, coming from Bina. She shook her head at him sternly. Then she gestured to the brane, and it began to recede from them. The ridges and pocks became smaller until he could no longer make them out. Eventually, it became harder to perceive the overall warping of the brane.

As the brane continued to move away from them, he saw where it was interacting with the resistance field. He knew the point was defined by a change in the universe. Its shape changed from a two-dimensional wall to a four-dimensional space that evolved into a nine-dimensional manifold, which bled outwards into a tenth dimension, and possibly more.

The whorls in the geometry were breathtaking to behold as they spread out from the two-dimensional brane and twisted in on themselves, disappeared into the body of the form, and re-emerged elsewhere. It was an amorphous, almost flowery form. Ridges in the form dipped in and out, reminding Amos of the edge of a scallop shell, only much more intricate and elaborate.

The feeling that permeated Amos as he took it in was a complex mixture of joy, humility, fear, and awe. It was like he was viewing truth in its purest form. Truth of life, truth of existence, truth of being. It was glorious, and Amos was overwhelmed by its existence.

Bina drew him away from the form and shifted his focus toward her. Emotionally drained, he was having a hard time focusing his thoughts. It was like he finally understood how miniscule he was within the greater structure. His ego was shattered, spent, humbled beyond anything he thought possible. He began to fold in on himself, unwilling or unable to take in anything more.

Bina enveloped him again, cradled him in the feelings of warmth, safety, and understanding. Amos was an infant, completely dependent on her for emotional nourishment, support, even life.

She held her embrace for what seemed like an eternity, nurturing him back to health and strength. Eventually, Amos regained control of himself and stretched from the embrace. Bina let go and allowed him to separate from her.

He focused on her, and she held a look of compassion on her face, understanding mixed with a tinge of fear. She nodded and looked over at a portal that had opened. Amos nodded back at her and then passed through the doorway.

He found himself back on the rock by the pond. His eyes filled with tears, and he wept uncontrollably, his body convulsing as each new round of tears flooded his eyes. He hung his head between his knees, his hands clasped in front. It felt like he had purged everything he felt about the world through his tears and convulsing gasps. His soul emptied and re-filled during that blink of an eye.

When the tears finally stopped rolling down his cheeks, his chest unclasped.

"Bina, what was that?"

"A representation of the Real."

"The Real?"

"Real, Truth, One, perhaps even God. Yes, it is our existence, our real existence."

"God? I thought humankind gave up on such notions a long time ago."

"Well, if it helps, I prefer to think of it as the One. It's difficult for me to understand as well. There's too much of myself in the way. But I have come to believe the False shattered the One, which yearns to re-unify itself. If you look and listen deeply, you will see the Truth."

"I don't understand. What is the False?"

"You, Amos. You are the False, as am I."

"Me? You're speaking in riddles."

"Not riddles, images. And this is why the subconscious is better."

"I don't understand."

"The truth remains hidden to me as well. I do know that you cannot touch the Real while encased in yourself."

"Is this to protect me?"

"Yes," she replied after a pause. "To protect yourself. We live in the world of space and time, but to live only in that world is not to truly live."

"That makes no—"

"Again, I don't really understand either. What I've shown you only scratches the surface of what exists below the conscious, available in the supraconscious. While I don't understand it, I believe it represents how everything is connected."

"Connected? Supraconscious? You mean a type of subconscious network?"

"No, well, yes but much more. More like how all of us are ultimately the same thing. I've come to believe our minds are feeble receptors of . . . a greater consciousness. There are hints of it all around us, protrusions of it in the form of life. It's why eye contact with another person means so much more than eye contact with a silicon life form, the voice of a machine doesn't quite resonate properly, and the touch of a lover reaches something deeper. We are all connected beneath this physical reality by something greater, or maybe it's better to say there is something greater."

"I don't think I follow you. What you showed me appeared more like a mathematical equation than something spiritual. The textured brane that defines our universe was familiar from my navigation studies, but you're saying even it is part of something greater, a ten-dimensional form. Maybe even more than that. You make it sound spiritual."

"I haven't figured it out yet, Amos. There are many unanswered questions. I needed to show you what I believe is real. Listen to your heart as well as your head. Your habitat is a product of human manipulation, convincing but ultimately a poor representation of what matters. Don't let it fool you."

Amos was silent for a moment before replying. "But Bina, the habitat provides for me, gives me nourishment, and develops me. The world around me, I helped create it, to make me happy."

"Don't you see what I've shown you, Amos? What you have created within the shell of the habitat has nothing to do with the habitat itself. Before rising to your consciousness, words are formed in the space between your self and the One. It is the source of all human inspiration and creativity. The fact you created what you did in the habitat shows you have already touched the One. Nothing is ever added by the codified silicon superconscious, only greater granularization of what is already there."

Amos lay back on the rock with his hands behind his head and looked up at the metallic blue sky above, struggling to make sense of it. His emotions were still raw from the cathartic experience. His face scrunched up when a thought struck him. "Bina, why was it so urgent to show me that?"

"Simple. It is time."

Amos shifted his shoulders in an attempt to avoid a ridge in the rock crossing his shoulder blades. "Time?"

"Yes. You were not ready before now, are still not ready, but I couldn't wait any longer."

"You couldn't wait? Unusually impatient of you," Amos observed.

"I believe your parents are waiting for you. You should go."

Amos checked the habitat's systems and realized Bina was right. He was overdue for his meeting with them.

"Oh crap!"

He sprang to his feet and hopped down from the rock into the soft mud by the pond, splashing muck onto his pants. He paused for a moment, considering the muddy spots on his pants and the superficial feeling of disgust they inspired.

Lifting his eyes to the pond, he followed a water strider as it danced across the surface. Whirligig beetles swarmed past the strider, swirling on the surface, diving periodically into the world below. Suddenly, he felt sad for the water striders, their world was so two-dimensional, so shallow.

An empty feeling consumed him, his gut carved out as he scanned the representation of life created by the habitat he had programmed. What had been his pride and joy and had filled his time with wonder had become a façade, an empty display meant to amuse but not fulfil. Worse, he felt imprisoned, trapped in a made-up world of his own design.

Disgusted with the pond that had once offered refuge, Amos turned his back on it and ran along the trail that led to his parents' room.

———————

"What the hell just happened, Sarah?"

Sarah stood stone-stiff, analyzing Amos's actions. "Sir, we may have a problem. Something's different, but I'm not sure what."

"Hell of a time for 'something' to change," Captain Melville. "Do we delay? Try to sort it out? Or do we pull the plug altogether and develop another evolved?"

Sarah hesitated, trying to push her emotions aside as she analyzed the facts and weighed the risks. Her position on the ship was to observe and develop Amos's emotional side, and this was the first time she was unsure of it.

"No, sir. I think we can manage him. We're too close now to pull out."

"But what happened there? It was like his mind disappeared for a moment, and then he started weeping like a baby. I could swear it looked like he was communicating with someone."

"I know, sir. I thought the same thing. But nothing showed up on the network, and all monitors suggested he was simply thinking. He is the evolved, the most evolved human in history. We are still studying how his brain works. I believe the answers will come as we understand more about how his brain operates."

A long, dead pause preceded Captain Melville's reply. "All right, we carry on as planned. But I want Dr. Daman up to speed on all of this."

Sarah cringed mentally. "Yes, sir."

7.

The blank door slid sideways, revealing what Amos saw now as his parents' fantasy refuge. He reminded himself that they were in this as much as he was, stuck here to advance evolution. Yet, somehow they didn't seem to mind it. Maybe it was easier if you chose your situation.

His parents' room was three times the size of his portion of the quadrant. As co-administrators of the habitat, they could afford a larger-than-necessary space. Their ceiling was not as high, reaching only fifteen feet instead of the twenty Amos preferred. Amos thought the low ceiling provided a more cave-like feel, but he accepted his parents' preference.

One wall was a floor-to-ceiling window, offering a cloud-level view of Eridu, his parents' home city. The tops of apartment buildings huddled together, seemingly floating on a layer of clouds. Some of the tallest building in Eridu had over five hundred floors, providing real rooms and homes for people. Many people on E-3 preferred the security of living in actual structures, arguing there was a more authentic feel to their homes.

Eridu was the capital of E-3 and considered the last great city, was at least five years of travel away. It was where the government bodies deliberated, including the Syndicate, and the administrators controlled the vast network of settlements spread around the galaxy. It was also where the evolutionary process was researched and managed, directing habitats like this one on critical decisions to move forward.

Amos's youthful idealism found the waste of resources these buildings represented disturbing, especially when the home software could replicate the feel so completely. Heck, his parents had even programed in a slight sway to the room, as if the building was rocking a bit in the wind.

Eridu was the last great city precisely because technology enabled people to live comfortably in much closer quarters. No longer was there a need to build upwards. Instead, populations could be grouped in any protected environment, from a ship traveling through space to an underground cavern, to a large dome in a field. All the resources required to provide a perception of space had been removed.

This city was a remnant of a more exuberant time, when the population as a whole had evolved to take full advantage of neodymium, enabling mind-to-computer communication. The total number of people was surpassing previous all-time highs, and the future looked limitless. Amos wondered at how the human race could keep making the same over-consumption mistake over and over again.

The walls on either side of the Eridu window were covered in reproduced paintings, a personal passion of his mother's and appreciated by his father. The paintings rotated through the typical masterpieces throughout history, including "Mona Lisa" by da Vinci, "Irises" by van Gogh, and "Galaxy" by VandenAkker.

One painting never rotated. It was displayed on a stand in a corner of the room, a George Inness painting of Niagara Falls. Amos was told it was an original painting, an item collected during the evacuation of E-1 and passed down through the generations of his family. Despite its age, the colors were more alive, more real. His mother cherished this original piece of art above all else, because it reminded her that a computer-generated world could never inspire the same raw emotional reaction as an original piece, reminding Amos that real eye contact and real touch could never be mimicked precisely.

As Amos's eyes were drawn inevitably to the painting, he wondered again at the beauty of the ancient natural wonder of E-1 as well as the sheer excess water on that planet at one time. Niagara Falls had stopped flowing well before humans left the planet. The end of the falls was viewed as the "canary in the coal mine," foretelling the end of the planet. No excess water, no primitive humans.

The painting itself was magnificent, but it also reminded his parents of their ancestral connection to E-1 and the Niagara region in particular. Amos had been told he could trace his ancestors all the way back to the Niagara region, where they had settled in the late eighteenth century after fleeing from the America Revolution. Their ancestor, who had settled in the area originally, was a member of

Butler's Rangers, a fearsome group loyal to the British Crown. Amos's father always claimed this fierceness and loyalty remained in their bloodline, although loyalty during this conflicted time in history was often considered disloyalty by those whom one abandoned. Amos took the lesson that in a complicated world, one must choose carefully to what—and to whom—one is loyal.

Despite the beauty of the view out the windows and the masterpieces on the walls, Amos enjoyed the display in the center of the room the most, where a computer-generated Dale Chihuly rested. The artwork was titled "Violet Persian Set with Red Lip Wraps Glass." The vibrant colors and waves made the artwork mesmerizing and added a sense of whimsical playfulness to his parents' room.

For the first time, it struck Amos that his parents' room was a perfect reflection of their values, which were succinctly: an outward view of the world from the center of power, a celebration of human masterpieces, family, loyalty, and a willingness to consider the absurd. Everything was consistent with societal values, except maybe the latter point

Along the fourth wall, from where Amos had entered through the door, were a series of private doors that allowed his parents to use the bathroom, go to bed without disturbing the other, or access a private food replicator room with the family's table and chairs. As administrators, they had a more permanent location on the quadrant that kept them close to basic facilities like a toilet and the food preparation machine. Apparently, they chose in-person meetings often, arguing that they preferred direct human contact. However, Amos realized suddenly that he had never actually seen his parents interact with another person.

Before he had processed the thought completely, Amos's mother greeted him with a warm, extended hug. After the initial squeeze had passed and his mother continued to crush his chest, Amos began to squirm and pull back.

"Oh Amos, as much as I enjoy our talks through the net, they can never replace a hug from my only son."

"Mother, it's good to see you."

She examined his mouth as he spoke. "I'll have to tweak the program for the hygiene center. It looks like you haven't flossed your teeth in some time."

"Yes, Mother." Amos flushed slightly as he offered a screwed up smile in a vain attempt to keep his teeth covered by his lips.

"Also, why can't you tell the computer to lengthen your pants? And really, a tank top? Here let me. . . . "

Amos felt the computer change the length of his pants, and suddenly his neck felt constricted as his mother over-rode his controls and put a collared shirt and tie on him.

"Mother! Stop it!" Amos jumped back and told the computer to change his clothes back. As much as he pressed his will toward the computer though, he knew his mother's administrative rights would override any attempt he might make to revert his clothes back to his choosing.

"But Amos, you always look so much cuter in a tie. Just be happy I don't put you in those wool pants you detest so much."

Amos thought back to how the computer would make his legs itch terribly when she put those pants on him. He always wondered as a toddler why the feel of the pants could not be altered to make them comfortable. It was only later that his mother confessed to giving the virtual pants that feeling in order to teach him how to act in uncomfortable situations. No wonder he had a rebellious streak!

Amos shot his mother an exasperated look. "Please, Mother! Can we at least take off the tie?"

"Oh, all right."

The constricted feeling around Amos's neck relaxed as the tie was removed and the top button undone.

"Thank you."

Amos's father turned away from the window out of which he had been staring and addressed Amos. "How would you efficiently plot a course back to Eridu if a supernova were in quadrant E-8?"

"Navigation? Nuts! That was last semester. I thought you had finished quizzing me on that material. Besides, you know I aced that class. I can load my notes from the quasi-crystals if you give me a moment."

"You should know this basic stuff off the top of your head. What happens if you're asked to do a course correction plot for a black hole? Or a two-dimensional sinkhole?"

"Come on, Father! I have plenty of time before I leave here to learn navigation."

His father's worried eyes clashed with his soothing answer. "Yes, but sometimes time progresses differently than we expect."

His father always seemed worried that he wasn't preparing Amos well enough for all of the challenges ahead.

"I'll make sure I review my navigation notes again," Amos offered in an effort to calm his father's concerns.

His father held his hand up to his chin, eyeing Amos closely. "Perhaps you're right, son, you still have time to master navigation."

Amos smiled brightly, trying to cheer up his father's typically sober mood. "Don't worry, Father, I have more time in this paradise of yours."

His father kept is eyes on Amos, seemingly trying to determine whether Amos was serious. "Son, you know your status as an evolved brought your mother and I here. It's not uncommon for the parents of the most evolved to administer the habitat dedicated to the development process."

A teasing smirk crossed Amos's lips. "You were given the difficult, no, impossible, challenge of developing an ungrateful brat. Hardly the highest calling within our society."

His father stood taller, taking a more defensive stance. "Raising an evolved is the most honorable. . . . " His face flushed as he realized Amos was mocking him.

Amos's smirk blossomed into a smile at his father, who chuckled to himself.

"Sorry, son. I'm just a bit worked up right now."

"Habitat problems?"

Amos's smile disappeared as he stared at his father, who was looking at Amos's feet, his thoughts somewhere else.

"What's the matter, Father? Why did you need to see me?"

"Your mother and I were put in this position to move evolution forward. A lot of resources were committed to this planet, to this habitat, to this colony. All of that commitment was with the understanding that we would help push evolution forward. This installation is not a simple colony on a distant planet; it is a managed effort to push humanity over what is hopefully the final hurdle."

Amos held up his hands as if the habitat had created a glass wall between them. "I know. You don't need to put any more pressure on me. Jeez, I'll go through my navigation notes!"

"No, son. I just wish I could explain . . . no."

A look of angst, mixed with a strange hesitation, almost like a computer glitch, came over his father's face. "What I'm trying to say is our work for this colony may finish sooner than expected."

"Okay, do we need to move to another habitat to finish my development?" Amos had heard that evolved changed their habitats when they entered new phases of their development. "What does that mean for everyone in the habitat? Are we all re-assigned to other missions? What happens to us?"

"Well. . . . "

His father seemed to be struggling to find the correct words, almost as if numerous voices in his head were squabbling, each offering alternative answers. "We will continue to live on this planet but without some of the . . . luxuries of the habitat."

"What does that mean? What 'luxuries' can be removed from an empty dome? And, does that 'we' include me or just you and Mother?"

His father's face became stern, and his voice flattened. "Son, as the evolved, your destiny lies outside this colony. Suffice to say that nothing would bring greater joy to your mother and me than knowing you can fulfill what is required of you."

Amos stared intently at his father, glanced at his mother, who offered a blank stare, and then returned his attention to his father. "Wait! There's something you are not telling me. You look pale, Father!"

His father shifted uncomfortably and glanced at Amos's mother. "Son, I can't tell you. In fact, the elders are likely displeased with what I've told you already. All I can say is that I have a wonderful surprise for you. Your freedom from this habitat is close."

Amos's face twisted into a mash-up of elation, confusion, and worry. Thoughts of experiencing worlds, real worlds that he could see, touch, and even smell bubbled up in his mind. "That's wonderful! I knew all the talk of four more years of study was a test of some sort!" Then Amos's triumphant look wilted. "But . . . what are you not telling me?"

His father's left eye flashed pink briefly, followed by a tear rolling down his cheek.

"Father! What is it?"

Amos's father closed his eyes and let out a deep breath. He looked upwards with tears in his eyes. After a few seconds, he looked back at his son. "You are being assigned to a science ship. The *U.S.S. Randall*. You will be a civilian intern in their navigation systems department. In another year or two, when you are old enough to enter the military, you will pursue the answers humanity must find. Son, you leave immediately."

Amos let out a girlish shriek, leaping in the air and pumping his fists. "Seriously? You mean it? This is incredible! No more studying? Real adventure? Oh, I can't wait to tell my friends!"

Amos paused, looked at his parents, and felt nervous suddenly. He knew that look. Their mouths were smiling, but their eyes gave away their worry. His mother turned away, stifling a sniff. His father's eyes became glassy, and it was obvious he was fighting back tears.

"Mom, Dad. Don't worry. We can still communicate often, and I'll come back here for vacations. It will feel like I never left!"

His parents shared a glance and a sad smile.

"What is it? What aren't you telling me?"

"Son, we are very happy for you," his mother said. "But we are sad, because you are leaving us for the first time. And to be honest, we're worried about you. Not because you aren't ready. You've earned this opportunity. It's just, well, it's a complicated world out there, and we hope you find your way."

Amos's mother stepped closer to Amos and gave him another long hug. "We are so proud of you. You have a good heart and your father's brain. You will do great in this world!" She held him at arm's length and looked him in the eyes. "Remember where you come from, Amos. Trust your instinct." She turned him toward the painting of Niagara Falls. "Remember what is important."

Amos's father walked over and hugged him. "Goodbye, son. We love you very much! Make us proud."

A door opened in the window, and two men dressed in military uniforms entered.

Amos looked at the guard on the right, puzzled by his appearance. His cold, dark eyes fixated on Amos, sending a shiver down his spine—and something else. A feeling stirred in Amos, almost imperceptible. Amos looked back at his parents, and his uneasiness dissipated for a moment. The guard on the right cleared his throat, drawing Amos's attention back. Their eyes connected, and then Amos's insides twisted violently. A desperate thought spasmed up to his consciousness.

Who am I?

"Dad? Mom?" He looked at his parents, who appeared flatter now, almost lifeless.

Amos's mother gave him another hug. "I choose to believe we will see each other again. I love you! Now, you must go."

Tears sprang from Amos's eyes as the weight of the moment hit him. "What aren't telling me?" Amos asked again.

The guards walked to Amos, stepping through his parents in their approach.

"Goodbye, son!"

Amos's father sniffed. His mother clutched his father's arm and buried her face into his shoulder.

A message from the guard on Amos's left entered his mind. "Son, let's make this easy."

With that, the guards took hold of Amos's arms and lifted him slightly, effectively carrying him out the door and into a long, dark hallway. The door closed behind him with deep, loud, all too real metallic clang.

8.

*Every spirit makes its house, but afterwards the
house confines the spirit.*

RALPH WALDO EMERSON (THE CONDUCT OF LIFE)

Shock gripped Amos, his body as unresponsive as his mind. The hallway they had entered was lit by a pair of flickering lights about every twenty meters. It was cold, a damp coldness that only reinforced his realization that he was outside the only home he had even known. Amos couldn't be sure, but he was fairly certain the raw, grey concrete walls on either side were one hundred percent real. The color touched off a deeper sense of foreboding within him.

The guards moved swiftly, almost forcing Amos to run to keep his feet beneath him. They had a firm hold on his upper arms, which made resisting the pace futile.

Suddenly, the weight of the moment landed on his shoulders, and his knees buckled. Without slowing their stride, the guards simply dragged him to keep him moving down the hallway, seemingly ignorant that his legs refused to carry his weight.

A flurry of emotions raged inside him. Confusion at why he was being escorted forcibly from his parents' room. Fear about what might happen to them. A background of elation at the thought this might lead to the opportunity to explore space. Nervousness about leaving the only home he had ever known. Terror of the unknown and what would be asked of him. Overwhelming these other emotions, however, was a heart-wrenching ache about leaving his parents—or the people he had always thought were his parents.

Amos reached out mentally to his parents in desperation for answers and to feel that familiar connection. What he felt instead shocked him to his core. Icy, empty silence. It was like the fingernails of his mind were scraping against the concrete walls that pressed in from both sides.

Even if his parents were busy in communication with a full array of people, Amos had always been able to feel their presence. Most of the time his parents would send a quick thought to let him know they would reach out when they had time. The loss of that connection was like an arm or a leg that had been severed, a cord cut. His brain struggled to come to terms with the connection loss as his thoughts wrestled to regain control of the lost appendage.

"No!" Amos cried, thrusting his legs wildly in front of him in an attempt to dig his heels into the slick concrete floor.

The soldiers simply lifted him higher. The physical feeling of being lifted was a shock. Despite all the advancements of virtual habitats, they still could not actually lift a person. For that, physical force was still required.

Stunned for a moment, Amos recovered, and then he began to kick wildly as he struggled to stop his forward momentum. His left foot kicked the back of the right knee of the guard on his left. The soldier's knee buckled slightly, but he recovered and kept moving forward. A thought pushed into Amos's mind.

"Let's not do this, son."

The word "son" snapped Amos out of his bewilderment, and he flailed his legs spastically in an effort to kick at the guards. He caught the guard on his right in the hip. It was like striking granite, and the guard barely reacted. However, it did give Amos a bit of leverage against the hold on his arms, and he pushed himself up and twisted his torso toward the left guard in an effort to break their hold. This caught the right guard by surprise, and Amos was able to slip his arm from the guard's grip.

Without the right guard holding his arm, Amos twisted and fell into the left guard, who squeezed his arm but fell forward, because he couldn't recover from the shifting weight. Amos landed hard on the concrete floor, and the left guard landed on top of him, knocking the wind out of him. A message from the left guard pushed its way into Amos's head.

"Hard way!"

A feeling like lightning bolts screamed through Amos's cortex. His muscles, from his back to his toes, spasmed, making Amos as rigid as a board. His back muscles contracted hard, arching him backwards. Amos let out a primal scream. The muscle spasms lasted about two seconds, but the psychological impact lingered, his mind recoiling at the momentary loss of control. Amos curled up on the ground and surrendered. The guards picked him up by the arms, and Amos's body went limp, devoid of resistance. The guards continued their march down the hallway, holding Amos high enough so that his toes scraped the ground.

For the rest of the march along the lifeless hallway, Amos hung his head forward and sobbed uncontrollably. He called out mentally to his parents, his friends, the guards, anyone who would listen. "Why? What's happening? Why like this?" Why couldn't he simply have kissed his parents goodbye and walked into the next stage of his life? It didn't make sense. His whole world had been stripped from him. What was happening?

Amos's mind sank into a trance as the cold, white lights passed in strobe-like fashion. After an immeasurable amount of time, just as drool began to fall from his mouth, the guards stopped abruptly in front of another large, imposing steel door.

Amos lifted his head, his eyes bloodshot, his cheeks wet from his tears, tacky snot hanging from his nose and drool collecting on his chin.

The left guard looked over at him. "Welcome to reality."

The door shuddered and opened inwards toward Amos. A high-pitched screech made Amos wince as the steel scraped against the concrete floor. A whoosh of cold, noxious air hit him in the face, causing his head to jerk back at the strong smell of ammonia.

The guard on the right took in a deep breath. "Ah, wakes you up, but I won't miss the stench of this planet."

"Grabs your senses, doesn't it? These habitats and their purified air put me to sleep," the guard on Amos's left replied.

The door continued to swing open, and Amos noticed a cold, bright light spreading out on the tunnel's walls and floor.

The left guard straightened up. "Look sharp. Let's finish our last task and report to the sergeant."

The insides of the room were revealed slowly, like a steel curtain had been pulled back illuminating the world. Once the door was open three quarters of the way, the guards lifted Amos slightly and walked across the threshold. Beyond the door was a huge, cone-like enclosure, almost what Amos imagined the inside of a wasp nest would look like. As the guards walked him into the hangar-like room, Amos looked around in wonder. He could not see the ceiling, as the room appeared to extend upwards into space itself. Horizontally, the room appeared to extend a half a kilometer in each direction.

The wall that encircled the space seemed to be made of tubes that extended upwards as far as Amos could see. At the bottom of each tube was a door. Amos saw periodic movement up and down individual tubes. Bewildered, he noticed a light source descend from the sky down a tube. It slowed as it reached the bottom. After it stopped at floor level, the door opened, and a person exited.

"What in the world is that?" Amos asked.

"That, son, is one of the shuttles that will take you off this rock," the guard to his left replied.

"What do you mean?" Amos felt his anxiety rise again, and he tried desperately to fight down the urge to try to escape back inside the habitat.

The guard on the right glanced at his partner.

"Don't worry," the left guard replied. "I know this process is a disorienting, but you'll be just fine."

Amos looked behind him, and the massive steel door through which they had entered the hanger had already closed. A wave of fear overtook him, and he tried to reach out to his parents again. Nothing. In fact, he couldn't feel any of his friends either. Amos sank to his knees.

"If you won't tell me what has happened to my parents, will you at least tell me what will happen to me?"

The left guard leaned over and put a hand on Amos's shoulder. "Son, just what your father told you. You have been assigned to the navigation department as an intern aboard the *U.S.S. Randall.* You will complete a two-year program and then enter the military to complete your mandatory service." After a pause, the guard added, "Leaving mother's womb is always hard for new evolved. But remember, you were created for this purpose, a purpose that will be explained to you more fully once aboard the ship. I have said too much. The rest will be answered by your commanding officer."

The guards lifted Amos to his feet and released his arms. Amos rubbed his triceps where their fingers had dug in. He looked around again and marveled at how this structure could have been so close to him his entire life and yet he hadn't realized it.

The left guard put his hand on Amos's shoulder and directed him to walk toward one of the doors at the base of a tube. Amos focused on the charcoal-grey structure and wondered at where it would take him. A brief thought entered his head that maybe he could escape during the shuttle ride. He would be alone, after all. After looking at the smooth, continuous surface of each tube though, he decided that escape was hopeless.

"What's that humming sound?" he asked the left guard. "I feel it as much as I hear it."

After an unusual delay the reply came through the network. "That, son, is the sound of the muon-catalyzed fusion reactors and electro-magnetic systems. The reactors provide the energy for the habitats on this planet and the electromagnetic propulsion, or EMPs, in the shuttle pods."

"Wait, habitats with an 's'?"

"Correct. Your habitat was one of four specially constructed for this planet, although your habitat has been the only one in operation for some time. While the atmosphere on this planet is practically non-existent and the fuel sources minimal, the location was ideal for the purpose."

"I never knew there were other habitats on this planet."

"Not just on this planet," the guard continued, "right next door. The purpose of this colony is high-end evolution. There's a whole city dedicated to researching reproduction and supporting human evolution."

"High-end evolution? Am I just an object to you?"

"Until you prove you're worth the effort. But enough, these questions should be answered on the ship."

Worth the effort? Fear seeped back into Amos, crawling down his spine. He was completely overwhelmed that so much existed in the physical world around him. He had spent most of his life sharing thoughts and conversing across vast expanses of space. The fact that there were people just outside his habitat, much less other habitats, was shocking.

Amos returned another thought through the network. "Is it always this busy—and loud?" He stopped short and realized there were actual people around him. Real people, not just objects filling perceived space. The musky smell of sweat soaked uniforms suddenly awakened his senses to the bustle of life surrounding him.

Hundreds of people were running around, moving even faster with the help of the dynamic floor that shuffled cargo and equipment around. People were actually yelling at each other, which was shocking in and of itself, since they could be sending thoughts much more efficiently. It was like he had entered a wasp nest after someone had stepped on it.

"People are yelling, because all the communication connections are at capacity. This is a huge logistical challenge to set up for the next evolved."

"Next evolved? You mean another is on the planet? But wait! Where are my parents going?"

The guards shared another look. This time, both of their eyes sparkled pink. "Those questions will be answered on the ship."

"Wait! What does that mean?"

"Your commanding officer will explain the rest."

Amos felt weak in the knees and almost collapsed from the realization of the enormity of the world and his situation. The guards grabbed his arms once again and held him up.

A message from the network pushed into Amos's mind. "Don't worry, son. You'll be all right. I know this is a lot to process at first, but it will begin to make sense in time."

With that, the guards carried Amos over to the door at the base of the tube that had just released another person. The slightly concave door slid open as they approached the tall, charcoal-colored tube, revealing a bulbous cone-like structure inside. The base of the structure was flat and emitted a humming sound. As Amos looked closer, he realized the structure was floating above the floor.

"The shuttle is propelled by EMP, right? I've seen these work through mind videos but never in real life."

"Correct. Although the truth is, you haven't experienced anything in real life. The base has a muon reactor and EMP system. The tubes provide the structure the EMP works against, as well as shielding the surrounding area from the effects of the EMP. Once the shuttle reaches the escape velocity required for this planet, the shuttle exits the tube. From there, the ship takes over control of the EMP system and guides you to the appropriate landing bay. At that point, your commanding officer will greet you and answer your questions."

"Should I be nervous?"

"No. The mass of this planet is relatively small, so the escape velocity is not very high. These tubes were designed for a much larger planet and thus are longer than needed. Those two factors and the advanced control system managing the rate of your acceleration should mean you experience a fairly comfortable acceleration."

The second guard opened his mouth as if to protest but snapped it shut again, and a smile appeared on his face.

Amos knew enough about EMPs to know they had a low rate of failure and were a fairly standard method of transporting people and cargo between a planet and a ship.

"No, I meant about meeting my commanding officer."

A quick twitch at the sides of both guards' mouths suggested he should be terrified.

"Good luck, son," the guard on his left said.

The guards turned Amos around, and Amos twisted his neck to see another concave door in the shuttle slide open, revealing a basic black seat. The guards backed him into the shuttle, pushing him into the seat.

"Try to keep your back straight. If you don't, you may end up with a herniated disk, or even a broken back. Nothing that can't be fixed, but it will make meeting your commanding officer even more painful."

"Wait! I thought you said this ride had little risk!"

The guards stepped back with smiles on their faces, and the door to the shuttle slid closed.

———————

"This may have been a mistake, sir." Sarah shifted her focus away from the monitoring sensors and pushed a worried thought to the captain.

"Doesn't matter. I've got my orders from the Syndicate directly."

"Directly? They've taken a close interest in this one. Previously they went through the chain of command."

"Ensign, you focus on Mr. Hare. I'll focus on chain of command."

"Yes sir."

9.

Sweat rolled down Amos's back as the door slid shut. He knitted his fingers together in his lap, cracking his knuckles as each finger flexed and squeezed. After a moment, he released his grip, leaving his fingers as white as the surrounding walls. He closed his eyes and took a few calming breaths, fighting back the anxiety that was growing inside.

"Mother?" Amos whimpered. The same empty coldness he felt in the tunnel confronted his senses again, like his life in the habitat had been switched off. Nothing felt familiar. Any warmth extended by his parents, friends, or community had disappeared.

An uneasy feeling sprouted in his stomach that a part of him had actually been cut off, like an umbilical cord. Any access he had had to storage crystals, computer arrays, or friends was simply gone. He had never felt so alone, so removed from others. He began to gasp for air.

An eager female voice broke Amos's thoughts. "Mr. Hare, please sit up and allow the safety restraints to engage."

Bewildered, Amos looked around for the source of the voice, remembered where he was, and straightened his spine. His eyes focused on a small green dot that had appeared on the wall about two feet from in front of his nose.

"Thank you," the voice said. "Please prepare for transport."

Amos felt a vibration go up his spine as a hum grew in his ears. The pod shuddered slightly, and Amos felt his back compress, applying pressure to his shoulders as they tried to roll forward.

"Sit up straight, Mr. Hare," the female voice ordered.

Amos straightened his back again and pushed his shoulders back against the seat. A screen appeared in front of him where the green dot had been. The head and neck of a young woman with red hair pulled back tightly greeted him.

"Mr. Hare, you should arrive aboard the *U.S.S. Randall* momentarily. The navigation officer, Lieutenant Jahan, will greet you upon your arrival. We will see you soon."

The screen blinked out.

Warm reception, Amos thought sullenly. *Maybe they'll have a cake for me as well.*

Suddenly, Amos's stomach dropped, and cake didn't sound like such a good idea. The restraints over his shoulders tightened, pulling him back into his seat. It felt like two boulders had been placed on his shoulders and weights attached to his arms.

Should . . . have . . . peed, he thought, and then he passed out.

When Amos awoke, he was lying on a bunk with a blanket draped over him. A warm white light glared into his eyes as he opened them. He went to sit up but rolled over instead, fell about a foot off the bunk, and crashed into a bucket, knocking it over. After a moment of bewilderment, he questioned the motive of putting a bucket next to the bunk. Then his stomach turned inside-out all over the floor.

"The bucket was a good idea, in theory." Amos lamented before he collapsed into his own vomit.

"Welcome aboard, Mr. Hare," a male voice said.

Amos lifted his head, puke and drool stringing from the side of his face. His arms were tangled in a blanket, so he rolled over slightly and looked up. His eyes glazed, all he could see was a dark blur of a figure standing over him.

"Not many new arrivals are carried aboard," the figure continued. "Some are carried off, but most can at least manage to report for duty before losing their lunch."

Amos groaned and rolled onto his back. "What happened to me? What's happening . . . to me?"

"A new life, Amos. Birth is always traumatic, so we'll give you some leeway. But your talents are in great demand, so we can't be too patient."

Amos lifted himself off his stomach and onto his hands and knees. "Birth? What are you talking about? I'm fourteen years old." Amos's stomach churned up another round, which also missed the bucket. He rolled over and sat in the vomit, one hand propping him up. He tried to focus, but his head wouldn't stop spinning.

"Ensign, please clean up Mr. Hare. See if he can keep down a meal, and familiarize him with his accommodations."

"Yes, Captain," a female voice purred.

The man walked away, and Amos heard a door slide open and closed with a low whoosh.

Amos looked at where the female voice had come from. His eyes fought his efforts to focus, but after a second, the image sharpened. The same redhead that had appeared on the screen in the shuttle was walking toward him. Suddenly, Amos was conscious that only the blanket was covering him.

He pushed a thought command toward the computer. "Clothing, standard preference."

Nothing.

Amos repeated the command out loud. "Clothing, standard preference!"

The redhead stood directly over him, and the sides of her mouth twitched upward in a mild form of mockery, or was it amusement?

"Until you are officially processed, you do not have access to the computer. I apologize for the lack of clothing, but the clothes you were wearing were . . . spoiled. Needless to say, it was the right decision to leave you in this state while your body adjusts."

Amos blushed and raked at the blanket with his fingers, trying in vain to cover himself. *Great,* he thought. *Sounds like I made quite the entrance onto the ship. Maybe they'll offer me a diaper.*

"Mr. Hare, you will find your uniform on the chair in the corner. However, I suggest that you clean yourself up first by taking a shower."

Her eyes darted down briefly at his exposed legs before looking into his eyes again. "Sir, would you like some assistance getting up?" Again, a small smile crept toward the edges of her pursed lips.

Amos turned a deeper shade of purple. "No, thank you. I can manage."

Her mouth maintained the sly grin, and her eyes sparkled. "Let me help you up."

A look of shock, then understanding, overcame Amos. She couldn't communicate mind-to-mind, and he didn't have access to the ship's network. She hadn't heard his thought.

"No, no, thank you. I think I can manage it," he said a little too hastily. "Please leave me."

Amos rolled onto his knees, put one hand on the bunk, and pushed himself upright as he clutched the blanket. He looked around for the bathroom, or at least a door to a bathroom, but found only what appeared to be solid walls. Amos started to send a request to the computer, but then he remembered where he was.

The redhead continued to stand in the corner. "I can help you do that, Mr. Hare. You are not familiar with the shower, and besides, you've never actually put on clothes before."

Amos was still sitting on the floor, leaning against one hand. "I have so!" he replied in a belligerent voice, but then he stopped to think if he had ever put on real clothes. "Well, how hard can it be?" he asked in an indignant voice. "I've felt covered my whole life. I think I understand how to put it together."

The woman sighed and extended her right hand. "Give me your blanket, and I'll wait over there while you get cleaned up, and then I'll take you to get some food."

Amos looked around the small room, which was similar to his room in the habitat, only smaller. "Er, here? You're waiting . . . here?"

"Of course. Now come on. You look like you just crawled through a Mype's jelly field, and you don't smell much better."

She extended her hand in an effort to help him up. Amos gripped the sheet with his left hand and reached up awkwardly with his right. She clasped his hand and yanked him to his feet. However, in the process of rising, the blanket fell off his shoulders, and Amos was left clutching it in front of his groin with the rest of the blanket pooling around his feet.

She smirked. "Not bad—for a baby."

Amos turned red again and glared at her. "I'm *not* a baby!"

Chagrined at the shrill sound of his own voice, he pressed further. "You can't communicate with your mind. What is that like?"

A blank look shadowed her face before she let out a wild laugh. "I imagine a lot of people are going to ask you that same question but in reverse. It will all be explained to you shortly. I'm here now to help you manage the basics of life, such as showering and getting dressed."

"Forgive me, this has all been very sudden," Amos replied in a petulant voice, frustrated at his impotence. "When I awoke this morning, I thought my main task was to finish a school report."

The woman took a step back. "No, I apologize. I forget how disorienting this process can be. Let's start simply. My name is Sarah."

She reached out her right hand. Amos regarded it cautiously and then looked up at Sarah's eyes, which seemed fiendishly friendly, like she knew the joke but wouldn't share it. He extended his right hand tentatively toward her.

"Amos, call me Amos."

She grabbed his hand and gave it a brief shake. "Good to meet finally you in person."

Amos gave her a puzzled look.

She turned and pulled him over to the corner of the room where there was a drain was in the floor.

"Stand here."

Before he could react, she yanked the blanket off him.

"Sorry. I don't have patience, and, well, living on a ship in close quarters means we're not shy." After a pause, she continued in a stern, motherly voice. "Get used to having someone real around."

Amos started to protest and tried to cover himself, but then he nearly jumped out of his skin as water shot from holes placed above and to the side of his body. The water didn't fall though. Instead, it moved back and forth in a scrubbing motion, took on a fragrance, and after about thirty seconds, fell to the floor and went down the drain.

"Hold your breath for this part."

Amos began to open his mouth to ask why when water shot out from the holes and engulfed his head. He choked as the water went up his nose and down his windpipe. The water moved swiftly around his head, but this time it only lasted a few seconds before it fell to the floor. Amos doubled over, fell on his hands and knees, and coughed up the water from his lungs.

"I told you to hold your breath. Given your state, I used twice the normal amount of water in the quantum shower."

After another attempt to turn his now empty stomach inside-out, followed by some fitful coughing, Amos looked up with vengeful eyes from his exposed position on the floor. He began to protest again but remembered he was still completely naked.

Sarah reached out to the wall where two towels hung on hooks. She pulled off the smaller one and waved it teasingly at him. Her eyes slid down over his body, leaving the feeling of an oil slick. She tossed the towel to him and then pointed at the chair in the corner. "Put your clothes on, and I'll start to answer your questions."

Amos looked over at the chair with his clothes lying on it. He noticed the smooth, carved eboney surfaces. "Hey! That's my family chair! How did it get here?"

"We had it transferred to the ship once you left your room in the habitat."

"It was moved up here before I saw my parents? Why?"

"Are you looking to start a fight in your birthday suit? Admit you're not in the strongest position to take moral stands, and then get dressed so we can talk."

Amos began a vain attempt to dry his body with what turned out to be a hand towel while keeping his private parts covered. Sarah glanced down, smiled slightly, and then looked back at Amos. Amos shot her an angry look, but when that didn't stop her, his face turned to pleading.

"Oh, all right, I'll look away," she said finally. "For someone who walked around for fourteen years in nothing at all, you sure are a prude."

"Huh? What do mean no clothes? The computer covered us from one another. How do you know. . . ?"

Sarah looked pointedly at his clothes. Amos tried to wrap the hand towel around his waist but ended up simply holding himself with the towel. He stalked over to the chair. His spirits lifted momentarily as he studied the intricately carved armrests. He glided his hand over the familiar backrest and admired the ribs running down to the seat. Just touching something that connected him to his family and the habitat made him feel sane.

After a moment, he turned and stared at Sarah. Her eyes rose to meet his.

"What? Oh fine, I'll turn around, prude, but I'll have you know I've seen most of the men on this ship naked, despite my sixteen years. So you're nothing new."

As Sarah turned her back to him, Amos looked down at his clothes. They appeared to be some sort of a uniform.

"Your clothes should fit perfectly," Sarah said over her shoulder. "Your measurements were taken just before you left the habitat. I'm afraid you won't be allowed to wear a tank top though, because it's not acceptable dress on the ship. Also, your pants will need to fit appropriately. We allowed you some flexibility but also tried to encourage you to conform to social norms."

Amos shivered. "You talk like you've been watching me my whole life. Like you know me."

"We have, and yes, I do. Just as you have also been training for your role your entire life, I have been trained my entire life to partner with you after your birth from the habitat. While you do not know me, I have watched and learned about you every day since I was six and you were four"

Amos blanched. "Again, you talk of my birth like it just happened. You've been watching? Too many questions in my head. I . . . I'm feeling overwhelmed."

"Put your clothes on, and we'll continue."

Amos picked up the collared shirt. It had a blue breast and black stripes down the side, and the fabric was thick and stretchy. The collar looked like it would extend up to his ears.

"Most people put on underwear first."

Amos turned and realized Sarah was watching him in the mirror hanging on the side wall.

She giggled. "Sorry, it's just that I've watched you walk around completely naked your whole life. It's strange to look away now."

Amos panicked when he thought of all the things he did in what he thought was the privacy of his room. "You've watched me at *all* times?"

"Yes, of course."

"Including in the bathroom and . . . before I fell asleep?"

"Yes. Oh! That? Completely normal for a fourteen-year-old boy. In fact, most of the officers were quite impressed by your virility."

Amos shot her an exasperated look. "Officers? Does everyone know?"

"Oh yes. Not much remains a secret on this ship. But don't worry. It's a very positive sign, since we will eventually have to reproduce." Sarah peeked slyly over her shoulder and gave him a wink.

"Reproduce? You? Me?" Amos dropped back into the chair with a shocked look on his face. "What is my life? Do I even *have* a life of my own?"

Anxiety flooded up from his gut and threatening to overwhelm him.

Sarah walked over calmly, picked up a sleek pair of shimmery blue underwear, and handed them to him. "Put these on first. These are a gift from me to welcome you aboard. They cost me a pretty penny, too. The fabric is Covarian silk."

Amos stared at the underwear. He sat down and lifted his hand slowly to take the offered present. Leaning forward and resting his forearms on his knees, he dropped his head. "What am I?"

Sarah took the underwear from him, bent down on her knees, and placed his feet through the holes. "You are the evolved. Come on. Enough chit-chat. We need to get moving if we're going to get something to eat before you meet the captain."

Amos watched Sarah tend to him with a melancholy feel inside his belly.

10.

"Clothing, I mean real clothing, feels, well, different."

Sarah and Amos stood shoulder-to-shoulder in a lift that was taking them up to see the captain. Amos was wearing the utilitarian uniform that had been issued to him. It was mostly black with blue across the chest. The fit was snug but not uncomfortable, allowing the right amount of room for a full range of movement. Amos puffed out his chest, rolled his shoulders back, and flexed his triceps.

"It kind of tickles in some places and scratches in others," he observed. "The collar makes me feel like you've clapped me in irons!"

Sarah offered a wry smile. "Well, maybe we did."

Amos tucked a finger in the collar and tried yet again to stretch the fabric away from his skin.

"Oh, quit your complaining. Everyone wears clothes. You'll get use to them." Sarah's eyes traveled over the entirety of his body, appraising the fit approvingly. "And besides, you'll appreciate the temperature control they provide."

She explained that the uniform's fabric was programmed to provide warmth when the body felt cold through wireless communication with the environmental control or EC system.

"Look, I get that the climate on the ship varies significantly," Amos said, "but I don't plan to crawl down a support tunnel next to the outer hull! I'll be quite happy to carry out my duties in my room."

"First off, your duties will require your actual presence around other people. Second, your uniform lets people know your rank, providing a secondary method by which to identify you. Finally, most, but definitely not all, people want to see you clothed!" Sarah's face turned innocent as she batted her eyelashes.

She went on to explain that the blue band across his chest meant that he was a non-commissioned warrant officer. His formal rank and responsibilities had not been given to him yet. Sarah also provided a brief overview of the colors associated with ranks. Black for commanding officers, dark blue with a subdued sparkle for Navigation, and light blue for science. Civilians onboard the ship also wore the same basic uniforms, although they could alter the cut and colored bar across the chest to suit their personal taste, just so long as it didn't conflict with military issue.

Sarah wore a uniform with a dark blue band across her chest. Light reflecting off the fabric gave the impression of a constellation of stars. Like Amos, her uniform signified that she was a navigation officer. Upon completion of officer training, a navigation officer could choose the constellation on his or her uniform, which typically matched the quadrant in which they had trained. Sarah also had a diamond lapel pin that designated her rank as ensign. Like Amos's uniform, her collar extended high up around the neck, providing additional warmth, if needed.

Amos continued to fidget. "And another thing, Sarah, thank you for the gift. I really appreciate it. However, would it be possible to find some more comfortable underwear? This underwear is kind of distracting, especially since I'm not used to real clothes."

Sarah gave him a hurt look. "All right. I'll have the standard issue delivered to the room. I just thought you'd like the silky feel."

"Thank you." Amos shifted and stretched his hips in an effort to remove the underwear from an entirely too intimate location.

"Please don't do that in front of the captain. He'll think your development went wrong."

"Well, maybe it did," Amos replied indignantly. His *development?* It was like he had emerged from a test tube!

The door to the lift slid open to reveal a large, well-lit room. The first thing that struck Amos was the energy coming from the room. While he couldn't tap into it, he felt it. It was a powerful vibe, almost like a deep hum that pressed against his senses. It was the kind of energy created by powerful silicon and organic systems working together. The layout was organized to enable information sharing with as many people and systems as possible.

While some people moved about, the crew were mostly sitting in chairs that conformed to their bodies. The chairs were arranged in clusters around the floor. Each cluster, or pod, surrounded a pillar that flashed general information to the room, providing anyone on the floor with a visual status update of the pod.

The crew members in the chairs focused mostly on their assigned pillars. Amos assumed each person had numerous communication channels open with the silicon systems in their pod. The visual cues on the pillars were probably a secondary system.

Amos shivered slightly. The temperature in the room was a few degrees cooler than in the lift. Without a mental prompt, he felt his uniform warm up slightly, taking the shiver out of his muscles.

Sarah noticed his discomfort. "The captain likes it cooler on the bridge. It keeps everyone alert."

Another shiver ran up his spine. "The shiver wasn't completely due to the cold. This room feels, well, daunting!"

Sarah nodded. "It's a lot to take in the first time."

A smile crept across Amos's lips.

She cocked her head at him. "What's so funny?"

"I'm just imagining everyone naked."

Sarah let out a giggle. "Well, that humanizes this place. Now that's all I'm going to think about when I'm up here. Thanks a lot!"

"You're welcome—for being humanized."

Sarah took a couple of steps forward and began a brief tour. "The room is laid out quite logically. The design ensures immediate information sharing, team building, and redundancies. For example, the commanding officers are in constant mind-to-computer communications with each pillar. However, they only receive high-level reports from each pillar according to the capacity limits of their minds to accept data feeds. The visual displays offer a redundant communication method for officers in case their remote links to the pillars are disrupted. So, for example, if the captain is devoting additional mental resources to navigation, at the expense of engineering, he can keep an eye on the engineering tower as he works with navigation."

Amos nodded. "Makes sense."

"The data pillar to our right is devoted to engineering," Sarah continued. "The display screens and holograms show the status of the engines, life support, and structural integrity."

Amos focused on the data pillar and noted that all of the systems appeared to display green with a scrolling text of system updates and routine test results. Surrounding the pillar were four officers seated in chairs. Three of them were chatting in a hushed tone with each other, glancing over at Amos and Sarah, while the fourth was focused intently on the pillar.

Sarah continued with her tour, walking slowly toward the back of the chair closest to the lift. "Each of these stations on the bridge has a minimum of four individuals at all times. Typically, only one person is required to administer routine maintenance and operations. The other three troubleshoot, jump in if a problem arises, and serve as the primary administrator during shifts. Each station has a ranking officer, who may or may not be present at the pillar. Typically, the ranking officer monitors operations remotely while tending to other requirements of their position."

"Why do they need to sit in pods? Why couldn't they sit in their rooms and work remotely?"

"Good question. The data pillars mirror information displayed on similar pillars in each of their respective areas on the ship. But the short answer is what I explained before. Effective information sharing, team building, and redundancy. Occasionally, an officer assigned to a pillar is allowed to work remotely, but most prefer to sit in close proximity to each other. By sitting close to each other, a more cohesive team is built as subtle body language signals can be picked up by others. It also provides a more social atmosphere for the individuals. We are social animals. Something is lost when all communication goes through the filter of a network computer."

"You mean none of them can communicate mind-to-mind?"

"No, only the most evolved can do that." Sarah gave Amos a pointed look.

Amos focused intently on the people seated around the engineering pod, watching how they interacted with each other. He had never really watched people before. He had spent most of his time in his room. It wasn't like he was a hermit; he had talked constantly with friends, teachers, and his parents. Besides, his room wasn't even really a room. He changed the walls and views often to suit his mood. Even when he chose to eat in the communal hall, he was usually interacting with others in his mind, leaving the people around him in the background. A sense of loss crept into Amos's mind as he thought of his home, causing his chest to constrict slightly. Was that what his home was? Background?

"Sarah, how many fully evolved people are on this ship?"

When Sarah didn't answer, Amos glanced over at her and found her eyes were looking forward, focused on a person approaching.

"Lieutenant Guan, sir. The captain has requested to see Mr. Hare."

A tall, light-skinned man strode up and stopped in front of Sarah and Amos. He was like a double eclipse on Kepler-47c. Their view of the room was obscured by his chest and shoulders, which were almost as wide as Sarah and Amos put together. Amos couldn't help but stare at his arm with the thought that Guan had evolved somehow to incorporate iron into his physique. Guan's frame looked like he could have been one of Atlas's pillars, holding Earth and sky asunder.

Amos moved his eyes up to a surprisingly youthful face despite the worry lines that creased Guan's brow. Guan's eyes were piercing, searching and evaluating Sarah as she stood at attention. After a moment, he relaxed his shoulders, and his mouth stretched wide into what was either a smile or a precursor to a snap of his jaws around unsuspecting prey.

"Yes, of course Ensign Laka," Guan said in a deep voice that seemed to resonate at a cellular level, demanding Amos's full attention. He shifted his stare to Amos. "Welcome aboard, Mr. Hare. We have eagerly anticipated your arrival. The captain is busy at the moment but will meet with you when he's done."

Amos stood awkwardly, unsure of how to reply. He fought down a nervous urge to crack a joke. "Ah, thank you sir," he squeaked out.

"Don't let him intimidate you," Sarah said. "He's nothing but a crusty creampuff."

Guan furled his brow and looked back at Sarah, letting out a low growl. Sarah giggled, and the sides of her mouth twitched upward.

"Ensign, how am I supposed to gain any respect if you don't allow me to intimidate people?" Guan asked, and then he let out a bark of a laugh. He turned back to Amos. "We are excited to finally have you aboard. I, for one, have been eagerly anticipating the start of our mission. I was getting tired of constantly talking about the Boron Bane with you."

Stunned, Amos took a closer look at Guan. "You . . . you mean you were one of my friends?"

Guan chuckled. "Yes, and your obsession with history was becoming quite tedious. Much more interesting to look forward, explore, save humanity and all that."

Amos continued to stare dumbly at Guan, trying to connect his hardened face with the young fresh faces of his friends, or the friends he thought he had. A deep sense of loneliness welled up in him. He knew all too well reality was about perception, but it didn't make reprogramming his own account any easier. He tried to re-imagine his friends here on the ship in different forms, merely actors for his development.

Guan nodded at Sarah, then turned and strode back to his station near the far end of the room.

Sarah leaned over to Amos. "He's one of the best weapons and defense officers in the military. If he comes across as a hard-ass, it's because he is one. He finished at the top of his class in special operations. He could have had a very successful career in tactical insertion, but he chose to transfer to space exploration instead. He's the one person I would want on this ship if we had any trouble. He's a brilliant leader and one of the most loyal people you will ever find. He considers everyone on this ship his family, and he will fight to the end to defend them. Oh, and don't ever call him a crusty creampuff. That really pisses him off."

Amos shot her a confused look. "How come you can get away with it?"

"Because we dated for a while when I was into muscle."

Amos's mouth opened slightly and then closed. Sarah kept her eyes forward, but her mouth formed into a sly smile.

"Don't worry. Now I like mental muscle. So much more stimulating!" Sarah tilted her head and batted her eyes at Amos.

Amos blushed and turned his attention back to the room. "So, Engineering is over here, and the Weapons station is at the far end. What are the other four pillars?"

"To our left is Intelligence. They control all the sensors and perform any required evaluations of the surrounding space, offering recommendations of risks to the ship and crew. A little further down from them is Communications, which can monitor any conversation on board and control bandwidths to central command. To our right, across from Communications, is Operations. They oversee all the basic necessities of the ship and crew, including medical, dental, food, and waste. Beyond them at the far end of the room on the right is Navigation, and you already know that on the left is Tactical Weapons and Defense."

"Where's the captain?"

"Where he can best command," a voice boomed from above.

Startled, Amos looked up and saw a slim man standing at a railing above them.

11.

"Ensign, please escort Mr. Hare up to the bridge." The captain's deep, baritone voice rolled down the stairs to where Amos and Sarah were standing.

"Yes, sir!" Sarah turned to Amos and smiled nervously. She held out her arm toward the stairs next to the lift door that led up to the bridge.

Amos looked at Sarah with desperate eyes, pleading for some unspoken guidance on how to approach the captain. All he heard were his own thoughts. *Nothing? No guidance on what to expect? How to act? Not even a word of encouragement, 'Break a leg'?* The lack of connectedness to anyone made Amos unsure about everything, like he had lost a vital sense like sight that allowed him to interpret his environment.

Sarah's eyes seemed to convey some message, and then she nodded toward the stairs. "After you, Mr. Hare."

Amos knitted his eyebrows at Sarah, sent an unkind one-word mental message to her just to make sure she really couldn't hear him, and then turned toward the steps. The captain watched silently as Amos walked to the bottom of the sweeping set of stairs that arced around from the base of the elevator doors up to where the captain was standing at a handrail overlooking the floor below.

"Well, at least now I'll get some answers," Amos telegraphed mentally to no one in particular.

A familiar voice sounded inside Amos's head, "Your life truly begins at this moment. Embrace it, but be cautious."

"Bina? Bina!" Amos reached out mentally and almost tripped on the first step. Then a calming feeling pressed against him, like a reassuring hand on his shoulder.

"Amos, this may be the last time we communicate. Trust in yourself. You are entering a wondrous but dangerous world. Your abilities will be critical to guiding life forward and overcoming its greatest challenge. You will find things that appear strange and baffling to humans. It will be up to you to find the path forward."

Amos sucked in a quick, shallow breath as Bina continued.

"Know that I will be watching but will be unable to correct your mistakes, for a mistake today may be the necessary path toward your ultimate goal. I don't know the path that must be taken. That will only be unveiled by the passage of time. Instead, know that you possess the inner strength and ability to overcome most obstacles in your path. But you cannot do it alone. You will need to find allies, friends, and even rivals who can help you attain your goal. Above all else, remain open."

"Goal? Bina, you're talking in riddles."

Amos's foot struck the front of the second step, and he pitched forward onto his hands. A cold sweat burst from his pores and stained his uniform. Any sense of Bina was gone.

"Amos, are you all right?" Sarah, who had been following him, bent down to help him get up. "What happened? You're sweating! Is your uniform malfunctioning?"

"No, no, it's fine. Just give me a second. I just feel a bit light-headed. A lot to process today, and I fear my mind is still overwhelmed."

"Understandable. For a moment there you looked like you had seen a ghost."

Amos looked up at Sarah with haunted eyes. "Maybe I did."

Sarah gave Amos a nervous look and then glanced up at the captain with a look of concern on her face. "Amos, please get up. The captain is waiting and watching you."

"Yes . . . yes, of course." Amos pushed himself back onto his feet. His uniform had become decidedly cold as it worked to offset his sweating body. A chill went down his spine, which resulted in a warming of his uniform.

"The temperature of your uniform is jumping all over the place. I think it may be malfunctioning. Do you want to change before talking with the captain?"

"No." Amos looked around nervously, fearful he would actually see a ghost but hoping that Bina would appear on the bridge or anywhere else in the room.

A flurry of confused thoughts streamed through his mind. What was happening to him? To his world? To his life?

As Sarah put her hand under Amos's arm, a look of concern on her face, his mind churned through possibilities but then returned to his current predicament, which was kneeling on the stairs with Sarah trying to lift him up.

Come on, pull it together. You can have your freak out moment later in your room. Try not to embarrass yourself anymore in front of the captain.

Amos realized it wasn't just the feeling of being disconnected, it was also the feeling of people. People surrounding him, with their energy and various subconscious ways of communicating. He felt like he had been pushed into a room where everyone spoke a language he couldn't understand.

One last feeling came over him that he wasn't entirely sure was his own. The feeling was that he should continue to keep Bina a secret. Once he had sorted through everything that had happened, he could decide if it was safe to talk about her.

Putting his right hand on the handrail, Amos let Sarah lift him back up. Then he proceeded to climb the rest of the way up the staircase. Sarah climbed the stairs next to him on his left. When they reached the landing at the top, she turned to Captain Melville. and stiffened.

"Captain Melville, may I present Mr. Hare," she announced, her voice wavering a bit.

Amos was greeted by a ghastly, contorted, twisted face. Captain Melville's right cheek was a pit in his face, the result of some horrific battle or accident. The left side of his face was covered by a black tattoo, causing Amos to recoil as he tried to determine which side was less terrifying. The tattoo only seemed to mirror the physical horror of the missing right side. Maybe it was a vain attempt to regain symmetry.

Conscious that he was staring, Amos forced himself to look away from Melville's probing eyes. He was dressed in black. He wore his service dress uniform, a tight-fitting jacket tailored to accentuate his broad shoulders and provide a sense of authority. The crisp, clean look of his uniform was a striking contrast to his ruined face.

The jacket's neckline was tight with the top of the left side extending and wrapping around over his right shoulder with no obvious button or zipper. His pants were also cut precisely to his body, with a flat front and a leg that tapered down to fit tightly around the knee and ankle. The only obvious decoration that denoted his rank was a thin, multi-colored ribbon embedded into the fabric on the left side of his chest.

Captain Melville's eyes blazed as they sized up Amos, who lifted his eyes nervously to the captain's face for a few seconds. The muscles around the captain's cold eyes twitched slightly, and his eyes sparkled with pink. What looked like concern crept into the captain's eyes, but Amos got the uncomfortable feeling it wasn't for his well-being.

"Are you all right?" Melville asked. "If you need some time to adjust, we can postpone our meeting until you're well."

Amos shifted nervously. "No, sir. Thank you. The energy in this room is overwhelming and confusing to me, but I'm fine."

"Are you sure?" Melville pressed. "For a moment, it appeared as though you were trying to connect with your past life in the habitat. It can take time to . . . move on."

Amos tried to deflect the line of questioning, not wanting to discuss Bina. "No, sir. Just not used to real stairs, I think."

Melville continued to stare at Amos, as if trying to read him, apparently concluding he wouldn't get a straight answer. "Welcome aboard, Mr. Hare. Since you're okay, given your status as a civilian, I will excuse your rather unorthodox boarding and reporting for duty. In the future, I expect you to present yourself appropriately on the bridge."

Amos grimaced. "Yes, sir."

Melville's eyes shifted to Sarah, who stood rigidly next to Amos. "Please make sure that both of you are better prepared in the future."

"Yes, sir!" Sarah replied sharply, her cheeks flushing.

Melville's focus returned to Amos. "Mr. Hare, I am not a difficult person to serve under. While this is a military operation, our primary mission is scientific research. Because a large component of the mission is focused on discovery, and even creativity, a slightly more relaxed environment is beneficial. That said, a certain degree of formality and decorum is required to ensure this ship operates smoothly. I need to know that I have your full attention when addressing you and that you fully comprehend my orders and requests. If I do not feel my messages are received, then I must take action to ensure they are understood and executed flawlessly. Understood?"

Amos mimicked Sarah's rigid stance, lifting his chin slightly while maintaining eye contact. "Yes sir!" he replied as sharply as Sarah had previously.

"At ease, Mr. Hare." Melville relaxed his own stance slightly. "My orders are to support you in your efforts. I realize that you do not even understand what your role entails. This will be explained to you by the appropriate ship personnel." His eyes sharpened again. "While my orders are to support you, my responsibility to the safety of this ship and its crew take precedent. Make no mistake, I am in charge of this ship. So long as your efforts are productive to the cause and do not place this ship in jeopardy, we will get along just fine. If I believe you are not performing your duties or are acting in a manner that counters my command, I will confine you to your quarters. If you continue to refuse to cooperate, we will take you to E-3 to stand before the Syndicate, where you will answer for insubordination. Understood?"

Amos went rigid as he tried to swallow the bile that had worked its way into his mouth. "Yes sir!" Inside, he was churning, floating freely in a world he did not understand.

"Good." Melville swiveled on the balls of his feet, shifting his body so that he faced the officers at their stations on the bridge. He extended his right arm with an open hand. "Mr. Hare, this is the bridge of my ship."

Amos looked beyond where Melville was standing. Five officers were at their posts. While a few chairs were present, they all stood and appeared to be busy.

The bridge itself was smaller than Amos would have expected. A single screen wrapped 180 degrees around in a semi-circle against the back wall. In the middle of the bridge was a table with various holograms floating over it. Three command chairs were positioned in front of the table, closest to the front that faced outward over the floor below. On either end of the screen was a closed door that separated the end of the screen from the staircase that extended up from both sides of the lift below.

"Mr. Hare, may I present Commander Din, my second in command."

If the captain appeared stern, Commander Din appeared like fire could erupt from his eyes at any moment. As Din stepped toward him, Amos felt him do a quick appraisal from feet to head. Din's lips pinched together, mimicking the puckering sensation Amos felt in his tail end.

"Welcome aboard, Mr. Hare," Din said through pursed lips. "We have been awaiting your arrival."

"Uh, thank you, sir." Amos's will melted, and he felt his knees weaken.

Captain Melville moved past Din to introduce the next officer, but Din's stare held Amos in place. Amos could not feel any communication coming from him. It was like watching a mute try to shout obscenities.

"Mr. Hare, let me present Lieutenant Jahan," the captain offered. After a moment of silence, he pivoted to look back at Amos. "Mr. Hare, at your convenience."

Amos tore his eyes away from Din and looked over at the captain. "Sorry, sir." Amos took three quick steps toward the captain, stood rigidly, and wiped his hands down the front of his uniform.

"Lieutenant Jahan is the navigation officer and your commanding officer."

Lieutenant Jahan stood next to the captain with a warm smile on his face, looking like he was suppressing a laugh. His eyes seemed welcoming but also probing. "Welcome aboard, Mr. Hare. We're excited to finally have you join us in person."

Amos shifted awkwardly, wondering at the number of ways his stomach could flutter based on the range of emotions he was experiencing. "Thank you, sir. I look forward to working with you."

Jahan nodded approvingly. "After Ensign Laka has finished her tour, please report to me so that I can bring you up to speed."

"Yes, sir." Amos didn't quite know what to do with his hands, whether he should salute, stand at attention with them by his sides, or something else. As a compromise, he held his arms straight down by his sides and flexed his hands open and closed.

Jahan noticed Amos's discomfort. "And Mr. Hare, don't let Lieutenant Din scare you. I believe you will find him an invaluable leader during our mission."

Amos relaxed slightly. "Yes, sir. I will, sir."

Amos focused on Jahan. Something about him was different, familiar somehow, but Amos couldn't put his finger on it.

Captain Melville gave Jahan a pat on the shoulder and moved around the table toward the back of the room where the remaining three officers stood. Amos smiled and nodded to Jahan before hurrying to keep up.

Captain Melville approached the next officer, smiled, and turned toward Amos. "Mr. Hare, may I present Lieutenant Mal, who runs Engineering."

A radiant, tall, blond woman stepped toward Amos and extended her hand. "A pleasure to meet you, Mr. Hare."

A feeling of ease and happiness overcame Amos as he approached Mal, like finding a long-lost friend. What Amos felt around Mal was the opposite of what he felt around Din. How strange to feel so differently around organic humans.

"Lieutenant Mal keeps the systems on this ship running flawlessly," Melville said. "Her knowledge of the ship and its limitations is unparalleled. With her and her team on board, I believe we have a decent chance of overcoming the many challenges we will face on our journey."

Amos looked quizzically at the captain, but his stare returned to Mal. In turn, Mal's attention was focused on him. She continued to smile with her mouth and her eyes.

"Mr. Hare, the captain exaggerates my ability to pull his ass out of the fires he falls into so often. He and the entire crew have an uncanny ability to pull together and find solutions to difficult challenges. I merely help us down the proper path."

"Lieutenant Mal may not give life, but she's damn good at protecting it," Melville said, smiling.

Amos tilted his head towards the captain, waiting for him to elaborate. When none was offered he continued. "An honor to meet you, Lieutenant Mal," he said in a warm voice.

"I'm glad your development in the habitat is over, Mr. Hare," she replied. "I look forward to our journey together." She smiled again before turning back to the screen on the back wall.

"Our next introduction is to Lieutenant Reilly, our communications officer."

Reilly stood up from his hunched position, where he had been staring intently at a spot near the bottom of his screen, and looked at the captain. "Sir." Then he turned to Amos and gave a brief nod. "Welcome aboard, Mr. Hare. As the captain said, I am the communications officer. Together with the intelligence officer, we oversee all signal processing. My focus is on known sources that involve direct, one-to-one signals."

The last unintroduced officer, who was stationed next to Reilly, stepped into the conversation. "Mr. Hare, I'm Lieutenant Commander Sig, the intelligence officer. As Lieutenant Reilly explained, we work closely together. My expertise is interpreting broad sensor signals and identifying unexplained signals."

Both Reilly and Sig were taller than anyone else on the bridge, almost a foot taller than Amos.

"Good to meet both of you," Amos said, looking up.

The two officers gave a brief nod of confirmation and turned back to their respective stations.

Completing the tour around the bridge, Captain Melville led Amos and Sarah to the door at the top of the stairs they had climbed. The door opened as the captain approached, revealing a conference room.

"Mr. Hare, with the formalities out of the way, I think a more casual conversation is in order," he said over his shoulder.

12.

Captain Melville sat down at the head of a rich wood-looking oval table in the chair closest to the door. Commander Din sat to his right while Sarah pulled out the chair to the captain's left for Amos. Once he was settled, Sarah sat down on the other side of Amos. The chairs had high backs and conformed to Amos's body as he sat down.

The walls surrounding the room were video screens, offering an array of views of activities on board the ship. These included a view of the data pillars from the bridge, a cargo bay with containers moving around, and the engine room. What looked initially like a window to the outside was displayed in one place on the far wall but shifted to an internal wall when they entered the room. Amos was unsure whether the captain had a personal preference or if that particular part of the wall where the window had been would be used for another purpose.

An uneasiness crept into Amos as he tried to relax in his chair. He was about to find out his fate, or at least the course of his life. Inside, he was still reeling from the loss of what had been his life, but he tried his best to push down those emotions. Instead, he focused on what was ahead, which brought enough angst in his gut. At least it would offer some relief to know what was in his future. That thought only made his stomach tighten further.

"Mr. Hare, I realize that all of this is overwhelming, and we will try to be patient with you as you adjust," Captain Melville began.

A little unsure of what to expect, Amos gave an agreeable nod as the captain continued.

"Please understand that any impatience on our part is due to an urgency to begin the mission. We have some of the best minds in the universe on this ship, and to delay our departure much longer would be a disservice to them."

Sarah leaned forward. "Sir, given everything that Mr. Hare has experienced over the past day, I believe he is holding up remarkably well. This demonstrates both his stability and the success of recent modifications to the development environment in the habitat."

Captain Melville looked over at Sarah and appeared to share an unspoken thought with her. "Yes, of course, ensign. However," he gave Amos a pointed look, "the weakest link in this entire mission is sitting at this table."

That knot in Amos's stomach turned into a molten ball of iron. He began to sweat. This only caused his uniform to become colder, providing an extra shiver down his spine. He tasted acid in his mouth. On top of that, he was beginning to get pissed off. Why the urgency? Why so abrupt? These and a thousand other questions swirled in his mind until he settled on: *Why me?*

Amos straightened up in his chair, his face flushed despite the cold uniform, and opened his mouth to provide a voice to the jumbled emotions inside of him.

Before he could speak, Sarah jumped in, more forcibly this time. "Maybe now, but I believe the potential is there for what you call our 'weakest link' to become humanity's greatest asset."

She put her hand on Amos's arm, holding it in place against the armrest. Amos snapped his mouth shut, thinking better of telling off the captain during his first day.

Captain Melville looked over at Sarah again, and after a momentary pause, nodded at her. "All right, I'll give you the benefit of the doubt. But the success of the mission rests on his shoulders, and, ultimately, yours. Let me remind you that your primary responsibility is supporting Amos during his adjustment period. I know the emotional support comes easily to you, but the psychology has me concerned." Melville returned his gaze to Amos. "Now, Mr. Hare. Shall we go over the mission?"

Amos leaned forward, his back still tense, and put his arms on the table. "Please," he said with a twinge of teenage mockery.

The captain either ignored his tone or chose to overlook it. "I take it you are well versed on the laws of thermodynamics?"

Amos looked at Sarah and then back at the captain. "Basically, the first law states that energy is conserved, the second states that entropy increases in systems not in equilibrium, the third law—"

"Yes, the first two suffice in making the point. Our universe is not in equilibrium, and thus, entropy is increasing. Why is this important? Because the ultimate end state of our universe is a high-entropy diffuse gas, unable to support life. Life exists because it uses relatively low-entropy energy and produces high-entropy energy. In short, life accelerates the time to which the universe becomes a diffuse gas."

Amos had heard the argument before during his time in the habitat. Was this part of his programmed development?

"When you say 'universe,' you mean the brane in which we live, right?"

Melville nodded. "Yes, thank you. We should be very specific in how we describe our surroundings. Our brane is a multi-dimensional membrane-like object in a larger space, or what is referred to as the 'bulk.' It holds almost all the matter and energy with which we observe and interact. The entropy within our brane is increasing."

Amos picked up the topic to help soothe his raw emotions with something familiar. "Entropy is a measure of disorder. The second law is one of the basic observations of humans. A plate shatters when it hits the floor."

Melville rounded out the rest of the basics. "We're not entirely sure what is happening in the bulk surrounding our brane, since our ability to explore it is significantly constrained by our attachment to our brane. Learning about the bulk is of interest."

Melville paused as if waiting for a response from Amos, but Amos merely waited for him to continue.

"If entropy continues as it has since the creation of our brane, the ultimate end state of our brane is a diffuse gas, unable to support life, because there will be no suns, no planets, nothing that produces or stores the free energy on which life relies."

"The entropy barrier."

Melville nodded. "No one would have expected this to become an issue a thousand years ago when space exploration seemed unlimited. The problem stems from some basic laws of physics. The first is we can only use the free energy in the area accessible to us. The second has to do with our consumption rate."

Amos added a point from his teachings in the habitat. "As we have progressed down the path of managed evolution, we have become more and more complex life forms, with numerous levels of hierarchy for information processing. More complexity requires more energy to sustain it."

Melville nodded. "Right. Our ability to communicate with computers and our heightened intellectual abilities means the average person aboard this ship uses about a hundred times as much energy as a human from a couple millennia before."

Amos sat back and considered the issue, pulling all the information from his teachings to arrive at the obvious missing data point to complete the analysis. "And how much more energy do I require, given my status as evolved?"

Captain Melville looked over at Din and then returned his focus to Amos. "You consume about ten times more energy than the rest of us, a hundred times more when you're working at the limit of your capability. If it wasn't for advancements in synthetic food production, a ship of this size could not support you for an extended period of time. In short, you are highly efficient at creating high-entropy energy, or energy that is effectively useless to life after you have discarded it. This means you are a very expensive person to have on board the ship."

Stunned, Amos stared at the captain. Everyone else around the table remained silent, watching him.

After a moment, Melville continued. "You see, Mr. Hare, with your birth from the habitat, the clock has started. When you were inside the habitat, the resources to support you could be gathered efficiently and stored on the planet. Time is not on our side as we search for an answer to our problem."

Amos leaned back with a bewildered look, trying to comprehend himself in relation to everyone else. More questions swirled in his mind. What about his friends? Bina? How could they also be supported? Were there other ships then, like this one? He verbalized the simplest and most obvious question.

"Why do it? Why develop me?"

Melville relaxed slightly and let out a small sigh as he considered his response. "While you are an expensive investment, the issue remains for humanity. Even if you didn't exist, humanity would have to find a solution to the problem before it consumed all available energy within the few solar systems we populate. We hope your expanded mental capabilities from the adoption of neodymium will allow you to communicate mind-to-mind with life forms and possibly perceive more of the dimensions that surround us."

"How long?" Amos asked in a low voice. "How long for this ship? How long for humanity?"

Captain Melville looked down at his hands, which were resting on the table in front of him. "Based on current estimates of the energy available to us and our consumption patterns, we estimate about a decade for this ship. This assumes we find locations with modest amounts of free energy that we can use to replenish our supplies."

"Ten years? That's it?"

Melville shrugged. "It's the catch-twenty-two of our mission. We need your capabilities to have a chance of finding a solution to the high-entropy barrier, but your very existence accelerates the problem."

Amos sat silently for a few seconds, staring vacantly at the table in front of him. "How long for humanity?"

"That's a bit more flexible, and undetermined. Depending on how many evolved, like yourself, are produced, the time could be anywhere from one hundred to one thousand years. Of course, there may be pockets of humanity where there is more excess energy for them to access locally. Thus, the majority of humanity may die, but a small colony at the edge of humanity could survive for considerably longer."

Tension gripped Amos as he contemplated the ramifications. "What about my friends? Jemma?" Amos stopped before mentioning Bina. "They must consume similar amounts of energy."

Sarah took Amos by the hand. "They were all created by the habitat to foster your development," she said softly. "Jemma was based on me, Andrew on Guan, and Karla on Jahan."

Amos stared at Sarah in stunned silence. He broke down as his mind processed a world completely gone, that never even existed. Angry thoughts bubbled up in his mind. Lies! So many lies! But then a calmer feeling came over him, like when a final piece of a challenging puzzle was finally put in place, revealing the entire picture. Somehow he had known, not on a conscious level, but at another, deeper level in his mind. The sliver of a feeling that something was perversely wrong with his life had finally been removed.

Amos remained silent for a few seconds, then let out a couple of slow breaths. "It's all beginning to make sense."

Everyone around the table looked at Amos, unsure of what he meant or if they had even heard him correctly.

"What makes sense?" Sarah asked.

Amos remained focused on the table. "Looking back on my time in the habitat, all the studying, all the conversations prompted by friends who I thought were real. It all revolved back to this issue."

Sarah nodded. "Most of it did, yes. It was also decided that you should have a fairly well-rounded education. From previous attempts, it was learned that developing someone with too narrow a focus led to less creative solutions and more isolationism."

Amos looked up. "Others?"

"Previous attempts to develop an evolved. A topic for another time," Sarah replied.

Amos nodded and looked at the captain. "So, what are the immediate plans for the mission?"

Melville shifted in his chair as he gathered his thoughts. "Well, the next few days are devoted to the final preparations. The plan is to give you this time to learn about the ship and adjust to your new life."

Amos leaned back in his chair. "A few days?"

Melville fixed his eyes on Amos. "Our first destination will take us some time to reach. During that period, you will have the opportunity to work with navigation, learn everything about the ship, and take whatever time you need to for yourself."

Relief washed over Amos. "Okay. Thank you. That time will be helpful."

A look of apparent compassion came over Melville's face. "Look, Mr. Hare, no one expects you to solve our problem in the next few days, much less the next few years. You will have plenty of time to get up to speed, gather yourself, and begin your work by looking for interesting anomalies for us to research. I've found that keeping the mind engaged is the best medicine sometimes."

Amos shot him a doubtful look.

"But, then again," Melville continued, "if you need to simply lie in your bunk to sort through everything for a while, that's fine, too. Sarah will provide us with updates on your progress."

Amos looked over at Sarah, who offered a smile.

"Let's start with getting me up to speed on the ship," Amos replied. "How I deal with the . . . adjustment will likely take some time. I have a lot to think about and sort through. Maybe learning about the ship will provide a positive distraction for me."

Melville stood up, straightened his uniform, and smiled. "Good. It's the first step we were hoping for. We can only ask that you make an effort through this tough time. We will help you in any way we can."

"I don't have much of a choice," Amos said sullenly, still sitting, "but maybe that's a good thing." He stood up and nodded at the captain. "Thank you, sir."

Melville turned to Sarah. "Ensign, please continue Mr. Hare's tour of the ship. Mr. Hare, I look forward to working with you."

Sarah grinned, "Aye-aye, Captain."

13.

Sarah and Amos descended in the lift, falling away through countless decks of the ship, away from the bridge. Amos stood in deep thought, fingers knitted in front of him, his focus on some nondescript point at the base of the lift door.

Sarah bumped him with her elbow. "So, what happened up there on the stairs? Your face went completely white, like you had seen a ghost."

Amos looked up at her and saw her nervous smile. He took a deep breath and closed his eyes for a moment before opening them. "I don't know. Something surprised me. Sarah, what systems am I connected to now?"

"You can't tell? The links should be obvious."

Amos looked at Sarah, trying to read her thoughts. "Yes, of course. I know that I can access my personal memory quasi-crystals. Some of the same systems I could access in the habitat are also still available, allowing me to dig into the collective memory banks of humanity. However, Captain Melville has not yet authorized any connections aboard the ship, and I seem cut off from the system that allowed me to communicate with other people through the network."

Sarah shifted her weight nervously, and her smile faded a bit. "Yes, we have discontinued your access to systems that were designed to foster your development."

She reached for his arm, hesitated for a moment, and then pulled back. "Are you sure you want to have this conversation now? The captain just dropped a mental bomb on you, effectively telling you the future of humankind rests on your shoulders. Don't you think a little time to process your thoughts would be better?"

Amos gave Sarah a stoic look, but the worry lines around his eyes gave away the raging emotions inside. "No, tell me the whole story now," he said weakly. "I need to know where I stand if I have any chance of moving forward."

Sarah offered an unconvinced look in return.

Amos steeled himself. "How can I even start to work on my assignment if I have no idea what's real and what's virtual?"

Sarah's shoulders sagged a bit, and the worry returned to her face. She held his stare. Then she took a deep breath, straightened her spine, and stuck out her chest, shifting her weight onto the balls of her feet. It was the "officer pose" Amos had noticed many in senior command had assumed on the bridge, stiff and distant.

"You're right. This may be hard to accept, but I'll tell you straight out. Your friends in the habitat were simply simulations created by the network. Each of your friends was designed to infuse certain characteristics into your personality. They also helped you absorb all the material we were teaching you."

Amos's eyes saddened, and his shoulders slumped forward. "That's what I feared. They were so . . . real. I guess I kind of knew, but it's still hard to believe they were simply computer programs."

"Computer programs based on the personalities of Jahan, Guan, and myself, who have been connected to the network."

"So they do exist?"

"Well, your friends had the raw traits of desirable aspects of our personalities. The scientists tweaked those raw traits to become more compatible and to help develop traits in you. None of our experiences match up with your friends from the habitat though."

"Yes, of course. It's silly, but it's almost like you just told me they all died in some freak accident. I feel like I'm in mourning, which doesn't make much sense, since they never actually existed."

"There's nothing abnormal about that reaction at all. From your perspective, those 'people' shared their thoughts and desires with you. You grew up with them. Maybe even loved one of them?" Sarah's right eyebrow lifted as she asked the final question.

"Cared for, but no, not loved," Amos replied sullenly.

A look of disappointment crossed Sarah's face, which she masked quickly. "Look, we all have history. It's what makes us who we are.

Does it really matter that your history is possibly a new paradigm for human development?"

Amos's head jerked up, and he stared at Sarah with a hardness, almost cruelty, in his moist eyes. "Yes! Everything I've known up until now hasn't been real. Everything I've felt has been based on lies! How can you say that doesn't matter?"

Sarah looked back at him with hurt in her eyes. "We live in a world where reality and simulation are blurred. The senses we have inherited through evolution were built for a world of light, soundwaves, molecule recognition, and touch. They were not built for a world where we can connect our thoughts through networks, where these networks can simulate sensory inputs directly inside our brain. It's a wonderful world, but one where one's sense of self can easily become confused. Part of anyone's development is figuring out who they are. The habitat was set up to allow you to explore your sense of self."

Sarah paused and softened her voice before continuing. "Don't discount those experiences simply because your feelings were reactions to a computer simulation instead of real people. Jahan, Guan, and I feel we are your friends based on what we devoted to your development. Each of us is different from your habitat friends, but maybe you'll find the kernel that drew us together."

The anger in Amos's eyes softened slightly, but his intensity remained. "How do I trust anything? Anyone? All of my experiences have been based on deception."

Sarah's voice took on a sterner tone. "What you experienced in the habitat isn't that different from what is normal for any child's development. I had virtual friends as a child. They were a comfort; somebody I could always talk to. Think of it this way: At some point we simply figured out how to transform the imaginary friends in the mind of every child into something more real."

Amos's stance softened a bit more. "But at least you had real friends, lived in a real world. You may think virtual friends and imaginary friends are similar, but I don't!"

"Like everyone else, you analyze all the information available, draw on your past experiences, and decide to either trust or not."

"But all of my experiences have been lies!"

The heat rose in Sarah's face as quickly as the decks blinked by the lift's small window. "That's not true! Everything in your coursework was based on humanity's knowledge base. All of that is true. For topics under debate, you were provided the intellectual tools to analyze and appreciate all sides, ultimately coming to your own conclusion. The primary goal of your development was to put as many tools into your toolbox as possible and to develop characteristics like perseverance and the desire to protect."

Amos felt the lift slow as it prepared to stop at their floor. "So, basically my 'self' was developed in a lab and molded in the habitat."

Sarah paused to send a thought to the lift to keep the door closed when they reached their deck, causing the lift to shudder. "Don't look at it that way. Yes, the scientists worked to develop certain traits in you, which was no different than a mother who takes her baby to music class to encourage its brain to develop in a certain way. Both come from a desire to raise their child's potential as much as possible."

"But even a baby benefits from having other babies around them, to mimic and learn to empathize," Amos protested. "I didn't have that!"

Sarah's shoulders sagged slightly, and she shifted her stare to Amos's chest. "Yes, that is maybe the greatest challenge for you, learning how to act in a world where you are the first, the most advanced, the superior over all others."

Sarah lifted her eyes up to Amos's face. He saw sadness in them as she continued. "But know this, Amos. I am here to support you, to help you handle these challenges. Please understand that I have watched you develop over the past few years. My development was managed to make me as compatible with you as possible. Maybe that seems artificial, but it's still real."

Feeling the conversation was over, Sarah sent a command to open the lift door. It revealed a warmly lit hallway with a dark carpet stretching about one hundred feet away from the lift door.

Sarah held up her hand, serving as a message to keep the door open as well as a signal to Amos. "Do you trust me?"

Amos stared flatly at her. "No, not entirely. In fact, I don't trust anything about my life right now. For all I know, I'm simply in another habitat structured to develop me through my teenage years."

Sarah nodded slowly, demonstrating a bit of the hurt she felt by the comment while realizing it wasn't anything personal toward her. "Forgive me. You have no reason to trust me. Let's proceed this way," she said after a brief pause. "I'll follow my orders of showing you the ship and getting you online with the network. Through this process, I ask only that you maintain an open mind and work with me. Okay?"

Amos thought back to Bina's final message to remain open. He gave a stiff nod, but his body remained rigid, and his shoulders and hips stayed turned slightly away from Sarah. "Fine. Where are we going now?"

"Mr. Hare, er, Amos, hopefully I can still call you by your name. We begin your tour at the bottom of the ship, where the power for the engines is produced and many of the basic operations occur."

Sarah led Amos out of the lift, and they proceeded down a hallway through what Amos thought must be the belly of the beast. He tried to re-focus on the task.

"How many people are on the ship?"

"Good question," Sarah said, glancing over her shoulder, "which reminds me, we need to get you online with the ship's basic operations."

After a moment of silence, Amos's eyes glittered pink, and he let out a brief gasp. "Oh my, I almost forgot what it feels like to find a new resource for information. There are five hundred and twenty-three individuals currently on the ship, three of which are not assigned to the ship but will remain on the planet when we depart in three days, twenty-one minutes."

Amos stopped walking and bowed his head while closing his eyes slightly. He opened his eyes and turned to Sarah. "You were born on this ship sixteen years ago. You were assigned to this planet shortly after your birth and put in a habitat, like mine, for the first five years of your life. After you left that habitat, you lived on the planet. You only came back on board this ship when it returned about a month ago."

"Yes, Amos. Like I said, my development has also been highly controlled, preparing me throughout my life to work with you. The biggest difference is that I was removed from my habitat at age five, longer than the one year of development that is typical for most people in society. The reason for the longer development was to enhance my empathetic capabilities and fully develop my brain potential, given my less evolved status. We are very similar. I'm just further along in my adjustment to the real world than you."

Amos stared at Sarah for a second, then continued walking down the hallway. "So everything has been arranged? Our friendship, marriage, love?"

Sarah tilted her head. "As much as I would like to think we will develop toward that goal, in reality, much of it is up to you. I was developed with high empathy, to be open emotionally. Love comes fairly easily to me. I enjoy connecting with others and building intimate relationships. Love, however, and emotions in general, remain a tricky part of the human brain. Scientists have not yet figured out how to make someone fall in love. No 'magic potion number nine,' if you will."

"Madame Ruth was more advanced than scientists today?" Amos's eyebrows shot up in a sign of mock astonishment.

Sarah giggled. "Well, at least we don't have to worry about you kissing the security guards."

Amos smiled. "I'll do my best to work with you, Sarah. Though I can't promise to love your tendency to tilt your head when you talk—or your smell after you work out."

Sarah tilted her head and gave him a hurt look. "But my development taught me an empathetic head tilt helped connect with someone. However, I will be sure to shower appropriately after I work out. Thank you for the tip." Her expression changed from hurt to a warm smile.

Amos nodded and extended his arm toward the end of the hallway. "And so, to Engineering?"

Sarah smiled, let out a brief titter, and began walking down the hallway. "There's one more thing you should know about me, something that's not in the network, or at least not in the network you can access."

Amos's full attention fell on Sarah as they walked. Finally, he couldn't stand the anticipation any longer. "Yes?"

"I'm not easy. You have to wine and dine me before anything happens."

Amos blushed slightly. "Why do you . . . What in the universe . . .?" Amos let out a flustered breath through extended lips. "What makes you think. . . . "

Sarah giggled. "Relax, Amos, I'm just setting the ground rules for courting me."

Amos stopped and turned toward her, but Sarah continued walking down the hallway, head held high and swinging her hips in exaggerated fashion. After a few strides, she glanced over her shoulder with mischief in her eyes. "Coming, Mr. Hare?"

Amos grinned, "Okay, I'll follow."

For now, he thought.

14.

The door slid open, revealing a cavernous room. When they stepped through, Amos found himself on an observation deck that looked down upon the operations below. A white metal railing ran along the edge of the deck. The deck itself looked like a partially exposed disc protruding from the wall.

Similar to the bridge, a number of data pillars were spread out around the room, each manned by two to six individuals. Catwalks and ladders spanned the room, enabling engineers to find a direct route to every part.

Sarah walked up to the railing, Amos trailing on her left. "This is Engineering," she said proudly, "where all the power is created to propel the ship, run all life-support systems, and basically enable all systems aboard the ship to function properly."

Amos's eyes scanned the room. "It looks like this ship, like most ships in the fleet, is powered by muon-catalyzed fusion."

Sarah nodded. "Correct. This ship utilizes deuterium-tritium, or d-t, fusion. A few newer ships in the fleet have upgraded to the latest, most efficient, muon fusion, but the technology in these engines have long proven their reliability to the fleet. Given that our mission may require us to travel great distances from any outpost, the captain wanted the most reliable power system."

Amos scanned the layout of the floor below, assessing it using a few of the courses on ship power systems and engineering he had taken while in the habitat. "Makes sense. It looks like there are six reactors in this room. I'm assuming that provides redundancy should one or more fail?"

"Yes. The ship only needs two reactors to function at peak performance, and only one most of time. The other four reactors provide us with plenty of backup should we have any problems during the mission. The captain had the additional two reactors installed in case any of the abnormalities we discover cause us problems."

Amos nodded as if agreeing with Melville's decision. "What about the engineering crew? How well are they trained?"

"The crew also has extra personnel to allow for any complications along the way."

Amos looked sideways at Sarah. "You mean 'deaths'?"

Sarah's posture deflated slightly, but she remained focused on Engineering. "Yes. Given our mission, the chances of crew members dying is quite high."

Amos turned and looked at Sarah's profile, trying to read as much from her body language as possible. "What are we going to be doing?"

Sarah looked sideways at Amos. "The simple answer is we will go wherever your talent is best utilized. Eventually, we will investigate what you judge is most critical."

Amos's face went white as he stared at her. "You mean that people may die because of me?"

Sarah turned to face Amos. "Don't think of it that way. The fleet commanders hand-picked the finest personnel in the fleet for this mission. Everyone who has been assigned to this ship is aware of the risks. Everyone said they would have volunteered for the position. This ship has the most important mission in the history of humanity, the most difficult challenge to overcome. Everyone aboard, including me, is willing to die to ensure a successful mission. It's an honor to be on this ship with you!"

Amos stared silently at Sarah for a moment, absorbing all the ramifications, before letting out a nervous chuckle. "Well, that takes the pressure off!"

He turned back to the railing, leaned forward, and rested his hands on it, letting his head hang between his arms.

Sarah stepped closer and put her hand over his hand. "One day at a time, Amos. No one expects you to fulfill the mission today. In fact, many people believe this mission may take generations."

Amos turned his head to look at her. "Generations? What does that mean?"

"It means that others, like you, are expected to join us in the future."

Amos jerked upright. "There are others like me? I thought everything in my development was virtual!"

Sarah squeezed his hand. "Don't get too excited. No one else like you exists at the moment. Based on the expected success of your development, the scientists started another fourteen-year development cycle with a number of individuals. So, at the earliest, it will be about thirteen years before another like you joins us."

"Thirteen years?" Amos moaned and hung his head again.

"Amos, for now, you are our hope, our best chance to succeed in our mission."

Amos's knees bent as his body began to collapse.

Sarah put her arm around his waist, supporting him, "Know this Amos. . . . "

Amos's body continued to sag.

With a sharp crack to her voice, Sarah dug her nails into his hand. "Everyone on this ship is here to help you. You are not alone! We will support you. We understand that it will take time for you to get up to speed."

When Amos didn't straighten up, Sarah took her left hand from his and wrapped it around his waist. Then she squeezed his waist and lifted his body slightly. When he began to support more of his own weight she leaned her head toward his ear.

"Now look up, Amos."

Amos squeezed his eyes shut, gathering himself, and then lifted his head. What he saw startled him. Everyone on the engineering floor was looking up at them. Some stood at attention, others had a more relaxed posture, and still others remained seated at their station. But they all looked up at him with an intensity that he found unnerving. He had never felt the focus of so many people on him. It was unsettling and empowering.

Amos straightened up slowly, looking around the floor at all of the people, taking in their collective strength.

"They believe in you, Amos," Sarah whispered. "They believe you will continue to develop into the person who can complete this mission. They also understand that you are young and that it will take time. They have patience, but they want to see that you are trying."

Amos continued to look at the individuals around the floor. They all held the same unwavering focus on him. A few gave a brief nod when his eyes met theirs.

"What if I can't?" Amos whispered without taking his eyes off the people below. "What if I can't do it?"

"Then it won't be for lack of trying! Not if I have anything to say about it." Sarah took her arm away from Amos and stepped back from the railing, leaving him alone in front of the engineering room.

After a moment, when Amos felt nothing but sheer terror, he pushed down his fear, straightened his body so he stood erect, and then puffed his chest out slightly, mimicking the officer pose he had observed on the bridge. As he continued to move from each set of eyes, Amos gave a brief nod to each individual.

After a few seconds, the people below broke their focus on Amos and returned to their work. Eventually, the room returned to normal, and Amos was left looking down at the floor and appreciating the efficiency of the teams.

"These are good people but with a false sense of hope," Amos said.

"The best people!" Sarah countered. "And perhaps a little desperate to find some hope."

Startled, Amos looked over at her. He tried to read her thoughts, but he found it unnerving that her thoughts were shielded from him, like he was looking only at the surface. And yet, looking at her revealed so much more than he had ever seen in the habitat. "Can you make that happen?"

Sarah smiled broadly. A pink twinkle in her eye let Amos know she was granting him access. Or was it something else?

A second later, Amos was alerted to his access to the engineering network. He shifted his attention from puzzling over Sarah's thoughts to the new information source.

"The two reactors online are running at minimal capacity," he said. "The engineering teams have been completing drills on transferring power sources from one reactor to another, improving the time it takes to bring a reactor online. There was a malfunction in reactor five, but that was caused by a faulty relay switch, which has been replaced. The inventory of spare parts is consistent with a multi-year voyage for a ship with six reactors. Six people were recognized for above-average work during the past months. Two were re-assigned to provide new challenges."

Sarah took his right hand in hers. "You have plenty of time to learn everything."

Amos snapped his head toward her. "Why are the reactors still using an old quantum clock based on entangled strontium atoms? More precise and reliable clocks have been developed."

Sarah hesitated and dropped his hand while looking slightly puzzled as she conferred with the ship's network. "I suppose since the reactors are based on the older, more reliable, muon d-t fusion that the supporting systems also reflect the older systems. Generally, engineers don't like to mix older technologies with too much of the latest technologies until everything has been fully tested. I'm assuming the captain was hesitant to tinker too much with the reactors, preferring to maintain what has worked. Besides, isn't a quantum clock that only loses a second every billion years precise enough?"

Amos considered the issue before replying. "Maybe, probably. I understand that these are very complex systems, and the risk of catastrophic failure must be minimized. But updating the quantum clocks is a relatively minor issue that could make a significant difference."

Sarah gave Amos a concerned look. "Why is that?"

"Look, I understand that, under normal conditions, the existing quantum clocks are highly reliable. If the ship's mission is to seek out anomalies, including, I assume, anomalies in time that could hold hints of how to overcome the high-entropy barrier, under those extreme circumstances, having the most advanced timing technology supporting our mission-critical systems is of paramount importance."

Sarah held his stare while she considered his argument.

"May I add that a more precise clock will also enable more exact navigation and a finer mapping capability," he added, "possibly helping to identify small anomalies?"

Sarah tilted her head slightly as she processed his words.

Exasperated, Amos went on. "If the timing is even one billionth of a second off between reactors, they could inadvertently shut down. If that happens when we're close to an anomaly in space, it could mean the end of us all, or something even worse."

Sarah nodded. "Okay, Amos, I'll pass along your concern to the Lieutenant Mal."

Amos relaxed and nodded. "Thank you. I don't mean to push, but this issue seems relatively obvious to me."

Sarah's face softened. "No, you did exactly what we all hope you will continue to do. You identified an issue that we need to address. That is your primary role. I don't know how Lieutenant Mal will respond, but she will likely want to talk to you directly about the issue to ensure she understands it completely."

Amos received a signal from the network, similar to someone calling his name. At first, he looked around for another person on the observation deck. Sarah tilted her head in confusion at Amos's perceived reaction to her comment. Then Amos realized it was a communication from Lieutenant Mal. He focused his attention on the signal, similar to how a person would try to listen to a bird call.

"Mr. Hare, Lieutenant Mal. Ensign Laka notified me that you have a concern with the quantum clock associated with the reactors."

Amos replied through the communications channel setup in the network. "Yes, ma'am. The quantum clock associated with the reactors is based on dated technology. I understand this clock is considered highly reliable and stable, but I believe more precise clocks are available that would not be too difficult to install in place of the existing clocks."

The initial communication from Lieutenant Mal had the feel of a person replying in a relatively emotionless manner, which could have reflected the lieutenant's feelings toward the matter or could have been due to the sterility of using the network for communication. Amos wasn't quite sure which was true and was admittedly nervous after the end of his sentence was sent.

"Thank you, Mr. Hare. Your concern is well founded, and it was one of the issues that the captain and I discussed while preparing this ship for the mission. The captain places a heavy emphasis on reliability, hence his decision to not upgrade the clocks. I will bring up the issue with him again."

"Thank you, ma'am."

Amos felt the communication channel close between them. The entire communication had occurred faster than if they had been talking but somewhat similar to how long it would take the brain to re-create the conversation. Once the channel was closed, Amos looked at Sarah, who was watching him intently.

"Well?" Sarah asked.

"Lieutenant Mal will bring it up with the captain. She was . . . supportive."

"Not surprising. She, like most of the officers on this ship, can be intimidating. But if you bring up a worthwhile concern, especially one that impacts the mission directly, all of the officers will respond immediately."

Amos felt another communication channel open to his brain.

"Mr. Hare, Lieutenant Mal again. The captain has changed his mind, and the clock will be upgraded. Lieutenant Mal out."

Amos felt the communication channel close. He was still looking at Sarah, who had begun to open her mouth when she noticed the twinkle in Amos's right eye.

Amos's mouth fell open. "The captain has ordered the clock to be upgraded."

Sarah smiled broadly, "And we are the safer for it. Good work, Amos! Your first successful input into our mission."

Amos smiled sheepishly. "Well, small beginnings, right?"

Sarah shrugged. "Could be small, could be significant. Either way, a start."

Sarah opened a discreet secure channel to the captain, completely hidden from Amos.

"Sir, I'm happy to report Mr. Hare is making progress. He is showing interest in the well-being of the ship and crew.

"Thank-you Ensign. Mal reported to me that Mr. Hare passed the first test. The Syndicate is pleased with his progress. They've ordered us to continue to Kairos."

"Is pleased', sir?"

"Sorry Ensign, I don't understand. About what are you confused?"

"You said 'is pleased.' Don't you mean 'will be pleased' given our distance from E-3?"

"Yes, of course. Keep up the good work Ensign."

Sarah quickly suppressed the uneasy feeling in her stomach and turned to Amos while motioning towards the exit.

15.

Amos and Sarah were back in the lift, but this time Amos knew the direction of the lift, its speed, maintenance record, and even who had worked on it. Now that he had access to the operations network, he knew with a thought everything about the ship's operations. In fact, if he inquired, he could determine the status of every lift on board, even who was on each lift and who was walking in a specific corridor.

He couldn't access system information inside private rooms, but through his access to the sensitive air sensors in public spaces on the ship, he could deduce a great deal of information. This took a bit of work to figure out. He wasn't sure if the average person on the ship could figure out private information, but his mind did it easily. In short, his access privileges, combined with his brain's processing capacity, enabled him to know when every person aboard the ship was eating, sleeping, or taking a piss.

As Amos assessed the ship's status, he realized the captain was in his room. He had returned to his room after a meal in the dining area with a few other officers. Amos could not hear their conversation, which was restricted, but he knew that most conversations were recorded aboard the ship. The records of these conversations were stored in a highly encrypted and secure portion of the quasi-crystals.

If he put his mind to it, he could probably crack the system, but Amos had no interest in listening in on everyone's conversation. He was, however, puzzled a bit by this secure portion of the quasi-crystals. He couldn't help but analyze the periphery of the secured system. He realized quickly that there was much more activity on the ship than he understood. The amount of power consumed by the secure portion of the crystals seemed excessive. Even if every conversation, every movement, every thought of every crew member was recorded continuously, it would only require a fraction of the energy these crystals were consuming. As Amos was considering what could require such large energy consumption, the lift stopped.

"This is our next stop," Sarah said as the door slid open. A corridor similar to the one on the engineering level stretched out before them. However, while the lighting in Engineering had an earthy, yellowish tone to it, the lighting in this corridor had a bluish, clinical feel.

Amos looked at Sarah. "Medical? Is this the next stop on our tour?"

Sarah stepped into the corridor, Amos behind her. "Yes, but not so much for a tour. You have an appointment with the chief scientist aboard the ship, Dr. Daman. He oversaw your development in the habitat and can begin to explain how you are unique."

Amos stopped short, forcing Sarah to turn back to him. "Wait! The person who controlled me for the past fourteen years is aboard this ship?"

Sarah gave him a confused look. "Yes, of course. Why wouldn't he be?"

Amos started to respond, then snapped his mouth shut, shifted his weight. "Yes, of course he would be. My development is not yet complete."

"The development of your brain and its capabilities is largely complete, but the psychological support to ensure those wires in your brain don't get fried is far from finished. In Engineering, you saw how important reliability is to this mission. Dr. Daman is on board to ensure you remain reliable."

Amos's face soured at the thought. "What am I?" he replied tersely. "A machine to be tinkered with and maintained?" He narrowed his eyes slightly. "Are there spare parts in inventory?"

Sarah giggled. "Yes, of course. Don't be silly! Aren't we all machines? We take useful energy and information in, utilize it toward a specific goal, and then release the useless energy and information back into the environment. Is that not a machine?"

Amos's face contorted as he wrestled with her argument, trying to find some flaw. "Well, that is a sterile view of humanity!"

"Dr. Daman will explain to you how your brain is different from the rest of ours," Sarah continued. "He'll help you to understand your role. He can also help you to understand yourself."

Amos continued to shift his weight and look around the hallway, as if the answers were written on the walls. Finally, his eyes returned to Sarah. "He has information that I can't access. I have no access to the networks with information about me. In fact, there is extremely limited information about me. Outside of the personnel files, which simply give my name, age, and sleeping quarters, I haven't been able to find anything." Amos noted Sarah had assumed the officer stance in front of him.

"And for good reason. Your meeting with the doctor will open up access to information about yourself. I can't promise you will have access to everything, but I trust there is a plan in place to help you as much as possible. As with many things, there are things we are all better off not knowing."

"What does that mean?" Amos's eyes opened wide.

"Only that you have what most people would consider an overwhelming amount of information to process ahead of you. Just understanding yourself will take a while. The captain and the scientists have tried to construct a schedule for its delivery that helps you process it in the most efficient manner. When the time is right, I expect the captain and the doctor will reveal everything they know."

Amos scowled at Sarah. "Why not just give me everything at once and let me go through it?"

"In short, context. If you were granted access to your full files and you began sifting through the information without the necessary context, you could misinterpret pieces of information that would cause more problems."

Amos scowled again and lifted his eyes away from Sarah. "The administrators of brainwashing offer similar arguments!"

Sarah gave Amos a disappointed look. "Once again, you must trust us. I know it takes time to earn trust, but you must believe we are trying to help you adjust to your new life as well as possible."

Anger burned behind Amos's eyes, but he forced it down. His shoulders relaxed, and he knit his fingers in front of him. His head bowed as his eyes focused on his fingers. "Maybe eventually, Sarah. Maybe someday I can trust completely." He shook his head. "But not yet."

Amos lifted his eyes back up to Sarah. She offered no emotion in return. Instead she simply nodded, turned on her heel and began walking down the corridor.

"Dr. Daman is expecting us."

A door slid open on the left side of the corridor slightly ahead of them. As they approached it, a short, slender man stepped into the hallway. His hair was grey, combed straight back, revealing a balding pattern that left most of the front of his head bare. He turned to face them, a welcoming smile spreading across his face as he looked over Amos. He eyes were sharp, but the dark circles under them revealed his lack of sleep. The man looked like he was in his late seventies, which was startling, since this meant either that he had not chosen any of the procedures to tighten and lift his skin or he was much older and these procedures had been less effective.

He stepped toward Amos and Sarah and spread his arms in a welcoming gesture. "Mr. Hare, Ensign Laka, welcome! Please come in. Mr. Hare, I am Dr. Daman."

He swept his right arm toward the room from which he had just exited and offered a modest bow.

"Hello, Doctor," Sarah replied in a warm and friendly voice. "Good to see you again. It has been a while. Have you solved the five cottages puzzle I gave you for your birthday?"

Dr. Daman smiled. "A devilish puzzle that many claim to be impossible, even in six dimensions. You do love to torture me, don't you?"

Sarah smiled innocently as she walked past him. "Just trying to challenge your great mind."

Dr. Daman scrunched up his eyebrows and then turned his attention to Amos. "Mr. Hare! Welcome! It's wonderful to finally have the opportunity to sit down with you and talk in person."

Amos stopped in front of the doctor, folded his arms, and gave him a hard, distrustful stare. "Everyone keeps adding 'in person.' I feel like an unwrapped toy."

After a few seconds, during which the smile on the doctor's face never changed, Amos grunted and stepped into the room.

He found himself in a small sitting area, which resembled what he envisioned a psychiatric ward might look like. Sarah stood in the middle of the room eyeing him. When Amos looked at her, she gave him a warning look.

Amos looked around the room. It had three cushioned chairs, all light blue. The walls appeared grey, but the lighting from above gave them a cool, bluish feel. Another door was across the room from the entrance. As Amos looked at it, the door slid open, revealing a second room with a table and chairs.

Dr. Daman walked around Amos and addressed Sarah. "Please remain here as Mr. Hare and I have a talk."

Sarah nodded and then shifted her focus back to Amos with cautious eyes. Amos interpreted the momentary pause as she focused on him as another warning. Then she turned and took a seat.

Dr. Daman extended his arm toward the back room. Amos looked at him, shrugged indignantly, and walked through the door. Dr. Daman followed , the door sliding shut behind him with a whoosh.

Amos found himself in an even smaller room, with similar walls as the seating area. In the middle of the room was a round, black table with two metal chairs, one on the far side of the room facing the door and the other across the table from it, closest to Amos.

"Please, take a seat, Mr. Hare." Doctor Daman extended his arm to the chair on the far side of the room. Amos shuffled his feet as he moved around the table and sat down.

Dr. Daman smiled at Amos as he pulled out his chair and took a seat across the table. "How are you adjusting, Mr. Hare? I know all of this has been a lot to absorb."

Amos scowled and offered no response.

After a couple seconds the smile on the doctor's face vanished and his lips were drawn tight in a serious frown. "Right to it then. Mr. Hare, what I am about to tell you is going to feel like a proverbial slap in the face." His tone was thoughtful, tinged with empathy, but firm and direct. He leaned back in his chair, adopting a ponderous pose.

Amos sat sullenly in his chair with his arms on the conference table in front of him. His eyes focused on his hands.

Dr. Daman continued to lean back in his chair, but his focus intensified as he spoke. "Let's start with your family, since I know they mean a lot to you. As you have probably figured out, you were the only person inside the habitat. Everybody else was created by the habitat."

Amos lifted his head at the mention of his parents and focused on the doctor. He gave little reaction to the news of his parents, feeling completely numb inside. He felt as hollow and empty as the habitat he had called home.

Dr. Daman paused to watch Amos take in the news. After Amos did not react, he continued in the same clinical tone. "Your parents are alive and are currently on the other side of our galactic zone, approximately five light years away. They live together aboard a science ship. They have not had any contact with you since your physical birth. By turning you over to the H-Plus Project, they fulfilled their obligation of providing offspring to further humanity."

Amos was distantly surprised he actually had parents. "Was anything real about my parents . . . I mean, the images of them in the habitat?"

"Yes. In fact, your parents both uploaded a significant portion of their memories and values into the computer in order to help instill their values in you. Of course, the project also guided your development by slight modifications to enable your development toward your ultimate state. Take solace in that your parents do love you, are still alive, and that they passed on what they could to you."

Amos leaned forward his chair, anger flashing across his face. "Love? What kind of love led them to abandon me to some desolate world to be an experiment?"

Doctor Daman shifted slightly in his chair, but he held Amos's stare. "The kind of love that wants something better for their son. The kind of love for their fellow man that demands great sacrifice. Mr. Hare, you are the evolved. The first of your kind. Feel fortunate. Humanity has been trying to produce your level of evolution for over a hundred years. There have been many failures, many unfortunate results, many near successes. It is from all these iterations that we finally learned how to make you. Your parents were carefully selected for their ability to produce a high potential offspring. If truth be told, they did not even know each other before they were selected, but as a fortunate sign, they fell in love instantly before creating you. In hindsight, maybe that was the missing ingredient in previous efforts."

Amos rested his forehead on the table in front of him. "They still left," he replied in the same hard, angry tone. "Why didn't they stay?"

Doctor Daman leaned forward and directed his voice at the crown of Amos's head. "Mr. Hare, you have been inside a highly-controlled environment for fourteen years. Everything from your diet to your studies to your shits have been closely monitored and managed. The habitat was built to support one individual. We have found trying to place more than one individual in such a habitat results in problems, especially individuals who know about the outside world. Imagine if it were physically possible to return to your mother's womb after growing up in the outside world. No one could manage the restrictions placed on them in such an environment. Furthermore, if another fetus was also present, the mature individual would likely kill it. The habitat is a similar situation. Your parents simply could not live in such a world, nor could you return to it now that you have experienced the outside world."

Amos lifted his head from the table but did not meet the doctor's eyes. "Can I contact my parents now?"

"There are no restrictions on who you can contact. However, communicating with their ship is approximately two neutrino years away as these particles move through the bulk between the folds of the brane. For this reason, any communication is difficult."

Amos looked up from his hunched position. "Then I want to go to them."

Dr. Daman let out an exasperated breath. "Mr. Hare, you have your mission, and that mission is focused on exploring this side of the humanity zone."

Amos pushed back in his chair so that it rocked slightly on the back legs. "What if I don't accept this mission? What if I refuse?"

Dr. Daman lowered his head and took another breath. "First, your mission is probably the most important mission in the history of humanity, the history of life. To give it anything less than your full commitment may mean the death of us all. Second, your parents do not want you pursuing them. They want you to fulfill your destiny. Finally, you report to the captain, and his orders are to take you to regions of vital interest to humanity. Seeing your parents does not qualify."

Amos threw up his hands in exasperation. "I don't want this! I have had no say! You can't just predetermine the course of someone's life." Amos's eyes darted around the room like he was caught in a trap. "It's my life!"

"Actually, we could program your brain to act in certain ways, all but assuring your cooperation," Dr. Daman said, unmoved. "We have done that in the past during previous iterations to minimize the risk of rebellious individuals. What we found was by restricting the person's will, even if not perceptible by the individual, the evolved individual failed. Failed to mature into a viable individual or failed to provide the creative thinking that is needed for the challenges confronting humanity."

Amos slammed his hands onto the table and leaned forward in his chair. "Well, then I invoke my free will to tell you to kiss my ass!"

Dr. Daman stared back calmly before replying. "You may not like us, Amos. You may even hate us, but please try to see why we did what we did. Maybe in that insight you'll see we're not all bad and your feelings of hatred are merely limitations on your capacity to see the whole of us."

Fury rose up in Amos. "You're telling me I should feel guilt for what you did to me? That it's my fault?"

Doctor Daman rocked back in his chair but remained composed. "Mr. Hare, I see you don't like me. You probably blame me for the pain you are experiencing right now. Your sense of loss, of betrayal, of anger at this pre-arranged life is likely all directed at me. And you know what? That's fine. It's helpful for you to direct it outwards, and that may be part of my role, to absorb it. But let me remind you, as you learned during the extraction process, we have methods that make disobedience the more painful option. And really, Mr. Hare, to what end? You accomplish nothing by fighting us."

Amos fixed the doctor with a hard stare, sending a thought message to his thick head. "Go screw yourself!"

Dr. Daman stared back with a kind but equally willful expression. "Look, Mr. Hare, you have an incredible opportunity ahead of you, a potentially highly fulfilling life. You will be free to socialize with whom you please. You have a well-defined purpose. All the ingredients are there for a wonderful life. At the same time, all the opportunity and capabilities are present in you to become a complete failure, maybe the biggest failure in history. The eyes of humanity are on you, Mr. Hare, for better or worse. Everyone on this ship is fully committed to helping you succeed and enjoy your life. The choice, as always, lies inside of you."

Amos balled his hands into fists and slammed then onto the table. "Except navigating this ship!"

"If you find interesting regions and can convince Captain Melville of their importance, your decisions will dictate the course of this ship. Once you're ready, you will have complete control over where we go."

Amos gave him a mocking look. "And if I want to spend the next twenty years smoking werk and chasing girls?"

Dr. Daman sighed, looked down at his hands, and then returned his focus to Amos's eyes. "Yes, Mr. Hare, you could waste your potential on such endeavors. While you are very much a teenager, in our eyes, you are an adult capable of making your own decisions. We need your full effort, because, believe me, it will take your full effort. If we force you, then your mission will be a failure as assuredly as if you choose to addle your brain with werk."

Amos rocked back in his chair, smirking as he diverted his focus to the ceiling. "Well, that settles it. Go fuck yourself!"

Amos stood up quickly, knocking the chair backwards behind him. "Everything I've known up to this point has been a lie! Hell, how do I know if you're real or even this room? This could just be the next habitat created to control me. I choose not to believe your 'end of humanity' arguments! I believe I'm still being manipulated, and it ends now!"

Amos jerked his head around, looking around the room frantically. His eyes settled on the wall behind Dr. Daman. He grinned at Dr. Daman and then ran around the table and launched himself head-first at the wall.

A sound similar to a coconut bouncing off a cement floor echoed around the room as Amos's head rebounded off the wall, followed by his shoulders and hips. He collapsed on the floor, unconscious.

16.

"Have we made a mistake?" a tense male voice asked.

"Give him time, he'll get there," a female voice replied.

"It might be simpler to pull the plug and move on to the next one. We have enough brain power on this ship to have a shot at success."

"Give him time!" the female voice pleaded. "It's only been a couple days. He's working through the shock of extraction from the habitat."

"But we must make a decision. Do we devote this ship, this entire crew, to a mission in which the most critical component might break?"

"Let me handle him. I can get him focused."

"Unraveling the mysteries of pregnant time, of Kairos, will take all of his mental ability."

The long pause in the conversation pulled Amos further into a conscious state as he strained to figure out his status. He sensed he was lying on his back in what felt like a bed. After checking with the ship's computer, he realized he was in his own room, and about ten hours had passed since his last memory of running into the doctor's carbon nanotube wall. Apparently, he had been carried back to his room, and there had been quite a bit of chatter about him since that incident. Captain Melville and Sarah were in his room. *Great,* Amos thought, *making a name for myself.*

Captain Melville's tone changed slightly, like he had turned to address Amos as well as Sarah. "I don't like this, Ensign. How can we possibly be successful if he is so unreliable?"

"He'll get better. I can't explain to you how I know, but I feel he is different from the previous attempts. Deep down, he wants to help. He's just struggling with trust issues right now."

"Well, you better be right. In two days, we're scheduled to depart, devoting a significant amount of resources to this mission. I have to give central command the final go, no-go decision a day from now. I'd really hate to go and then have to turn around and return."

Sarah's voice took on a sterner tone, but the plea remained. "You, yourself, said we don't have much of a choice. The next evolved is at least ten years away, even at a rushed pace. While we have many brilliant people on board, they can't do what he can potentially do. The decision was made long ago when the scientists decided to devote everything to his development, providing him fourteen years to mature. True, eighteen is ideal, but by accelerating the program, we jammed most of the important stuff into him. If we wait for the next one, there's a good chance that evolved will be even less reliable, or capable."

Melville sighed. "We really have all our eggs, or egg, in one basket."

"But what a basket!" Sarah replied, her tone cheery.

Melville chuckled. "Okay, but please try to make him more cooperative before we leave. The crew is already nervous about his state of mind, not to mention his age. This whole thing could go to shit very quickly if he doesn't at least make an effort."

"Yes sir."

Amos heard a door slide open, footsteps walk away, and then the door slide closed.

A moment later, Sarah's voice came from directly over Amos's face. "Did you catch that?"

Amos opened his eyes to find her leaning over him. She had a warm smile on her face, but her eyes suggested suspicion, possibly even fear.

"Hear what?" Amos asked, trying to play innocent.

"Please. I know you woke up about a minute ago, and the captain knew as well. Until you prove you can take care of yourself, as your handler, I have full access to the status updates of your room and vitals monitors."

Amos offered a sheepish smile. "I heard most of it, I think. I at least caught the part about my unreliability."

"Yes, the topic of the day. Does this crew, heck, does humanity, place their trust in you?"

A metal fan in the vent above Amos's bed clattered to life, deadening the pitch of the conversation and pushing cold air into the room. Amos rolled his head away from Sarah.

"Trust seems to be in short supply around here."

Sarah sat back in the chair that was positioned next to the bed, keeping her eyes on him. "Yes, trust. How do you trust us and we trust you? That is the issue right now."

Amos rolled his head back toward Sarah. "My head is spinning!"

"Well, yes, that's what happens when you decide to try to prove your skull is thicker than a carbon nanotube wall."

Amos blushed, squeezed his eyes shut, and felt his head where it had impacted the wall. "Ow!"

"You'll live. We applied some freezing to it, but I told the doctor to leave the lump to remind you of your pig-headedness."

Amos opened his eyes. "I guess I deserve that."

Sarah let out an exasperated breath. "Deserve that? You're lucky I didn't give you another lump on the other side of your thick skull!"

Amos winced again, but this time from the tongue lashing. "All right, I get it. But I wasn't referring to the lump when I said my head was spinning. I'm still processing everything."

The fan screeched to a halt, relieving Amos of the chill running down his spine, his uniform apparently was removed when he was put to bed.

Sarah's eyes softened as she looked into his eyes, reading them. "Yes, I know. A lot for you to absorb. No one expects you to jump right into your role. But understand that when you hurt yourself willingly or rebel against the people trying to help you, the crew begins to doubt the choice to make you the key to the mission's success."

Amos winced again. "I know, but I didn't ask for this!"

Sarah smacked her palm on the lump on his head. "Enough!"

Amos jerked away and sheltered his head with his hands. "Ow!"

Sarah continued in a tone mixed with the authority of an officer and the concern of a friend, "You didn't ask for your role. Tough! You have no idea how much time, energy, and resources have been devoted to you. Instead of whining about it, understand how many people have sacrificed themselves to ensure your success."

Amos stared lasers back at her. "I didn't ask them to do that!"

"No, you didn't! But the fact is the best scientists poured all their effort into your development. The best officers volunteered to support you in this mission. The most resources were devoted to this ship to ensure the best chance of success."

Sarah paused, rubbing her temples with her eyes squeezed shut. "Honestly, Amos, I know this is difficult for you. But the way you're acting suggests you need to be sent to the nursery to re-learn how to work with others."

Amos continued to look at Sarah with hard eyes, but then his stare softened, and his eyes shifted to the white ceiling as he tried to clear his head. "I'll admit I haven't been very cooperative."

Sarah's expression also softened. "Look, Amos, all I ask is that you keep trying. I'm here for you. When you start to feel frustrated, rebellious, or angry, talk to me, okay? And don't run into a wall in front of the senior scientist, okay? It makes you look . . . childish."

Amos stared at the ceiling and then shifted his eyes to Sarah. "My problem is that I don't think I can trust you."

"Of course you can!"

Amos rolled slightly toward her. "No, I mean really trust you. You have your role that is devoted to this ship, to the captain. That can be at odds with my needs."

Sarah's face became pensive, and her eyes filled with what looked like fear as she considered his comment. "Amos, I'll tell you this: So long as your behavior is productive, or at least trying to fulfill your role on this mission, you can trust me completely. In that sense, our roles are one hundred percent aligned. If you try to subvert the mission in any way, I will have to report it to the captain."

"Perhaps, but I still don't think I can trust you. Will you answer my questions honestly? Will you give it to me straight, no matter how unpleasant the answer?"

Sarah leaned forward in her chair and looked at Amos with the officer's mask she wore on the bridge. "Yes, you can trust me. You may not always like what I say, but I will always defend you when I can see you are trying to help. But running into a wall is no way to help the mission."

Disappointed by her obvious lie, Amos's eyes dropped to the sheets in front of him. "Okay, I'll try," he said, offering his own lie in return. "It may take some time for me to trust you completely, but I'll do my best." Amos wasn't sure he meant that last part or not, but maybe he did need to show an effort.

Sarah's warmth returned. She leaned over and took his right hand in her hands. She waited until his eyes shifted up to look at her. "Amos, I'm here for you. Yes, I must fulfill my duty to this ship, just as you must, but my role is to help you. If that means some things are kept between us, then that's fine with me."

Sarah continued to hold Amos's hand. Amos looked back down at the sheet in front of him, fidgeting under it. After a moment, he looked back up at Sarah, who had a sly grin on her face. She continued to stare into Amos's eyes. While Amos could not read her thoughts, her facial expression made it clear what was going on inside her head.

"Err, uh, Sarah?"

"Yes?" Sarah's mouth curled up on the right side as she batted her long eyelashes. Why were her eyelashes so cute? Suddenly, he was aware that he wasn't wearing anything underneath the sheet—the thin, clingy sheet. He shifted to his side quickly and brought his knees up into a fetal position before he embarrassed himself in front of her.

Sarah's eyes glanced down at his hips as he rolled toward her before returning to his face. A broad smile blossomed across her face, followed quickly by a mischievous look in her eyes.

"We can keep this between us," Sarah offered with a slight purr in her voice. She lifted his right hand in hers and rubbed it gently.

Amos shifted again, this time away from her. He tried to pull his hand back from her grasp, but she held on firmly, using her middle finger to stroke the inside of his wrist.

Amos was left in the awkward position on his back, his right hand pulled by Sarah and his left arm offering little leverage to enable him to roll away from her. Once again, he became very self-conscious, finally sliding his body toward her and twisting his hips to his right, leaving his lower body pointing away from his, his torso lying uncomfortably flat, and his neck trying to follow the lead of his legs but stuck staring at the white ceiling.

Sarah continued to hold his hand. "When you're ready, I'm here for you," she said softly.

Amos's face flushed, but thankfully she released his hand. At first, he tried to finish his roll away from her, but then he became worried it would send the wrong message, so he rolled back toward her and swung his feet out while lifting himself into a sitting position on the bed, facing her. With his hands, he bunched the sheet in his lap. He looked at Sarah, who continued to hold a mischievous grin on her face.

"Look, Sarah, I like you, I think. In a way, you're beautiful. No, I mean, you look beautiful—er, I'm happy you were assigned to me."

Exasperated, Amos slumped his shoulders forward and stared at the floor. Sarah waited patiently, continuing to watch him.

Amos lifted his head but didn't meet her eyes. "Let me try again." He took a deep breath. "I like you, Sarah. I'm happy you're the one who is helping me. But, well, can we just focus on the mission for now?"

Sarah suppressed a giggle before replying. "On one condition."

"What's that?"

"You don't stare at my chest while you're talking to me."

Amos's eyes jumped up to the ceiling, shifted to the far wall, and then back to Sarah's face. She let out a laugh and smiled at him. His face went a bright red, and then he chuckled as well.

"Deal."

Sarah leaned forward and extended her right hand. Amos looked down at it. Sarah's face turned serious.

"Shake on it."

Amos took Sarah's hand and gave it a firm shake. "I promise to try not to stare at your chest."

"And I promise not to undress you again when you're unconscious."

A look of indignation flashed across Amos's face. "You did what?"

Sarah giggled. "Oh come on! Remember, I watched you prance around naked for fourteen years in the habitat."

Amos blushed again and let out a nervous laugh. "Yes, I keep forgetting that part. But I'm out of the habitat now. Let's start new, okay?"

"Okay," Sarah replied in a resigned tone while flashing her mischievous grin one last time. Then she stood up and headed toward the door.

"Goodnight, Amos. Get some rest. Tomorrow we bring you online with Communications and Intelligence. If you thought Engineering was intense, these two departments will blow your mind! You'll get your first glimpse of the universe around us."

Amos watched her walk to the door. He had almost leaped off the bed at the prospect of beginning to learn about where he was in the universe and what was around him. Maybe he could even gather some insight into the direction of the mission.

"Sarah?"

The door slid open as Sarah approached it. She stopped at the threshold and turned to look at him. "Yes?"

"Thank you."

"For what?"

"For your understanding . . . and patience."

"Of course. We're in this together, Amos. Tomorrow is a new day and a new opportunity to shine."

Amos smiled as Sarah turned and walked out the door, which slid closed behind her.

A new chance to shine, indeed, Amos thought.

———————

"You're shameless!" The doctor's message pushed into Sarah's brain through the network.

"Just doing my duty," Sarah replied. "You have your skills, and I have mine. One of them is seduction. If that's what it takes to get him to trust me, so be it!"

"Are you really that cold-hearted? Your powers of seduction are well known on board this ship, but I always thought they came from a place of genuine warmth."

Sarah offered the equivalent of a mental shrug. "Part of my training for handling Amos."

17.

"Are you ready to talk like an adult?"

Dr. Daman looked across the table at Amos, who sat forlornly in a chair. He looked like he was preparing for the most miserable experience, just short of torture.

Amos shifted uncomfortably while flexing his intertwined fingers, causing them to crack. "I . . . I'm sorry, Dr. Daman. I've gone through a lot in the past couple days. My world was literally taken away, and then I find out I'm supposed to save humanity. The enormity of it all is well, overwhelming."

Dr. Daman nodded approvingly, maintaining his calm expression and even tone. "Totally understandable. You've been through a lot. Admittedly, we expected your reaction. Maybe not the face-plant into the wall but some kind of outburst."

He paused to gauge Amos's reaction. Amos shifted again uncomfortably in his seat, using his hand to pull out the part of his uniform that continually found a way to pinch his most sensitive body parts, and stared glumly at the table in front of him.

"I wish we could have figured out some way to ease you through the transition," Dr. Daman continued. "But, like birth or puberty, much of who we are is formed during a few intense crucibles in our life. Either way, it would be a shock. This way you're forced to deal with your surroundings, and you have complete access to any resources you require to help you."

Amos looked up at the words "help you" and focused on the doctor, offering a sheepish smile. "Do I look like a person who can save humanity?"

Dr. Daman shifted in his seat, causing his chair to creak as he considered his answer. "Well, maybe not at the moment. You have a long path ahead of you, but with your brain, we believe you can do it. You see, Mr. Hare—"

"Amos, please, just call me Amos. I think that's part of what's throwing me off, everyone calling me 'Mr. Hare.' I know it's my proper name, but back in the habitat, no one called me that, or at least I never heard myself referred to in that way."

Dr. Daman offered a deep nod in recognition. "Fair enough, *Amos*. What I'm about to show you is some of the reason why you had a fourteen-year development inside the habitat—and the reason we hope you can save humanity."

Amos let out a nervous laugh. "Can I grow spikes out of my shoulders? Control other people's thoughts? Turn invisible? I've always wished for super powers."

Dr. Daman furled his brows and gave Amos a pointed stare. "You done?"

Amos dropped his eyes back to the table, falling into a slouch. "Yes, sorry. Apparently, I'm still differentiating between what is said in my mind versus what is said by my mouth. Weak attempt at humor." Amos looked back up at the doctor with a slight smile.

Ignoring the distraction, Dr. Daman leaned back in his chair, causing another creak to break through the tomb-like silence. "Actually, that reminds me that we felt one of the key criteria of your successful development was maintaining at least a minimal level of intelligence in all areas, such as linguistics, interpersonal communication, kinesthetic, and wisdom about yourself. Humor was a major topic of discussion. What was the right amount? As great as your mind is, you still need help. Your value as a part of a team will be greatly diminished if you can't interact properly. While we wanted to maximize your intelligence in the areas of logic, spatial, and naturalistic intelligence, we also wanted to make sure you were perceived as a normal person. No one will benefit if you isolate yourself and refuse to cooperate."

Emboldened by the seeming acceptance of his insolence, Amos straightened in his chair. "Well, thank you," he said mockingly. "So you'll accept some of my flippant remarks?"

Dr. Daman stared back with a flat, cool stare for a couple seconds and then broke into a smile. "I think you just used up your quota."

Amos's shoulders rolled forward again in defeat.

"All right then," Dr. Daman continued. "Let's begin with an overview of your ability to bring information into your brain." Dr. Daman touched part of the table next to his right hand. A hologram of a brain appeared above the table between the two of them. Despite himself, Amos smiled at the minor victory and focused on the image hovering in front of him.

Dr. Daman leaned toward the hologram. "This was your brain at birth, similar to most other babies' brains at birth. While not obvious in this display, your brain possessed a higher degree of potential than other babies' brains. On both your mother's side and your father's side, there is a long history of above-normal neuron generation during the first year after birth. Admittedly, there is also a higher than normal rate of neuron elimination in the first year, but this dynamic appears to enable your family to construct a more efficient brain through trial and error. In short, both of your parents, and most of your ancestors, started out with physical brain advantages."

"If the brains in my family eliminate neurons almost as quickly as they create them, why would my family be smarter?" Amos asked. "Why wouldn't the two cancel each other out?"

"Neurons grow rapidly in the early stages of life as the brain literally wires itself. Their growth is guided somewhat by genetics, but it also factors in a fair bit of apparent randomness. Extensions lengthen and connections are made. Some of these neurons prove essential, others non-essential. As neurons find a productive path and the connections are used more frequently, their signaling capabilities strengthen and solidify their value. Neurons that do not find productive paths are eliminated. Through this Darwinian process, the brain wires itself. By creating more neurons, your family has a greater chance of producing productive connections simply because the brain tries more combinations."

"So basically the brains in my family win the lottery by buying more tickets?"

"That would be one, extremely simplistic, way of explaining it."

"All right, based on my studies, the neurons act like the roots of a tree," Amos said. "Roots that find water and nutrients are expanded to increase flow while others that do not find water and nutrients either stop growing or are eliminated."

"In a very basic way, yes. But there are literally hundreds of types of neurons that serve a diverse range of functions and utilize a wide variety of chemicals or neurotransmitters. It is a very complex system, but yes, the maturation goes through many of the same random and natural selection criteria that impact other life forms. But it goes beyond that. Your ancestors have exhibited a high degree of cerebral flexibility, enabling their brains to adapt quickly to changing stimulus. This plasticity may be one of the key reasons you stand here now."

"Okay, so I've got good genes. Why are you so confident in my future?"

"Here, let me show you."

Dr. Daman touched the table again, and another image hovered next to the original hologram. He leaned forward, focusing so closely on the second image that his nose almost pushed into the hologram. "This is the scan we took of your brain just before you were extracted from the habitat. See how different it looks?"

Amos also leaned forward and looked over the image carefully before replying. "Not really. Besides the overall size, which I assume relates to my age, they look similar."

"Yes, when looking at a jumble of wires, it's difficult to see much difference, and potential. Let's start with what is consistent with other people today. First, all humans who made the evolutionary jump to computer communication have a new sensory array around their temples. These specialized neural cells act similar to the photoreceptors in your eyes, only they are sensitive to electromagnetic waves in the terahertz range. These 't-rays' can only penetrate a few millimeters below the skin. For this reason, these photoreceptors are just under a specialized type of skin that protects them."

Picking up the discussion, Amos thought back to his biology class. "These optical and t-receptors are really wonders of natural evolution. Quite extraordinary that life forms on Earth were able to develop the capability to capture a single photon."

"Well, Earth was awash in photons from their sun," Dr. Daman said. "Nature has an uncanny ability to find the right combination of atoms available to take advantage of the energy sources surrounding it. The retinal molecules that capture a single photon in your eyes are similar to the carotene molecules used in photosynthesis in plants."

"A good model to follow," Amos replied. "If my memory in the quasi-crystals serves me, the most challenging part of managed evolution was finding stable carbon chains that could tune into t-rays and have a low probability of activation when t-rays are not present. You don't want false positive signals sent continually to the brain."

"Yes, and also to find a good range of carbon chains so that humans could differentiate between wavelengths. This is where adaptation to neodymium was the final break-through. By incorporating neodymium into these carbon chains, the photo-mechanical transduction could occur in the terahertz range."

Amos leaned forward. "But doc—can I call you that?"

Dr. Daman nodded briefly.

"It's one thing to figure this out in a lab. What always seemed left out is how these neodymium carbon chains were incorporated into reproducible human biology."

Dr. Daman's shoulders sagged slightly. "The end of this process was a combination of DNA surgery trial and error, combined with simple and unyielding Darwinism."

"You mean survival of the fittest?"

Daman nodded. "Humanity has been pushing the limits of what population is sustainable for some time. This has been an intense ethical debate for millennia. I could justify the decision by saying the casualty rate during adoption of neodymium was much lower than expected. But the reality is, when faced with extinction, the ethics of humanity has shown a willful ability to adapt.

Amos nodded pensively as Dr. Daman continued.

"Returning to anatomy, the human eye has four distinct proteins tuned to different wavelengths of light, three of which are for the primary colors, blue, yellow and red. In the same way, every human has only three distinct proteins in their t-ray sensors. You, however, have six, thanks to new discoveries of proteins tuned to various wavelengths and our ability to introduce them into your development. This greater sensitivity to a broader range of terahertz wavelengths enables a broader and more nuanced understanding of signals. Furthermore, we have improved the amino acid dipoles around the carbon chains in your sensors, enabling better fine-tuning of the signal through electron quantum adjustments. This little trick was also copied from human eyes."

"How does the fine-tuning affect me?"

"The protein themselves react to photons in a wider range of wavelengths, broadening the spectrum you can tune in to. By introducing more amino acids, your sensors are able to shift the wavelengths to a more coherent structure for your brain, enabling a more efficient data transfer. Think of it as more flexibility at a higher resolution more perfectly tuned."

"Okay, how does that impact me?"

"Well, besides an ability to receive information on wavelengths others cannot, you are able to 'see' more details in signals sent from computers."

Amos straightened his back and smacked his forehead with the palm of his hand. "So that's where the voices are coming from!"

A look of shock crossed Dr. Daman's face. "What—"

"Just kidding." A sly grin grew across Amos's face.

Dr. Daman relaxed back into his chair and let out a chuckle. "Good one. You got me."

Amos smiled triumphantly.

18.

Amos stood next to Sarah in the midst of a giant room, located one level below the ship's bridge. Numerous data pillars were scattered around the floor, each with at least one person stationed next to it.

The room was well lit, bathed in a mild, reddish hue. Everywhere Amos looked, a data pillar, screen, or holograph filled his line of sight. Occasionally one display would flash, which seemed to require an individual's attention. Amos found it an overwhelming amount of information for his eyes to consume and process. In fact, he couldn't take it all in through his eyes, the sheer amount bringing on a mild headache.

The floor was covered in the same utilitarian carpet as the rest of the ship. While there was no elevated platform, the floor rose and fell gradually. The seats around the data pillars were in depressions that allowed Amos to view the data pillars over the crew members' heads. He stood with the officers on a bubble-like rise in the floor with a table placed on top. The elevated position allowed the officers to scan the entire room, taking in each station's status while in a seated position.

The air itself was even cooler than on the bridge. Whether this was to keep the computers or the crew from overheating was unclear. The crew members engaged at their stations were apparently deeply involved in their tasks. Some sat with their eyes closed while others showed some strain on their face as they presumably sifted through data collected by the sensors associated with their pillar. Some crew members even had beads of sweat rolling down their faces, which was unusual given that they were wearing their climate-controlled uniforms.

Even the space on the ceiling was used efficiently. The ceiling was shaped in a dome-like structure. At the moment, it simply displayed what Amos assumed was the view outside the ship, a constellation of stars that gave a feeling of openness. The direction of the received signals was mapped against the stars.

While Amos wondered at the room, the ache behind his eyes increased as the amount of data displayed went through his optical nerves. He could consume much more information when fed to him directly from the computer. His optical nerves were simply not accustomed to processing this volume of data. Human eyes remained constrained by how much information they could absorb and process, determined largely by the focal area.

Lieutenant Commander Sig strode up the elevated area on which Sarah and Amos stood. Even if Amos had not been introduced to Sig and had not learned how to interpret rank from uniforms, it was obvious Sig was the person in command. His back was straight, offering a sense of strength, but everything else seemed loose with a feline-like ability to react. As Sig walked up, Amos had the sense Sig knew everything that was happening on the floor. Rarely, if ever, had Amos felt at a disadvantage of knowledge. It unnerved him slightly.

When Sig reached the highest point of the rise in the floor, he stopped, his officer's mask still on. "Mr. Hare, Ensign Laka. Welcome to Intelligence. Mr. Hare. I look forward to showing you around and bringing you online with our systems."

Amos went rigid, gripped with nervous fear, and stood at attention, fixing his stare on a spot across the room. "Thank you, sir. I look forward to learning about Intelligence."

The mask on Sig's face broke, and he smiled and waved at Amos in a downward motion. "At ease, Mr. Hare. In here we try to keep the atmosphere more relaxed. There's enough stress associated with this job without getting worked up about formalities."

Amos relaxed and let out a breath. He looked at Sig nervously. "Yes, sir."

Sig glanced at Amos's head. "How's your head? I heard there's an outline of your body on the wall in Dr. Daman's office."

Amos winced. "Just fine, sir. Thank you for asking."

Sig chuckled. "Don't sweat it. In my youth, I tried to prove I could leap across a conference table, only to catch my foot on the nearest edge. I landed in a sprawled-out position on the table, my momentum carrying me across and over the table. I ended up in a heap on the floor."

A stunned look crossed Amos's face, unsure how to react.

Sarah giggled. "I believe there were other . . . circumstances to that story?"

Sig's eyes shifted to Sarah and softened into a warmth that matched his smile. He chuckled. "Yes, it was the evening before the start of officer training, and we had been enjoying some . . . freedoms before the intense program."

Sarah giggled again. "'Freedoms,' the drink of choice of the officers on the *Randall*."

Sig dropped his head as he stifled a laugh that might weaken his projection of authority. He lifted his head back up a moment later, and only a smile remained. "Someday, Mr. Hare, when you're ready, we'll enjoy some 'freedom' together."

Amos smiled back nervously, still trying to balance the officer with the person in his mind.

Sensing his nervousness, Sarah stepped forward. "The systems in this room will blow your mind, so no need to start sweating just yet."

Amos looked over at Sarah, who also held a pleasant smile on her face. Her eyes seemed to offer approval for making the effort to conform to ship protocol, but they also let him know it was okay to relax.

Sig returned to his officer pose, although the smile remained on his face. "Let's start with a general overview. Each data pillar is specialized for a specific type of information gathering. The largest amount of information is gathered through neutrino signals. There is an abundance of neutrinos passing through us constantly, and they store information about their interactions with masses, even though they only interact with them weakly. For this reason, we devote a significant amount of resources to processing their signal."

Sig swept his left arm across a quarter of the room. "This general area is devoted to neutrino signal processing."

Amos scanned the half dozen data pillars in the area, which seemed to operate in normal ranges, based on the relatively low-key interactions in which the crew members were engaged.

"Of course, we also process the full spectrum of electromagnetic signals," Sig continued, "from radio to gamma rays. Through this monitoring, we pick up all communications between ships and planets. We also monitor communications on the ship, although there are protocols set up to allow for privacy. Unless we have reason to suspect a person might be trying to subvert ship operations, we are not allowed to monitor a crew member's communication. Even if we suspect an individual, we need approval from the captain."

Amos gave Sig a suspicious look. "Are my communications being monitored?"

Sig looked Amos in the eye. "Yes," he said without a hint of apology. "Just as we monitored all your communications while you lived in the habitat, we continue to monitor your communications while aboard this ship."

Amos felt a surge of anger rise inside, but he pushed it back down. "So much for freedom. Am I considered a potential threat?"

Sig continued to look at Amos in the eye as he responded in the same blunt tone. "Yes. Until you demonstrate a full commitment and devotion to the mission, you are considered a threat."

Amos winced at the truth in his words. After a moment of consideration, he nodded. "I understand."

Sarah let out a nervous breath. "Amos, every new crew member is monitored in the same way until they have proven their commitment. Even then, privacy is considered a luxury aboard a ship. Partly for obvious reasons given the tight quarters but also to protect the crew and the ship."

Amos looked at Sarah with cool eyes. "I understand." Then he turned back to Sig. "One question. Since I'm the evolved, if I could communicate directly with another person, would you be able to monitor it?"

Sig considered the question for a second, then looked back at Amos. "We would detect the signal sent. Whether we could understand the communication is another matter. Brain-to-brain communications could theoretically have completely different data structures than the more universal language of brain-to-computer. In essence, brain-to-brain communications are encrypted. Not to say we couldn't break the encryption, but given the limited history of this type of communication, I can't say for certain how difficult it would be under varying circumstances."

"Of course, this is all theoretical, given that you are one of a kind at the moment," Sarah added.

Amos held Sig's stare for half a second, trying to read if there was any more knowledge on the subject behind his eyes. After a moment he turned to Sarah. "Yes, of course." He nodded at Sig. "Thank you for the honest answer, sir. I appreciate it."

Sig nodded. "I would add that with your brain connected to our systems, the potential to process brain-to-brain communications is improved significantly. There remain certain signals that are better suited to processing in the human brain."

Feeling uncomfortable at where the statement might lead, Amos turned to look over the opposite side of the room. "What are these areas devoted to?"

Sig followed his gaze. "Various types of signal processing. We monitor all bosons and their associated fields in this area, excluding photons, which are monitored in the electromagnetic area." Sig swept his arm across about an eighth of the room, which began next to the electromagnetic area. Then he pointed to the area next to what he had just framed with his arm. "In this area, we monitor gravitons, which are tightly linked with the navigation operations."

Sig held out his arms to define the remaining quarter of the floor. "This area is devoted to detecting the harder to find or theoretical fermions and bosons, including the saxian, gluino, and skyrmions. It's an area that will likely become of vital importance to you as we search for anomalies to study."

Amos nodded as he scanned the area, which also had people stationed at about six different data pillars. They looked older, some even a bit frail. "Are the crew members stationed in this area different than those in other areas?"

Sig glanced sideways at Amos as they faced the area in question. "Yes, the crew members in this area all have advanced degrees. Most have completed cutting-edge research and have published their findings. A few have even won a Heliacal Prize for outshining science and math peers. Most of their backgrounds are in physics and mathematics but also in chemistry, engineering, and even philosophy. They represent many of the best minds in humanity, up until you boarded this ship."

Amos cringed and looked over at Sig. "Well, that isn't daunting! You talk like I'm more accomplished or smarter than all of these people."

Sig shifted uncomfortably and glanced at Sarah.

Sarah put her hand on Amos's shoulder. "Well, we hope that you prove that you are. Yes, you have not accomplished anything, but your intellect is measured as vastly superior to them. This potential, combined with the greater processing capacity of your brain, should mean you can easily surpass their accomplishments."

Amos looked around the room and noticed a few people were watching them. "Well, I guess I have a lot to prove."

Sig gave a quick nod, and Sarah's eyes lit up in approval.

"Well then, shall we move over to Communications?" Sig asked as he turned toward the lift.

Amos took a final look around the room, "One more question."

Sig stopped and turned back. "Yes?"

"Do I have a station on this floor?"

Sig straightened before replying. "Yes, of course. Your station is wherever you feel you can be the most effective. Crew members are instructed to make room for you should you choose their station and to provide any support you require. But, we assume that most of your work will be done through the network from either your primary station in Navigation, from the bridge, or from your room, should you require a quieter location."

Amos nodded in approval. "Most of the time that would be fine, but should we discover something of interest, then I would likely prefer to work on this level, surrounded by visual cues from the computers and, more importantly, the crew. Since arriving on board, I've realized how much nonverbal information is passed between humans."

"If that is your desire, then we will make sure the proper arrangements are made."

Amos pressed a little further. "Commander, since no one on board can communicate with me directly, without the aid of the network, speech, or visual cues, I must ensure these less efficient communication channels are maximized to avoid missing something. This room is set up to maximize all of these communication channels."

Sig rocked back a bit on his heels as he considered the request. "Yes, of course. Once you have completed your tour of the ship, we can figure out the best solution for you."

Amos nodded in approval. "One more thing, Commander. Can you please grant me access to the intelligence systems?"

Sig glanced over at Sarah. "We were going to bring you online in steps, in conjunction with Communications. We thought it would be easier for you if we stepped into it."

Amos shook his head in mild irritation. "Thank you for your concern, but I believe that if I'm to get up to speed quickly, I must have access to all the systems as soon as possible."

Sarah's eyes sparkled for an instant, and then she turned to Amos. "I believe we can do that, Amos. The captain has given his approval. But you will have no ability to alter systems or send commands to the crew until a later time."

Sig's eyes turned pink, and then he looked at Sarah and nodded. "Very well. Let me bring you online."

Sig went silent for a second and his eyes remained pink and he stared at Amos.

Amos felt a sudden rush as his brain was notified of the new systems he could access. His mind started working through all of the systems and sensors attached to the network, taking an inventory of what was available.

Suddenly, he squinted and let out a groan. Sarah and Sig watched nervously, and Sarah reached for him with her hand. However, he recovered, and his face relaxed. Amos raised his head slowly with his eyes closed, focused completely on the avalanche of information storming into his head. After a few seconds, he opened his eyes and looked at Sig, who watched him patiently.

"Impressive! This ship can sense every known signal, both natural and unnatural, that it comes in contact with."

Sig offered a small, prideful smile in response.

"There's too much information for me to process at the moment," Amos continued, "so I will work through everything later. But may I make one small suggestion?"

Sig straightened as he stumbled over his reply. "Well, we have tested and calibrated and . . . of course. What's your suggestion?"

"The neutrino sensors are a fraction off, probably too small to be caught in the routine testing. Almost all of the time this wouldn't be an issue, but it may cause some inaccurate readings when interpreting their pure mass eigenstate."

Sig's face turned faintly red. "We will have someone look at the sensors. Thank you."

Amos nodded. "Now, on to Communications?"

Sig hesitated, then nodded and began to walk toward an archway to the right of where the door to the lift was located. As Sarah and Amos followed, Sarah pushed a message to Amos through the network.

"Way to go! You just can't help yourself, can you?"

She gave Amos a quick elbow, causing him to glance over at her. Sarah offered a smile in return. Amos did not smile or offer a thought back to Sarah. His jaw was tense as he started working through some of the intelligence systems.

A humming sound came from the archway as they approached. It ceased, and then a beep sounded. A light Amos had not noticed changed from red to green above the archway. Sig looked back at Amos, apparently reading his thoughts.

"Since you do not have access to security systems, I should tell you that the archway is protected. If you approach it without the proper security clearances, you will feel a strong push away from the archway. I am told that if you continue to attempt to approach the archway, you will be stunned, likely knocking you out as your neural network is overwhelmed. I've never felt it, but it sounds unpleasant."

Amos thought back to the guards who had escorted him out of the habitat and shuddered. They had been able to shut down his brain at will. Just the thought of that experience caused him to slow his speed as he approached.

Sig walked through the archway, which led to a wide staircase that swept down and to the left, out of view. He paused on the first step and turned toward Amos. "Don't worry, it's safe. Now that you're online with the systems in intelligence, you should have no problem going through the archway."

Amos took a few shortened steps without sensing any push back. He scanned the entire arch and then stepped through, with no effect.

Sig nodded and turned back toward the stairs and began descending. He also continued with his straightforward way of presenting the tour. "This leads down to Communications. Of course we could also take the lift, but I prefer the exercise of the stairs. Besides, it's usually faster anyway."

As they continued down the stairway, Sarah let out a giggle. Amos and Sig looked at her.

"Sorry, I was just thinking how the staircase spirals to the left, adding another layer of defense from Communications."

Both Sig and Amos stopped and stared at her. Sarah also stopped and looked back with a quizzical expression.

"Oh, all right, let me spell it out. Spiral staircases in ancient castles of what was called Europe on Earth also went down to the left. They spiraled to the left so that the defenders would have the advantage should the enemy breach the defenses. The right arm of the defenders would be free to swing their sword downwards at the enemy as the defenders retreated up the stairs. Alternatively, the attacker's swing would be impeded by the height difference and the wall on the inside. I just had a funny vision of Communications storming Intelligence with swords."

Sig and Amos's mouths fell open slightly as they stared at her. She continued to chuckle to herself, realized she was being watched, and then suppressed her smile and straightened her back.

"Well, I know Reilly covets your role over Intelligence. Sorry. Carry on."

Amos's face broke into a smile as Sig returned his focus to the descent. He pushed a thought message to Sarah.

"Nerd!"

Sarah giggled again, causing Sig to glance toward her and then to Amos, who centered his attention on the steps.

19.

Sig, Amos, and Sarah continued down the curved staircase. After a few more steps, the Communications room came into view. The room was smaller than Intelligence with about a dozen doors to offices and conference rooms ringing the central area. Only one data pillar stood in the center of the room with two people stationed at it. In a ring around the pillar were six small workstations with displays.

As they stepped onto the floor, Lieutenant Reilly lifted his head from the display at the workstation closest to the stairs and smiled warmly. He strode over to greet them.

"Sig, Mr. Hare, Sarah, welcome to Communications." Reilly offered, smiling.

Sig stopped and turned sideways to allow Amos and Sarah pass. He looked at Reilly. "Lieutenant, I will let you take it from here." He turned his head back to Amos and Sarah. "I look forward to working with you in the future."

Amos nodded. "Thanks for the tour. I look forward to it as well."

Sig nodded and went back up the stairs.

Amos and Sarah turned their attention to Reilly, who stood in front of them, bouncing slightly on the balls of his feet like a giddy boy. When he began talking, he swung his arms around and used his hands to help articulate his points.

"Again, welcome. This is Communications." He swept his arms in a wide arc while he turned slightly, as if introducing a performance on a grand stage. "Amos, I hope Sig didn't burst your cortex already. He likes to have all his fancy lights blinking when giving a tour."

"Well, it was overwhelming for the visual cortex," Amos replied tepidly, "but once he opened up the direct data feed, it all made sense."

Reilly let out a laugh. "Oh, that must have irked him something fierce!" He continued to laugh to himself as if everyone was in on the joke.

Sarah chuckled along with him. "You should have seen his face when Amos offered a suggestion to improve one of his sensors after he was given access."

Reilly howled with laughter, bending over slightly and slapping his thigh. "I would have loved to have seen that!"

Amos stood silently, unsure how to react. Reilly and Sarah noticed his silence and pulled themselves together.

"For most people—no, for everyone besides you, Amos—that amount of data would have knocked them out," Reilly explained. "Sig likes to show off with his blinking lights and then scare everyone away by providing some level of access to the system. That way, everyone on the ship thinks he's a genius and leaves him alone."

Sarah continued to smile, offering an affirmative nod. "He doesn't like anyone poking around his systems."

Reilly slapped Amos on the back. "But you! You showed him up!"

Amos offered a sheepish smile. "I didn't mean to. I mean I didn't—"

Reilly waved him off. "Oh pshh, he deserves it. I love him, but he can be an arrogant ass at times."

Amos's smile broadened, conveying more confidence than he felt.

Reilly turned back to the floor before them and continued with another sweep of his arm. "If intelligence is about consuming and processing any and all signals, communications is about sending signals and ensuring only the intended party receives a clear signal and the message is understood fully."

Reilly paused and looked at Amos, leaving an opening for a question with an eager tilt of his head. When Amos remained silent, Reilly righted his head and continued.

"The central pillar is a direct feed from Intelligence. All incoming signals are processed by Intelligence initially to protect against corruption or other issues that may impact the ship's systems. Then Communications receives a clean and decrypted signal."

Reilly paused again and looked at Amos and then Sarah, who continued to stand patiently. When no response was offered his posture deflated slightly.

"Okay, let's walk around the floor."

Reilly turned to his left and began walking around the room in a clockwise direction. Amos and Sarah followed. As Reilly walked, he turned his upper body to look back at them.

"The people stationed at the data pillar are focused on ensuring that the signals coming from Intelligence and all signals sent from the personnel on the ship are processed effectively. Any communication, from the captain on the bridge to a crew member in his or her quarters, is processed through Communications. Any signals sent outside the ship go through the standard censorship process used by the military. This is to ensure that the ship and the crew are not inadvertently put at risk."

"What about communications between crew members aboard the ship?" Amos asked.

Reilly stopped and turned to Amos. "We have the capability to monitor all communications aboard the ship. Certain crew members, like the captain, are able to have private communications, although all are recorded. Once you have passed all the checks and completed a certain amount of time on board, any crew member can have a limited number of private communications when off duty. All communications while on duty over the ship's network are considered property of the military and thus are available for monitoring."

Reilly paused for a second, seemingly contemplating the question some more, and then continued in a lower voice. "Mr. Hare, we do not want to listen to exchanges of lovers and other highly personal communications. For the most part, the computers process the signals and flag potential threats for us to review. More seniority typically means more privacy, but we try to be highly conscious of a person's personal boundaries."

Amos nodded. "Understandable. All of my communications are monitored, correct?"

Reilly blanched slightly. He looked at Sarah and then back to Amos. "Yes. Until the captain is confident in your commitment to the mission and we believe we can trust your judgment."

Amos nodded. "Understood."

Sarah turned to Amos. "Didn't we clarify that point for you in Intelligence?"

"Yes. I'm just trying to understand something."

Sarah waited for him to complete his thought, finally growing impatient. "Which is. . . ?"

Amos held her stare with a seemingly blank mind. She squinted slightly as she tried to decipher the meaning of the statement. Then she let it drop.

Reilly hesitated awkwardly for a moment and then continued the tour. "The rooms you see surrounding the floor are for more focused work, such as crafting sensitive messages to command and speeches to the crew or foreign parties. Some of the rooms contain specialized systems when more confidential communications are required. Captain Melville has access to these specialized systems from a room off the bridge, but sometimes other crew members require the use of these systems."

"Specialized encryption systems?" Amos asked.

Reilly glanced back as he walked. "Intelligence handles all encryption and the specialized systems in these rooms. However, the rooms themselves are constructed in a manner to ensure confidential conversations. We would rather crew members come to Communications for these conversations than Intelligence, for obvious reasons."

Amos nodded. "Makes sense."

As Reilly walked closer to the data pillar, Amos focused on it and all of the various colored lights, a few of which were flashing. He counted at least four different colors: green, red, yellow and blue. Most of the lights did not blink. Others went through a slow flashing cycle lasting about two seconds. Still others flashed more rapidly. Three main groupings of lights were located at the top, middle, and bottom of the pillar. Within these groups, the lights were not fixed in any single position but seemed to adjust their position as new lights appeared or others disappeared. To someone unfamiliar with the system, it was bewildering to understand the information emitted by the lights.

"Each of the lights on the bottom third of the pillar represent an open communication channel between the ship's systems and an external partner," Reilly explained. "When we are in close orbit to a settled planet, like we are currently, many of these communication channels remain open as data is exchanged consistently between the ship and the planet. For these close-range channels, typically a distance of under a light week, the communication channel utilizes photons at various wavelengths, depending on the amount of data and the security requirements."

"What do all the colors mean?" Amos asked.

Reilly turned and pointed out the different colors in the lower third. "A range of things, but generally, green is within operating parameters. Yellow has one to three parameters outside guidelines, which could simply be a user going over an allotted amount of time granted or slower data transmission due to a technical problem. Red requires more immediate attention by the crew in communications, because either there are significant technical problems or security may have been breached. A rapid flashing light means the issue has not been addressed. A slower flashing light means the problem is being addressed."

"And the blue lights?"

"Blue means the channel is highly secure and controlled by another group on the ship. It could be the bridge, Intelligence, or another department with the appropriate security clearances. Here in Communications, we don't always know exactly. Our role on these channels is to watch for disturbances and handle technical problems, but we have limited ability to administer those channels."

"What happens if one of those channels has a problem?"

"Typically, if the channel is having significant technical problems or has been compromised, we shut it down and re-establish the party on a new communication channel. We are primarily the operators. We also assist with translations from and into different languages. And we support with crafting messages to the crew and external partners, should a crew member require it."

Amos nodded.

"When you're online with communications, most of the alerts behind these lights will become obvious. For right now, let me show you directly."

Reilly leaned down and touched one of the lights. A holographic display of the wavelength used by the channel appeared in the air near the light with various pieces of data about the status of the channel displayed around the wavelength. Amos made out tiny vibrations in the wavelengths as data was transmitted. Reilly touched the wavelength and spread it so that it focused on one part. Then he tapped it, and the wavelength froze in place.

"Here, I've taken a snapshot of the wavelength. This one is operating within normal parameters and is not encrypted, so it's pretty straightforward. You can see how we can drill down into specific segments of each communication channel and watch for problems, either technical or another signal trying to piggy-back or insert data to corrupt the system."

"Does that happen often?"

Reilly looked up at Amos from his crouched position. "No, not really anymore. But a long time ago, it was one way that an outsider could gain entry to systems."

Reilly stood up, and the display disappeared. "No system is completely secure, but a lot of our focus is on monitoring wavelengths for issues that reduce communication effectiveness."

Reilly pointed at the middle groupings of lights. "The lights in the middle region are monitoring our systems to ensure they're running within specifications. They also give information about the load on the overall system and summaries of usage patterns."

He motioned to the top of the pillar, which had fewer spaces for lights, but every space was filled by a blue light. "The lights at the top represent neutrino-based communications. These communication channels are used more for long-distance channels, typically over a distance of at least three light months. For these longer distances, communications can often determine a shorter distance between the points by utilizing right-handed neutrinos."

"That makes sense, because, unlike the photon, the right-handed neutrino has the ability to leave the constraints of our brane," Amos observed, "taking a more direct route through the bulk between the folds of the brane."

"Yes. Given your expertise in navigation, this little trick is completely obvious to you. While everyone who has adapted to neodymium can perceive our brane, it is very difficult to determine a more direct route. We rely heavily on the detailed maps of the brane in navigation to find the most effective route. Even then we lose the signal into the bulk or to some other distant portion of the brane."

Amos tilted his head as he focused on Reilly. "I can probably help you improve your performance. Once I'm up to speed on everything and have figured out what I'm looking for, it will become critical that we can communicate effectively back to home." Amos's voice trailed off at the mention of the word.

A quick nod from Reilly sent a message of appreciation. "We need a closer interaction between someone like you in Navigation and Communications, which isn't always obvious. I would appreciate your help very much."

Amos smiled back at him. He liked Reilly. "Of course. Maybe I can come up with some new methods of communications beyond photons and neutrinos. Who knows? Our brane could be constrained within a higher-dimensional brane, offering new particles that can find even shorter paths."

Reilly looked relieved. "If you could discover something like that, it could possibly alter the fate of humanity."

Amos's face turned serious. "We all have a lot of work to do, and who knows what we will discover on this mission. Branes, dimensions, particles, a higher level of consciousness? It's exciting—and scary."

Sarah stepped forward. "Let's not get ahead of ourselves. First, let's get Amos connected to communications and allow him time to process everything."

Reilly nodded. "All right, I'll grant you access to the systems, but that doesn't mean you can listen to communications. It simply means you will have the ability to open and close your own channels and have administrative rights to monitor operating parameters. If you want to change settings or other pieces of operations, I simply request you run it by me so that I understand any changes made to the system."

Amos nodded. "I understand."

Reilly's eyes twinkled, and Amos felt his brain open up to communications. He knew immediately that there were 153 communication channels open. Fifty-two were encrypted, of which twenty were controlled by a group outside of communications. At random, Amos chose an unencrypted channel and brought up the details behind the wavelength along with all of the descriptive data about the open channel. He let out a small gasp as he realized his brain could interpret the channel and understand what was being said. This particular wavelength was a conference call between engineering personnel on the ship and an officer on the planet. They were going over their checklists to make sure the final preparations for the ship were going smoothly.

The ends of Amos's mouth curled up slightly as a female in Engineering compared a particularly small tool to a part of "Jeff's" anatomy.

Sarah watched him closely for any reaction to the new data feed. "Something amusing that you'd like to share?"

Startled, Amos closed down the monitoring of that channel and turned to her. "No, why?"

Sarah's expression changed to a smirk. "Amos, you're turning pink. What's so funny?"

"Er, uh, I was just thinking back to your comment about communications storming up the stairs to Intelligence."

Reilly gave Sarah a quizzical look.

Sarah blushed. "That was . . . a bad joke while we were walking down here. Nothing was meant by it."

Reilly shrugged. "Okay, you should have full access to communications."

Amos smiled back. "Yes, everything seems in order."

Inside, he wondered at all the encrypted channels in use and what could possibly require that amount of bandwidth.

20.

Dr. Daman's bushy grey and black eyebrows bounced downward with each point he made. Amos imagined they were a silver fox, pouncing on the round orbs below in a valiant but ultimately fruitless effort to capture them.

He was finally getting answers and a better understanding of his life. As painful as it had been to discover that much of his life was an illusion, it was also satisfying to understand why he had felt discomfort with so much around him. Amos also began to appreciate that his development up to this point was quite similar to what humans had endured for millennia. While this knowledge didn't make up for the feeling of loss from the removal of his made-up parents, at least he had some perspective.

Throughout the meeting, Amos couldn't keep from asking himself whether all of this manufactured evolution was worth it or even the right course. The easy answer was that it allowed humanity to continue, but at what cost? And if humanity was doomed if Amos failed, maybe life shouldn't continue. Why couldn't humanity learn to live within its means?

Dr. Daman continued in more of a monologue than a discussion. "Converting the energy of the photon into a neural signal is also a wonder of nature. When developing t-ray sensors for humans, scientists borrowed heavily from nature's examples. These neurons are capable of a fair bit of quantum processing before sending the signal to the thalamus."

Amos responded in a "you've told me this already" tone mastered by teenagers. "Yes, this was one of the significant breakthroughs enabled by evolving the sensors organically as opposed to implanting them. The human eye has five basic types of neurons with around fifty specific neurons that process the information gathered from all of the photons hitting the retina. This processing sends a coherent signal into the brain."

Dr. Daman nodded twice in confirmation. "Yes, as you remember from your history of anatomy courses, at first humans used external devices linked to the brain to create this capability, then implants, then surgery to transform existing tissue, and finally DNA surgery and managed evolution to make it an inherent quality in humans."

Amos shook his head with narrowed eyes as he considered this evolutionary process. "What a barbaric time during those early attempts. Doctors and scientists did more damage at first as they butchered parts of the brain."

Dr. Daman shrugged nonchalantly. "Be thankful you never had to live through such horrendous experimentation. Starting with the photoreceptors in your temples, there's actually an extra type of neuron relative to the neurons in your retina. These neurons fine tune the temporal differences in the signal. In most humans, there are about twenty distinct neurons in this group. You've got closer to thirty."

Amos's eyes widened as he snapped up the new piece of information about himself. "So I can understand the more complex signal?"

"Exactly. In the average human, the signal must be kept relatively free of distortion, and the signal has an upper limit of data transmission. In your case, you can tease out the information from a more distorted signal, and you should be able to understand the subtler information it contains."

"So I'm listening to computers in high fidelity?"

Dr. Daman chuckled. "Yes, compared to what preceded that ancient technology, you are effectively listening in high fidelity. From the t-sensors, the information is transmitted to the thalamus. From the thalamus, the processing of the information often incorporates a wide range of the brain's functions, depending on the information. Your brain, however, has evolved to another level—more receptors, more neurons devoted to transporting and translating information, more connections between those neurons, and much greater sensitivity to temporal differences. This enables you to download more information at a greater speed than anyone else."

Amos leaned forward against the table. "Did the adaptation to neodymium enable humans to process these signals deeper in the brain as well?"

Dr. Daman nodded. "Yes. The element was incorporated primarily into the temple area, increasing sensitivity to electromagnetic waves, although neodymium has also been incorporated into other brain functions to improve processing capabilities. One of the most amazing things about the brain is its ability to adapt to new sensory inputs. Once the new sensitivity to t-rays evolved sufficiently to tune into specific frequencies, the neurons in the brain adapted quite readily to the new source of information. It took a little while to train the brain to interpret the signals, but again, the actual physical changes inside the brain largely took care of themselves."

Amos pondered this information for a moment. "So, does that mean more of the brain is devoted to signal processing?"

Dr. Daman nodded again, smiling faintly as he warmed up to the questions. "Yes, definitely, but maybe not in the way you might think. As you can imagine, the amount of data downloaded during a conversation with a computer is significant. This required the brain to increase its processing power at the expense of long-term memory. So the thalamus is much more significant in its size and its connections to other parts of the brain associated with intelligence and memory retrieval."

Amos's eyes focused on the wall behind the doctor as he took in the information. "Makes sense, however, most of this I already know from my studies."

Dr. Daman stared at Amos for a moment before continuing. "Digging a little deeper into your evolved brain, as I said before, your brain has much more capacity to download information from computers. Part of this is due to your family's well-documented adaptation to samarium, which increased the parallel processing capabilities of your auditory nerves. Part of it is also more neurons and greater sensitivity. But part of what is really unique to you is a highly efficient construction of neurons and connections that can carry this information. It's like we provided the highest quality materials, and your brain developed the most efficient way to incorporate them. We have not seen another develop in as efficient a manner as you. While we recognize the beneficial construction, we have had limited success in replicating it in other humans. It seems somewhat unique to your family."

"So I can carry on a few more conversations at a time?"

Dr. Daman chuckled. "Not only can you establish at least a half dozen connections with different computers about different subjects, your rate of data transfer is at least a hundred times what other proficient humans can achieve who have only one connection. In other words, you could plug into each of the information pillars on the bridge of this ship and exceed their existing rate of information processing power while also carrying on a casual conversation with the captain. No one else can manage more than one connection to a single pillar, and even that requires their complete focus."

Amos's jaw fell open. He had never considered that he was that much . . . smarter than everyone else. Noticing the doctor's gaze, Amos offered a hurried response. "That would explain why most of the people seem zoned out."

Doctor Daman smiled. "Trust me, they are not zoned out. If anything, they are zoned in and completely consumed by their tasks. That's why there's a rotation schedule at each pillar, providing back-up, redundancy, and necessary down time for each individual's brain to rest."

"I'll keep that in mind next time I'm on the bridge."

"Good idea," Dr. Daman replied. "Now, returning to your brain. The amount of data moving into your brain requires significantly more processing power. The plasticity of your brain is much greater than that of a child. This means it can adapt more readily to changing sensory inputs. It also suggests an ability for greater creativity and efficient data processing. This comes at a cost, at least to you internally. Because so much of your brain is devoted to brute processing strength, you have a significantly diminished internal memory capacity. You probably don't realize it, but most of your memories are stored in the memory processing quasi-crystals rather than your head. Your ability to access those memories is so advanced that it doesn't matter if they're stored internally or externally."

"Wait! How can that be?" Amos asked. "The method through which the brain stores memories is completely different from a computer. In a computer, there's a highly-structured system that relates data to each other. I know artificial intelligence is able to create meaningful new relationships in real time as it processes, but it still hasn't matched the brain. Dig down deep enough into the brain, and memories are objects without any meaning. The brain is able to process this type of information, but computers still need a layer of structure wrapping these data points. It remains the fundamental difference that separates humans from silicon systems."

Doctor Daman leaned in. "Good point. I'm glad you picked up on the issue. There was a piece of information left out of your education, largely because it's classified. Scientists have developed a special type of quasi-crystal that is able to use the extra dimension in a way that not only enables it to mimic how the brain stores and retrieves memories but also how it processes it. The technology is actually not that new; it's been around for hundreds of years, but it has been kept secret."

A questioning look came over Amos's face. "Why keep it secret? Sounds like it could have profound effects on commerce systems as well as human intelligence."

Dr. Daman leaned back in his chair while he pondered his answer. "I shouldn't tell you this, because you have not yet been granted access to this security level, but given your rate of improvement, I think it's only a matter of time before you are granted the necessary security clearance."

A subtle flash of pink appeared in his eyes that Amos only caught because he was fully focused on the doctor.

"Let's just say there are security concerns should this technology be misused. For this reason, the Syndicate has kept it secret."

Amos watched Dr. Daman closely for a moment, trying to read anything else from his body language. He was sure he had touched on something important, but it was also clear that Dr. Daman would offer no more on the subject. Deciding to not push it further, Amos took a different tack.

"So, what's the catch with my ability to access memories in the silicon systems?"

Amos noticed the tension in the doctor's shoulders subside.

"The catch is you must be connected to the computers at all times. If that connection is disrupted or you find yourself some distance from the computer network, you will be unable to access most of your long-term memories. You will also be unable to recall things like your studies, your past life in the habitat, possibly even your name."

Amos sat quietly for a moment, contemplating the ramifications of this reality. He chose to take a philosophical path. "Okay, but if I'm not my memories, who am I?"

Dr. Daman's shoulders relaxed further, relieved at the turn of the conversation. "Ah, the age-old question of self. As humanity has evolved, enabling more personal information to be stored outside of one's self, this has been an ongoing debate. Are we a collection of experiences unique to ourselves, or are we something deeper?"

He paused and looked up at the ceiling while putting together his next sentence. "Basically, I believe it boils down to how your brain processes experiences, stores memories, and reuses them. An interesting discovery was made during an early scientific experiment in which the brains of two people were hardwired to each other. The two people could not interpret each other's memories. When accessing the other person's brain, the individual saw images, but it felt more like a dream, confusing and difficult to interpret. Each person creates his or her own unique structures for creating and retrieving memories. Accessing someone else's memories is like trying to transfer data files out of one data structure into another. There is simply not enough similarity to allow an easy transfer."

"But then how do individuals share information?"

Doctor Daman shifted in his chair and appeared to look at a non-existent board on the side wall. "That was a significant challenge when the first generation evolved to communicate with computers. Each person could upload data and retrieve it, but sharing information through this method proved difficult. Again, you may not have noticed it, but when you worked on a school report, you were working in a more structured environment."

Amos thought back to his early years of classes. "Yes, at first it was annoying that I couldn't just upload my thoughts directly."

"That was so we could interpret your thoughts. No one is born speaking a language, much less the language of their parents. The brain has to be taught how to interpret its processes into a transferable form understandable to another person. Conversations may seem unstructured, but they are really highly-structured forms of sounds that enable another brain trained in the structure to understand. While this transfer is inefficient relative to the processing inside the brain, it is absolutely necessary. This is important. If you simply try to push a mass of thoughts at the computer when giving commands, the computer will react much slower, because it has to interpret your thoughts, often arriving at inaccurate conclusions about your commands. If you give clear commands in a language and structure it recognizes, it will be much more responsive."

Amos leaned back as he considered something he had known intuitively. "I'll try to keep that in mind—literally." Amos gave a weak smile. "Sorry."

Dr. Daman smiled. "Take solace in the fact that this same issue provides some level of personal privacy. It is challenging for someone to access your brain without you knowing it but even more difficult for them to understand your thoughts."

Amos fixed his eyes on the doctor. "What about my memories?"

Amos caught another brief pink sparkle in the doctor's eyes as he responded in a more clinical tone.

"While difficult, those more structured memories in the network can be interpreted. Know that in society there are strict ethical codes against accessing someone's personal memories without their approval. That said, you should also make sure that you set up the security in a manner that protects your memories and do regular checks and maintenance to ensure the system has not been violated."

Amos considered Dr. Daman's answer before responding. "Thank you for telling me. But, if I understand my evolved status correctly, what truly sets me apart is my ability to communicate brain-to-brain with others of my status. Of course, this ability seems useless without another person of my status. I feel like I'm shouting in German 'The horse does not eat cucumber salad.' I'd be lucky if anyone could understand it, and certainly no one could reply."

Doctor Daman let out a belly laugh. "Ah, a wonderful analogy! The connections your brain makes by having access to the history of humanity in the network is a wonder to watch. Yes, you are a singular entity built for an integrated community. Yes, your ability to communicate with others cannot possibly be tested and understood fully until another person of your status is developed. All I can say at this point is that your potential to communicate directly with others also offers advantages while communicating to computers. You are not even close to using your full potential, but your abilities far exceed any other person alive."

Amos refocused on the image of his brain floating before him. "Is that all I am? A brain that has been scanned and clinically displayed like an artifact floating over a wooden table?"

"A difficult question, Amos, for all of us. If you want my unscientific opinion, we are on the cusp of something special. You may open a door into a reality unfathomable by anyone before you. Just as humans began to perceive extra dimensions once they could communicate directly with computers and all the sensors attached to the network, your experiences may differ vastly from ours as your brain senses and possibly even communicates through dimensions hidden from our senses. Your brain is still developing and will likely continue to develop throughout your life as it adapts to your new environment."

Amos thought about Bina. He had been unable to communicate with her since shortly after he arrived on the ship. She had said she couldn't interfere. Could she simply be some control system put in place by Dr. Daman to trick him into discussing his innermost thoughts? Was she another evolved, secreted away, with whom he was able to communicate? Was she something more? Amos wished he could talk with her. She was the only one who really understood him and had been with him for as long as he could remember. Then again, maybe "she" was just some schizophrenic disorder he'd developed as a by-product of the evolution process. Was he crazy?

Dr. Daman watched Amos closely as he thought through these issues. "For a boy who may one day be capable of processing the dynamic quantum gravity fields inside a supernova, you seem very deep in thought."

Amos looked up at Dr. Daman, who offered a fatherly smile with a hint of remorse. *Strange,* Amos thought. *I wonder what he isn't telling me.*

"Amos, in some ways I feel we are alike," Dr. Daman said. "I know I can't possibly understand all your emotions and thought processes, despite our abilities to watch your brain function. You are going to experience feelings and intellectual challenges that no one has faced before. That said, the H-plus project has consumed most of my life, demanded long hours in which I communicate only with the computers. Just as you were developed to help humanity overcome the entropy barrier, I was developed to find solutions to the problems plaguing the project. It has been lonely at times, which was one of the reasons I insisted you have a rounded intellect. I hope you can find some human connections that help you."

Amos offered a weak smile at the doctor's empathetic words. "Thank you. As you said, we all have our role, and mine is important. I'm not sure developing human connections is as important."

"Don't discount your basic human emotions, Amos. You may be evolved, but you're still human, requiring love, touch, and emotional connections to others. History has shown that people who block out these basic human needs for too long become unstable, often lashing out in painful ways. In the end, it is these human emotions that make us who we are."

Amos thought about that argument, unable to find an obvious rebuttal but also not completely convinced it was the answer to what made him who he was. He simply nodded while looking down at his hands, his fingers still knitted together.

"Ensign, please respond."

"Yes captain?"

"The doctor reports that we may need to supplement Mr. Hare's preparation with some emotional handling. The Syndicate has requested you focus more on your relationship with him."

"You mean sleep with him, sir?"

"If you think it will help, yes. The Syndicate wants him to feel connected to us, the crew."

"I have tried flirting sir, but I'm not sure he wants anything physical. He's too mixed up right now."

"I don't care how you do it! Make him feel like he belongs."

"Yes sir."

21.

"Deep thoughts, Amos?"

Sarah gave him a nudge with her elbow as they stood beside each other in the lift. Amos had been standing silently, staring at the bottom of the doors for the entire ride and had offered little in conversation when Sarah had stopped by his room to escort him to meet his commanding officer.

His concentration broken, Amos offered Sarah a weak smile. "Sorry. Just thinking about everything Dr. Daman told me yesterday. A lot to absorb, even for me." Amos attempted to project a confidence he did not feel.

"Understood. Don't worry about it. I'm glad you had such a productive discussion with him. He said you seem willing to work with him now and that you made significant progress."

Amos looked back at the bottom of the lift doors and shrugged. "I don't have much choice, do I?"

Just as Sarah was about to respond, the lift stopped, and the doors slid open. Sarah extended her arm toward the open door, and they stepped off the lift onto the navigation level.

Amos looked around and saw a structure similar to the previous command floors but less packed with displays and data pillars. The room was also smaller than the other command rooms. The center was dominated by a huge table, over which was a three-dimensional display of the ship's current position. An image of the ship floated in the middle of the spherical display. Amos realized suddenly that he had not actually seen the ship from the outside. His eyes focused on the ship, which seemed fairly unremarkable from his perspective.

Amos's eyes shifted to the surface of the planet beneath the ship, just above the surface of the table. The planet's topography was displayed, along with a few bubble-like buildings. A tower stretched out of one of them, which Amos assumed was the shuttle launcher between the planet and the ship.

Seemingly confirming Amos's thought, a small, blue dot appeared from the top of the tower and began flashing green. The velocity with which it exited the tower was more than enough to carry it past the ship and into space. The dot changed its course as it lined up to to enter the cargo bay. Small arrows flashed around the dot, which Amos guessed was the shuttle's propulsion system, as the main ship controlled its navigation. The dot changed to green, and the arrows disappeared.

"Lieutenant Jahan, may I present Mr. Hare," Sarah announced in a strong, steady voice.

Amos's full concentration remained on the flashing green dot as it approached the ship. Its course appeared to head straight toward the lower side of the ship.

Sarah bumped Amos hard with her elbow as she spoke in an annoyed voice. "Mr. Hare is reporting for duty."

Amos gasped as her elbow connected with his lower ribs. He pulled his eyes away from the table and focused on Lieutenant Jahan, who was standing in front of him and Sarah and eyeing Amos patiently. Amos straightened his back, stiffened his arms by his side. "Mr. Hare reporting for duty, sir!" he said a bit too loudly.

Lieutenant Jahan gave a curt nod. "Welcome, Mr. Hare." He looked over his shoulder at the table and then looked back at Amos. "Another shuttle is about to arrive. It's transporting some of the last supplies we require for this mission, including, I believe, the latest quantum clock for engineering."

Startled at the impact his opinion had already had, Amos looked back at the shuttle. It was quite close to the ship. Suddenly, the flashing dot disappeared.

"Another routine shuttle launch and landing. The shuttle is safely aboard the ship," Jahan said in anticipation of Amos's question. "I assure you, Mr. Hare, that what you will learn today will make this routine shuttle landing appear quite boring."

Amos looked back at Jahan and held his arms rigidly at his sides. "Yes sir!" he responded, a little too loudly once again.

"At ease, Mr. Hare," Jahan said as he took a more relaxed stance himself. "Let me talk frankly. This is a somewhat awkward reporting structure. Your abilities will soon surpass mine as well as the captain's, making the normal command structure inadequate. So let's talk openly. Technically, you report to me, but my role is more to enable your eventual elevation to command. As you are able to take on more responsibility, I will step back. Initially though, I am in charge, understood?"

Amos gave a nervous nod, careful not to make the same mistake he made with Dr. Daman. As he stared into Jahan's eyes, a puzzled look came over Amos's face.

"Sir, you're . . . I mean, you're—"

"A silicon human? Yes, Mr. Hare. There are a number of us on this ship."

Amos blushed. "Sorry, sir. I mean, I know your kind are on the ship, obviously. I just haven't yet, or I mean, you're the first—"

"Understood, Mr. Hare. Then you know we prefer to emphasize the human part and not the silicon part. We're equals."

Amos stiffened and nodded curtly. "Of course, sir."

Inside, Amos felt uneasy. Something within him recoiled at the thought of Jahan. Why should he feel different about silicon life? After all, in the habitat, it was all fake. Maybe deep down Amos had always known it was fake and, therefore, simply accepted the display in front him. Or maybe everything was different now. He had entered into a community of organic life and was embracing it. Yet Jahan was part of that community, or was he? Amos continued to flip his thoughts around in his mind.

Acknowledging Amos's nod with a pointed stare, Jahan continued. "I am here to ensure things run smoothly and to handle your requests. But let me make one thing clear. You make requests of me, you do not give orders to me or to the crew. If this is to work, I must insist on this understanding."

"Yes sir," Amos replied in an even tone.

"Now that we have that clear, let me begin our tour."

Jahan turned promptly and walked to the center of the room. Sarah followed while Amos fell in line behind her. As he hurried to catch up, his right shoe scraped along the carpeted floor, causing him to pitch forward and almost bump into Sarah.

Sarah turned back with raised eyebrows. "Pick up your feet!" she hissed.

"I'm still not used to shoes, much less carpet," Amos whispered back, reddening slightly.

Sarah tilted her head and looked at him from the corner of her eyes, sending the message that that was not an adequate excuse.

Amos ignored the look and focused on where they were going, toward the table at the center of the room. He noticed that the table was placed on top of a rise in the floor that was about three feet higher than the rest of the room. Similar to Intelligence, this allowed the people at the table to see the entire room while standing at the table.

Jahan climbed the dome-like rise in the floor toward the central table. He turned his head back slightly as he walked. "This is the central command station of navigation. From here, we can evaluate the area surrounding us and plot the most efficient course."

Amos took in the table as he came closer and was impressed by the high degree of visual details in the display. He saw that the ship had a series of doors on the side of the sphere closest to the planet. He assumed that the shuttle had entered the ship through one of them.

The image of the ship was wiped clear, as if a large hand had washed it away. In its place appeared what looked like a mountain range, complete with innumerable peaks and ridges. It took a moment for Amos to recognize the image as a three-dimensional representation of the brane.

"As you probably recognize, Mr. Hare, this is our brane. The brane in which we live has three spatial dimensions, providing us with the length, width, and height of everything in our universe. The laws of general relativity that control our existence within this brane have been studied closely for thousands of years."

Amos nodded in understanding. "Yes. Most of these physical laws were well understood on E-One."

"Correct. It was only when we evolved to utilize neodymium that the actual texture of the universe became more obvious. While the theory of branes had been developed well before our first evolutionary jump, it was only when we could begin to perceive the extra dimension around our brane that we could really understand it."

Jahan looked over at Amos to gauge his response, but Amos's eyes remained fixed on the display of the brane over the table. Jahan returned his focus to the display as he continued. "While the brane defines our three spatial dimensions, we soon figured out there were additional dimensions. A good analogy is when humanity realized that E-One was not flat but round. Navigational skill increased, and new worlds were discovered."

Without shifting his focus from the display, Amos interrupted in a soft voice, almost like he was talking to himself. "It was the ancient Greeks who first argued that Earth was spherical. In fact, it's a popular myth carried down from around the nineteenth century that scholars living during the Renaissance believed Earth was flat. Almost all European scholars accepted a spherical planet after the third century BC. The myth they believed in a flat earth was more about a debate of evolution than anything truthful."

"Interesting. Is there a point? Or can I move on?" Jahan asked, mildly annoyed at the interruption.

"Yes. That at one time, the truth of evolution was questioned." Amos held his stare on Jahan for a moment longer than necessary.

Jahan looked back at Amos, trying to read a deeper meaning, but then broke eye contact and proceeded with his well-rehearsed presentation. "Yet even with our ability to sense the extra dimension, we still could not see our full brane. The reason was, our brane is not flat or even round. It is defined instead by peaks and ridges and even holes. These characteristics are due in part to an uneven charge across the brane itself. Yet our first view of the brane from E-One was similar to the view that confronted Lewis and Clark when they approached the Rocky Mountains, a seemingly impassible wall. But this wall confronting us in our brane appeared as an almost infinite distance."

"A wonder we ever survived that first jump from Earth to E-Two," Amos said, almost to himself.

Jahan looked at Amos with a mildly annoyed stare and then gave a measured nod. "Yes, a wonder given their rudimentary navigational system."

Jahan's focus returned to the display, and he continued with a slight rise in his voice, emphasizing that he was reaching the climax. "But what really blew their minds was the dynamic nature of the brane. They realized that it was interacting with an outside energy field. We think it's this dynamic relationship that created what we perceive as time."

Amos turned away from the display and looked at Jahan. He wasn't so sure the understanding of this dynamic was complete or that the theory was entirely correct. In fact, something deep inside him said understanding time might be a clue to something much greater. For the moment though, he played along with what he had been taught.

"While in the habitat I learned that our brane is as much an energy field as anything else. As outside energy waves pass through our brane, they meet resistance as they interact with the energy bound to our brane. The Higgs Field was the earliest discovery of the energy passing through the brane, although scientists didn't understand it completely until they could perceive the extra dimension."

Jahan nodded and continued the thought as he kept his eyes on the display. "The Higgs Field provides a resistance to energy confined to our brane, slowing it down and imparting mass to the particles. Einstein was the first scientist to recognize this relationship with his theory of relativity."

The holograph floating over the table displayed a closer view of the brane, allowing for the perception of massive objects distributed across it.

"The conversion of energy to mass enables our reality to exist," Amos added as he watched the display transform, "complete with our perception of time."

"Do you understand the theory of time we operate within?" Jahan asked, giving Amos a sideways glance. "It's vitally important, since navigation depends on it. I want to make sure you understand the theories completely."

Keeping his eyes on the display, Amos recited what he had been taught in the habitat. "Mass exists, can only exist, in the present. The present is defined as the moment when the Higgs Field interacts with the energy of our brane. This suggests that the Higgs Field itself is bound to another brane, and we are simply at the intersection point of the two branes, a universe in which Newtonian physics exists. The moment we call the present is when all sorts of interactions between energy wavelengths occur to impart mass and entangle the energy wavelengths."

"Good! You understand the basics." Jahan refocused on the display, which changed to a quantum level representation of a wavelength and what happens when it passes through the field. "Effectively, an energy wave that is everywhere at one time collapses into a singular position and becomes entwined with other waves."

Amos nodded numbly and recited his studies. "When the Higgs Field brane interacts with the energy brane, it causes energy waves to slow, imparting mass, which results in an intertwinement with other waves."

"And the past?"

"The past is simply a recording of the interactions of the present. But that sounds obvious. The violent interactions in the present bind the energy waves together, creating a singular wave. Photons are dispersed from the interactions, carrying information about the past that we can interpret in the present." After a moment of reflection. "We live in an odd corner of the universe."

Jahan nodded with a half-smile. "Yes, difficult concepts to grasp."

Amos's glanced at Jahan. "Mind bending? Yes. But the future is what intrigues me."

"Maybe we can't see the future," Jahan replied, "but we have a pretty good idea of how it's different from the past. The single wave of the past continues forward through the present into the future. It splits at the present moment into an infinite number of parallel energy waves extending into the future. This fissure explains why we can't perceive the future. The present is like a type of weaving loom. Multiple strings enter the loom, and a single fabric is produced. While the length of the strings in the fabric of the past are fixed in their relative position to one another, the strings of the future are free to move in relation to each other."

Amos continued his thought. "That freedom of movement of waves relative to one another allows for the possibility of a degree of free will in the universe."

Jahan grinned slightly. "We like to think so, don't we? Gives us a feeling of purpose. But how exactly does one alter the strings before the present moment passes? Is there anything inherent in the present moment that allows for an indeterminate future?"

Amos worked through the logic, as he had been taught. "Assuming we can't influence the future threads, to continue the loom analogy, the present is basically the shuttle. The shuttle is the point where the weft threads are interwoven with the warp threads, creating the fabric. So the question becomes: Is there some lever of control provided by the shuttle, or flaw or opportunity for chance inherent in these mechanisms that allows for free will?"

"Scientists have been looking for that at the quantum level for millennia," Sarah replied. "The probabilities associated with quantum mechanics represent the unknown about the future, not necessarily any room for chance in the actual system."

Both Amos and Jahan looked at Sarah, who blushed slightly. "Hey, you two aren't the only brainiacs around here you know."

Amos turned back to Jahan with a concerned look. "The near future to us is largely determined."

"This diminishing number of possibilities to our future is the primary reason for the urgency of our mission," Jahan replied grimly. "We can't simply jump across the brane, because the energy waves that define us in the present are extensions of the waves that have already passed through the Higgs brane at this location. Until we find a way to shift waves more dramatically in the present, we are bound by our historical reality."

"So, first we must figure out how to break from a potentially determinate universe, or at least learn how to control an indeterminate one," Amos said, summing up the challenge. "As we work on the problem, the number of possible futures for humanity are diminishing as our future becomes increasingly determined by our actions."

Jahan nodded sternly. "Good. You appreciate our basic challenge of existence. We are in a catch-twenty-two. We need to become more advanced, more evolved, to find new sources of free energy, but by becoming more complex, we deplete the free energy accessible to us more rapidly. A way to escape this trap is to discover the mechanism by which we can break free from what seems like a deterministic future."

Amos stared hard at the brane. "So we need to find new, abundant sources of free energy, ways to manage the passage of time or somehow disconnect from our brane."

Jahan nodded. "Those are the obvious potential answers, although none of them are trivial or less daunting. We want to look for other answers as well. The deeper you understand the make-up of the brane and the bulk surrounding it, the greater our chances of finding a solution."

"Don't be afraid. Our fate can't be taken from us. It's a gift."

Mouths open, Amos and Jahan stared at Sarah.

"What? *Dante's Inferno.* Seemed appropriate."

Amos smiled. "Well, personally I think a more optimistic quote from twentieth century author Amy Tan hits the mark better: 'We dream to give ourselves hope. To stop dreaming—well, that's like saying you can never change your fate.'"

"So you think we have a chance?" Jahan asked.

Amos nodded. "Yes, but we might be looking in the wrong places."

22.

Amos shivered. Cold anticipation built up inside as he prepared to enter the superconscious of the network. If it was anything like the supraconscious he had entered with Bina, he feared losing himself within it. As he considered it further, his fear of the superconscious was more centered on something else controlling him. Sarah wrapped a comforting arm around him.

"Really, Amos? The super should be trembling in fear at the thought of your big mind entering it."

The shivering continued, but Amos managed a small smile. "You make it sound like I'm trying to impregnate it."

Sarah giggled and squeezed his shoulders. "There's the spirit we've been missing."

Amos had to clasp his hands together to control the sudden onslaught of shakes in his arms. "Tell me again what happens to my body while I'm in there?"

"Simple. Your body's basic functions continue to perform normally. A technician monitors you while you're in the superconscious. Every precaution is taken to ensure your body and mind reunite properly."

A grimace on Amos's face showed he wasn't convinced.

"Amos, this has been done for centuries. Only in very rare cases is there a complication, and those issues are almost always rectified."

"What about the case in which a man's mind went in and a woman's came out?"

Sarah gave him a withering look. "Really, that was centuries ago, and at the time the scientists were convinced it was simply a hoax. The fact of the matter is that too much of yourself remains in the body for another mind to take it over."

Amos shook his head. "I don't know. You mix a bunch of ingredients in one bowl, and you're never able to completely separate the ingredients again. What if there's a power surge or a faulty silicon circuit we don't know about? What keeps me, me in there?"

"Enough! I'll be in there with you, guiding you and supporting you. You're only going in for a short period of time. Just enough to get your bearings, understand the environment, and get out. Just like the synapses in your brain keep you yourself, the dedicated circuits for you in the super keep you together."

A doubtful tilt of the head gave away Amos's true thoughts on the subject, but he wanted to get it over with. "All right, let's get on with it." Amos closed his eyes and opened up connections to the network, requesting access to the superconscious.

"Let me go in first," Sarah said. "I'll open the portal for you once I'm in."

Sarah's eyes went eerily distant as she leaned back in her chair.

Amos leaned back in his chair and closed his eyes before opening up his mind to the network. At first, he felt nothing, but an audible click in his head notified him Sarah had granted him access.

Amos felt the ship's network connect to his mind deeper than was standard. Conscious thoughts that were not his own began to patter against the periphery of his consciousness like raindrops hitting a window pane, splattering his thoughts into an unruly mess. The connection deepened, worming into his mind and overtaking his senses. He became an outsider in his own mind, watching the data from the network probe his mind and make the necessary connections. Panic surfaced from within, but he pushed it back down.

A random thought surfaced about how efficient the ship's system was at using his own neural network. He knew it was his, because it sent a spasm throughout his body.

"Relax, Amos," came the message along with a calming sensation from the network.

"Sarah? You sound . . . you feel different."

"Yes, the intimate links we have with the network enable us to share more emotions."

An emptiness filled the gap in the conversation.

"Amos, are you all right?" Sarah's asked nervously.

Cold steeliness gripped Amos. He felt permanent, immovable . . . cured? No, cemented. Like one of the high rises outside his parents' window.

Amos awoke in the superconscious, and a strange feeling gripped him, outside of time yet open to all possibilities. Upon further reflection, he decided he wasn't outside of time but frozen in the moment. There was an unblinking absence of all the little cues in his body that indicated the passage of time. No variation of touch, no sensation of air entering and leaving his lungs, no heartbeat. It was . . . deadening.

Strangest of all, he felt no fear. If anything, he felt sturdy, knew his place within the ship with a certainty he never expected. Everything was defined explicitly, from the size of every ceramic seam in the ship to the sensor file structures to the specific location of the crew. From his position, he simply knew everything accessible on the ship. It was strangely intoxicating. Where the supraconscious overwhelmed with its sense of oneness and possibility, humbling him, the superconscious overwhelmed in a singularly expansive way, like he could control the universe if only the right tools were provided.

Amos found his way around easily, simply because everything was coded, objectified. Metadata tags hung from every bit of data. Even the tags had tags to define them more explicitly. It was a world of words layered on words, obscuring the very object they were defining.

He focused on Sarah, causing a mild tremor in his now distant body. She appeared to him like a confetti-filled muon bomb frozen in time a moment after it had exploded. Every neural link, chemical concentration, and psychological diagnosis was defined and tagged in colorful codes spanning the spectrum. He considered analyzing the chaos but then decided against it, realizing he didn't want to know the mechanics of her brain. Instead, he simply took in the beauty of what appeared like a supernova of information before him.

Distantly, he felt his body shudder again, sending a rippling realization into the superconscious that the mechanics of his mind were also on full display. Amos attempted to mask that thought.

"Yes. Sorry, Sarah. It's just I've never really . . . known you this closely. It's awkward, like I'm standing in the room while you're in the shower."

A small ripple of pink flickered from Sarah. "Ah, a fantasy of yours. I get it."

Red permeated Amos's stumbling thought back. "You can . . . I didn't think, I—"

"Relax, Amos! An educated guess. I know when a guy's checking me out." Sarah's confetti nebula surged brighter with pride.

An unintended pulse of amusement, like a chuckle, came from Amos. He forced himself to relax his mind and began to explore the superconscious.

"Let's begin," Sarah said.

A confetti bomb imploded into Sarah's more familiar shape. It appeared now as though she was standing in front of him. A warm smile blossomed on her lips as she began to talk. "Think of the super simply as a deeper connection to the network. All of the normal functions are available to you, such as checking messages and commanding the ship's sensors."

"It doesn't feel right," Amos said.

A wrinkle representing fear rubbed against Sarah. "What doesn't feel right? Are you okay?"

"Yes," he said after a pause. "I'm okay. I meant the environment doesn't feel natural. It feels sterile."

"I don't follow, Amos. The purpose of the super is to provide a much more intimate connection. It overrides your senses, enabling you to experience the network as if you're living in it."

Amos looked around. He saw the same colors of the ship's corridors, felt the cool draft on his neck, even tasted a mild level of bile churned up from his stomach. In many respects, it was hard to discern that he was not simply walking around the ship, because the visual cues were so convincing. Yet, it was obvious he was not inside his head. His inner thoughts rattled like a gerbil placed in a ball. The supraconscious had a sense of fulfilment to it, while the superconscious had only objects warehoused in his mind. It was filled but empty of . . . purpose? The opposite of the supraconscious. Amos felt himself recoil.

"No. It feels like I've gone through a prism and come out only blue. It's weird, like my thoughts are mechanical, almost pre-programmed, simplified sequential steps toward a singular, pre-defined goal."

"Not much different than the real world, eh? Well, you'll get used to it."

"How? How does one get use to not feeling whole?"

"Well, you're not whole on purpose. Remember that most of you remains in your body. But don't worry. Here, see if this helps."

A sense of euphoria erupted within him, combined with a warmth seemingly coming from inside. His mind cleared, and his thoughts sped up as he worked through what was happening. "Whoa! I feel . . . amazing! Happier than I've ever felt! Whatever you did certainly made me feel better."

"A mild stimulation to certain parts of your brain mimicking a combination of drugs to make you feel more alive."

"More alive. . . . " Amos let his thoughts drift out into the super-conscious, batting playfully at pieces of data that he controlled with his mind.

"Careful, Amos, I'm going to dial it back a bit."

Amos felt the sensation dull slightly as Sarah continued.

"Most of the crew uses the highs available in the super to help them handle the monotony of daily tasks. But a few get hooked on it and spend too much time in the super chasing the high."

"Using?"

The word flashed in his mind despite his own thoughts slowing slightly. The changes in his mental state bewildered him.

"Chasing the high. Physically and mentally, using is perfectly safe. It's the psychological impact that's a danger to the ship. A hardcore user has a difficult time performing outside the super, because the person's thoughts become obsessively focused on returning to the feeling. More and more of their energy is focused on returning, leaving them less interested in and even less capable of performing their duties."

Sarah's words felt hollow despite the high he was riding. While happiness pervaded him, after experiencing the supraconscious, the super didn't hold the same allure. He couldn't understand how so many could get sucked into it.

Amos pulled his thoughts together. "No, not more alive, happier, that's for sure, but still not whole. You've made the part of me in the super happy, but I still feel cut off from the rest of . . . myself."

"Well, it's good you can manage the difference. We were concerned about how you would handle the super, possibly become addicted it. Good thing you're numb to its influence."

"Numb? That's how I feel already. Emotionless, zombie-like."

"Zombie? No. We have all the control and mental functionality of our brains plus the computing power of the network. If we're zombies, we're also on mental steroids."

"Even zombies control their mechanical movements, have a purpose, even if it is only singular." Amos's thoughts stopped as he struggled to broaden his perspective. "I don't like this. My thoughts are clear as a crystal, but I feel clumsy, like I can't coordinate them easily."

"Give it time, Amos. Think of the super as a new tool. You're a baby gumming a new rattle. Once you master it, you'll find it very effective."

Amos was not convinced, but he continued to work at it.

Sarah sensed an opening to move forward. "Right, let's try a few simple tasks that'll help you stay oriented and access the data you need."

Either the stimulant was wearing off or Amos's body was rejecting the situation. Either way, he became agitated. "No, Sarah. I think I need to leave—now!"

Sarah's form focused on Amos, and he felt the network crawl through the parts of him that existed in the superconscious like maggots consuming a corpse.

"No! I'm leaving now!" Amos retreated toward the point he knew was his body. He felt something resisting his retreat, trying to hold him in place like a brush stuck in paste. He pulled away violently, focused singularly on leaving the superconscious. Whatever was holding him released him, and Amos tumbled back into himself.

He awoke to Sarah leaning forward and staring intently at him.

––––––––––––––––

"Report Ensign."

Sarah shivered. "He started out okay but then he freaked out and practically tried to leap out of his own skin to escape the superconscious."

"The Syndicate tried to help hold him in but he's simply too strong."

"The Syndicate was in the superconscious of the ship? I had no idea that was possible at this distance."

"All will be revealed when you attain the rank of captain, Ensign. Until then, focus on your task."

"Sorry sir. I've never heard of anyone reacting like he did. Even the previous evolved seemed more capable of handling the environment."

"Why do you think he 'freaked out,' as you put it?"

After some hesitation Sarah responded. "Intellectually, I don't know. Emotionally, it felt like he feared dying. Like we were trying to poison him."

"Does he fear us?"

"Somewhat, yes. But that is not the cause of his reaction to the superconscious. More like we were trying to make him eat something he doesn't like."

"Well you better make him like it Sarah. The superconscious is critical to the Syndicate's plan for Kairos."

"Yes sir." Sarah again shivered.

23.

Amos sat quietly in Dr. Daman's conference room going over everything he had seen and learned in the superconscious. Humankind had come a long way after managing its own evolution, but a feeling of unease crept into his gut each time he considered the path everyone was on. He couldn't put his finger on what was bothering him. It was like the voice of doom was screaming in the back of his mind. As he tried again to reach out to this suppressed voice, the door slid open, and Dr. Daman strode in.

"Ah, Amos, it's been a while since our last conversation. I'm glad we have a chance to talk." Daman took his usual seat next to the door, directly across the table from Amos.

Amos straightened up in his chair and looked across the table with a slightly wary gaze. "Hello, Doctor."

Dr. Daman smiled in return. He looked almost giddy as he fidgeted in his chair. "So, how did it go in the superconscious? It can be a big challenge even to enter it, much less understand the environment."

Amos shrugged, suppressing his true feelings. "All of it seemed overly logical. It'll take some time to figure it all out. It was a larger space, but it isn't that different from connecting with silicon life systems."

Dr. Daman nodded, "Yes, I suppose you're well trained in that. Well, last time, we talked about your unique abilities to absorb information into your brain. That discussion was more mechanical, input/output type of stuff. What truly makes you unique, and what offers such potential, is your overall connectome."

A puzzled look came over Amos. "Connectome? You mean the wiring of my brain?"

Daman bounced slightly in his chair, as if his whole body was nodding in agreement. "Yes, exactly! A bit of an antiquated term, I know, but I prefer it, since it captures the essence of the brain." He paused to settle himself into a comfortable position. "How each brain develops determines who the person is as an individual. This development is largely due to genetics, experience, health, and chance, which is really just a scientific way of saying we can't explain it."

Amos gave him a dubious look. "Chance? You mean after centuries of managed evolution, my personality is determined by a game of chance?"

"Maybe a better way to explain it is an extremely complex system we don't fully understand. But that is largely how the brain has evolved from, single-celled organisms up to mammals and then humans. Sometimes it goes terribly wrong, producing a non-viable life form. Other times it produces a genius. In some cases, maybe both. But back to your connectome."

Amos pressed further. "Just strange to think that all this investment could go terribly wrong should one cell go the wrong way."

Daman sighed as he settled further into his seat and glanced at the table. "Yes, part of the reason we had many failures prior to you and an ongoing reason why silicon life is more reliable than organic." He straightened his back and looked at Amos. "Anyway, your connectome, your brain, is significantly more evolved than the brain of a present-day human and quite different than a pre-evolved human."

Amos leaned back in his chair, bored at the potential of reviewing more history. "I know our heads are bigger, although consistent with the increase in our overall body."

A bit of the giddiness returned to the doctor as he bounced slightly in his chair once again. "That's only scratching the surface—pardon the pun."

Amos shrugged, unimpressed.

"The reason for the larger brain size is our brains have developed a super-cortex, or a cortex that surrounds the neocortex of pre-evolved humans. The neocortex is responsible for much of the intelligence and consciousness that makes us human. That is still largely the case in humans today. The super-cortex evolved once humans adapted to external information sources. It has enabled a higher level of consciousness, the ability to perceive extra dimensions, and the capability of processing externally-sourced information from the network. It provides the processing power to interface directly with external sources separate from the traditional senses."

"And the recipe for super geniuses was discovered!"

Ignoring the comment, Daman pressed on. "Prior to the development of the super-cortex, the human brain consumed about twenty-five percent of the energy in the body. After the development of the super-cortex, this percentage went up to almost fifty percent. This development is the reason why our caloric intake has grown as much as it has and periodically placed significant burdens on the ability of society to produce enough food to support humanity."

Amos jumped to the punchline. "Yes, this is the catch-twenty-two of our existence. The more advanced humans become, the more energy we require to support life. The more energy we consume, the more advanced we need to become to overcome the challenges of producing additional free energy in a way that is beneficial to humans."

Dr. Daman leaned sideways in his chair, happy to jump forward through the lesson. "And we haven't even discussed your brain. I've heard your ability to devour platters of pasta is legendary in the food hall."

Amos smiled proudly. "Yes. Yesterday I was able to polish off three. Each platter is meant to feed a table of twenty."

"And yet you're one of the skinniest individuals on the ship."

Amos shrugged. "Inherited a good metabolism from my parents?"

"Your parents were quite healthy, but that is not the primary reason. Your super-cortex is significantly larger than others on the ship."

"So you're saying some people calling me 'Egghead' isn't just because of my scrambled brain?"

"No, your head is larger than average, but not the biggest ever recorded. Your super-cortex seems to have taken some space from your neocortex, but it is also the most efficient design we have ever seen."

Amos stifled a yawn. "Okay, what does that have to do with my records in the food hall?"

"Your brain consumes almost seventy-five percent of the energy produced in your body. You probably didn't notice it as much until recently, because we included high caloric tablets in your meals."

"That would explain why I get famished while working on difficult problems."

Dr. Daman leaned forward, resting his chest on his interlaced fingers. "Yes, besides the larger size and highly efficiently construction, your brain works on over-drive most of the time. The average human brainwave is around thirteen hertz when working efficiently. During times of complex information processing, the brain can rev itself up to over forty hertz, although this usually results in a higher degree of agitation. Your neocortex runs consistently at forty hertz when you're awake and typically thirteen hertz when asleep. Everyone else's drops to well below ten hertz."

"So my brain doesn't turn off?"

Doctor Daman looked down at the table as he considered his response. "In a way, yes. Although it's unclear to us how your brain can maintain that level of activity while asleep. It seems like your brain relaxes by processing information that the average person can only do when alert and focused."

Amos leaned forward in his chair. "I often find a solution in my brain when I first wake up. 'Sleeping on it' has always been helpful."

Dr. Daman nodded. "The amazing part is your super-cortex. It continually operates well above forty hertz but fluctuates more depending on your interaction with the network. During periods of heavy processing and memory access, your brain can ramp up to almost one hundred hertz. Quite amazing to watch."

Amos squinted slightly. "Okay, is there any problem with this level of activity? Am I cooking my brain?"

"Not that we can tell so far, but we do keep a close eye on you for any abnormal activity."

"And . . . anything?"

Dr. Daman contemplated his answer before continuing. "Occasionally in the habitat, we noticed periods of elevated activity when you were not accessing the network. The activity was similar to the activity exhibited while in communication with your friends."

"Did it stop once I came onto the ship?"

"Apart from once during the first couple days after your arrival, we haven't noticed anything. It could be some side effect of the habitat or possibly some developmental issue we haven't considered. Do you have any ideas?"

Amos thought of Bina but then banished the thought. "No, seems strange. I guess I'm just happy it stopped."

Dr. Daman stared intently at Amos for a couple of seconds, seemingly trying to read his thoughts through both his personal sensory perceptions and aid from the network. "Yes, we will let you know if we notice it again."

Amos and Dr. Daman held a long stare as each tried to read the other's thoughts.

"What's on your mind, Amos?"

Amos thought of Bina again. This was the longest period of time that he had not communicated with her. Was Dr. Daman behind the female voice? Was Bina simply another way to try and manipulate him? Was this some type of test to see if Amos was being truly open about his experiences? If Daman wasn't involved, why couldn't she connect with him? Was she listening at least? Watching? All of these questions filtered through his mind before he responded without any noticeable hesitation from Doctor Daman's point of view.

"Nothing," Amos said, adopting a nonchalant "I don't give a damn about anything" look that teenagers had mastered since the dawn of time.

Dr. Daman held his stare. Amos could almost feel the doctor's limited mind trying to reach out and connect to his, like he was trying to lift the cover off a muon-catalyst engine to see within. Something from the network he could not identify had been trying subtle probes since he arrived. Was it Dr. Daman? Feeling self-conscious he was giving something away, Amos finally broke the silence.

"Is that all for today? If you don't mind, I have a lot of information to process after reporting to duty in Navigation."

Dr. Daman nodded slowly, continuing to hold his gaze. "Of course. Now that you are actually taking on more responsibility, our chats will have to be more limited, but I want you to know that I'm here to help. I sense that you're suppressing something, covering up a feeling, possibly some inner turmoil, even something related to your responsibilities. I'm here to help, Amos. You can tell me anything."

Amos's stare hardened. "Tell you anything? I'm assuming you provide continuous updates to the captain. Why shouldn't I be guarded?"

Daman leaned back in his chair and looked sideways at the floor before speaking. "Fair enough. Yes, the captain demands updates about you, especially anything relating to your ability to perform your role. But I do not provide him with every detail, especially when it concerns your personal well-being. The captain simply wants to know you are stable and progressing."

Doctor Daman looked up at Amos, who shifted uncomfortably in his chair. "If you want to keep something between us, please let me know. It will stay between us."

Amos offered a noncommittal nod as he stood up and headed for the door.

24.

"Look, you pile of sand, I'm telling you, you're wrong!" Lieutenant Commander Sig taunted.

"Too much oxygen in that semi-evolved brain of yours?" Lieutenant Jahan fired back.

Sig's face turned scarlet as his voice rose. "That silicon between your ears may surpass my brain in sheer processing power, but it still only considers the world a list of objects to describe, analyze, and catalog. An aggregate of qualities. You only get a whiff of actual life."

"From where I sit, managed evolution hasn't made your organic ass much different," Jahan replied smugly.

Sig opened his mouth to respond when the door slid open, and the captain and Din strode into the bridge's conference room. They sat down in the chairs closest to the door. Sig, Jahan, Doctor Daman, and Sarah were already seated at the table. Sig and Jahan continued to stare neutrino beams at each other.

Captain Melville looked at each of them. "Are you two having this argument again?"

"Captain, how many representatives of the Syndicate are silicon-based life forms?" Jahan asked calmly.

"Really?" Melville replied. "Why are we back to this? Everyone knows that about a tenth of the Syndicate are silicon humans, and the rest are organic."

"Because it shows the biases that remain in this society," Jahan replied. "Silicon humans are equal to organic humans but hold only a small percentage of leadership roles. The data shows they are paid less as well, only about three-quarters that of organic humans, and this despite having higher intelligence!"

"Until you can actually produce an offspring naturally, you're not nearly as productive," Sig said.

Jahan shot out of his seat. "We can, you piece of preprocessed shit! We routinely combine the best of existing silicon humans into a new life form! And we do it much more elegantly than your disease-breeding methods."

"A fully grown silicon human, with the help of a lab."

"Organic humans are often made the same way! Why does it matter that you start out as babies? If anything, that's a mark against you, since society has to support you. Hell, an evolved takes sixteen years of nurturing after birth before they contribute anything. A silicon human can be fully functional in less than a month."

"It's important, because we have a soul! Something you can never match."

Sarah and the doctor shifted uncomfortably in their chairs while Jahan continued.

"A soul? What does that even mean? Silicon humans reached consciousness a long time ago. We process information and impact the environment around us. I don't see any evidence of a soul in organic humans or any other major difference. Someplace back in the muck you evolved out of, you convinced yourself you have a soul. This delusion is used to cast down all silicon humans, even though you can't even prove it exists!"

"You're just sore that you don't get the full enjoyment of reproducing."

"Fuck you! I feel love and hate just like you. I even have a larger dick than you! I'm happy to bend you over right here and show you pleasure! You're just jealous that most of the organic women on board choose me."

"Enough already!" Commander Din bellowed. "If you two want to go pleasure each other in another room, please do. Until then, can we please start this meeting?"

Din looked over at the captain, who was covering a smile with his hand. Melville looked back at Din with watering eyes as he held back a chortle.

"I've never noticed a difference between organic and silicon, if it makes you two feel any better," Sarah offered boldly.

Stunned silence filled the room as all eyes turned to Sarah, followed by roaring laughter. Sig and Jahan both chuckled and smiled at her.

"Just saying I think we're equal," she added sheepishly.

"All right, all right," Captain Melville said as he continued with a smile on his face. "Let's get to it. Doctor, can you fill us in?"

"Certainly." Dr. Daman used his hand to wipe the smile from his face. "Amos has made great progress. We've met on a regular basis, and each time he is a little further along. He's not yet fully developed, but I think we're moving past his mommy issues and making progress on his acceptance of his role."

"Excellent! Good work, Doctor." Melville leaned back in his chair and offered a small, stiff smile in recognition of Daman's efforts. "I've noticed his activity in the network has increased significantly as he continues to understand the ship and begins researching possible solutions."

Sarah leaned forward and put her hands on the table. "I've also seen significant improvement in his attitude. He seems to have moved past what happened in the habitat and is trying to understand his place on this ship."

"But you haven't slept with him yet, have you?" the captain asked casually.

She shook her head. "No, I'm still working to get over that hurdle."

"Please make sure it happens soon," Melville said.

"His 'place'? What do you mean?" Jahan asked.

"His place socially," Sarah replied. "We developed him so that he would be social, seek out the company of others, and empathize with others. He has a natural charisma about him that draws people in. That said, he has a hard time trusting anyone."

"Well, that's no surprise given what he's been through," Sig said.

"True, but I think he absolutely must find that person to trust," Sarah replied. "If he doesn't feel that we trust him or that he can trust us, I fear that he may not put the mission, the ship, or even society ahead of his own interests."

"What are you saying? He'll try to subvert us?" Din asked.

"Maybe not actively, but if he's faced with a difficult choice, I'm not sure it's clear to him that we're on his side."

"How do we handle it, Ensign?" Din asked.

"Well, I'll keep getting closer to him, building that trust. If I can pull him closer, then I should be able to convince him to act in our interest. Once I get him in bed, I think it will go smoother."

"If I can add," Daman interjected, "trust is the biggest challenge for him. It will be hard to earn it."

Sarah nodded at Dr. Daman.

"We trust you, Sarah," Captain Melville added. "Put yourself out there. Seduce him. Do whatever it takes."

Sarah's gaze returned to the captain. "Yes, sir. But I don't think seducing him is the answer. He's too smart. Sure, he probably enjoys a roll in the sheets as much as anyone, but to gain his trust I'll have to seduce his mind."

"Something you obviously have a talent for."

Sarah gave Sig a withering look. "I do my job just like the rest of you. My role simply has a few more perks associated with it."

She batted her eyelashes at Sig, causing him to look away.

"I don't care how it's done," Melville said, "just make sure he's ready for when the time comes."

Sarah nodded. "Understood, Captain."

Captain Melville turned to Jahan. "Lieutenant, how has he performed his duties?"

"Sir, he's up to speed on the systems and has a good understanding of cosmology. It will take a little time for him to understand the creative side of navigation, but I have no doubt he'll get there. Furthermore, his initial entry into the superconscious training module appeared to go smoothly. He has a long way to go, but he's making good progress."

"So, no complaints?" Din asked.

"Only that he seems a little distant at times, but that may just be his way of handling the volume of information."

"Distant, what do you mean?" Melville pressed.

Jahan paused as he considered his answer. "Only that he seems to disappear mentally for periods of time, goes inside of himself. During those moments, it's difficult to understand what he's working on or even what he's feeling."

Sarah and Dr. Daman shared a glance.

"This behavior was observed while he was in the habitat," Daman added. "It appears as though he has another layer of thought beyond what we can monitor."

"I don't think it's a threat or a problem," Sarah added quickly. "I think it's simply a way for his brain to process everything more efficiently."

Captain Melville shifted his gaze from Daman to Sarah. "Understood. But can you please try to explain what's going on in his brain? It might be his way of processing, or it could be a glitch. Sig, maybe you can help them. Look for any unusual signals coming from the ship that can be traced to him."

Sig nodded. "Yes, sir. We've been monitoring him closely, but we'll work it harder."

"Thank you." Melville turned to Daman and Sarah. "Anything else to add?"

Both shook their heads.

"Fine then. Thank you for your reports. Doctor, Ensign, you're dismissed."

Sarah and Dr. Daman stood and walked out of the room while the remaining officers began talking over possible risks on their current course.

25.

Amos lay in his bunk, eyes closed, working feverishly as he interfaced with the networks. He wasn't in the ship's superconscious, because it felt wrong to him, like he was missing some essence of living. Most of the work he could do outside the superconscious anyways.

Besides an elevated temperature, anyone watching him might think he was asleep, deep in a wondrous dream that was causing his eyes to dart around under his eyelids. The rapid eye movement was a by-product of his active brain.

His eyes flew open, revealing crackling pink light coursing across his eyeballs. The amount of pink light made his eyes appear bloodshot until the energy subsided.

"Amos . . . . "

The message came through the network, pushing into his thoughts like an unwelcome stranger wedging himself into an already full lift. Amos opened himself up to the message.

"Amos, can I stop by?"

Sarah's message interrupted his train of thought, which normally wouldn't have been an issue given his massive parallel processing capabilities. However, in this case, he had been maxing out the number of connections to the computers as he searched for an answer to a critical question. When Sarah's message pushed through, it forced him to disconnect from one network, momentarily distracting the rest of his brain.

"Yes."

Amos rubbed his eyes and ran his fingers through his hair, sitting up on his bunk in a bit of a daze. Just sitting up was becoming harder as his body weakened from the lack of physical activity over the past month. He had found that when we went that deep into work, it took a few moments for him to pull back to reality, the physical world. He would go so deep at times that he felt like a computer himself sometimes.

Even though he had been working for a month now, it was still jarring to move from the world in his head and the network to the physical world. He understood now how people could have major mental problems by engaging with the network too deeply and for too long.

"Yes, I was just finishing up a few things. When did you want to—"

A whoosh on the far wall alerted him that his door had slid open. He looked across the room and saw Sarah stride in.

Amos shielded his eyes from the brighter light of the hallway. When he was working, he preferred dim lights, which provided less distraction for his brain. "Jeez! A little more warning next time!"

Sarah stopped and put her hands on her hips. "What? I asked if I could come in! Besides, you have access to almost all of the systems on the ship. You should know who's outside your door."

Continuing to hold his hands up to protect his sensitive eyes, he rolled to one side and swung his legs over the side of his bed. "I didn't realize you meant right now! I could have been naked or something."

Sarah held her silent stare at Amos until he looked up at her.

"Maybe that was what I was hoping for," she said, and then offered a slight grin to reinforce her point.

Amos turned away, but a small smile appeared on his lips as well. "Well, next time just let me know before you open the door, or else you might get a big surprise."

Sarah gave him a doubtful look. "Please, we both know your brain is your biggest . . . asset."

Amos glared at her, making Sarah giggle.

"Oh, all right, your second biggest asset!"

Amos's face softened. "Thank you. I have a teenage boy's self-consciousness that requires a bit of ego inflating."

Still giggling slightly, Sarah walked further into the room and sat down in the chair next to his bed. "Noted. Now, it has taken me an hour to get my message through to you. I was about to override security and just come in here to check on you."

Amos dropped his head slightly, focusing on his knees. "Sorry. I've been working on a particular challenge, one that must be understood before we can make any realistic progress with our mission."

Sarah smiled. "Good! I'm happy to hear you're engaged during this time to our first destination. What have you been working on?"

"Chance," he replied in a serious tone.

A puzzled expression crossed her face. "Chance? As in gambling?"

Amos ran his fingers through his hair, as if it helped to smooth his thoughts. "No. Well, yes, but as it pertains to us."

"Okay, planning on hitting the casinos on Vegasvar?"

Amos gave Sarah a flat stare. "Please, I think I have other things on my mind."

Sarah leaned back into the chair and crossed her legs and arms. "Okay, sorry. Go on."

Amos took a deep breath. "Newtonian physics is completely deterministic."

Sarah nodded. "Force equals mass times acceleration."

"Yes, that is the law of motion. In theory, based on this law, if one knew the exact position, velocity, and direction of every particle in the universe, one could determine future macro conditions."

Sarah nodded again as Amos continued.

"The problem is, these laws of physics are symmetrical in that you could reverse all the directions of the particles in the system and time would theoretically run in reverse. Ice cubes would freeze in a glass of water, and supernovas would form stars."

Sarah shrugged. "You're touching on the second law of thermodynamics. Entropy of any isolated system not in thermal equilibrium increases."

Amos leaned forward on his bed, trying to press his argument onto Sarah. "Correct. This law is well understood and is the primary reason for our mission, since nobody expects this law to reverse itself. It is this asymmetrical nature of the order of systems that seems to define the one-way timeline of our universe."

Amos paused as he considered all of the implications of the next steps in the argument. "Our universe began in a relatively low-entropy big bang. Much of our understanding of the present time is based on Newtonian laws, the past hypothesis, and the statistical postulate."

Sarah waved her hand casually. "Okay fine. You're going over what is well understood through our studies. Am I missing something?"

"My point is that this view suggests everything is pre-determined."

Sarah folded her hands in her lap. "Okay, but it's different at the quantum level," she countered.

Amos jerked his head up. "True! And that's where I've been focused as I try to figure out how much wiggle room we have to alter the future—and our fate."

"So, will we make it, or are we all doomed?"

Amos's shoulders sagged as he refocused on his knees. "Not sure yet. A lot of events need to unfold. It's not like I'm peering into the future but instead trying to figure out the width of our path into the future. If we confront some huge hole in the floor, will we be able to step around it? Or are we destined to fall into it?"

Sarah leaned forward, smiling. "And if we do fall into a hole, will we be able to find a 'hole expert' to get us out?"

Amos stared at Sarah for a second, processing her comment, and then burst out laughing. "A hole expert! Hilarious!" He rocked back on the bunk, his face taking on a worried look. "Hopefully we won't need one."

Sarah pulled her chair closer to where Amos was sitting and took his hand. "We already have an asshole on board, so maybe we have a hole expert as well."

Amos smiled. "Hopefully we can avoid the need, because I think the answer lies at the quantum level."

Sarah released his hand and leaned back in her chair. "Well, there certainly is enough spooky dynamics at the quantum level that should allow for some flexibility in our future."

Amos nodded solemnly. "Yes, but not in the way you might think. The wave functions in quantum mechanics act like a type of guide for particles, and the laws that govern those wave functions through time make them deterministic. Therefore, on the surface, the quantum world appears as deterministic as the Newtonian world."

Sarah was engaged now, accessing her memory quasi-crystals from the classes she had taken. "Yes. It took a long time to understand the apparent interference that observations of wave functions caused."

Pulled from his train of thought, Amos looked over at her. "The measurement problem seemed to boil down to the fact that the act of measuring the wave function altered the wave itself. Either the wave function collapses when measured, or it doesn't."

"I always thought it strange to think the wave function didn't collapse, essentially arguing that the world continues to exist in all possibilities."

Amos nodded. "The problem with that interpretation was that it never seemed to coincide with observations in the world, but it did help work through the issue of entanglement."

Sarah wrapped up the argument triumphantly. "So, since the wave function remains probabilistic when unobserved, that means the future is undetermined, since the wave could move forward through time by following multiple paths."

Amos looked up at Sarah with a furled brow. "Wrong! That's what I've working through. The wave functions are held to the laws of physics and thus are deterministic. The probability inherent in these two interpretations reflects more our lack of understanding of quantum physics than any real randomness in the world. Furthermore, they require an intervention outside the system in order to occur, which is assumed outside the laws of physics."

"But wouldn't interference, entanglement, and decoherence alter things?"

Amos shook his head. "No. If all the information is known at the quantum level. Then following the laws of physics should allow us to see into the future as wave functions, as well as interference, occur in defined manners."

"Okay, so our fate is predetermined?"

"Well, that's where it gets interesting, and it's what I've been working out," Amos replied with a smile.

He lay down on the bed and closed his eyes as he worked through the final calculations.

Sarah sat there watching Amos, wondering at what was happening in his glorious mind. She thought about reporting her thoughts to the captain but decided against it.

26.

Sarah stared steadily at Amos, who had remained lying in his bed for an hour, trying to read his thoughts. Abruptly, Amos opened his eyes, sat up, and looked at her with a smug grin on his face.

When he didn't volunteer anything, Sarah gave in. "All right, I bite. Why aren't we living in a deterministic world?"

"I knew you'd ask that." His grin evolved into a full smile.

Sarah leaned forward and tried to punch him in the chest, but Amos rolled back onto the bed.

"Smartass!" she exclaimed and then leaned back in her chair.

"You're so predictable," he said, laughing.

Sarah crossed her arms and glared at him. "Finished?"

Amos sat up and faced Sarah. "You should know."

"Amos Hare! Get on with it!" she said angrily and then smiled.

"All right, all right." Amos continued to chuckle but then gathered himself. "Where were we? Oh yes, interventionism. The problem is that both the Copenhagen and many-world interpretations imply an intervention from outside the system. But we're all part of the larger system and bound by the law of conservation of energy. So this intervention is impossible in what we define as reality. Thus, we're back at the conclusion that we live in a deterministic world."

"Okay, but what about dark matter? Could it have some structural intelligence that influences our world? If not, we're back to puppet status."

"That's one possibility, and one I want to consider further. For now, I'm choosing another option."

The truth was, Amos believed dark matter, with its ability to hold energy, remain diffuse, and permeate our world, could explain a lot of what he perceived in the supraconscious. But he wasn't ready to go there with Sarah quite yet.

Sarah was about to counter, but Amos continued. "Reconsider the observation that we have a past hypothesis and not a future hypothesis. So, while the causality of the future is based on what we do in the present, the present has no impact on the past."

Sarah considered his argument before responding. "Implying that the future is not determined, unlike the past. But doesn't the resistance field knitting together the energy wavelengths on our brane explain determinism?"

"Precisely. But something has always felt wrong about the theory. The argument still leads to a deterministic universe. Something is off." Amos held his finger to his lips in a pensive pose before continuing. "I see three potential reasons why we may still have some hope of free will, or at least chance. The first is a higher force outside our dimension can actively choose the outcome of the measurement of quantum wave functions, thereby not violating the laws of physics."

Sarah rocked back. "You're talking about God coming to save us? Please, humanity gave up on him a looong time ago."

Amos held up his hands in protest. "Hear me out, if only to fully consider my reasoning."

Sarah shrugged. "Fine."

"Okay, think of 'God' simply as a unified being in a higher dimension that has been split by a resistance field. On one side is all the matter and energy of our universe. All of the other dimensions have been distorted so we can't perceive them. But they're still there. Evolution can be thought of as the 'One' trying to re-unify itself by guiding ever-increasing consciousness."

Sarah's expression softened slightly, but she remained unconvinced. "Seems like a big leap to me."

"Well, look at the human brain, in which there is clear evolution from reptilian, to mammalian, to human, to more axial thinking as communities developed. Primitive man thought more in terms of relations to himself rather than objects. It was a more spiritual encounter with the world as man understood his relationships with it. This is the essence of the One, pulling all of those relationships back together."

Sarah smirked. "You're not suggesting we go back to dancing around fires and painting our faces?"

Amos offered a flat stare before continuing. "As we increasingly viewed our world as a collection of objects to be catalogued and coordinated, the more enamored we became with the objects themselves and less with the relationship. The more we objectified our world, the less power we had to relate, eventually relying on relational silicon systems that made relationships themselves objects. We lost our power to relate spiritually. Eventually, we saw ourselves as nothing more than objects to be managed, ordered, evolved."

Sarah shifted her stare to the corner of the room. "Humans evolved to open up new possibilities for humankind, allowing us to escape the death of Earth and improve our lives. Humanity flourished only after it threw off the shackles of spirituality."

Amos looked at Sarah with sad eyes. "Or expanded our fantastical world at the expense of missing the bigger picture." He leaned forward to emphasize his point. "Science and religion are two sides of the same coin. Both seek to encounter the world around them, understand it. The common mistake is an overreliance on the mind to understand the world. It leads religious followers down a path of moralistic divisiveness and science into words upon words, explanations that remove the essence of it all. Ironically, these paths cover up what they ultimately seek, truth for the conservative and what is real for the liberal."

"All right, whatever. You're not convincing me, but how is it free will if God, or some external entity, is making the decision to alter pre-determined outcomes?"

"Well, if God is judging our actions, then he might pluck a few strings here or there to guide humanity forward. That said, if our actions are all pre-determined, then on what basis does he judge who is rewarded and who is punished? It implies that he's not so much judging individuals as simply steering all of humanity toward a certain goal. In this light, we have little control over whether we overcome the boundary. In short, we have an autopilot guiding our ship toward some unknown goal in the future."

Sarah leaned back. "Uplifting and demoralizing at the same time. Can we move on now to more reasonable options?"

"Interesting choice of words, but yes. The second is something proposed about two millennia ago. Basically, the argument is that the wave function itself contains an inherent probability that will cause it to reset itself randomly once every billion years or so. This introduces a randomness into the equation without breaking the laws of physics, even if the law behind this apparent randomness is not understood."

"Okay, if it's random, how do we use that information to our benefit?"

Amos shrugged. "I don't know. I'm working on that part. My sense is that if there's a trigger to reset the energy wave, then maybe I can find it in the wavelength itself, although if it truly is random, then there may not be a trigger."

Sarah leaned back again in her chair. "Well, I guess that's more encouraging than your autopilot scenario. So, what is the final path?"

"The last option I've figured out is that while the law of conservation of energy may hold for the energy and matter bound to our brane, it may be possible to use some energy or matter that is not bound to our brane to influence outcomes on our brane. This is just the interventionist argument again, but the trick is figuring out how to control energy and particles not attached to our brane."

Sarah turned thoughtful, considering theories on how to accomplish the task. "All right, well, we use sterile, or right-handed, neutrinos for communication shortcuts through the extra dimension between the folds in our brane. Could these qualify as a way to intervene at the quantum level of wave functions attached to our brane?"

Amos nodded approvingly. "It has the best chance of success. As you point out, we already know how to send signals outside the confines of our brane using these sterile neutrinos."

"Okay, so what next?"

Amos looked up at Sarah. His eyes were watering slightly, probably from lack of sleep. "I have a lot of work to do with the other scientists on board this ship."

"Maybe you should get some sleep first."

Amos rubbed his eyes. "You're probably right, but first I want to plan out my next steps. The first step is to analyze wave functions in more detail. I'm probably the only person who can do that because of my extra sensitivity to signals. Hopefully I can find some piece that isn't deterministic, a switch I can manipulate."

"What happens if you find the switch? How will you know how, or when, to use it? And how will you know you have the right switch?"

Amos dropped his head into his hands, rubbing his hair into a wild arrangement that looked very much like the iconic Einstein picture. He looked up at Sarah. "Not to mention understanding how one wave function could be entangled with another and not entangle myself into the wave function. Who knows? I flip the wrong switch, and our entire world could disappear!"

Sarah giggled.

Amos looked at her with confusion on his face. "You think that's funny?"

"No, but I think you have the worst case of bedhead I've ever seen."

Amos let out an exasperated sigh but then smiled. "Put it this way. If the wave functions of all the particles attached to our brane are as entangled as the hair on my head, we're screwed!"

Sarah nodded. "I get the picture. Literally."

A moment of silence followed as they both looked at one another with serious faces. Then they burst out laughing.

"Do you think the energy waves in our brane have lice?" Sarah asked between cackles.

Amos doubled over, howling. He looked up at Sarah with tears in his eyes. "Hopefully! They could be our saviors!"

Both Sarah and Amos fell into hysterics, laughing so hard their stomachs hurt.

"What we need is a lice comb," Sarah said as their fits began to subside, then continued laughing.

Amos, however, stopped laughing as he considered her comment. After a few seconds, she noticed he had stopped laughing and looked up through teary eyes.

"What? Not funny?"

"No, I mean, yes, funny. It just gave me an idea on how to untangle quantum wave functions. It doesn't solve all the challenges, and it may even create new ones, but at least it's another tool in our toolbox. At the right time, it may prove critical."

"Care to share?"

Amos shook his head, not looking up. "Not yet."

Sarah let it pass. "So, we made some progress on analyzing and possibly altering wave functions of particles on our brane. How about the sterile neutrinos not held to our brane?"

Amos closed his eyes for a second. "For that I can probably work with the scientists and engineers in both navigation and communication systems. They understand the laws of physics for neutrinos as well as the theories about manipulating them. The engineers who understand the current neutrino systems will hopefully be able to create some mock-ups of equipment on which we can experiment."

Sarah nodded. "Sounds promising. That would also free you up to focus on other areas."

Amos's eyes lit up. "Yes, if I ask them to focus on neutrino oscillations between their three flavors of electron, muon, and tau, maybe we can figure out a way to send a signal that impacts the quantum functions of particles on our brane. Of course, that's a big 'if.' Trying to get the right signal to the right wave function at the right time and place. . . . . " Amos's shoulders sagged as the extent of the challenge overwhelmed him.

Sarah leaned forward and put a hand on his shoulder. "One step at a time, Amos."

He looked up at Sarah and nodded. "Yes, one step at a time. I'll let the scientists know they have a big challenge ahead of them."

Sarah put her other hand on Amos's other shoulder so that their faces were close together. "I have no doubt they will embrace the challenge. They've wanted to get more involved, have some direction. This plan will excite them, make them feel like they're helping."

Amos nodded silently.

"It's a good plan, Amos."

"Yes, it is."

He appreciated Sarah's intelligence as well as her ability to calm him and help him think through problems. However, he wished he could talk to Bina. She could help him work through all the challenges, keep him on track. Heck, if she was truly something greater than what existed in the universe, maybe she could even manipulate the wave functions herself. His thoughts floated around Bina. She had said she would be watching. Amos sent out a thought message to her.

"Bina? Bina? If you're listening, I need some help, some sign, some direction, anything."

Amos waited a moment for a reply, listening intently for any signs that she was out there. The only noise was the cold air coming in through the vent, mirroring the same cold, empty void inside him since he had been removed from the habitat, and Bina.

"What is it, Amos?" Sarah asked. "Your eyes look sad, like you're remembering something you loved and lost."

Amos looked up at her and shivered slightly. "Lost? Hopefully not. Just . . . missing."

Sarah gave him a confused look but remained silent.

"Sarah, can you leave me now? I need to get some sleep. I have a lot of work to do, and I'm exhausted. I can't seem to think right now."

Sarah stood up and looked at Amos with worried eyes. "Of course. I'll check on you tomorrow, okay?"

Amos nodded before falling back onto his bunk, falling asleep immediately.

Sarah bent over and adjusted the sheet to cover him and then slipped out the door. She turned back before she left, a warm smile blooming on her face.

"Sleep well my brain stud," she whispered before going out.

27.

Amos sat comfortably next to the data pillar devoted to neutrino sensors and analysis. The head scientist, Dr. Brown, sat next to him. He had devoted his life to studying neutrinos and the secrets they could offer about the universe.

"See! See that?"

Dr. Brown looked off into the space across the room with unfocused eyes. Amos also looked around the room, but he used it as an opportunity to see what else was going on around them.

"Yes, there was a slight alteration in the wavelength of the right-handed neutrino we're following. The fluctuation seems to coincide with previous fluctuations of other right-handed neutrinos in the same area."

Dr. Brown focused his eyes on Amos. "You see? There's something there! Something not attached to our brane. It has to be something massive to cause that level of oscillation."

Amos turned his head slightly toward the doctor. "I get it. There's something there. But we've been looking at the same coordinates for months with similar results. The phenomenon of right-handed neutrinos localizing off our brane is well understood. Their wavelength suppression of left-handed neutrinos attached to our brane is also understood. Is there something more to it?"

The scientist's face dropped in disappointment. "Sorry, of course. It's just . . . I still get excited by the ability to sense particles off our brane. One day, maybe we can create detailed maps of off-brane space. It would be like sailing off the edge of the known world."

The truth was that Amos had already started to do just that. His brain was developing an ability to sense a sixth dimension, and possibly more. This ability gave him huge insight into the nature of their surroundings. The problem was that he couldn't make sense of it all. The amount of data was more than even his mind could process effectively.

Furthermore, complex interactions were occurring between energy fields off the brane that would require an army of evolved a lifetime to study in order to understand.

Feeling guilty at deflating Dr. Brown's enthusiasm, Amos offered some encouragement. "Could it be a sign that our brane has folded over itself like a blanket and that this point is quite close to itself?"

The doctor's face perked up immediately as he considered the theory. "Yes, yes, quite possibly. If we could only stop for a while, we could study it and see if we could send a particle through the bulk to the brane on the other side. Might open up the possibility of a wormhole or even time travel."

Amos was fairly certain that it was not their brane folded over itself at this point, much less the possibility of creating a wormhole. However, it warmed him to see the enthusiasm return to Dr. Brown.

"Unfortunately, Captain Melville is hell-bent on specific coordinates," Amos said, "and thus the possibility of stopping, or even slowing down, is remote."

Dr. Brown's face turned serious. "What has the captain told you about our destination?"

Amos turned toward the doctor, trying to determine if he knew more than he was letting on. "Apparently, it's called Kairos, which means 'pregnant time' in ancient Greek. The captain hasn't told me much. He described it as a singularity but not like a black hole."

"Hmm . . . a low-entropy singularity? Is it considered dangerous?" Dr. Brown asked a little too nonchalantly.

Alarms went off in Amos's head. "A low-entropy singularity? What does that even mean? Is it alive? What energy is it consuming?"

"All excellent questions, and ones we don't have an answer for. It seems to consume light, but there isn't the Hawking radiation or firewall that has been observed from other black holes. These observations suggest this singularity is as dangerous as it is potentially our savior."

A message broke in to their conversation. It was encrypted at the highest level of security, which meant it was from the Syndicate. Both Dr. Brown and Amos received the message simultaneously, causing them to look at each other. Dr. Brown responded first.

"I passed along your analysis of the right-handed neutrinos to the Syndicate, as I do with all anomalies."

Amos offered a questioning look, waiting for more of an explanation.

"You know I have to report everything," Dr. Brown explained.

Amos diverted his gaze. "Yes. I'm just surprised sometimes at the efficiency of the military command structure and the Syndicate's ability to respond to such mundane messages in a timely manner."

Dr. Brown shrugged and looked away, pretending to focus on the data pillar in front of them. "Guess we're just that important."

He looked sideways at Amos and winked. Amos smiled back, but there was no amusement behind his expression, only worry that something was amiss. He decided to change the subject.

"So, you've been onboard this ship for numerous missions. What do you think of Commander Din? I can't seem to get a good read on him other than he always seems angry."

Dr. Brown nodded in agreement. "He's tough, demands nothing but the best from everyone at all times. But there is no one else I'd rather have next to the captain."

Amos gave Dr. Brown a sideways look. "But not as captain?"

Dr. Brown sighed. "Commander Din is incredible at keeping the ship running at peak performance, getting the most out of everyone. He's a born leader, makes sound decisions at all times, and is extremely smart—well, smart for as evolved as he is."

Amos held his focus on the doctor. "But. . . . "

"But he sees everything in black and white. To him, there is very little grey in the universe. If he believes you've made a mistake, or even worse, crossed him, his wrath is relentless. It's like you've been banished from the ship."

Amos shifted slightly in his seat. "Has that happened to you?"

A startled look came over the doctor's face. "Me? Lord no! If something like that had happened, I wouldn't be on the ship."

Amos looked past the doctor at the far wall. "I can see that. However, I feel like I've already been judged. He makes me uncomfortable despite all the work I've put in since coming on board."

Dr. Brown offered a sympathetic smile. "Don't take it personally. There's a lot of history on this ship, and you may simply remind him of someone who crossed him."

Amos looked at Dr. Brown as he waited for him to elaborate, but the doctor only shifted back into his chair and focused on the data pillar.

"Doesn't seem fair," Amos replied finally.

"Maybe not," Dr. Brown admitted, "but it's hard for experience not to shadow how one perceives the world."

Amos pondered the comment for a while, but Dr. Brown seemed intent on letting it drop.

"Who's your favorite officer?" Amos asked.

A smile bloomed on Dr. Brown's face. "Favorite? That's easy. Lieutenant Mal. She's full of life and compassion, a real counter-balance to Commander Din. The fact that she runs Engineering only makes her that much more interesting."

A mirroring smile came to Amos's face. "Why's that?"

Dr. Brown looked at Amos. "Well, any person who can combine technical knowledge with a human touch is special. Most engineers are cold-hearted SOBs, toiling away on their engines and systematically developing and maintaining systems. They're typically happier tinkering in the world of silicon than in the organic world."

"Organic? Why do you say that?" Amos asked, genuinely intrigued.

Dr. Brown shrugged. "A figure of speech."

Amos waited patiently as Dr. Brown tried to pretend he was listening to some communication. Finally, he looked at back at Amos. "I just mean we have the ability to love and develop emotional relationships. For whatever reason, only organic life has the ability to feel emotional attachment. Silicon life forms connect but only at a superficial level. If the soul is an ingredient to life, they're missing it. But that's just my opinion."

Amos shifted his gaze toward the data pillar, as if considering it as a potential life form. "Interesting thought. I never considered the difference between a silicon person versus an organic person."

Dr. Brown gave Amos a curious look. "No? You never wondered why managed evolution programs focused only on organic life? I mean, these days it's hard to tell the difference between silicon and organic from the outside. Heck, they even sound similar when communicating through the network."

"Just always thought we're two sides of the same coin, complementary," Amos said. "We service them just like they service us. The only real difference is the way we reproduce."

A laugh rolled up from the doctor's belly. "A key missing ingredient. Wouldn't you agree?"

28.

Amos's mind was empty, exhausted. He had been pushing himself hard for months, trying to understand all the signals the ship was collecting. Almost daily now he was entering the ship's superconscious to help find a key that led to an enlightened view of the universe. It had taken him a couple months simply to understand all of the signals available despite his evolved brain.

The volume of raw data was simply overwhelming, even for him. He could utilize the filters or the processors like everyone else on the ship to help sort through it all. However, he was worried about an algorithm that created a bias, a missing piece of data that could offer a clue by its absence more than any single piece of available data. Maybe it was a hangover from his time in the habitat, but he simply didn't trust silicon-based systems. He felt he needed to go through every piece of code to look for bugs and fix inefficiencies. There were too many unrecognized irregularities, irrational thoughts that could overlook the key data piece. This immersion in the structured environment of the superconscious left him exhausted, drained, and numb. Lately, he had found his mind grinding through the data but not really absorbing it. He realized this was a signal from his mind to take a break, let his overheated circuits cool down.

He had started by taking a walk around the ship, looking for a change of scenery from his room, Navigation, or other officer-infested decks. He even found the dull colors and low hum of the ship distracting. He simply needed to find a quiet place where his mind could turn off or at least wander on its own for a while.

Eventually, he found his way to the observation deck, with its magnificent views of the surrounding space. He stared out the window at what appeared to be an electrified nebulae, a supernova remnant. He reveled in its mix of radiating pinks, purples, and oranges on the edges. Taking in the view with only his eyes provided a sense of awe, of wonder, of endless opportunity. Strangely, the same uplifting feelings weren't there when he looked at the nebulae through the data provided by the sensors. Somehow, information was lost in the transfer, like the silicon sensor systems were filtering out the essence of the information.

"Beautiful, isn't it?"

Startled, Amos turned from the window to find Sarah standing next to him. The fact she was able to walk up next to him unnoticed was testament to his mind's exhausted state. Amos turned slightly and offered a weak smile as his mind struggled to muster a basic courteous response.

Sarah smiled back at Amos, a hint of amusement in her eyes. "I'm happy to find you're taking a break. You've been pushing yourself so hard. Even you can benefit from taking a step back and re-charging."

She had kept her distance as he had been working these past few months, but she had watched him with a growing sense of awe. His brain was beyond anything humanity had developed, but his drive was what surprised her. At first, she had tried to seduce him, joined in the betting pools on when Amos would crack and run into another wall. But as time went by, she found herself defending him to the crew. Only recently had she realized what had driven him so hard. It was empathy, of all things, love for humanity.

Amos lowered his head, leaned forward to put his hands on the railing that encircled the observation deck, and gave a weak nod.

Sarah put her hand on his, giving it a small, comforting squeeze. Amos focused his eyes on her hand and then looked out the window again. Sarah followed his stare. They stood in silence taking in the view.

After an extended time, Amos was finally able to pull two thoughts together. "Ever wonder if life forms as advanced as humans existed before us? Maybe they faced the same fate we do."

Sarah gave his hand another squeeze and looked at him. "Perhaps, but I thought you didn't believe in predestination."

Amos dropped his head as a pained expression overtook his face. "Don't I? Maybe hope is a better descriptor than belief. Hope is what we have, even if we live in a deterministic universe. Hope is a hard thing to rely on."

Sarah shifted her hand to his shoulder. She pushed his shoulder back slightly to straighten him up and force him to face her. "If hope is all we have, then we better make the most of it. It has served humans well in the past, and I believe it will serve us best in the future, because the alternative leads to failure."

Amos looked searchingly at Sarah, like he was trying to find the essence of humanity within her. She looked deeply into his eyes, offering the hint of a door open for him. Neither said anything, but Amos felt an emotion inside of him grow. Unnerved at the intrusion, he wondered what it meant. Finally, he decided what he felt was hope, hope that there was something more.

He broke eye contact with her and looked around the observation deck, as if he was watching to see if anyone else had appeared on the deck without his notice.

Sarah dropped her hand from his shoulder. "You know, Amos, you have to make sure you eat properly. Your body can't rely on the energy provided directly from the system."

"I'm fine," Amos replied absently. "It's my mind doing most of the work, and it can tap directly into the ship's system through the superconscious and pull energy from the engines."

A worried look grew on Sarah's face. "Yes, but your body can't live off that energy. It needs nourishment, vitamins. Your mind isn't of much use if your body falters."

Amos looked sideways at Sarah. "I'm not so sure about that, but I agree that relying on silicon systems for support is . . . perverted."

"Perverted? Not sure I follow you." Sarah turned to face Amos, but he turned his gaze to the nebula.

"Perverted in the sense of a deviation of the natural, even amoral." Amos enunciated the last word, marking the emphasis of his thoughts.

"Amoral? Since when have morals factored into your thoughts about saving humanity? I think saving the universe places you on fairly high moral ground." Sarah let the last phrase come out in a teasing manner, an attempt to lighten the conversation.

Amos ignored the jest. "You're in a ship about to crash into a densely populated area of a planet. You have a lever in front of you. If you pull it, the ship will avoid killing millions of people on the planet, but at the expense of killing everyone on board, including yourself. Do you pull it?"

Sarah shifted her gaze outwards again, taking a moment to consider her answer. "Depends who's on the planet and who's on the ship."

Amos turned toward her. "Does it? Is any one life more valuable than another?"

"Of course! If the ship has you on it, it's worth is far greater than anyone on the planet. This is the moral code humanity has lived with throughout managed evolution. The many are willing to make sacrifices to lift up the few who can overcome the obstacles ahead. It has perpetuated the existence of humanity in the face of certain extinction."

Amos dropped his gaze to the black floor. "Yes, it is, isn't it?" he whispered. "It's this moral code that has guided us to this point."

Sarah tilted her head forward in an effort to pull his eyes back up to hers. "What other course is possible?"

Amos lifted his eyes, but not his head. "That our strength, the collective strength of humanity, is largely untapped. That we do not understand its true nature. Therefore, by sacrificing the many for the few, we ultimately make ourselves weaker."

When Sarah did not answer, he continued. "I don't have the answers right now. All I know is that when I drop into the superconscious, I feel like I'm missing something. It's like information is filtered out. It's the difference between standing here looking at the nebula with our eyes, and going back to Navigation and looking at it as a hologram. Somehow, the feel of it is diminished, reduced."

Sarah was silent as she worked through Amos's words and tried to read any signals coming off him. She felt his seriousness; therefore, she decided not to make light of what he had said. "But wouldn't we get a more complete understanding of the nebula by utilizing the vast array of sensors that can analyze the signals? Don't our computers provide a deeper understanding than we can perceive?"

"Maybe. Again, I don't have all the answers. All I know is that it feels . . . more complete when I view it with my eyes, even though I can't tell you its mass, vectors, or energy levels." Amos broke the stare between them and looked out at the nebula again.

Sarah was trying to sympathize, to understand Amos, even if she was more confused by him. "I get that. It's the same reason why a poem can bring one to tears and a person can sit for hours exploring a master's artwork. It's what ultimately separates us from computers, from silicon-based systems."

Amos looked back at Sarah with a small smile on his lips and nodded slowly. "Yes, these emotions hint at an inner depth within humans. An untapped potential."

Sarah nodded in harmony with him. "Okay, so what's your point?"

Frustrated, Amos looked back out the window. "My point? My point is that maybe we're on the wrong path. Maybe the path to salvation doesn't involve ships, sensors, computers—hell, maybe it doesn't even involve me, an evolved!"

"Don't doubt yourself, your ability. You'll figure this out." Sarah put her hand back on his shoulder.

Amos stood looking out the window for a long moment before responding. "I don't doubt my ability—well, maybe I doubt my ability within the constructs of this mission." He let out an exasperated breath and hung his head in defeat.

Sarah moved closer and wrapped her arm around him. "Amos, trust yourself. Don't give up hope."

"Trust myself? Do you trust that I can find the answer?"

Sarah pull his body close and turned his ear toward her mouth. "Amos, I trust you," she whispered. "I've watched you work yourself almost to death. I believe in you."

Amos breathed heavily as he worked to rein in his emotions. He lifted his head and turned to face Sarah. Her hands were clasped behind his neck as she held him close. Not knowing what to do with his hands, he placed them on her hips and lowered his eyes to the floor.

"Thank you," he mumbled.

"What was that?" Sarah lowered her head and looked up into his eyes. "I didn't quite catch that."

Amos let out a nervous laugh and lifted his eyes to meet hers. "Thank you, Sarah. Thank you for trusting me."

A broad smile took over her face, and before she could stop herself, she brought her lips to his and kissed him.

Amos did not pull away. Instead, he pressed his lips to hers, tentatively at first, then hungrily as the flavor of her lip balm touched his tongue. She pulled him closer and then unclasped her hands and moved them to his face, holding it tenderly as she tried to control his eagerness.

He pulled away abruptly and looked away from her, down at the floor. She tried to hold his head, pull it back toward her. He twisted his body and pushed her away, taking her hands and pulling them away from his face.

"I'm sorry, Sarah, I shouldn't have done that."

"Sorry? I did it, Amos. Don't be sorry." She slid her hand down from his shoulder to his arm, hooking her fingers around his tricep and pulling him toward her. He resisted while looking at her terror-filled eyes. It was the look a teenager gives when he thinks he's done something wrong, something he may regret. Sarah pulled harder, stepped toward him, and placed her hands on his face.

"Amos, how are you going to understand the deeper strength in humans if you don't allow yourself to feel it?"

Startled, Amos began to sputter a few words but nothing intelligible. He retreated as if to re-form his thoughts as he dropped his eyes. Finally, he pushed his hand out. "I don't think I can afford this . . . complication. I have to devote my full effort to the mission. You must be able to understand that!" He looked at her with pleading eyes, hoping she would release him.

Sarah continued to stare for a few more moments before dropping her hands from his face. She stepped back and straightened into a more formal posture. "Of course."

Amos noticed her officer mask had returned, and his heart sank. "Sarah, I . . . I appreciate all you've done."

Sarah continued to watch him closely, giving no signal of her inner feelings. Inside, her heart was beating rapidly. What had she done? Her moves hadn't been calculated to seduce him but instead came from a place deep inside her. What was this feeling overtaking her?

"It's . . . I . . . . " Amos looked out the window again as if what he wanted to say was written in space. Finally, he pulled himself together enough to reply, "Sarah, you mean a great deal to me. I couldn't do this without you. Maybe later, when I'm in a better place. But for now, I need to work."

Sarah's eyes softened slightly through her mask. "I understand," she said.

Inside, her heart twisted.

29.

Captain Melville screamed and doubled over, falling forward out of his chair on the bridge. An onslaught of data signals pushed into his mind to alert him the ship was in immediate peril. The overwhelming amount of information assaulting his mind put him on the verge of blacking out.

Through sheer willpower, he sorted and analyzed the information, producing a wave of sweat that dripped from his forehead despite his uniform's best efforts to cool him. He hung his head as he remained kneeling on the floor, leaning forward and placing his hands in front of him. A groan escaped his lips as he forced his head up and took in the visual information surrounding him. What he saw jolted him into action.

Everyone on the bridge was also on the floor. Commander Din and Lieutenant Guan were in a similar state, sweat saturating their uniforms and their eyes crackling pink as they struggled to comprehend what had happened. The rest of the officers on the bridge were unconscious, lying on the floor like marionettes whose strings had been cut mid-performance.

Captain Melville lifted himself into a standing position and surveyed the data pillars below him. Navigation, Weapons, and Engineering were consumed in flashing red and yellow lights. The pillars for Communications and Intelligence were sending out signals that everything was normal, although the lack of activity suggested a diagnostic test was required to ensure the systems were operating properly. Most of the crew surrounding the pillars were unconscious in their seats or lying on the floor in positions similar to the officers on the bridge.

"What the fuck?"

"Captain!"

Disoriented, Melville looked around, expecting to find one of his officers talking to him. Instead, he saw Din and Guan looking at him with wide eyes, trying to determine whether he was hurt and if they themselves were functional.

"Captain! Please respond!" A desperate voice resonated in his mind, drowning out every other urgent signal pushing into his brain.

Melville groaned again as his brain strained to comprehend the situation. He squeezed his eyes shut and shut down all communications from the computer. It was an act of sheer desperation and possibly put the ship in jeopardy, but it was necessary for him to regain control of his thoughts.

It was like a large, ringing bell was silenced in his head. The ringing in his ears remained, but at least he could begin to organize his thoughts. He looked around at the bridge, trying to take in visual clues that would explain the situation.

Din and Guan were struggling to stand up, but their eyes remained fixed on his. It didn't take any communication through the computer to tell Melville that both men were extremely worried. The fact that he was now effectively unplugged from the systems probably only heightened their fears.

Melville focused on Din, who appeared to be shouting at him. In a fog, Melville tried to reconcile the movement of Din's mouth with the lack of sound processed by his brain.

As Melville's mind worked through these conflicting sensory signals, Din and Guan ran over and lifted him by his arms. With his feet beneath him, Melville tried to stand up, only to find that his knees had buckled, and he collapsed again.

Din and Guan lifted Captain Melville and placed him in his chair. Din was still shouting at him as Melville's head rolled around on his shoulders. Din leaned forward and held Melville's head in his hands, forcing the captain to look him in the eyes.

After a moment of evaluating the captain, Din turned to Guan to say something while still holding Melville's head.

"Captain!"

Din's voice screamed inside of Melville's brain. This shook his thoughts into some order, as if restarting his mind. His began to regain control over his head and body as he looked at Din.

"Status report, Commander," he said weakly.

Din looked back Melville with a sense of relief on his face. "Sir, are you okay? Are you back with us?"

"Yes, Commander . . . Just give me a moment."

Din nodded and stepped back from the captain's chair. He turned away and looked out over the data pillars to try to collect information about their current situation.

"Captain! Are you there?"

"Yes! Give me a damn status report!"

"Yes, sir. We have come to a full stop."

"I know that! Why?"

"Captain! I need to talk to you, immediately!" The voice in his head pleaded.

Melville was about to scream at his commander to talk sense when he stopped. He checked his own status and found that all communication channels with the computers were closed. Confused, he looked around the bridge to find out who was talking to him besides Din.

Din's look of concern grew as he watched Melville look around aimlessly, like he was searching for a ghost.

"Sir, are you sure you're okay?"

Melville's head spun back to Din. A look of fear crept into his eyes as he realized some other person was talking to him. "Commander, please get me a full status update."

Din nodded and then turned back toward the data pillars.

Melville pushed out a thought through no particular communication channel. "Who is this?"

"Oh, thank God! You're okay!"

"Who is this?" Melville repeated.

"Sorry, sir, this is Amos."

"Amos? How are you communicating with me?"

"Through the network. I bypassed a few security controls. Given the urgency of the situation, I felt it was necessary."

Melville ground his teeth. Guan, who was helping Din put together a status update, glanced over his shoulder with a worried look. Seeing a look of fury on the captain's face, he turned back to his task.

"Amos, this invasion of my mind is beyond repugnant. I'll have you blown into space for this intrusion! The fact we're in a state of emergency only makes it worse!"

"Captain, please! You closed yourself off from the computer. It was the only way. Please open one private channel to me so that we can communicate."

"Mr. Hare! I have a situation right now that demands my full attention. We can talk later."

"Captain, I stopped your ship. Please! There's something important we need to discuss."

Melville leaned back in his chair and rubbed his temples, attempting to will away the oncoming migraine. His already stunned brain was trying to process this latest act of betrayal.

"Lieutenant Guan! Take Mr. Hare and put him in the brig!"

Guan spun around and was about to ask a question when he saw the blind rage in Melville's eyes and thought better of it. "Yes sir." Guan eye's crackled pink as he sent out an order to all security personnel to take Amos into custody.

"Mr. Hare, I will shut down every synapse in your brain if I have to! You will spend the rest of your life in the brig under heavy sedation!"

After a moment, Amos replied with a simple message. "We have arrived at the edge of Kairos."

Melville took a couple of deep breaths as he let the news sink into his mind. It also allowed him to regain control of his emotions and process how he planned to handle the situation. He pushed thoughts of Amos and his feelings about being violated out of his mind and focused on the task of ensuring the ship was safe.

He walked forward and stood next to Din. Together, they looked out over the data pillars, trying to piece together the data to determine their status. Despite feeling like his head would explode, he re-connected his brain to the different systems, Engineering first followed by Intelligence and then Navigation.

"Do you see anything?" Melville asked Din without looking at him. "Any piece of information that suggests we're near anything? Any explanation for our emergency stop?"

"Nothing," Din responded while maintaining his focus on the pillars. "From what I can tell, there is absolutely nothing in our path forward for light years. It appears as though more star systems have disappeared."

"Are the sensors working properly? Any malfunction?"

"I don't think so. The brane looks quite normal from where we came. All the systems appear consistent with our maps. Based on the lack of even background energy in space ahead of us, I think we've reached the edge of Kairos."

"But we're nowhere near the coordinates of our last visit to Kairos. We should have another six months of travel before reaching it. Did it move? Nothing from our previous missions implied that it moved."

"No, there is nothing to suggest it changed its position over time. Maybe it's grown?"

Melville glanced over at Din. A look of concern passed between them.

"Sir, look at these coordinates." Din sent the coordinates over to the captain's mind.

"What about them?"

"We use them to navigate by a pair of binary stars located at those coordinates."

Melville's eyes widened. "There's nothing there."

"Yes, sir. In fact, we get the same lack of signals from that region, similar to what we observed at Kairos during our previous missions."

"Is there a threat? Is the ship at risk?"

"Not sure, sir," Din replied. "For the moment, I suggest that we stay at our current location until we figure out what's happening."

Captain Melville nodded in agreement.

Din looked down at the railing in front of them and then back at the captain. "Sir, does Mr. Hare know anything?"

Melville continued to scan the data pillars, going over what he had already scanned a half dozen times, looking for some new clue. Then he took a deep breath and focused back on Din. "Yes."

He collapsed on the floor as blood ran from his eyes and a clear liquid seeped from his ears.

30.

Amos sat in a well-lit cell looking glumly at the grey floor. A cool, raw breeze blew out of the vent near the ceiling, seemingly directed perfectly so that anywhere he stood, the draft ran down his spine and gave him the shivers. The walls were similar to his quarters, although smoother. The room itself was much smaller, only long enough for a bunk. Amos was sitting on the bunk and staring vacantly at the common room beyond his cell. There was no door, but Amos knew that if he tried to walk through the opening to the cell, he would feel the same excruciating pain he had felt when leaving the habitat.

Amos's thoughts drifted to what he imagined was the now lifeless habitat that had been his entire world. Had there ever been any real life in it? Had he even been alive in that place? He felt like he had died with the habitat, switched off like another failed attempt at evolution. He was different now, only beginning to understand himself. He was outside, which terrified him. He had no support in this world in which he found himself.

Given the security systems in place, there was really no need to keep him in the cell, but a guard was posted outside the opening. The guard was facing Amos, watching and likely communicating every one of Amos's moves.

Amos had been disconnected from the ship's systems. In a way, the quiet in his mind was a welcome relief. He had been pushing himself hard for months and was mentally exhausted. To his surprise, he actually felt a bit rejuvenated by the incarceration.

Of course, the drug-induced sleep helped quite a bit, as had eating a couple of large meals since he had woken up, boosting his energy level. He was a little surprised at how thin his body had become from pushing himself to work non-stop. Unsurprisingly, the combination of sleep and food helped him tie a few more things together, possibly pushing him one step closer to a solution for figuring out Kairos. The problem with the apparent solution was that it wouldn't save human-ity. In fact, it could actually wipe it out.

Some solution, Amos. If everyone dies, the problem goes away, he thought.

Amos went through the facts again, trying to identify an inaccuracy. Not finding any, he moved on to the theories and tried to find a flaw in his reasoning. While all the arguments were logical, they were only theories. Amos leaned back on the bunk, resting his head against the wall. It boiled down to a leap of faith, trading one reality for another. Even if this leap worked, it could destroy him and humanity. It was a hell of a thing after all the advancements in science to be reduced to hope, to believing.

"Mr. Hare," a message entered Amos's mind from someone he did not know.

Amos sighed and sat back up. Maybe he could just stay in this cell. Let them try to figure it out.

"Mr. Hare, please respond."

"Mr. Hare here. Who is this?"

The guard outside the room moved to the center of the opening, crossing the threshold of the cell. "To me," came the reply through the network.

Amos stood up and faced the guard. "Good to meet you," he responded verbally. "Me. Is that name short for anything? Meathead, perhaps?"

The guard scowled at Amos but then regained control. "You will come with me to meet the captain."

"No, thank you. I'm actually quite happy in this room. It allows me to relax. It's almost like a vacation. The only thing that you could improve is my view through the doorway. Don't take this personally, but you really are quite ugly."

The guard's face went red, and his hands balled into fists, but he didn't move toward Amos. He took one step backwards, stepped aside, and extended his arm to show that Amos could pass.

A smug smile formed on Amos's face as he walked toward the door. He continued to look at the guard with a feeling of triumph as he went to pass him.

The next moment, Amos found himself lying on his back in the cell, mentally stunned. A wicked migraine was just beginning to develop at the back of his head. He groaned and rolled over, lifted himself onto all fours, and proceeded to throw up the remnants of his last large meal.

After a few rounds of emptying his stomach, Amos was quite sure he had nothing left. Puke dripped from his nose while his hands and arms were covered in bits of synthetic beef and what must have been green beans. He lifted his head, and the stomach acid in his nasal passage ran back down his throat, causing him to gag again.

The guard's voice entered his mind. "Whenever you're ready. I made sure the security portal is turned off. Sorry about that."

Amos looked up from his position on all fours and shot a look of hatred at the guard. However, the guard was still standing sideways, his focus straight ahead.

Amos pushed himself up, using the bunk to help steady himself as he stood. Then he went over to the tiny sink in the corner to wash his hands and rinse off his uniform as best he could. He filled his mouth with water, swished it around, and spat it out in the direction of the sink. Most of the water missed the sink and splashed off the wall onto the bunk. Amos cupped his hands and filled them with water. He splashed it onto his face to rinse off any residue and to revive himself.

Feeling somewhat normal again, Amos faced the portal and walked forward. At the threshold, he extended his index finger tentatively. When his entire hand passed through the portal, he stepped over the threshold and looked at the guard. The guard's mouth was set in a tight, straight line, but his eyes revealed his feeling of satisfaction.

Amos thought about saying some smart remark but kept his mouth in check. "Shall we?"

"The captain is on the bridge. You are free to walk up on your own."

Amos gave the guard a puzzled look and then turned and walked out into the hallway, only to discover Sarah, who had a worried look on her face.

"That was one hell of a stunt you pulled!" Her face changed to anger as her voiced cracked. "The captain is furious and doubts you can be trusted. I share his concern!"

Amos gave her a hard stare, not willing to back down. "We came on it quite suddenly. Maybe I should have been more focused on the intelligence signals, but our systems don't sense it very well."

Sarah's face softened. "See what? What haven't you told us?"

Amos took a deep breath. "Hard to explain. It's like a black hole in that light doesn't return from it, but there's something more."

"What do you mean?"

He shook his head, still trying to figure it out. "Again, I'm not sure. It's like space is shrinking in this area, pulling in the surrounding space. Like a black hole but without gravity causing the stretched space time."

Sarah stared at Amos for a moment. "How do you know this? Our sensors see only a void. A strange void, but a void. We have very little hard data."

Amos was pensive for a few moments, then looked at Sarah. "I believe I'm starting to perceive an extra dimension."

A startled look came over her face. "What? What kind of dimension? How?"

Amos ran his hands through his hair as he considered how to explain it. "I don't know. It is more a feeling than anything else. I did a little research, and the first people who evolved to adapt to neodymium also recorded strange feelings, like the world was bigger somehow. It wasn't until their brain adapted to fully control their new sensory capabilities that they were able to explain it and then utilize it."

"What does that mean? Is our brane held within another brane?"

Amos held up a hand. "I don't have all the answers yet. All I know is that I had a terrifying feeling that the ship was about to be lost. When I focused on the intelligence systems, I found enough data to support that feeling. Then I overrode all functions on the ship and had it stop."

Sarah's eyebrows knitted together. "Yeah, another nice trick. How did you manage to override all the security systems in the ship to take control? You just about killed fifty crew members who were engaged at their stations. Ten probably won't recover much of their brain functions. The pulse of energy going through the system and the ship's defenses almost blew everyone's mind. The captain himself needed twenty-four hours in intensive care to repair parts of his cortex that were effectively reduced to goo."

Amos gave Sarah a startled look and then hung his head. "I . . . I'm sorry. I didn't know. I've been cut off from all systems since right after I told the captain where we were."

Sarah leaned toward Amos with a stern look on her face. "Why not simply do your little trick again and override security?"

Lifting his head, he gave her a worried look. "I did what I did, because otherwise the ship would have been lost! I accept my punishment, but you have to trust me that I was acting in the best interest of everyone on board."

Sarah focused intently on Amos, and he felt the network itself probing him for some additional signs that he was lying. After a few moments, her look softened. "All right, I believe you. But you're going to have hell to pay with the captain. Not to mention Commander Din, who thinks you tried to murder Captain Melville."

Fear engulfed Amos as he thought of confronting both Captain Melville and Commander Din. "Shit! It was the only way, Sarah! Honestly! If I'm right, we have to tread very carefully from here."

Sarah nodded. "Well, you've convinced me, but the hard part is still ahead."

You have no idea, Amos thought to himself.

31

Amos and Sarah took the lift to the bridge, which was vacant except for one petty officer who fidgeted nervously at the sight of Amos while pointing toward the conference room. It was like he thought Amos was going to strike him down with his mind.

Amos dismissed the thought and turned without acknowledging the officer and walked over to the entrance to the conference room, followed by Sarah. The door slid open to reveal the ship's senior officers seated around the table engaged in a tense conversation. A wave of feral, pent-up energy poured from the room, causing the hair on the back of Amos's neck to stand on end.

"He almost killed the captain!" Commander Din's face was red as he looked up from addressing the officers around the table. A look of total disgust smoked across his face when he saw Amos, which was all the more unnerving, because he typically wore the officer's mask of emotional detachment.

Sarah gave Amos a nudge as she walked into the room. Amos's feet were stuck momentarily to the floor, and he almost fell forward when Sarah pushed from behind.

"Come on, they won't bite," she whispered.

Amos stood flat-footed, staring into the room. Din was sitting to the right of Captain Melville, on the far side of the table, and staring at Amos with absolute hatred.

"I'm not so sure about that," Amos replied.

He walked in and looked tentatively around the room, trying to find a friendly face who might offer some support. Captain Melville remained seated at the head of the table, his left arm resting on his chair's armrest with his hand held up to his mouth. He appeared to be deep in thought. Guan sat in the chair closest to the door through which they had entered. He had turned his chair toward Amos, coiling his body. His weight was forward in his chair, positioned into an ophidian-like warning. Amos had the impression he was ready to lunge at Amos at any moment.

Sig sat on the far side of the table. He was clearly displeased but held a more neutral expression. Next to Sig sat Reilly with more of a hurt look on his face. He also didn't seem happy to see Amos, but for a different reason. Amos wasn't sure if it was betrayal or disappointment.

Guan was at the foot of the table, farthest from the captain. Surprisingly, he offered Amos a slight nod when their eyes met. Amos took that tiny gesture as an encouraging sign that he might not simply be thrown back into the brig.

Mal looked like she hadn't slept in days. She sat with her head bowed forward over the table. Her face and uniform were dirty, probably from sweating while working to get the engines back in order and handling causalities under her command. Amos knew that what he had done had likely destroyed at least one engine and most likely the crew managing that engine. A feeling of remorse flooded over him as he looked at her.

Lastly, Jahan sat between Mal and Guan on the near side of the table. He had not looked over when Amos and Sarah entered. Instead, his focus remained on the far wall, offering no signal to Amos as to how he felt.

Amos tried briefly to reach out to Jahan through the network, only to be reminded that he was disconnected from all systems. He became painfully aware that it was just him, alone. He had no allies in this room. The best he could hope for was a chance to state his case before they threw him back in the brig or maybe even out into space. He would have to rely on the skills he had developed interacting with computer images in the habitat to persuade these highly experienced officers of the dangers they faced.

"Mr. Hare," Din began in a growl that evolved into a bark as he proceeded, "do you have any idea—"

"Amos, please take a seat." The captain's voice cut through the room like the crack of a whip, silencing Din.

Din looked at Melville, who held one hand out in front of him is a gesture for silence. His other hand was pinching his temples as he tried to subdue what appeared to be a migraine. Din straightened up and considered pressing his point, looked between Amos and the captain, who lowered his hand from his forehead to reveal a face straining to control whatever internal pain and emotions were surging through him. Din settled reluctantly back into his chair.

"Yes, sir." Amos moved to take a seat but hesitated when he noticed only one chair. He looked over at Sarah, who nodded and moved to take a seat against the wall.

What did you expect? Amos thought glumly. *That she would hold your hand?*

Amos pulled out the chair, which let out an audible squeak in the silent room, and swiveled it around awkwardly to face the crowded table. He could almost feel the fire shooting from Din's eyes.

The room remained silent as everyone waited for the captain to begin. Amos felt his uniform start to cool his body in response to the sweat that was running down his spine. He shivered.

After what seemed like a lifetime, Captain Melville regained his composure and started to talk in a deliberate monotone. "Mr. Hare, you have caused great damage to this ship. You have killed fifty-three crew members, possibly destroyed an engine, and most of us are suffering from some degree of brain damage. The entire mission is in jeopardy, and I am strongly considering aborting it."

Amos began to speak, but Mal cut him off. "Fifty-four, sir. Andrea Shep just passed away in intensive care."

All eyes moved to Mal, who bowed her head and fought back tears. Jahan leaned over and put his hand on her shoulder, offering what little comfort he could. Mal straightened, composing herself, and looked up at Amos. Her eyes were filled with sorrow.

Amos felt his heart strain at the thought that his actions had killed people, people who had pledged to save his life. He fought back tears and used all of his energy to pull his thoughts together. He shivered again despite the thin comfort of his uniform.

"Mr. Hare, while we are all wondering at how you did what you did, and I am personally outraged at your intrusion into my mind, we would very much like to hear your reason for doing it." The captain lifted his head and focused his eyes on Amos.

Now that Amos was able to take a good look at Captain Melville, he was shocked at what he saw. His eyes were sunken, surrounded by dark circles. It looked like he had aged about twenty years as the skin on his face hung loosely under his eyes and chin. As Amos looked him over, he realized that the captain looked extremely frail, like he had simply been placed in the chair. Amos would be shocked if Captain Melville had the strength, or energy, to actually stand. Even raising his arm must have taken an incredible amount of willpower.

Amos's awareness expanded out from the captain, and he realized suddenly that all eyes were focused intensely on him, awaiting his explanation. Looking around the table, he sought some hint that he had an ally in the room. What he found was less than encouraging. Amos took a deep breath and decided the best approach was a direct one.

"The ship is on the edge of the influence of a singularity in space. If we had gone any closer, we would have been consumed into the singularity, and all of us would now be dead."

Din let out an exasperated breath. "Singularity? Our sensors show no such thing. Gravitational fields appear within normal expectations in all directions."

Amos looked at Din. "Not a black hole. The singularity in not gravitational in nature. It's something different."

Sig leaned forward and looked at Amos. "Amos, Din is right. We have completed extensive sensor sweeps of the area. There are anomalies but nothing to suggest that the ship is in immediate peril."

Amos looked down at the table as he struggled to organize his thoughts. "I don't understand it completely. The best way I can explain it is a feeling I have. The sensors don't recognize anything strange, I agree, but when I analyze all the information, I'm left with this . . . feeling."

"Feeling?" Din asked. "We're supposed to accept some random pubescent feeling you're having as an immediate threat? For all we know, your hormones could be producing this feeling."

Amos felt the tension in the room rising as the officers' doubt increased. He struggled to come up with some way to explain it, something tangible that would allow them to understand the threat—not so much a threat as a quarantined area. If anything, the feeling Amos had from the area was positive, welcoming. But was that a trap? Could he trust his feelings?

"Do you feel a welcoming warmth, Amos?"

The tension in the room relaxed slightly and Amos looked around bewildered, wondering if the question came from anyone in the room. He found Jahan looking at him with intense eyes.

"Do you feel like we are welcomed to this space?" Jahan repeated, "or are we in imminent danger?"

Amos's mouth fell open as his brain worked to understand why the hatred he'd felt a moment earlier had not exploded toward him. The hatred was still there, primarily coming from Din, but the honest question gave Amos the room to think and respond thoughtfully. A life raft had been thrown to him, for which he was eternally grateful. "It . . . That's part of it. I feel like a door is open in front of us, if that makes any sense. Through the door lies some sort of happiness but also great risk. Are we in imminent danger, like something is about to attack or consume us? No."

Amos paused as he continued to collect his thoughts. "Imagine standing on top of a mountain with your toes curled over the edge. In front of you stretches an endless landscape of beauty and freedom. You feel the warm sun on your face, and it seems to want to draw you closer to it. You want to step toward it, but that would mean certain death as you fell into an abyss."

"It is this . . . 'abyss' that made you stop the ship?" Captain Melville asked, his eyes riveted on Amos.

"Yes . . . and no. The abyss *feels* like it represents complete freedom, another existence. But it's an existence that may not be available to all of us."

The officers looked at each other, many of them shifting uncomfortably. Even Din was sitting back in his chair as he listened.

"Has it moved? Can it move? Is there a new one?" Jahan looked at the captain as he asked the question.

Captain Melville had returned to his pensive pose, working through all the information. He lifted his head slightly from the hand on which it was resting. "Two of these singularities in the same general region of space? I find that unlikely. The other answer is that it has grown."

"Forgive me for stating the obvious, but none of these answers are particularly illuminating," Jahan said.

"We still don't know what it is. If it has grown, or even moved, is it alive?" Sig asked. "Pushed by some force we don't know? Or does that mean she did it? Is it possible she's still alive in some way?" Sig's voice took on an excited tone for the last question.

The atmosphere in the room changed from outrage to a mixture of fear and excitement.

"If she is present, then maybe it actually worked! Maybe we've found the answer!" Mal had perked up at the turn of the discussion and looked around the room excitedly.

"Hold on!" Sig exclaimed. "Even if it is her, and we have not received any signal to suggest it is, then what does it mean for us? What do we do?"

Confused, Amos leaned forward to ask who *she* was but was interrupted.

Guan held his hands up. "Everyone calm down! We have nothing to go on except Amos's feelings."

"Not entirely true," Din replied. "There are multiple anomalies that we're trying to understand."

"I thought you said we didn't have any signals that suggested anything was out there." Guan said.

"Well, that's the anomaly," Jahan explained. "In this region of space, there's nothing. A complete lack of signals coming from the region. Not even background energy."

"A black hole?" Guan suggested.

Din shook his head. "No. As I said before, we aren't seeing the changes in gravitons that you would find around a black hole. Besides, if we were this close to a black hole, we'd already be lost, but we can communicate normally with other ships and planets. In fact, there are stars that appear to have vanished when we scan further into the region ahead."

"Vanished?" Mal and Guan replied together.

"How can that be?" Mal continued. "This region of space appeared quite stable the last time we came through it."

Captain Melville leaned forward. "Yes, it was stable. Now that I've had some time to look over the sensor data more closely, it still appears to be stable. Yet, there are changes in the mass and energy distribution in the region that we cannot explain. We did not recognize these changes at first because of the distance we still must travel to the next star system, and the lack of readings was not enough to warn us of a danger to the ship."

Amos looked around in confusion, waiting for someone to explain what they were talking about. Every officer seemed consumed in their thoughts. "Excuse me, but what are we talking about?"

All eyes turned to Amos, surprise showing on their faces like he had just appeared out of thin air.

Melville turned to address Amos directly. "Amos, I apologize. You saved this ship and we are in your debt. You are returned to active duty and all charges are dropped."

Amos offered a guarded nod in return.

"This ship and this crew already did this mission once before to study Kairos," Captain Melville explained. "We did it with another evolved."

Amos sat back in stunned disbelief. "Another evolved? Who? Where is he—she—now?"

"Her name was Bina, and we believe she died."

32.

Amos struggled to assemble the pieces of the puzzle in his mind as the conversation continued around him. Bina was dead? She was alive? She was an evolved? Amos spent a few moments processing these three components. On one hand, it made sense, on the other, it made no sense. How could she be dead?

Finally, Amos's mouth started to work again in sync with his mind. "Who is—was—she?" Amos asked quietly, almost to himself. When the conversation around him didn't stop, he repeated his question. "Who was she?"

At first, Captain Melville looked puzzled at the interruption by such a basic question as he studied the stunned look on Amos's face. He seemingly brushed it off by the fact it was the first knowledge Amos had of an actual evolved besides himself. Amos continued to stare back earnestly, ignoring all the hushed stares around the room. A tired look returned to the captain's face as he rested his head on his hand and looked into Amos's eyes.

"She, like you, was developed for the purpose of overcoming the entropy barrier."

Amos stared blankly at Captain Melville. He was consumed by the rush of emotions inside. Elation at finding out another like him existed, or at least had existed. Worry that something unnatural had changed her. Puzzlement about how he had communicated with her. Most of all, fear that the same fate awaited him.

"What happened to her?" Amos asked quietly.

A moment of silence followed the question as the officers looked at each other. Captain Melville looked down at the table and then returned his gaze to Amos.

"Simple. She fulfilled her mission. She did what she felt was the answer."

Amos leaned forward, anticipating more of an answer, but Captain Melville did not offer anything further.

"And? What happened?"

"Let's back up a bit," Jahan suggested. "Maybe a bit of background will help you understand what happened."

The captain nodded. "Like you, Amos, Bina came out of the habitat. She was pulled out when she was ten years old. The plan was to keep you in the habitat for sixteen years, because we felt a longer duration might help prepare you better, but the urgency of the situation demanded we pull you out sooner."

Amos's mouth fell open. "She grew up in the same habitat? We lived in the same place?"

Captain Melville nodded. "Yes. She was the most successful of the evolved. She was the one who found Kairos initially."

"Most successful? You mean there were more evolved before her?"

"Yes." Captain Melville watched Amos as he spoke, trying to gauge his reaction. "Perhaps a better description is 'evolving' instead of 'evolved.' Each iteration produced a slightly more evolved person, able to accomplish more. Humanity has been working on the entropy problem by managing evolution for a few hundred years. Initial attempts involved a large number of individuals in order to create a large reproducing group. However, the slow progress toward adoption of tellurium and energy usage by these groups proved unsustainable. Eventually, as the scientists improved the development cycle, the effort became more focused."

"So, what happened to Bina?"

Din shifted uncomfortably in his seat. Captain Melville paused to take a breath before continuing.

"Fourteen years ago, Bina was on this ship in much the same capacity as you. The mission back then was to identify anomalies in space and time, research them if close enough, and try to identify a method to escape our seemingly pre-determined destiny."

Amos's eyes squeezed shut for a moment. "The destiny of high entropy, in which there is not enough usable energy in our area of space to support life."

Melville nodded. "Yes. After about ten years of exploration we, or really Bina, discovered a point in space that we now call Kairos. She gave it that name, because the best way she could describe it was 'pregnant time.' That point was about one light year from here."

"But my orders were to search for anomalies as well, to help direct the ship to regions of interest," Amos said. "All along we were going to one point?"

Captain Melville shifted his weight in his chair. "You were given the same orders as Bina. These orders successfully identified Kairos. We felt it was prudent to give you the same open-ended orders to see if you could discover another anomaly, or, at least, we didn't want you too narrowly focused on something you wouldn't be able to study while we traveled to Kairos."

"Are there files on the anomaly? Is Bina's research stored somewhere?"

"Yes, but those files have been partitioned from the main network by orders of the Syndicate. Scientists have continued to work through the data, but we did not give you access."

"Why not? Why hide it from me?"

Melville glanced at Jahan, who shrugged. "Might as well tell him."

Melville turned back to Amos. "We kept this information from you because of what Bina did. We did not want you to do the same thing."

Worry bubbled up in Amos's stomach. "What did she do?"

The captain looked down at the table and then returned his gaze to Amos. "She killed herself."

Jahan leaned forward. "From our perspective, it appeared as though she killed herself. We don't truly know what happened to her."

Amos sat back in disbelief.

"We spent a considerable amount of time studying Kairos," Melville continued. "Bina was engrossed by the project. As the weeks went by, she became increasingly harder to reach, often locking herself in her room for days, similar to what you have done recently. At the time, we thought she was simply working on the problem. We had no idea the depth of the psychological problems she was encountering."

Amos sat up. "What do you mean?"

"After she killed herself, we went through her records looking for some clue as to what had happened. During those final weeks, when she was locked away in her room, she was not communicating with the network. As best, we can tell she was communicating with herself and living out some life completely separate from reality."

Amos tilted his head. "She was delusional?"

"More psychotic than anything else. She just seemed to lose it. Lose herself. Lose any connection to her handler, the ship and its crew."

"What happened to her handler? Wouldn't they know?"

"The handler killed himself. We're not sure why."

Sarah looked down and shifted in her seat.

Amos's eyebrows furrowed. "And there's no record of what was going on in her mind? How can that be with all the systems and connections?"

"Well, it appears as if she detached herself completely." Melville paused as he considered something. "Here, let's just show you."

Sarah stood up abruptly. "Is that wise, sir?"

Captain Melville looked at Sarah as he considered his decision. "Maybe not, but I think if we're going to truly understand Kairos, Amos needs to know the truth."

Sarah sat down reluctantly and leaned forward in her chair.

A hologram appeared above the table showing a young woman in a small room that looked much like Amos's current quarters. She was lying on her bed with her eyes open. Initially, it looked like she was simply daydreaming, but as Amos focused more intently, he heard her talking and saw that her lips were moving. Amos strained to understand her, but he couldn't make out the words. The harder he listened, the more it sounded like a completely different language.

"Can you increase the volume, enhance it? What's she saying?"

"I'll warn you," Captain Melville said, "we have tried to understand it, but we can't even come close. It's like she's talking in some code, like the noises coming out of her mouth are the audible interpretations of the data streaming through her mind."

The sound from the hologram increased, filling the room. It was a series of crackles, pops, and hisses. It sounded like the background noise from a radio telescope. How her mouth was capable of making such sounds was bewildering.

Amos looked around the room. Every officer was focused on him with a look of hope that he would be able to crack the code and explain what Bina had been working on.

Sitting back in his chair, Amos rested his arms on the armrests and looked down at the table. "Why do you think she was talking to someone?"

He looked up and found all eyes focused on him. Another wave of fear swept over him, and he considered all possible explanations and how the crew might interpret them.

"She must have been talking to someone. Why else would she be talking?" Captain Melville leaned back and exhaled. "She was probably talking to herself, having some mental breakdown given the heavy workload and strain put on her brain by the network. We were working her pretty hard, pressing her to provide a solution."

Amos pondered the captain's answer for a few moments. "How long ago did this happen?"

A confused murmur went around the table. The captain stared at Amos thoughtfully.

"About five years before you emerged from the habitat."

Amos thought back to when he had first spoken with Bina, which was only about three years before he was taken from the habitat. She had simply reached out one day, asking him how he liked the view out his window. At the time, Amos couldn't tell what communications were coming through the network versus direct contact. Her question felt the same as his other friends, although she never spoke with anybody else. It was like an old friend had walked up next to him and shared an interest. It was odd that he had never questioned where she had come from. She had always seemed familiar to him. At any rate, this recording predated when he had begun speaking with her.

"When did she die?" Amos asked after puzzling over it a little longer.

"The day after this recording was taken," Captain Melville replied, his eyes fixed on Amos.

"The next day? What happened?"

Captain Melville shrugged. "We don't know. She just vanished."

Amos gave him an incredulous look. "Vanished? How did she vanish?"

"Well, maybe 'vanished' isn't completely accurate. Her mind vanished. Her conscious thoughts disappeared."

Even more confused, Amos pressed further. "I don't understand. You mean she died?"

Captain Melville looked around the room once again as the officers shifted uncomfortably. "This is where there's a difference of opinion. Din here, and a few others, believe that she died. She had a mental breakdown, and something unstable inside of her resulted in a seizure, heart attack, or maybe even a cortex shutdown."

"But you disagree."

"Jahan and I believe she transformed."

Amos knitted his eyebrows together. "Into what?"

Captain Melville shook his head. "We don't know."

33.

"Well, that was vitalizing!" Amos deadpanned as he collapsed into one of the two chairs in his room.

Sarah responded with a withering stare. Both were exhausted after a long debate amongst the officers.

After the captain had offered his theory about Bina's fate, a seemingly well-rehearsed discussion broke out. Both sides were firmly entrenched with only speculation separating the key points. They really only had two firm facts. The first was that after a lengthy time, Bina could interpret the sensor data through her mind, illustrating the strange energy and mass dynamic surrounding Kairos. The second was that Bina seemed increasingly unstable. A couple of the officers thought she was "losing it."

Since the crew's explanation was unhelpful, Amos decided to turn inward for answers. While he had only touched the periphery of Kairos, he felt his mind drawn to it. It was hard to interpret, but he felt like his mind wanted to flow out of him and toward Kairos. It seemed to offer a type of utopia, but a utopia from which there was no return. The fact he was following in Bina's footsteps scared him more than he was willing to admit.

"If I tell you something, you must promise to keep it between us for now," he said while staring at the floor.

Sarah had been watching Amos carefully. A look of relief crossed her face, combined with hope that he might finally open up to her and that he had discovered something that could make the mission successful. She realized that he was beginning to trust her, even love her. Love? When did she want that? She pushed the distraction back down.

"Amos, you know I can't promise that before knowing what it is. My first obligation is to the ship, then to you."

Amos looked into Sarah's eyes. "What about humankind?"

Sarah tilted her head in puzzlement. "What do mean?"

Amos leaned forward in his chair, maintaining his focus on Sarah. "Do you put humankind ahead of this ship?"

"Well, yes," she said, her voice wavering slightly, "since destroying humankind more than likely destroys this ship."

Amos's stare intensified. "What if this ship has to be sacrificed to save humankind?"

"Then I think that's something the captain should be aware of."

Amos nodded pensively. "Yes, of course." He shifted his focus to his hands, flipping them slowly back and forth to look at his palms and then the back of his hands. "You know we're mostly empty space, right?"

Sarah's face scrunched up in confusion as she tried to process the change of topic. "Are you saying we're worthless? Is this some way to justify putting us in peril?"

Amos gave her a puzzled look. "No. I mean the actual matter in the atoms incorporated into our body is mostly empty space."

Sarah looked relieved. "Oh yes, of course. Everyone knows that."

Amos returned his gaze to his hands, as if trying to see through them. "It's amazing when you think about it."

Sarah looked down at his hands at well, as if he had discovered a new way to look at them. "What? That we're empty space?"

Amos shook his head as he made a fist with his right hand, rotating it as if he could see through it. "No, that we even exist. The universe seems finely tuned to enable our existence. If just a few variables were slightly different, neither we nor the universe would exist as we know it."

Sarah leaned back in her chair, clearly exasperated. "What are you talking about?"

Amos tilted his head up at the ceiling. "We're in a strange existence. It just seems like we're incredibly fortunate that we can even have this conversation."

Sarah crossed her arms. "I'm confused. You're getting philosophical on me."

"Maybe another way to describe our existence is our spirit takes the physical form required in this corner of the universe."

Sarah looked up at the ceiling in an effort to calm herself and see what Amos saw. Amos brought his focus back down to Sarah, who also lowered her eyes. He appeared to be trying to read her thoughts for a moment. Then he looked back down at his hands, opening his palms and then squeezing them into white fists. Sarah waited patiently for a moment. Then she leaned forward and took Amos's hands in hers.

"What's going on in that big mind of yours, Amos?"

Amos hung his head in surrender. "I'm trying to figure that out Sarah. But I need help."

Sarah squeezed his left hand. "I'm here to help you."

Amos looked up and studied her face. "Yes, I suppose you think you are."

Sarah dropped his hands and grabbed his chin. "Amos, we're on the same side. We have the same goals. You can trust me."

"Why do you think the first generation of evolved, the generation that successfully adapted to neodymium, left all the non-evolved on the original earth? They abandoned them. Worse, they committed genocide on an unprecedented scale."

Caught off guard, Sarah released Amos and leaned back in her chair, exasperated. "Because they couldn't take them when they moved to E-Two. There simply wasn't enough time and energy to transport everyone."

"Yes, that's what the records teach us. That decision weakened us, set us on a path that diminished us."

Sarah studied Amos for a moment. "Weakened us? Even before managed evolution, there were many examples of genocide throughout history. Humanity often looked the other way, and we seem to have survived okay."

"Maybe genocide is simply a symptom of a deeper problem, a problem that started long before managed evolution, something that has been festering in humanity since the dawn of civilization."

"What are you talking about?"

"Division, splitting, judgement, anything that pulls us apart."

"You think managed evolution is evil?"

Amos shrugged. "Evil? No, although some may use that term to describe it. It's simply motive-driven, something fundamental to our existence. A split within us, a division between who we truly are and who we need to be to survive in the universe. As our minds evolved naturally, this split developed between our mind and soul, with civilization gradually placing more emphasis on the mind. This growing ignorance of our true selves increased our fear of death, because, after all, our minds do die eventually. Civilizations were built on this fissure, resulting in division amongst us, separation of belief systems as our minds worried about this world. Religion, the very thing that is supposed to bind us together, became so fractured it collapsed when the mind seemingly succeeded in overcoming death through conscious uploads."

Sarah shook her head. "Very few people choose that option now. I know I don't want to be uploaded into some computer to spend eternity."

Amos nodded in approval. "It does seem to allow for immortality at the expense of your soul." His gaze dropped back down to the floor as he continued. "In a way, the progression was determined a long time ago. I suspect that first generation of evolved simply saw the universe differently. They saw only the limitations of the non-evolved, not the beauty. They thought the non-evolved were closed-minded, or perhaps small-minded. They made a choice that saved themselves."

"Okay, so maybe the first evolved were protecting their interests first. If you really want to take it to extremes, maybe they were responsible for genocide."

Amos watched Sarah as she said these last few words, noting how she seemed relatively nonchalant about their ancestors' choices. A pleading look came into his eyes. "Are we worth saving?"

"What do mean? Of course we are. We're among the highest evolved. You are the evolved!"

"No, I'm not talking about you and me."

"The crew? Most are also highly evolved, and they're the finest in the fleet. Amos, they're good people."

Amos shook his head in frustration. "No, no, I mean humanity."

Sarah sat in stunned silence, looking at Amos with horrified eyes. Her chest tightened as she pushed out her response in a hushed voice. "What are you saying?"

Amos looked down at his hands. He twisted his ring finger slightly, causing it to crack. Then he squeezed his hands into fists and stretched his fingers outwards again. "We're a wicked race, Sarah. Our ancestors have committed unspeakable atrocities, justifying the decisions by the result."

"But many of those decisions were made to save the human race. No doubt they were hard decisions, but they were also necessary decisions. If those decisions weren't made, you and I wouldn't exist! There's a good chance humanity wouldn't exist!"

Amos looked at her. "How can you know that? Sure, you and I may not exist but how can you say humanity wouldn't exist? The present would be different, but maybe it would be better, more harmonious with the universe."

"You're asking me if it would be better if we never evolved? That seems silly, because we never would have escaped Earth, never expanded our reach out into the universe. We would have no understanding of our brane. Think of all the wonderful things we have now because of those hard decisions."

"I'm not saying that our lives aren't amazing in what we understand and the opportunities open to us," Amos replied. "I'm just saying that it could have been different. Less sacrifice, less death, maybe more happiness."

"We can't go back and change history, Amos. Those decisions and actions are written into the very fabric of the universe now."

Amos looked down at his hands. "Maybe. At any rate, I'm most worried about learning the right lessons from the past mistakes to help guide me in the future."

"Okay. What have you learned?"

Amos took a deep breath as he gathered his thoughts. "That some things, maybe even most or all things, are inevitable."

Sarah watched Amos as he struggled to articulate his argument.

"Take the Native Americans," he continued. "The Europeans decimated their culture and killed many of them in either direct battles or through disease. The Europeans removed a beautifully spiritual way of life that existed on Earth. Yet, it was probably inevitable that that way of life would go away as technology advancements in Europe progressed faster and faster. Given the abundance of natural resources in the Americas, those technological advancements were bound to consume them eventually, at the expense of local cultures."

Sarah crossed her arms. "Later, governments tried to compensate the descendants of Native Americans."

Amos looked at Sarah before dropping his eyes again. "True, but their culture was largely assimilated by that point, and their land was being used by others. In many ways, they were treated like second-class citizens for centuries afterwards, marginalized by society."

Sarah held up her hands in confusion. "Why are we talking about ancient history?"

"Because it's relevant to our situation."

"How? We aren't about to wipe out a civilization. We're trying to save our civilization! Who are we hurting by our actions?"

Amos's voice revealed some of the torture he felt inside. "Not our actions, my actions. What I might have to do."

Sarah saw the misery in his eyes, and her heart broke for him. Her mouth started to move, but then she clamped it shut. She squinted slightly as she tried to read more information on Amos's face as he looked at her with pleading eyes. Again, Sarah pushed her heart aside before it overwhelmed her.

"Once again, Sarah, can I trust you? I need someone to help me."

Sarah leaned back and threw up her arms. "This is maddening! We're going in circles here! Yes, Amos! You can trust me."

Amos continued to stare at her, saying nothing. After a few moments, she fidgeted as the silence made her more nervous.

"What? What do you want me say?"

The lines on his forehead hardened. "I want you to recognize that the mission of ship, our mission, may ultimately doom humanity."

Sarah's eyes scanned the ceiling as she responded in a terse voice. "How can I say that when the mission is specifically to save humanity?"

"All right, let me rephrase that. The methods this ship is using to try and save humanity could ultimately wipe it out."

"Okay, but you have the captain's ear. Why can't you simply tell him that? I'm pretty sure he'd want to know."

"I can't tell him, because he won't accept the alternative."

"Which is?"

"We turn back, find another way."

"Do you have another way?"

"No. And I don't think any other way will prove attractive."

"So what, we're fucked?"

Amos rubbed his hands over his face and ran his fingers through his hair. Since he had not cut his hair in about four months, it left him looking like a crazed maniac. "I didn't say that. My question is, can I trust you?"

Exasperated, Sarah stood up and walked around her chair. She paused while on the far side, looking at the doorway to the room. She turned abruptly to look at Amos. "Fine! I'll keep this to myself. Even if it means the mission is jeopardized."

Amos nodded and smiled. Then he stood up and walked over to Sarah, taking her hands in his. "I believe Bina was trying to complete the mission the best way she could. It was this dilemma about fulfilling the mission while saving humanity that led to her . . . change. I believe she sent her consciousness into Kairos."

Sarah's mouth fell open. "So she's not dead?"

Amos shook his head. "No, she's not dead. In fact, I believe she began to transform into something much greater but is stuck, a perversion."

A look of excitement came over Sarah, which changed abruptly to concern as she read the worry on Amos's face. "Is that a good thing?"

"For her, possibly. For us, it may mean the end."

"Why is that?"

"I think Bina was wrong on at least one thing. She couldn't enter Kairos until she let go of herself. Because she still exists, attached but unique from Kairos, all of us are in great danger."

"How does one let go one's self, Amos?"

He looked her straight in the eye. "I can only think of one way. Death."

34.

"Think like a photon," Amos said, staring into Sarah's eyes like he could follow the photons passing through to her retinas.

Amos and Sarah had been at it for hours, going through possible solutions and theories. Finally, Amos decided to take a different approach. They sat on either side of a small table that lifted up and away from the wall.

Sarah closed her eyes and rubbed her temples as she tried to stimulate her brain. "How does one think like a photon?"

Amos watched her closely. "Well, think of its purpose, to transmit information."

Sarah opened her eyes and looked at Amos. "I never really considered it that way."

Amos let a small smile cross his lips. "Your eyes are the end result of about a million years of evolution to catch photons and translate the information they carry into something useful. The fact we can see each other, see the room we're in, is a testament to their ability to carry information."

Sarah nodded. "Okay, I get it. The photon is the basic means of transmission enabling our understanding of the universe."

His smile broadened. "Yes. It allows us to peer deep into the heart of galaxies and begin to understand the black holes at their center."

Sarah offered another mocking nod. "So, what's your point?"

Amos leaned back in his chair and crossed his arms. "A photon carries the history of one interaction to its next interaction. It is the basis of why we can perceive colors and the details of the environment surrounding us."

Sarah shrugged. "Yes, I get that."

The smile remained on Amos's lips, but he looked across the room as he gathered his patience. "All right, let me take a different approach. What is entropy?"

Sarah narrowed her eyes as she tried to pull out the subtle point in a forest of the obvious. "Entropy is a measure of disorder in a system."

Shifting his eyes back to Sarah, Amos leaned forward. "Correct. But let's put it another way. Entropy is the amount of information required to explain a system. Thus, a system defined by low entropy would take less information to explain than a system with higher entropy."

"Makes sense," Sarah replied, pondering his words. "A smashed glass takes much more information, and energy, to explain than a whole glass."

Amos slapped his hands on the table. "There you go! Now, think of energy and information as interchangeable."

Sarah jumped in her seat at the sudden noise. "Okay, so the energy surrounding us is simply information?"

Continuing to lean forward with his hands on the table, a small smile crept back onto Amos's lips. "Yes. But even with all our sensors and senses, we capture only a fraction of the information available."

"Is that important?"

Amos slapped his hands on the table again. "It's critical! But let me back up a bit. What system reduces entropy within it?"

Sarah frowned in confusion. "What?"

"Life."

Sarah closed her eyes and rubbed her temples. "Life? What do you mean? I thought life increased the rate of disorder in our environment. Isn't our growing energy needs the whole reason that our existence is threatened by the exhaustion of free energy available to us?"

Amos nodded. "We use energy to create order within our bodies to prolong our lives."

Sarah saw a look of triumph in Amos's eyes. "Right. Like I said, life consumes the available energy in its environment at a higher rate, producing less usable energy. It defines life. We are entropy producers. We eat food, extract the nutrients, and dispose of our shit, since we can't use it directly to sustain us."

Amos mirrored her look. "Not exactly. Overall, yes, but the whole purpose of our senses, our being, is to understand our environment. Our shit is a by-product of a deeper purpose."

Sarah opened her mouth to reply but Amos pushed on. "Our senses, our body, our brain, is built to gather information about the environment and make sense of it. Our eyes capture photons in the visible spectrum. Our temples collect them in the terahertz spectrum. The sensors that are connected to our brain communicate information to us across the spectrum. We are tantalizingly close to being able to interpret all the information scattered around us."

Sarah thought for a moment before replying. "Why is that important?"

A triumphant grin bloomed across Amos's face. "Because this process of collecting the information and making order out of it reduces entropy."

Sarah was silent for a moment, staring at Amos. Then she straightened up, and her smile returned. "That's nice, but how does it help? Our bodies are tiny specks in the universe, utterly irrelevant in the greater scheme of things. Furthermore, our brain cannot possibly process all the information bombarding it, dumping most of it as not useful to our survival. Thus, we forget most of what we're exposed to during our lives."

Amos raised a hand as he started to refute a point, but Sarah pressed on.

"And the cherry on top is we're mortal, thus, any information collected during our lifetime gets dispersed back into the environment in the form of higher entropy."

Sarah paused for a moment. "Does uploading our consciousness allow us to continue the process?"

"I don't think so. The superconscious is simply data layered on data in order to keep it organized. The amount of energy required to maintain that order is extremely inefficient. From what I can tell, this ship consumes a ridiculous amount of energy to support the systems onboard."

"That would explain why we're regularly harvesting solar fuel."

"No simple answer there," Amos admitted, "and the reason why we, humanity, find ourselves in our current predicament."

He leaned back in his chair, crossed his arms, and stared at Sarah with mischievous eyes. Sarah stared back for a few moments. She had to admit it was at these times when his mind was fully engaged that she could barely hold herself back from jumping on him.

"All right," she said finally, "I'll bite. What's the answer?"

Amos leaned forward, resting his elbows on his knees. "We live in an unusual corner of the universe, one where mass is created, where our senses are naturally tuned to perceive three spatial dimensions. After adapting to neodymium, we learned that we actually live on a brane, which defines the four dimensions we perceive. We could perceive an extra dimension that allowed us to view the topography of our brane."

Exasperated, Sarah threw her hands up. "Honestly, Amos! I know that! Get to the point, will you?"

"The reason, I believe, our world is four-dimensional is because we exist on a brane in a localized gravity island. Gravity affects how we perceive our three spatial dimensions as well as time. If we could move ourselves off our brane, we would see dimensions differently. Gravity could become more powerful, or less, expanding or contracting our sense of time and space."

"Amos, this is a well-documented theory, supported by navigational observations as well as neutrino communications. That said, there are other theories as well. Why this one?"

"Because my personal observation is that the extra dimension surrounding our four-dimensional brane is actually held within a ten, eleven, or even higher dimensional bulk or universe. My ability to utilize tellurium allows me to perceive extra dimensions and sense signals from them. It was confusing at first, like a faint echo or background noise, but the more I think about it, the more convinced I am that I'm right."

"You can perceive extra dimensions? With an 's'?"

"Yes."

"Got it. So what do the extra dimensions tell you about the universe?"

Amos shrugged. "Besides we're living in a sink hole? Not much. I haven't worked out everything yet. All I know is that I can sense them. The more I study it, the more obvious it is to me that they exist, but that doesn't mean I've put together a structure that explains them and how they interact."

"Neat. You'll probably win your first of many Heliacal prizes for this discovery, but how does that help us?"

"Well, I think Bina could sense the extra dimensions as well. In fact, I believe she was studying them intently during the recording before her apparent suicide."

"So, why did she do what she did?"

"I've been struggling with that question, especially in light of our proximity to Kairos." Amos paused as he reconsidered a thought.

Sarah leaned forward in her chair. "And?"

"She was trying to determine on which side she could help the most."

Confusion contorted Sarah's face. "Which side? You've lost me again. What other side is there?"

Amos continued to stare at the table between them, bringing his hands up to his mouth as he thought. Finally, he looked up at Sarah. "Which side of existence, of course."

35.

Sarah sat in stunned silence, processing what he meant by "existence." Her mouth hung slightly open as she looked at Amos, waiting for him to explain more. However, it was like he had receded back into another world. He sat with a vacant stare, either deep in thought or simply absent. The look on his face unnerved her slightly. It was all too familiar from watching the Bina files. Not knowing what else to do, she waited patiently for him.

After what seemed like an eternity Amos looked up at Sarah. "It comes back to thinking like a photon."

Sarah rolled her head back, relieved he was present again but also exhausted at following the bread crumbs his mind left for her to follow. "Are we back to that? How do I think like a photon? They can't think!"

Amos smiled. "No, but they transmit information."

"Yes, yes, I get that!" Sarah said impatiently.

"In no time, from their perspective." Amos paused to let Sarah consider it for a moment before continuing. "From a photon's perspective, there is no time, or maybe a better way to think about it, no distance. If it could process, it could not perceive our dimensions even though it was interacting with them, from our perspective."

Sarah leaned forward and put her arms on the table. "Wait, hold on. Let me work through it in my mind. A photon, which by definition travels at the speed of light, does not perceive distance or time. This is because of the theory of relativity, in which the closer one gets to the speed of the light, the shorter one's perception of time is relative to an outside observer. Thus, if you are traveling near the speed of light, what you perceive as a year passing would be something like ten thousand years to someone who is stationary relative to light. Correct?"

"Pretty much. Alternatively, distance appears to shrink as you approach the speed of light, which is simply the other way of saying time is shorter for you relative to an outside observer."

"Okay, so a photon wouldn't perceive time or distance. So what?"

"They feel like they're in a single point, a singularity. The only reason we're different is because we have mass and can't move at the speed of light or anywhere close to it. As we try to accelerate to the speed of light, our mass increases exponentially, mass that is influenced by gravity, the gravity defined by our location on our brane."

"You're losing me again."

Amos took a deep breath before continuing. "The laws of physics don't allow us to come close to approaching the speed of light. It simply takes too much energy to accelerate something with mass to that point. All the energy in the universe, in fact."

"Got it. This is well understood and taught in first-year navigation."

"Exactly. But what if one could leave one's mass behind? Effectively transform our consciousness into energy?"

"How would that be possible without some structure to hold it together?" Sarah asked. "Wouldn't the energy dissipate into space, basically leading to death?"

Amos smiled weakly. "That's where I'm stuck, and I believe Bina was stuck as well. It requires a leap of faith."

Sarah was fully engaged now, but she leaned back again in her chair. "Faith? Oh boy, after all the centuries of managed evolution, are we back to faith?"

Amos shrugged. "I believe we are. Look, if I'm right and Bina transformed into something else, effectively moved into a higher-dimensional world, then it's clearly possible."

"That's a big *if*, especially since the only possible hint we have that something, or anything at all, happened after Bina was lost is the change in the size and location of Kairos. In fact, we don't even understand Kairos! It could have expanded or moved independent of anything Bina did."

Amos winced slightly at Sarah's last comment.

"Bina could have simply had a psychotic breakdown," Sarah continued, "and the feelings you are having about the area ahead of us could be totally unrelated. This entire area could be something very simple but extremely dangerous. Hell, you still haven't proven the region of space in front of us is even safe."

Amos nodded in recognition of Sarah's argument. "Yes, but here's my theory as to why she decided to do what she did."

"Okay, I'm listening."

"Let me return to my argument that life has the ability to lower entropy but is limited by the four-dimensional world we live in with mass and dispersed energy."

Amos waited for a response, but Sarah just crossed her arms, so he continued. "All right, as the abilities of our ancestors' brain grew, they began to perceive more about their environment. They started by seeing more of the universe by using new instruments like radio telescopes, expanded into all sorts of sensing devices that picked up every available signal, and eventually pieced together the quantum laws. But it wasn't until they were able to integrate signals directly into their brains, avoiding the filters inherent in their eyeballs, that they could perceive an extra dimension."

Again Amos looked at Sarah to make sure she was with him. She offered nothing but silence, which Amos took as a positive. "Thinking about it differently, our ancestors' work enhanced our senses. Managed evolution enabled us to capture more of the pure information traveling around us in the form of photons. We became much more effective at collecting that information. We use the information provided by photons that interact with us to reduce disorder in the small part the universe called our minds."

Amos paused as he reconsidered his argument. "What if natural evolution is simply the multi-dimensional universe trying to reunify itself within this three-dimensional sinkhole of the cosmos? You have to admit the general trend is toward binding information together."

Sarah remained unconvinced. "Are we back to this mystical argument? Really? What does that say about managed evolution?"

"I don't know. Maybe we're doing God's will, or maybe our ego is subverting it."

"Religion? You mean the scattering of groups that believe in God?"

"Well, yes. Although I agree it's hard to discern anything from their teachings. They all seem more intent on preaching moralistic virtues and damning outsiders than providing any clear insight or vision on spirituality."

"Most of humanity gave up on religion a long time ago," Sarah reminded him. "It's hard to believe in a God who seems so petty and divisive. How many people died simply because one side had built up a different belief system?"

"I agree with you. The spirituality underlying religion was lost long ago, replaced by humankind's perverted value system. One century it was a sin to charge interest on debt, another century it was judging same-sex relationships. I think the final straw was when billions of people were sacrificed to 'elevate' the evolved. Any remnants of spirituality died then, replaced by a morality that emphasized the pursuit of happiness through minor pleasures over deeper spirituality."

Sarah nodded. "Right. Now that's settled, going back to your photon argument, since our mind is housed in a body with mass, all this collected information is lost when we die."

Amos stood up and waved his arms excitedly. "Correct, but what if two things could happen? You could become effectively immortal, where time wouldn't exist for you, and secondly, you could capture more information, or distances would not exist for you."

Amos saw the light go on in Sarah's brain.

"If you transform into energy but maintain your consciousness," she said, "it would be possible to lower entropy."

Amos jumped up on his chair and thrust his fist into the air as if knocking out an opponent. "And that is what Bina did! Or, at least what I think she did. If you look at the sensor readings, the space itself does not have any energy, no photons. Now, this could be because of some strange ripple in our brane, a black hole, or it could be because something, or some consciousness, is consuming all the information in that space, not allowing any to escape."

"But how is it stable? Why aren't we simply devoured into it? Assuming it is Bina, how can she define the space she influences?"

Amos stepped down off his chair and paced around the room as he spoke. "I don't know. That's what I've been trying to puzzle out. Why wouldn't it simply expand and consume everything in a big flash? I've come up with a few possible reasons. The first is that, just as it has taken time for the universe to unfold, it takes time on this gravity brane to 'fold' it back up. The second is that in her higher-dimensional universe, she has held onto enough of herself that she can exert control to expand the singularity at a controlled rate. In essence, she's offering time to humans. The final possibility is that she is unstable, or she doesn't have the full capability to control the consciousness outward. This last one is worrying, because it may mean the singularity will jump outward at any moment, consuming us."

"What happens if we enter Kairos, er, Bina?" Sarah's face twisted as she said the last part of the sentence.

Amos stopped walking and let out a chuckle. "Sounds erotic, doesn't it? In a way, it's the most intimate joining possible. But Bina isn't Kairos. If anything, she's a perverted offshoot of Kairos."

"Why has she maintained a separation? How did she do it?"

"I'm not sure. Maybe she's holding back somehow, not giving herself fully to it. However, I digress. You're referring to our current existence in which we have mass, correct? In theory, something similar to what would happen if we were pulled into a black hole. We would get torn apart as our bodies were pulled into the singularity and then crushed and converted into energy."

Sarah winced. "Ouch. Sounds unpleasant."

Amos returned to his chair. "To say the least! But if someone converted themselves into a coherent consciousness that was pure energy before entering the singularity, then it would be possible to survive—or at least understand that you are transforming into something else."

Sarah rolled her eyes. "Big if, coherent, massless consciousness."

Amos shrugged, looked across the room as if the answer existed around him. "A better question is what happens when Bina consumes us."

Sarah gave him a startled look. "Consumes us? Is she a threat?"

"No, not in the way you think. But as the consciousness expands outward and consumes information, anything within that sphere effectively becomes part of the singularity. Again, by Kairos expanding outward, it is effectively lowering the entropy of the universe, pulling the fragmented mass and energy back into a coherent structure."

Sarah gave him a doubtful look. "You assume that this consciousness has a great deal of control over itself. Given our understanding of physics, I find this . . . unlikely."

"Yes, but I told you before I believe I can perceive extra dimensions."

Sarah raised her eyebrows. "Okay. And how does that help?"

"I believe I can perceive a field, similar to an electromagnetic field, in the higher dimensions that allows for the structure of energy. In short, it allows for consciousness in those higher dimensions."

Sarah's mouth fell open. "You mean there's such a thing as God—or gods?"

Amos hesitated, unwilling to commit to that final step. "I suppose that's one way to interpret it. Assuming there's a higher level of consciousness, it's not certain whether they would even perceive, much less understand, us."

"But if they're basically omniscient, wouldn't they know about us?"

"If we found an entire universe inside a space smaller than a quark in an atom, would we know how to determine if there was life inside of it, much less know how to communicate with it?"

"Good point. So we're effectively irrelevant to them. But if Bina has transformed into one of these higher-dimensional entities, is she even aware of our predicament? She may have lost us in the proverbial haystack, or maybe she doesn't even care now that she's moved on."

Amos stood up and walked across the room. He stopped at the far side and stared at a point on the wall. He bowed his head as he appeared to come to a decision. Then he turned slowly to face Sarah. "I've spoken with Bina."

Sarah went to stand up, but her chair was pushed in under the table, so her thighs hit the table, and she fell back. She put her hands on the table and raised herself out of her seat. "What?"

A sheepish smile crossed his face. Then he winced. "It occurred while I was still in the habitat and once when I first came aboard this ship. I'm not sure why she hasn't reached out since then, but she did say that her influence could cause problems."

"And you're only telling me this now? Why have you kept this from me? From the captain? Do you realize this information could have saved the lives of all those crew members who died when you stopped the ship?" Sarah's face turned red as her anger boiled over.

Amos shot an angry look at her. "Don't add that guilt to what I already feel about causing those deaths! I don't see how that information could have saved them."

"My god, Amos, there's a reason you're not the captain or even an officer on this ship. These are the decisions you do not make!"

"This is why I kept it to myself!" Amos's face grew heated as he confronted Sarah. "Don't you understand? Even the knowledge that Bina is inside Kairos could pull us in. Remember how she works, where her consciousness expands the information in that universe is consumed into the highly ordered energy singularity. If we tried to probe her or, worse yet, contact her, her consciousness could expand to engulf us before we even finish. In our current state of existence, it would have been the end."

Sarah's face contorted into a frustrated grimace. "So what do we do? If Bina is offering us time, to what end?"

Amos relaxed and sat down, gesturing to Sarah to do the same.

"Assuming she is stalling," he said, "there are a few different reasons."

"Such as?"

"Let me tell you one thing first: none of the answers are good for humankind."

"Okay. . . ."

"The first reason is basic but should at least be considered. She might be holding back Kairos somehow, allowing us to move away before it continues to expand."

"Sounds unlikely, since that would just put off the inevitable."

"Possibly, but maybe she can leave certain regions unaffected, essentially restricting humans to their current region."

"But that dooms us, because we'll use up all of our available energy!"

"Not if humans devolved, managed their evolution to reduce their energy consumption."

"That doesn't sound like a solution."

"It depends on your values. A society that tries to live in harmony with its environment, like early Native Americans or the Amish, probably view it as an ideal solution."

"Are you saying we need to go native?"

"Well, there is one more way, but we need to talk to the captain first."

"I thought you wanted to keep it between us for now."

"Yes, but there's one unknown for me still on board this ship."

36.

Captain Melville's eye sockets and cheeks were deep, dark caves in his face. It appeared his brain had been sucked out, leaving a vacuum inside his skull that the skin stretched to fill. Both Amos and Sarah struggled to stifle gasps at the sight of him when they met him on the observation deck.

No one else was on the deck, which had been cleared of people. The observation deck was a large, suspended disc with a railing around the edge, which the captain leaned against for support. The lift was in the middle of the disc and a continuous window to space that encircled the deck.

In previous visits, Amos had found that by standing at the rail, especially if plugged into the ship's sensor arrays, he could almost believe he lived outside the ship in space itself. It had felt glorious before, but at this moment, his mood was more somber.

"You're looking better, Captain," Sarah said as they approached. "Did you get some sleep?"

Captain Melville looked at Sarah with a small smile of gratitude. "Yes, thank you. Amazing what a little sleep, nourishment, and the good doctor's care can do for a man."

Both Sarah and Amos forced a smile to suppress the worry on their faces.

"I'm glad to see you walking," Amos said. "Again, I—"

"Please, we're past it," he said, waving his hand dismissively. "We have larger things to think about now." He turned slightly to look back out into space. "Hard to believe there's something out there. It looks so empty to our primitive eyes."

"So much is hidden from our eyes," Amos said. "We evolved in a simple world, where knowing all the details of the universe was immaterial."

Captain Melville nodded as he continued to gaze out the window. "You're right. Even with all of our advanced technology and abilities to perceive the fifth dimension we remain . . . basic."

"There's a lot that is not shared."

Captain Melville gave Amos a questioning look. "Not shared or simply hidden from our senses?"

Amos shifted his stance slightly but held the captain's gaze. "Maybe purposely hidden, and definitely not shared."

Captain Melville turned to face Amos. "Is there something you'd like to know, Amos?"

"Yes, a few things have not added up." Amos hesitated before continuing, "Does the crew know about Mal?"

"Know what?" Sarah asked before she could help herself.

Melville glanced at Sarah before narrowing his eyes back on Amos. "Careful Amos. Some things are personal even if you question if they are a person."

"But, she's organic, right? It's the ship that provides her consciousness. Am I wrong?"

"We're not discussing personal issues now. After we figure out Kairos, then you can ask her directly."

Nervous sweat began to trickle down the spine of Amos. Straightening up, he changed tactics. "Okay then, why is so much of the network blocked from me?"

The captain maintained his officer mask, revealing only the tiniest flicker of uncertainty. "What are talking about? You have access to almost all of it."

Amos's stare hardened. "At first I agreed, but the power consumption of the ship does not sync with the size of the network."

Another flicker of concern crossed Melville's eyes, or was that pink?

"What are you talking about? The engines, life support, synthetic food creation, other systems; all of them consume a considerable amount of power." He gave Amos a warning look, trying to get him to back off from his line of questioning.

Amos persisted, taking a deliberate step forward. "I've added up all the power needs of those systems, and I can't even get to half of the power consumed by this ship. In fact, the amount of excess power consumption on this ship would support about hundred evolved like me. There is something large, and hungry, on this ship."

Captain Melville stared at Amos for a moment, glanced at Sarah for some signal, but she just shrugged. Then he turned away from them and walked along the rail. Amos and Sarah followed.

They had almost walked completely around the observation deck before Captain Melville began talking in a soft voice while keeping his eyes on the window. "Amos, you have had access to everything you need to do your job."

Amos's eyes followed the captain's focus to the area where Kairos was most likely located.

"Up to this point, yes. But I believe we're at a point where a decision must be made that is bigger than you and me."

Melville continued to walk, shifting his focus to the railing he slid his hand along it. "You may be correct. But you must understand that only I and Commander Din are aware of the full extent of the . . . systems on board."

Sarah gave him a confused look, but she kept her mouth shut.

Amos looked down at the captain's hand on the rail. "I figured as much," he replied firmly but gently, like a parent trying to coax the truth from a child. "If I'm right, some crew members might find what's on this ship disagreeable."

Melville nodded. "Truth be told, Amos, I'm not one hundred percent comfortable with it either, but I have my orders."

Amos offered him a grim smile. "Thank you for saying that. I believe you."

Melville stopped walking and turned to face Amos. Sarah stopped next to him.

"What I'm about to tell you has been approved should the need arise, but understand it is viewed as a last resort. Once I tell you, I have to assume it will trigger a larger discussion that involves the officers and likely the entire crew."

"Yes, that is likely to happen," Amos replied. "This choice is larger than any of us. However, know that I have tried to come up with other solutions to avoid this situation. The alternatives are probably less attractive to the crew than the one in front of us."

Melville's face softened, and his shoulders rolled forward like a weight had slid off them. His eyes settled into a sad, resigned look as his body sagged slightly. "Thank you for at least considering other alternatives. I appreciate it."

Amos rocked forward onto the balls of feet. "So, what do we do about them?"

Sarah shot a look at Amos, wondering who he was talking about. Then she looked at the captain, who offered no surprise, only a pensive look.

"We start by talking to them. But I think I know what they will want."

Amos leaned forward in his stance, lowering his head slightly as he tried to move into Melville's field of view. "Even if it means risking their death?"

Melville looked up with weary eyes that gave away a leeriness to proceed. Amos wasn't sure if the wariness came from what he had done or what they had done afterwards to the captain.

"Even if it means that," Melville said. "This is probably the best chance they'll ever have."

"What are you talking about?" Sarah asked. "Who are they?"

Amos turned his head toward Sarah, but his eyes remained focused on Melville. The captain gave a nod of approval. Then Amos looked at Sarah.

"The Syndicate."

Sarah let out a brief laugh. "The Syndicate? Here? On this ship? That's impossible! We would have seen them walking around. They would have been sitting in meetings, offering their wisdom."

Amos looked at Melville to respond.

"It's true," Melville said. "The Syndicate is on board this ship. In fact, this ship is their home."

Confused, Sarah furled her eyebrows. "How can that be? I saw all the records of who came on board. There were no large ships that met us during that time." After a moment, during which she seemed to check a few things on the network, she continued. "The food consumption is consistent with the current number of crew on board since we departed."

"Their bodies are not on board the ship," Melville said, "thus, food is not required to sustain them."

"Their bodies are not—" She stopped as a look of recognition spread across her face. "You mean the Syndicate is a hive of minds? There have always been rumors, but I thought that was only theoretical!"

Melville nodded. "Actually, a better description would be a hive of consciousness. Each member retains his or her own thoughts and memories partitioned from the others. However, like the honeybees that use to live on E-One, they work together quite effectively. Their collective thoughts can almost match that of Amos, albeit much less efficiently."

Amos looked out through the window. "I always wondered a bit at how quickly decisions seemed to come back from the Syndicate, despite the increasing distance. At first I brushed it aside, thinking a particularly smart individual in Communications had found a more direct route in the fifth dimension. But as we traveled around folds in the brane, I knew that something else was going on. After looking through the power consumption details, it became the only available explanation."

Melville looked at Amos. "I assumed you would figure it out sooner or later. I told them that, but they insisted it remain a secret for as long as possible."

"So, who are they then?" Sarah asked. "What happened to their bodies back in Eridu?"

"A collection of some of the greatest minds humankind has known over the past few centuries," Melville replied.

Sarah stared at him in shock. "Past few *centuries*? How have they lived that long?"

"It's how the hive was constructed. When a particularly brilliant individual was nearing the end of his or her natural life, they were offered a permanent home in the hive, essentially making the person immortal."

"Not really immortal," Amos added. "They can die, or maybe a better term is 'turn off.' They are, after all, reliant on the computer systems and networks for their existence."

Sarah looked at Amos, still somewhat confused. "But are they alive?"

"Think of them as part of the super-consciousness on board this ship," Melville explained. "The same superconscious that Amos has trained in, just a different partition."

"But they're elected officials!" Sarah exclaimed. "How is all of this possible?"

"Well, not all of them are represented at any one time," Melville said. "They run against each other in elections, offering ideas and visions to make society better. We vote on their ideas and visions, with the winners elevated to a more prominent role in the hive, effectively allowing their ideas to be heard above the background buzz."

"But I've watched holograms of them! Their faces and names are not the same as the geniuses of the past!"

"Simply avatars. Right, Captain?" Amos asked.

Melville nodded in agreement. "But, to be clear, these avatars are not gods descending to Earth in a human form. As much as they might like to think of themselves as gods, I consider them people trying to elevate themselves to the status of gods."

Amos and Sarah both looked at the captain.

"So, you don't agree with the Syndicate?" Amos asked.

"Agree with the Syndicate? That's politics, and my command doesn't worry about politics. My command reports directly to the Syndicate. I follow orders."

"Not the politics, the attempt at artificial immortality."

Melville blinked, but his voice held the same force, "Careful, son, you're treading into dangerous waters."

Amos stepped back and changed the direction of the conversation as he addressed Sarah. "For millennia, a minority of people has been trying to achieve immortality. The ancient Egyptians' tombs were designed to ensure safe passage to the afterlife. Later, cryogenics was used to freeze the body in hopes that someday a person could come back to life, and nousgenics is the effort to preserve one's mind after death."

Melville shifted his weight, and Amos sensed he might have disconnected from the ship.

"My personal feeling is that it's unnatural, and unethical, for them to hide their true . . . nature from society," Melville said. "But they are the governing body and, therefore, they set the rules."

Sarah was incredulous at the discovery. "How can this be? How can this information be hidden from everyone in an open civilization?"

Amos shrugged. "Is it really so surprising? Once society figured out how to upload a person's consciousness into the network, preserving them effectively forever, it became almost pre-determined that they would eventually take control of the government due to their intelligence and intimate access to information."

Melville looked at Sarah, "Humans used to worry about computers taking over the world. Instead, they should have looked at their history and realized the largest threat was themselves."

"Are they a threat though?" Sarah asked. "I mean, all of us seem to be okay, and there's a quasi-democratic process with each individual able to vote freely."

"For the most part, no, they are not a threat," Amos replied. "In fact, their intelligence and efficient manner of communicating has probably benefited society as a whole. Yet, there is a hidden agenda, enabled by allocated resources that many people may find undesirable. It's the lack of transparency about their true nature that most would find offensive, including, apparently, the captain."

Melville nodded as he stared at Amos's chest.

A message from the network entered all three of their minds simultaneously. "Captain, please escort Mr. Hare and Ms. Laka to Level Thirteen-C."

Sarah looked around, confused. "Level Thirteen-C? I didn't think there was even a level thirteen. Who wants us there?"

Melville and Amos looked at each other before Amos replied. "I think we are about to meet the Syndicate. We'll see how much of a threat they truly are."

Sarah's face turned white as all of the blood drained from it.

37

Captain Melville led Amos and Sarah back into the lift. His eyes sparkled an electric pink as he sent the required security codes to the network in order to access the level with the Syndicate. The lift started to descend.

Sarah fidgeted awkwardly in the corner of the lift, causing Melville and Amos to look over.

"What do you think they want?" Sarah asked nervously.

"To talk to us," Amos replied.

A look bordering on panic took over her face. "Why? What will they do to us?"

"Do?" Amos asked. "It all depends if we can give them what they want."

Sarah's eyes widened. "But what could they want?"

The lift stopped abruptly, and the door slid open. Amos could feel the hum coming from the room as much as hear it when the door slid open. Melville extended his arm out of the elevator to allow Amos and Sarah to pass. Amos took two long strides, after which Sarah jumped slightly and took a few quick steps to catch up.

They walked out into a walkway that was suspended about three floors above the ground. The room itself was a huge dome, with the peak of the ceiling ten floors above their heads. The walkways extended in both directions around the outside of the room.

In the middle of the room was a cylindrical structure. Its base took up most of the space on the floor below. The radius of the cylinder tapered until it ended in a cone-like shape near the ceiling. On the surface of the cylinder was a faint pattern of hexagons, each one dark gray and outlined by a black line. The size of the hexagons was similar to that of a humans head.

After a few quick calculations, Amos concluded there were about one hundred thousand hexagons on the surface of the cylinder. From looking at the structure, he was not sure if there were also layers of hexagons beneath the surface.

A message pushed into their minds, spoken in a strong female voice. "Welcome, Captain Melville. Thank you for bringing Mr. Hare and Ms. Laka to meet us."

"You're welcome, Ms. President. I believe they are here to help."

"Most definitely," she replied. "We have been watching their progress intently. I believe they may finally have found a solution, unlike the previous evolved."

Amos assumed she meant Bina, and he winced slightly at the thought of her. The focus of the president's voice centered on Amos, similar to the feeling when an individual looked directly at him when talking.

"Amos, you have questions. Please proceed."

Amos cleared his throat, more a stall tactic than anything, to allow him to collect his thoughts. Of course this conversation would take place through the network, so there was no need for vocal chords. "Allow me to be direct."

"Please do," the president's voice boomed. The entire structure flashed yellow in synchronization with her voice.

Amos shifted his weight slightly in an effort to relax. He found his butt muscles had cramped uncomfortably, causing more fidgeting. Melville glanced sideways at him. Ignoring him, Amos proceeded. "I believe I understand your ultimate goal. But in order to determine if that goal is even possible, I must gather some information about the Syndicate. You see, while I have speculated about your existence onboard this ship, I do not really know anything about you."

A warm tone resonated inside Amos's head. "Of course. What would you like to know?"

Amos straightened up slightly while clasping his hands behind his back. While likely irrelevant when talking to the hive, Sarah noticed he had assumed his own officer's mask.

"First, how many of you are there?"

"Elected to the Syndicate, one thousand. In the hive, about two hundred thousand."

"How many of you are seeking a solution?"

What sounded like a thousand voices responded at once, almost pushing Amos back on his heels.

"All of us. We are unanimous on this decision."

A couple flickers appeared on the surface of the hive-like structure in front of them. Amos was unsure what they meant.

"Let me rephrase my answer," the president said. "All of us wish to know if the solution is possible, but there are a couple who do not wish to be part of the solution. Their role remains undetermined."

A few more flickers of light appeared before they were extinguished.

"Does a choice need to be unanimous?" Amos asked.

"No, only a simple majority."

"And if a majority vote in favor, do all enter into the solution?"

"That would be ideal."

Amos paused to consider the answer. He unclasped his hands from behind him and leaned forward onto the railing. "Why?"

"To make us as strong as possible. Mr. Hare, our minds are not as evolved as yours. We find our strength in numbers. To reduce our numbers would weaken the whole."

"Understood. You understand there are great risks to the solution."

"Yes."

Amos lowered his head in a reflexive show of mild frustration. "These risks might be reduced if we spent more time studying Kairos."

"That may be the case, Mr. Hare, but more time also means more energy usage. Given the reserve power sources on this ship, the available energy in our vicinity, and our consumption needs, time is running out."

Suddenly, Amos realized the full extent of the mission. "This is a one-way trip for you, isn't it?"

After a few moments of silence, the president replied. "Yes."

"What if it fails? What then?"

"We have taken every conceivable precaution to ensure the mission's success."

Amos began to feel nervous. There was something he was not fully understanding.

"Excuse me," Sarah interrupted, "but what is this solution you're discussing?"

When president did not respond, Amos stepped in. "They want to be 'beamed,' for lack of a better term, into the center of Kairos, to become part of the singularity."

Alarm showed on Sarah's face, but she masked it quickly. "Oh, okay. Is that all?"

Amos turned his attention back to the Syndicate. "Why do you believe you will be successful?"

"Because Bina was sent into Kairos, and she survived."

Sarah shot a look at Amos while the captain reacted in shock.

"She survived?" Melville asked. "How do you know?"

"Because Mr. Hare told us."

Both Sarah and Melville looked at Amos, who continued to focus on the hive. After a moment, he turned to Sarah.

"When I told you, I assumed that I was also telling the Syndicate. They have full access to all systems on this ship, so it seemed reasonable that they would be listening. It was the only way I could think of to get an audience with them."

A look of horror crossed Sarah's face, followed by resignation as her body slouched slightly. "Oh."

Amos returned to his conversation with the Syndicate. "A couple technical things. How much data will be sent?"

"About ten exabytes per person."

Amos wondered momentarily at her reaction but did the calculation in his head. "That will take some time to transmit, likely days, if not weeks. Is that amount really necessary? Do you need all that baggage?"

"Again, Mr. Hare, our strength comes in our numbers. To attempt to enter Kairos at only partial strength, or as a partial consciousness, seems foolhardy. Wouldn't you agree?"

Amos nodded absent-mindedly. "Yes, of course."

His mind continued to work through the calculations as he communicated through the network. "Keeping a communication channel open that large for that long will be difficult to keep stable. Any fluctuation in power, location, or signal strength, and we could lose all of you."

"We know, so we've come up with a more efficient way to transmit."

That nervous feeling returned to Amos's stomach. "Oh? What's that?"

"You."

Sarah gasped as the final piece of the puzzle clicked into place. "Of course. That makes perfect sense."

"Mr. Hare, you have demonstrated an ability to communicate directly with Bina in a highly efficient manner, so efficient that our systems are unable to pick it up. We have calculated that your mind can transmit almost one hundred exabytes per second. By queuing us efficiently, you should be able to send about ten of us per second."

Amos began to sweat, despite his uniform. "Assuming I can even handle that amount of data running through my brain, that still will take almost six hours. I don't think my body could hold up for that amount time under such pressure."

"I agree," Captain Melville said. "The amount of stress that that would place on his body would likely shatter him in the first minute, much less sustaining it for six hours."

"We have considered that problem as well, and we believe we have a solution."

The nervous acid in Amos's stomach boiled into full on panic. "I don't think I'm going to like this."

"Mr. Hare, you will first upload your consciousness into the hive. Your consciousness will make the initial contact. From there, your role is to maintain the connection while the rest of us piggy back on your signal into Kairos."

"But my communication with Bina has not been through the ship's systems; it's been through my subconscious. If I load my consciousness into the hive, I don't know if I'll still have access to my subconscious."

A pause proceeded the president's response. "A detail to be worked out. But the only way for us to enter Kairos is through the superconscious. You must find a way through the superconscious that is acceptable to us."

Amos leaned forward and gripped the railing, the sweat on his palms allowing his hands to slide outward as he put more weight onto the railing.

Sarah stepped forward and put her arm around his shoulders. "You don't have to do it," she whispered. "You have a choice."

"Actually, Mr. Hare, you don't have a choice. While you were still in the habitat, we voted on and approved a decree that this is your role to help humanity take that final evolutionary step."

Sarah looked up at the hive. "But this will likely kill him! That amount of data riding over his consciousness will destroy his mind. He might get you there, but he'll have no idea where to turn once the transmission is complete."

"That is a risk, yes, but we believe the potential payoff makes the risk worthwhile. Besides, the benefit to society—"

"Benefit to you, not society! Society doesn't benefit from this. In fact, you risk destroying humankind by even attempting this leap! Kairos is unstable. By sending that much energy and information into it, the singularity could expand abruptly, consuming the ship or even the galaxy. You risk killing everyone for your own benefit!"

After a pause to make sure Sarah had finished, the president continued. "Benefits to society, because if successful, it will provide a path for others to follow. Humanity will finally escape its dependence on new sources of energy, because we will become energy, pure information that can observe any part of the universe, any dimension, we desire."

"You're insane!" Sarah cried.

Amos raised his head. "I'll do it," he said quietly.

A look of shock took over Sarah's face. "You will not! Amos, this will destroy you! This isn't right! We'll talk to someone, get this changed."

Amos straightened up and looked at Sarah. "Talk to who? Who's going to override the Syndicate? I'm sure the announcement has already gone out that I'm willing to sacrifice myself so that humanity can evolve to its final destiny, overcoming the entropy barrier."

"You are correct," the president said. "Although we do not use the word 'sacrifice,' because we believe there is a chance you can survive and join us in Kairos. Once humanity develops another evolved, then more can follow. Amos, you will be like Moses, leading humanity to their salvation."

Sarah grabbed Amos's face, forcing him to look at her. "No! This is insanity!"

Amos shrugged. "For the past two millennia, humankind has been willing to make great sacrifices to push evolution forward. What am I in the greater scope of that sacrifice? Just a speck."

Sarah started crying. "Don't use my words against me, you bastard!"

Amos took Sarah's hands in his and pulled them down off his face. They stood there for a moment looking into each other's eyes, Sarah pleading silently for him to figure out some way to change things.

Finally, Amos turned to the hive. "When shall we begin?"

38.

"Do you think Stephen Hawking is in there?" Reilly asked eagerly.

"No, he lived too long ago. The current hive of consciousness wasn't created for at least another thousand years," Jahan replied dismissively.

"All right everyone, let's stay focused here," Din interjected.

"Commander, you may have known, but the rest of us are still coming to terms with the fact the Syndicate is a hive of consciousness, much less that this ship is devoted to it," Reilly said, leaning forward in his seat.

"I understand, but we have pressing matters to discuss," Din replied, trying to regain control over his officers.

"Wait, let me get this straight," Reilly continued. "The . . . people in the hive don't use their real names, right? They make up new characters to mask their identity."

"Correct. This is necessary to create the illusion of mortality and the passage of leadership," Din answered patiently.

"But that means we could have had one person governing us for the past three hundred years!" Reilly pressed.

"No, there are thousands of people loaded into the hive. Each has to declare their interest in running for office and then go through the democratic process just like in our reality," Jahan explained.

"Who checks those processes?" Sig asked.

"Excuse me?"

"Who checks that it isn't the same 'person' changing identities to make us think there's a transition of control over the Syndicate?"

"Well, the galactic constitution defines the checks and balances between the congressional, judicial, and administrative sides of the government—"

"So they know?" Sig interrupted.

"Does who know what?" Din asked impatiently.

"Do the judges know the Syndicate is a hive?"

"Well, no—"

"And the CEO? I understand the position is more of an administrator who signs off on legislation created by the Syndicate. But would that person know?"

"No, because technically, this ship falls under the control of the Syndicate's armed forces and not the military." Din was growing more agitated.

"I always wondered about that!" Reilly said to no one in particular. "Why the Syndicate required its own military structure."

"We're more of a science ship than a military ship," Sig pushed back.

"No, we're more of self-sustaining fortress than a science ship," Guan interjected. "Anything scientific is focused on the entropy barrier."

"That explains why we've always been able to determine our own course," Jahan replied. "I always wondered why we didn't need to remain closer to E-Three and the supposed Syndicate home."

"Silence!" Commander Din's voice reverberated against the walls of the bridge's conference room. "If the captain was here he could answer your questions, but he is tending to Amos."

"Amos. Are we really going to support his plan? He's only fourteen, and this plan will likely destroy us, if not all of humanity," Guan said with a sneer in his voice.

"Not to mention he already almost killed us with that last stunt!" Sig added.

"That last 'stunt' probably saved all of us," Mal broke in. "He may be fourteen, but he is the evolved. His brain works well beyond anything our combined efforts could muster."

"He's a traitor!" Guan yelled. "Almost killed the captain, and now he'll likely destroy the Syndicate."

"The Syndicate," Sig said with a sneer. "I don't see why I should care about a bunch of people who are at best deceitful, at worst, not even human anymore."

"Are you saying that because they're not organic they are somehow less than human, that their opinions don't matter?" Jahan asked.

"No! I'm not saying that," Sig replied angrily.

"There is a long history of silicon life forms elected to the Syndicate. Why is the hive any different?" Jahan pressed.

"For starters, because now they're all silicon-based life forms!"

"Based on organic life forms," Mal said in an attempt to offer a bridge between the two.

"But still silicon life forms that have lost their humanness," Sig said, shooting a warning look at Mal.

"What does that mean?" Jahan asked, continuing to stare at Sig.

"Look, whether any of us like it or not, the Syndicate remains our governing body. All of you voted during the last election—"

"I voted, but I didn't know for what!" Sig said, turning his attention to Mal.

"Enough!" Commander Din pounded his fist on the table, silencing everyone. He eyeballed all of the officers around the table before proceeding. "I realize this is a lot to take in. When this over, we will either all be dead, rendering this discussion moot, or have plenty of time to debate political science. For now, I need your full attention on the task at hand. The Syndicate remains our freely elected governing body and our primary interest. Let me remind you we all swore an oath to the Syndicate to uphold their decisions."

Din paused and looked around the table. Slowly each officer straightened and put on his or her officer mask. When everyone was focused on him, he proceeded. "All right. This plan will require all of our focus and all of the ship's energy. Mal, we're going to need all available engines online. Four running at peak should suffice, but let's have the remaining one ready to go should we need it. Also, what's the status of engine two?"

"Understood, sir. We're already going through the ramp-up procedures to make sure engine five and six are ready to go. Engine two is likely still inoperable after the sudden stop next to Kairos."

"Work on getting it operational. If this whole thing blows, it may offer our only power to get away from here."

"Yes, sir."

"Reilly, let us know what you need for power. I have a feeling this is going to consume every channel we have available. Keeping everything running and synchronized is going to take a minor miracle. If there's even one hiccup, we risk losing the Syndicate completely. I'll work with you to ensure you have everything you need."

Reilly took a long breath before replying. "Understood." He shifted slightly in his chair. "Sir, I'd like access to the hive so I can double check the hardwiring. It's not that I don't trust—"

"Granted. I agree with you that we need to check and double check all connections and systems. The systems are already in place for the Syndicate to do an emergency upload out of the ship, but this scenario is unique."

Reilly shifted again in his seat.

"Anything else?" Din asked. "Please speak up now."

"Sorry, sir. It's a personal concern," Reilly said. "I just didn't realize everyone in the Syndicate is silicon-based. I've always voted to support policies supporting silicon life forms, but now that I know all of them are silicon, I'm a little overwhelmed at the importance—"

"Just trust the systems are in place, trust your fellow officers, and trust your crew. After that, all there is to do is your job. Can you do your job?"

Reilly gazed up at Din with a lost look in his eyes.

"Reilly, we need your best effort. You need to focus on the task. Do not allow other issues to distract you. Understood?"

Reilly's eyes focused on Din, and his look hardened. "Yes, sir. I will do my job."

"Thank you. Now, doctor, are the systems ready to handle any injuries?

"Yes, sir. Everyone is ready for any problems that may occur," Doctor Daman replied.

Din turned to Sig. "I want our sensors open to anything while this is going on. If you see any unusual or unexpected fluctuations in signals coming from anywhere around us, I want to be notified. Also, I want everything recorded. Assuming this is successful, we're going to want to analyze everything that happened."

Sig nodded. "We'll have it covered."

"Guan, we'll need our defenses lowered during the process, but I want weapons available if anything or anyone unexpected show up."

"Roger that."

"Finally, navigation. I want a clear exit away from here should this sector become unstable. Chances are if it goes wrong, we won't even have time to react, but I want to be prepared with a way out."

Jahan nodded. "Got it."

"The situation may become . . . dynamic, so I want a constant evaluation process underway determining the best course of action."

"Yes, sir."

Din gazed proudly at his officers. "We've trained for these types of situations. Everyone remain focused on your task and trust that Amos can pull this off. Beyond that, I believe Bina is on the other side looking out for us." Din paused as he looked around the room. "That gives us two evolved, twice as many as the last time we tried reaching out to Kairos. In my book, that doubles our chances."

39.

Amos lay on his bed staring up at the ceiling. His mind, for once, was completely empty. If he was going to accomplish what he needed to do, he needed to be completely focused and rested. Focus he could muster, but sleep eluded him.

Restless, he rolled onto his side and checked in with the ship's computer, to which he had been re-connected. He'd been lying there for the total time he usually slept, which had seemed like three times that amount. Annoyed, he sat up and swung his legs over the edge of the bed so that he was in a seated position.

Come on, Amos, he thought to himself. *This is going to take all of you, possibly even consume you.* He pushed that final thought from his mind. It was not helpful to think of all the "what ifs."

He stood up and walked over to his sink. He filled it with cold water and splashed it onto his face. Thanks to his connection to the ship's power source, he felt somewhat energetic, even if he was not rested mentally. It was his mental energy that he needed. Maybe when his mind was uploaded he would feel refreshed.

How strange it must be to upload yourself into a computer, he thought. Then he laughed. As opposed to beaming your consciousness out into space. That was normal, apparently.

He stared at his wet face in the mirror. His eyes were bloodshot, and his face looked tired with large puffy sleep sacks under his eyes. He thought he looked like a war refugee, slightly malnourished despite his rich diet on board the ship.

Lots of luck fulfilling your plus-two requirement with a face like that, he joked to himself.

"Ms. President." Amos pushed the message out to the network to the Syndicate.

"Yes. Are you rested?" her calm, feminine voice replied. "We weren't expecting to begin for another few hours."

"Another few hours will not help. I've finished making all the necessary preparations. Might as well get this going."

"Understood. I will notify the captain to prepare the upload program. You should report to Dr. Daman's office."

Amos bowed his head. The truth was, that was the last place he wanted to perform this task, but it was also the best due to its immediate access to medical support should something go wrong.

"Understood. I will make my way there now."

Amos looked around his room, wondering if he was seeing it for the last time, and then left through the door.

Sarah was waiting for him by the door leading to Dr. Daman's office. She had not slept either, and she looked like she had been crying. When she saw Amos walk out of the lift, she ran over and threw her arms around him.

"Tell me you've come up with another way!" she said, sobbing as they hugged.

"You know as well as me that this is the only way. My only hope is to fulfill the mission and hope that I find myself in a better place."

Sarah buried her face in his shoulder, continuing to sob. Amos put his hands on her shoulders and pushed her back gently. His face was like stone as he tried to remain focused on the challenge ahead. When Sarah lifted her wet eyes up to his though, he melted slightly.

"Sarah, please! It will work out."

"I . . . I want . . . to go with you. Please, take me too!" she blubbered between tears.

Amos's face changed to concern. "Sarah, I'm not sure what I'm about to try is even possible. It's very dangerous, could kill all of us. I need you next to me, or at least next to my body, to help add strength and watch over me."

Tears streamed down her face, but she nodded in understanding.

Amos took his hands off her shoulders and clasped her hands. "Sarah, I need your strength right now. Please, can you do this?"

After a moment, Sarah straightened up, sniffed away her tears, wiped her eyes with her hands, and transformed her face into a mask of stability. Amos watched the transformation, and, when it was complete, gave her a curt nod.

He turned to the door, which slid open, and strode through into the doctor's office, Sarah behind him.

Waiting inside were Doctor Daman and Captain Melville. They broke off their conversation and turned toward the door as Amos and Sarah entered.

"Are we ready to do this?" Captain Melville asked in a voice that conveyed only a tinge of concern. Amos nodded to him and then looked at the doctor.

"Doctor Daman, have you made all the preparations I requested?"

Dr. Daman nodded. "They all seem quite reasonable and understandable. We will do our best to provide the necessary energy and strength to you during the transmission."

"Thank you."

"There's just one more detail that must be answered," Daman continued.

Amos looked at him. "Yes?"

"Since this is possibly a one-way trip, what would you like us to do with your body if—"

"I leave that decision up to Ms. Laka."

Amos turned to Sarah, who looked like she was about to lose it again. "Sarah, I trust you will know what to do when the time is right."

Sarah looked up at Amos with watery eyes. She seemed to gather strength from his stare. The more she focused, the more she was able to pull herself together. The look in his eyes effectively grabbed her shoulders and pulled her up straight. She still let out a sniff to catch an uncooperative runny nose as she nodded at Amos.

Amos turned back to Dr. Daman. "Is the Syndicate prepared?"

"Yes. They have started to queue up for the passage. The first ones have already been compacted into the smallest data files possible."

Amos shook his head. "No. They must go in parallel. It is absolutely necessary if they are to have any chance."

Daman and Melville both opened their mouths to question the request, only to be interrupted by a message from the president.

"Why parallel transmissions? This request increases the risk if something goes wrong during the transmission, potentially losing the

Syndicate completely. We have always queued to minimize the risk of loss during transmissions."

"Ms. President, as you said before, your numbers are your strength," Amos replied. "Since none of you were fully evolved before entering the hive, and many are even less evolved than that, you need your collective numbers to hold your structure when you enter Kairos. To beam each of you one at a time likely means you would be lost as the relatively small amount of information each consciousness represents was consumed by the larger consciousness inside Kairos. Each of you would be torn apart, losing your feeling of self in the process before the next person could be beamed in. Think of it as holding hands."

A moment of silence followed as Amos assumed a discussion ensued within the hive. Whether they accepted this request was absolutely critical in Amos's mind. If they declined, then all of them would likely be lost, but it would also make his chances more remote.

"We have decided to divide ourselves into two batches. This should provide enough strength to maintain our consciousness," she said finally, "but also ensure that none of us are lost."

Amos had expected this reply. "I'm sorry, Ms. President, but I must insist. You want to go in at full strength, not half strength. By splitting yourselves up, you reduce your chances significantly."

She was silent for another moment. "We have discussed the proposal, compared our views, debated amongst ourselves, and finally reached a unanimous decision. We accept your proposal, because you will also be part of the parallel transmission as part of the hive. We agree it should ensure the strongest possible structure inside Kairos."

"I'm sorry, but that's not possible. I simply cannot be inside the hive and provide the transmission highway over which the hive must travel. I cannot be in two places at once."

More silence followed, during which Amos grew nervous. If they didn't accept his argument, then he might be forced to upload himself into the hive. The thought of spending eternity with these people was not pleasant.

The silence stretched on longer than before. Amos looked over at Sarah, who was watching him intently. Her face was a mask of strength, although her eyes hinted at some confusion about his requests. Amos turned to Melville, who was also watching him carefully. He seemed more suspicious but held back from saying anything. He gave Amos a questioning look, almost like a warning. Amos wondered how his actions would be judged: sabotage, betrayal, or salvation. He saw nothing but precipices on all sides. Dr. Daman appeared focused on setting up the instruments for the transmission. He was looking at the far wall, his mind connected deeply to the network. Amos started to get an uneasy feeling in his stomach that something was wrong when the reply finally came back.

"After much debate, we agree to your requests. I don't agree with them, because I think you risk the Syndicate's existence, but our rules dictate that the will of the majority decides, and a small majority has accepted your request."

Amos let out the air in his lungs that he had not realized he was holding in. "Thank you. I believe this solution provides the best possible outcome for all of us."

"The best solution for the Syndicate is the best solution for you," she replied. "Now, we will need a few minutes to pack up everyone for the transmission. I hope to see you on the other side."

"Good luck, Ms. President," Amos replied.

Silence followed. Amos was a bit stunned that his request had been accepted. He turned to Sarah, who continued to maintain a mask of composure, although her eyes suggested questions were swirling in her mind.

"I hope you know what you're doing, Mr. Hare," Captain Melville said. "It would be a shame if my orders from the Syndicate of protecting them led to harming you."

Amos shuddered as he felt the captain's piercing eyes. "As I said, this is the best way for all of us."

Melville held his stare on Amos and then nodded. "Okay. Let's get on with it."

40.

Amos followed Dr. Daman through the doorway that led to the back room in his office. Instead of a table, there was a bed in the room. The room looked like mission control central with layers of holographic displays encircling the bed.

"We have routed all of the ship's systems into this room," Daman explained. "From here, we have complete control over the ship, from Communications to Engineering. All personnel are in a state of readiness, monitoring the progress and able to respond in a flash. I will be able to monitor your progress and adjust systems to help your effort. We chose this room to make you the most comfortable."

Amos winced slightly at the last comment as he looked around the room and couldn't help but notice the wall he had run into during his first meeting with the doctor. He looked back at Dr. Daman and offered a weak smile.

"We also have complete control over Weapons should something unexpected happen," Melville added.

Amos gave him a nervous look before replying, "I certainly hope that doesn't happen."

Melville locked eyes with Amos. "Me, too."

"Amos, please lie down on the bed," Daman said, motioning to it.

Amos bent over the bed, moving through another holographic display that floated over it. "Honestly? I thought we had progressed past all this holographic stuff," Amos said to no one in particular as he squirmed into a semi-comfortable position just under the display.

"Most of this stuff is for back-up purposes," Daman explained. "We need to make sure we can watch your progress as well as our communication directly through the network."

Amos nodded as he continued to wiggle his shoulders to try and loosen some of the tension in them and find a comfortable position.

"Could I please have a chair next to the bed?" Sarah asked in a stern voice, making it more of an order. Amos had found that tone highly successful at making him do things he did not want to.

Daman opened his mouth to protest, but Melville gave a small nod. "All right, Ms. Laka. Please bring in one chair from the reception room. Be careful not to disturb any of the displays though."

Sarah walked out of the room and returned, arms straining while carrying the eboney chair made by Amos's distant grandfather. She stoically lifted it over her head, a quiver in her brow hinting at its weight, and followed the path Amos had taken through the holographic displays and between the doctor and captain. When she reached the bed, she continued to hold the chair over her head while she looked down at Amos, who lay slack mouthed staring at the chair.

A tear rolled down the side of his face. She stood over him with chair held aloft, reminding Amos of the strength and sacrifices of his family. For a moment he thought she might drop the chair onto him, wrecking any immediate possibility of the transmission occurring in some perverse attempt to rescue him. A firm resoluteness in his eyes seemed to make her think twice and she lowered the chair into place next to his bed.

She sat down, and Amos extended his hand. She took it in hers, squeezing it as a show of strength. Amos smiled up at her, which brought a smile to her face.

"All right, I'm ready." Amos announced.

"I'll let everyone know to begin the process," Melville replied.

Amos felt the communications systems reach out and offer connections to him. He accepted their request, and his mind engaged directly with them. The Syndicate would be transmitted to him through Communications. Their systems provided the most bandwidth, and the officers could monitor their progress, making adjustments if necessary.

"We're set up on our end," Amos heard Reilly announce to everyone. "Awaiting your instructions, Amos."

A shiver ran down his spine. He was about to try something that might be impossible—push the silicon-based superconscious through his subconscious. In theory, it should work, but Amos wasn't sure how the highly structured hive would flow through his mind's unstructured subconscious. Worse yet, the collective supraconscious of Kairos might reject the hive and destroy him in the process.

Pushing doubt aside, Amos squeezed Sarah's hand before relaxing his mind to enter the subconscious. Once accomplished, he reached out toward Kairos, trying to determine its exact location. This took some time, because Amos had to go slowly, methodically. He only wanted to touch the outside of Kairos with his mind. If he rushed and jumped into the middle of Kairos, his mind would be sucked in, and he would be lost. He needed to find the boundary, establish a transmission channel to the edge, and then push the signal over the final distance and into Kairos.

"Amos! What are you doing?! This isn't what you want!" The words hit Amos like a sledgehammer, causing him to falter and almost lose the signal.

"What was that?" Melville's question pushed into his mind, followed immediately by Sarah's.

"Are you all right?"

Apparently, they were able to monitor him somewhat in the subconscious. He had grimaced at the sudden and direct intrusion from the superconscious. It felt like razors spinning through his mind.

Amos gave Sarah's hand another slight squeeze and then responded to Melville through the superconscious. "I've found Kairos. Working to stabilize the connection."

Amos turned his full attention back to the supraconscious. "Bina?"

Bina's alarmed thought came back, shaking his resolve. "Amos! Don't make the same mistake I made! I am incomplete! I cannot fully control Kairos, so it is very dangerous to come this close!"

Amos struggled to calm himself. "Bina, can I help?"

"Possibly," she replied after a moment of hesitation, "but then humanity will be lost. Is that what you want?"

After a pause, Amos sent out a multi-layered message to Bina. He was trying to use the emotional messages they had worked on back in the habitat to create a message richer and deeper in meaning. He mixed in a feeling of confidence combined with a slight feeling of knowing, similar to what one might send with a look to another. He wasn't sure now if Captain Melville or the Syndicate was listening, and he wanted this conversation to remain private.

"Understood. I hope to save humanity."

Alarm mixed with confusion, transforming into reluctance came back to him. "Then you must pull back! I can't help you without significant consequences! I can't reach out to you without sucking in the very existence around you."

A feeling of understanding and pleading accompanied his thought. "That's what I feared. However, I still need you to help with what I am about to send."

Alarm again hit him. "Amos, no! By sending information to me, Kairos becomes unstable and may expand and consume you."

Amos sent another pleading message. "There's no other way. Do what you believe is best."

Amos closed the conversation with Bina, effectively hitting mute while keeping the transmission channel open. Then he sent a command to Captain Melville. "Proceed."

Amos felt the data begin to enter his mind from Communications. It started slowly but ramped up quickly. Amos struggled not to lose himself in the torrent of data. It was like a river of acid had been diverted toward him, and he was trying to build a dam to hold it back. His mind strained under the pressure, struggled to work as his thoughts and commands were drowned by the swirling pool of information growing in his head.

Voices sounded in his mind, some panicked, others authoritative in their demands for concentration and calm. Amos did his best to ignore them, contain them into the vessel he imagined in his mind to avoid the information spilling out across his synapses and destroying him. His skull throbbed. His head felt like it was about to explode.

"I'm lost!" a thought came bubbling up from some deeper level of his consciousness.

"An abomination!" was another unintentional thought he wasn't sure was his own.

He couldn't control his thoughts; they were completely swamped. It was like the supraconscious was rising up in full-scale rebellion against what the conscious part of his mind was attempting.

Suddenly, he realized the pain wasn't only in his head but also in his hand. It was excruciating, like his hand was about to snap off, but it gave him something to focus on outside his head. It may have saved him as he struggled to determine the source of the pain.

It was caused by someone hurting his body, crushing his hand. Illumination entered his mind as he realized that Sarah was still holding his hand, watching him. His body must be exhibiting enormous strain, and her worry was causing her to almost break his hand as she squeezed it.

Rather than push the pain away, he embraced it, made it part of his consciousness. Somehow, this helped him to ignore the acidic pain in his head. It also helped him to focus his thoughts momentarily, releasing the data out of his mind and into the thin, tenuous channel connected to Kairos. The release was orgasmic, especially after the pain he had felt, holding onto the data from the superconscious. While still struggling, he felt like he had regained some control over his thoughts.

But it wasn't working. Amos focused on the stream of data. He realized the information wasn't flowing properly. The start of the data stream had entered the connection but then seemed plugged up. Was Kairos rejecting it? Could the structured data even flow through his subconscious?

Struggling to form his thoughts, Amos remembered that he had set up the connection to Kairos from his body on the ship. The connection was not fully formed all the way to Kairos. He needed to force his consciousness down the channel right to the edge of Kairos and push the data through the last barrier.

Gradually, Amos crept out into the subconscious channel with his consciousness. It felt like the powers of existence were pushing against him, attempting to prevent what he was trying to do.

The structured energy and data of the superconscious and the Syndicate screamed past him, trying to find an outlet. More voices in the stream were panicked as they sensed something was wrong. He felt pieces of the Syndicate in the stream attempt to pull back and swim back against the current to the apparent safety of the hive. If Amos didn't push it through the final barrier soon, the channel would disintegrate, releasing everything into empty space and losing himself.

The synapses in his brain burned from the acidic Syndicate consciousness running through it. Amos extended his mind outward, probing until he felt the edge of Kairos. A small amount of resistance pushing back on him defined Kairos, similar to the surface of a bubble.

Hope I don't pop Kairos, Amos mused grimly. He felt his body shudder at the thought. With a final effort, he pushed a single thought through the barrier into Kairos.

Ready.

It was mostly a thought to himself, a way to reinforce his will and hold himself, his mind, together.

The surface of Kairos changed slightly in response to him. At first, Amos thought Kairos had withdrawn, possibly making the connection unstable and flinging him out into space as diffusing energy. But when the connection held, he realized a passage into Kairos had been created, or at least a hole for the data to pass through. The data swirling in the connection found the opening and leapt into it.

Relief flooded Amos as the pressure in his brain subsided. The relief was short-lived as Amos felt himself pulled toward the hole. It was like a whirlpool had been created as data swirled around him and fell away into the hole.

Panicking, Amos reached desperately for the thin line of consciousness that connected him to his body and the ship. It took all of his concentration to maintain his grasp on the thin strand. He felt like he was on the end of a whip, flailing back and forth over the abyss of his subconscious. He struggled to maintain his grip on his reality, his mind. Amos felt himself weaken due to the strain. The thought bubbled up to simply let go and fall away into the hole to Kairos.

His close proximity to Kairos was weakening his resolve. Kairos was like the mythical Sirens, calling out to him, luring him, pulling him toward a promised utopia. It seemed to whisper about a better existence through the portal. All the mysteries of the universe revealed, offering the ability to explore every dimension, to see the dark matter permeating existence. What would it matter if he entered Kairos? He would likely survive, join Bina, and leave this four-dimensional sinkhole to return to the truth in the universe.

Amos began to release his strand of consciousness, letting it slip from his mind as he was pulled toward Kairos. A sense of calm, serene emptiness flowed into him. Objects in his reality seemed irrelevant. Why fight it? Utopia was there. All he had to do was let go.

An image of Sarah tumbled into his mind. She was crying. Ignoring it at first, Amos found himself drawn back to the image. He focused on it, and a twinge reverberated from somewhere deep inside his subconscious.

Expanding his scope, he saw Captain Melville working frantically to save the ship from disaster, and then. . . nothing. Their images were consumed by Kairos, reduced to fluctuations in the fabric of space time. They were simply objects that dissolved back into the four-dimensional sinkhole he had escaped.

Panic fluttered up inside him. No, not simply objects. Relationships! How could he abandon Sarah? Humanity? That momentary flicker of images had reminded him of something. Was it already too late? Had he glimpse the future or the present? Confused, his mind spun as he lost his sense of space and time.

Amos pulled together what remained of his mind through sheer willpower. He focused intently on the weakening strand that led back to his world, repeating to himself with all the strength he could muster that it was his world, where he belonged. It was this thinnest of threads back to his mind that Amos used to pull himself back to the edge of the reality he knew. He felt like a salmon fighting upstream, only making progress through sheer determination.

Yet the Sirens continued to wail, and the acidic river of sewage that was the Syndicate coursed through him. It was too much. He couldn't move against the torrent of information flowing past, couldn't resist the whirlpool sucking him into Kairos. He was tired, depleted to the depths of his soul. His willpower was weakening; he simply didn't have the energy left to fight it.

Amos closed his consciousness, severed the thread that led back to his world, and prepared to enter Kairos. As he did, a sense of relief, of excitement, filled him. Joy at joining with Bina. Elation at learning about the true nature of the universe. Satisfied he had fulfilled his mission for humanity, or at least that he had done his best, he let go of himself completely.

41.

Emptiness. Amos was empty. Void of mindful thoughts yet clear. He was at peace, floating with Kairos but separate from it. Kairos made sense to him. It was alive . . . in a way. No, more like it was what gave life, creation, into what was a perversion of reality in which humanity existed.

Without Kairos, there was no life as we knew it. While separate, it also surrounded and pervaded the only reality humans knew, or at least thought they knew. Without Kairos, humanity's four dimensions were only a series of pre-determined mechanical sequences of physical interaction without purpose. Humanity's reality had no purpose without Kairos and would simply disperse into space, lifeless.

Euphoria filled Amos with emptiness.

42

Confusion surfaced in Amos, filled his emptiness, and tore it apart. Searing pain consumed him, shredding his essence. Panic overtook confusion. Darkness.

––––––––––

Amos wondered at his place. He was still in the torrent stream of data outside Kairos. This shouldn't be. He should have been sucked into Kairos by now. He spread out his reawakened consciousness, looking desperately at his predicament. He found a thin, tenuous strand attached to his consciousness that was straining, about to snap. Had it always been there?

He explored the strand, tried to understand it. How had it come to him? What should he do with it? He pushed his consciousness into the strand, trying to understand it. A feeling of astonishment overtook him.

It was Sarah! She was holding onto him with all of her energy, not letting go. But she couldn't hold on for much longer. She had already used up most of herself. It was a wonder that the strand had not snapped already or that she had not been pulled into Kairos with him.

Amos began to panic. The strain was killing her. She had to let go, or her conscious self would shatter, leaving her an empty shell. He considered pulling her into Kairos with him. At least that way it would end her completely, put her out of misery.

Then a thought rose up inside Amos, weak and so garbled that he didn't understand it as first. He tried to ignore it, but the thought persisted, pressing on his consciousness. He focused on it, tried to interpret it, but it was like translating gibberish.

"Sarah! Let go! Let me go!" Amos pushed the thought toward Sarah, but she didn't respond. Either his message was lost in the flood of data or she was ignoring his plea, refusing to obey.

Amos was about to try again, make one last effort to cut her free, when he realized the thought that had bubbled up wasn't so much a thought as an emotion, primal and raw. Furthermore, the emotion wasn't his. It was coming from Sarah, from the most ancient of sources inside her brain, within the area typically considered instinctive. As he reached out to the emotion, he felt intense pain that grabbed the very core of his being, threatening to shut down his will to survive. He pulled back, stunned at first at the intensity of the feeling.

Pain? It made sense she was in pain, but this pain was not physical, not even conscious. It came from deep within her. Amos puzzled over it, which relieved him momentarily from his own torture. He reached out again cautiously, trying to confirm what he had felt, analyze what it meant.

When he touched her, he confirmed the pain was not from anything physical, which surprised him, given the strain Sarah was feeling. Instead, the pain was from loss, or fear of loss. The emotion was rich, deeper than any communication he had ever shared before. Just by touching the emotion, more information about Sarah passed to him than he had shared even with Bina. It felt like this raw emotion reached out and enveloped him, consuming him within it. He struggled at first to push away, to escape the pain she was feeling, but found he could not. Trapped, he sought to explore his predicament, understand it.

He realized quickly he wasn't so much trapped as connected. Connected like two magnets might connect, each unable to pull away from the other. His essence was pressed against the strand of her essence, not letting him release and enter Kairos. Finding that he couldn't separate, Amos lowered his boundaries to try and communicate with Sarah instead. He hoped that, together, they could discover a way out, a path to salvation.

Instead, he found himself hopelessly intertwined with her, like each of them were a pile of string that had become knotted together. The more intertwined they became, the more Amos realized the true source of the pain.

Love.

Sarah was deeply in love with him, couldn't imagine her life without him. He discovered one more thing that shocked him even more.

He loved her, though maybe not as deeply. His was only the seed of love, a friendship with infinite promise. He realized that pulling apart from her was as hopeless as two lovers trying to avoid making eye contact.

Unable to untie the knot, and understanding the situation better, Amos opened himself further. He lowered his emotional defenses, the walls that defined his self. Instead of helping disengage, he became one with Sarah, understood her completely, realizing her wants and desires.

The intimacy grew between them until they were like one entity. The love she felt for him was like water and soil to the seed inside of him. It sprouted, grew magnificently inside him. It was like the strength of an ancient sequoia tree from E-1 had planted itself inside of him, drove its roots deep into his self, forever. The feeling was powerful, like he could do anything, take on any challenge. His soul soared at the positive energy from his love for Sarah.

Amos knew he was unable to separate who he was with who Sarah was. His existence depended on her survival, on her happiness. A feeling of joy hit him, overwhelming him more than the initial feeling of pain. The joy was coming from Sarah as she recognized his touch, his essence mixing with hers.

Amos felt himself shudder, and something cracked within him. An ecstatic, even erotic feeling overtook him as he saw himself as Sarah saw him, the love she held for him. He opened himself up to her, embraced her, and pulled her closer to him.

He felt his body go through painful convulsions as it was overwhelmed by his joyful soul, which wept uncontrollably. He and Sarah embraced again, intermingled, bound to one another. Amos couldn't explain the feeling. Ecstasy was too tame, any other word too weak. All he knew was that, combined, they were more than what they were as individuals.

He saw himself through Sarah, how she felt when she looked at him, felt him. He finally understood what she saw, her wonder at his abilities, her desire to have him as a lover. Her dreams of their union overtook his mind. Visions of children floated through his perspective. He even saw himself as a grandfather, bouncing his grandchildren on his knee in some romanticized look into the future. This was Sarah's deepest desire, what she had kept hidden from him, fearful of how he would react.

Sorrow filled Amos's soul, almost crippling him. How could he have been so blind? So uncaring? So thoughtless toward this beautiful creature who loved him? Amos felt a warmth flood through him, coming from Sarah as she tried to comfort him. She knew everything about him now, his dreams, fears, and desires. She accepted them just as he accepted her completely. His sorrow changed to joy at finding someone special, a perfect match to him.

A clear thought came to him. He wasn't sure if it originated within him or if it came from Sarah, but the meaning was unmistakable.

"Come home!"

In a flash, the true purpose of his life filled him. He had to get back to the ship, find a way to lead humanity to salvation, whatever that may be. For him to enter Kairos was failure, selfish, even dangerous. If he allowed himself to enter Kairos, he would be no better than the Syndicate.

Had Bina been trying to tell him that all along? Trying to ride the fine line between guiding him without influencing him? Bina had made that mistake, allowed herself to become seduced by Kairos. Maybe another time, another existence, he could use Kairos. Bina could help him when the time was right. But for now, the fact that she was inside Kairos, had become part of it, represented a massive risk to humanity, to the structure of the universe around them.

Kairos was unstable and uncontrollable. Bina was doing her best to minimize the risk, to provide time for humanity to find a solution, if there was one. But her existence, her efforts, ultimately increased the risk. Amos had limited time to escape and find another way.

He focused his energy on the thin strand that connected them back to their bodies. Sarah was barely holding onto it, pushing herself to the breaking point. He pushed himself toward the strand, toward Sarah. The reaction was immediate. Sarah grew stronger, more assertive. Her feeling of attachment to him, while complete, strengthened. It felt like Amos's essence was wrapped in an irresistible force. He could not break free, even if he wanted to.

The torrent of information that continued to flow past him forced Amos back to the present. He heard the members of the Syndicate screaming past him and through him toward Kairos. The feel of the information flow was changing. Initially, it had been excitement, eagerness. Now it was nervousness. The information wasn't pushed toward Kairos anymore; it was actually being sucked voraciously into the singularity. Amos didn't think he could stop the transfer even if he wanted to.

The speed of information increased steadily. Amos was surprised the ship's network could even send out that much information at once. He thought the captain must be using every available resource on the ship to reach this rate. It was like a raging river flowing past him, twisting and turning in various directions as he clung to a tree limb held out from the shore. If it wasn't for Sarah, he would have been lost long ago.

Sarah was pulling him now, giving him direction, sharing what little strength she had left to save him. Amos's energy was diminishing. He was struggling to keep moving upstream back to the ship. Concern blossoming into alarm was overtaking Sarah. He didn't think he was going to make it. He simply couldn't focus his remaining energy on moving in a coherent direction.

The torrent of data began to rip through his mind, his consciousness. It caused a different kind of pain. It felt like a bitterly cold wind on his face, a feeling he knew would cause frostbite and leave scars. It was intensely painful, but it also felt like the flow of data was destroying the very fibers of his being.

Amos pushed back against the flow of information, tried to hold together the strings of his mind that enabled rational thought. But he couldn't stop the flow from entering his mind. If he tried to wall it off, it pooled in his mind again, causing additional pain.

Changing strategies, Amos tried to divert the river through specific pathways, protecting the critical areas of himself while sacrificing others. It was killing parts of him, he knew, but he had no choice.

Slowly, Amos was able to put up some buffers in his brain that redirected the data, relieving some of his pain. But now his mind was growing increasingly numb as shock sank in. His time was running out.

Blackness closed in, darkening his mind. He gathered himself for one last push. The fear of what might happen to him, to Sarah, if he lost consciousness kept him present. A secondary worry loomed in his mind. If he passed out, the connection would be severed, destroying everything in the channel, destabilizing the ship's systems and potentially even Kairos. This entire part of the universe might collapse, explode, or worse. He could not let that happen.

Desperate to find something firm to hold onto with his mind, he returned to the pain he felt in his hand. The pain had grown, feeling like his bones had been crushed. The pain was intense but it was only a fraction of what he felt inside his head. Amos flung his conscious thoughts toward the pain in his hand, knowing it was his connection to the reality he knew, to life.

The pain in his head increased. He felt what must have been neurons inside his physical head explode, synapses flood with chemicals as they struggled to handle the data flowing through them. In a final desperate move to hold onto his sanity, he screamed inside his mind.

Then everything went white.

43.

In the pursuit of learning, every day something is acquired. In pursuit of Tao, every day something is dropped.

LAO TZU

Amos awoke to nothing. No sound, no smell, not even a feeling. His mind, his being, was divorced from his body, from any form with mass. All of the signals his body typically sent were absent, even the tiniest of sensations, like a heartbeat or a breath.

A thought fluttered through his mind. Was the absence of everything . . . something? Like the concept of absence has some form? No, there was something.

I think, therefore I am . . . what?

That question stumped him. It was like the question about the kernel of what defined him had blundered up from some amorphous abyss.

The thought of laughter intruded into his mind, burbling up from deep inside like a drunk juggler falling face-first into his consciousness. There was nothing attached to it though, no emotion or physical response. It was like watching someone else laugh when he didn't get the joke.

Amos puzzled over the concept of laughter. He felt no surprise, joy, fear, or elation. None of the physical sensations, like tears running down his face. He had no face. His lungs should have gasped for air, his stomach tightening at the laughter. There was nothing physical about him like lungs or a mouth to provide those sensations though, only silence and emptiness.

He paused as another thought floated into his mind. This place was strange. Shouldn't he feel something? Shouldn't his chest tighten with fear? His vision constrict in panic and confusion? Was this what death felt like? But if this was the end, shouldn't he feel a sense of calm, of acceptance? He didn't even feel that. Since it didn't feel like death, perhaps he wasn't dead.

An emotion surged up from within, pushing its way through from a deeper, darker, more primal part of his mind. His thoughts blurred as rage overtook him. Logical thoughts were pushed aside as his very being seemed to flex outwards. It was the type of anger that accompanied caring for something deeply, with his very being. Rage at the complete sense of loss, like his soul had been violated, shredded into something perverse.

What's happening to me? What happened to me?

Anger transformed into wonder.

Why am I here? Where is here? How did I come to . . . this?

His mind churned, trying to make sense of things. He reached again for a familiar feeling. He tried to move an arm, a leg, nothing. A feeling of despair crept into his thoughts, growing inside as his impotence sank in deeper.

Then a calm, foreign thought pushed into his mind. "Open yourself, Amos."

Who was that? There should be no one else! Why would he think that?

Fear surged into his mind.

"Flee!"

But where? How?

Pushing aside his fear, his singular feeling changed to puzzlement. He realized he wasn't sure if he was more scared of the foreign thought, opening his eyes to reveal this world, or because he'd find he had no eyes. Fear consumed him. What was around him?

Light pushed into his consciousness, but he still couldn't feel his eyes, hadn't tried to open them. Instead, it was like someone was turning up the lights slowly, announcing "Behold!" like some god.

As the light intensified, he found there was nothing but light, everywhere, surrounding him. As it brightened, it tried to push into his mind, overwhelm him. The volume of light kept increasing uncontrollably. The illumination was becoming too painful to handle, like trying to comprehend billions upon billions of conversations at once. His mind could not absorb the volume of information pushing its way into him.

He fought to repel the light, close himself to it, but he couldn't turn it away. He changed strategies and strained to focus, to filter the light entering his mind. This strategy seemed to work better, the intensity dimming behind the filters. Slowly, individual light sources became recognizable, helping him to orient his mind.

Now with some bearings, Amos found he could change the focal point of his concentration with his thoughts. But so many lights were still pressing into his consciousness. Amos struggled to hold onto any coherent thought. It was still too much information, all of it trying to penetrate him, pushing into him with a survivalist's desperation. Amos felt his very being strain, the piercing pain of his essence pulling apart.

In a vain attempt to maintain his sanity, Amos picked out one light on which to concentrate. He strained against the intensity, like staring into the sun without eyelids. The sheer magnitude and power of the light threatened to burn through him.

He shifted his focus from the single point, searching desperately for a void of blackness, to find the emptiness that provided wisdom. But the light was everywhere. The lights were gaining clarity, but he had no control over them, could not block them out.

As he took it all in, he began to discern more and more points of lights, billions and billions. A feeling of slowness overtook him, like his momentum was retarded somehow. Accompanying the sensation was a sense of orientation, a sense that he existed in space. Lights were in front of him, behind him, above him, and below him. Disoriented, Amos struggled to make sense of it all. It felt wrong, like he was looking at himself inside-out.

Another emotion surged up into his mind: panic. Terror upon realizing he was a singular point of mass in space. How did he get there? Was he lost? How could he possibly find his way back home? Home? What was that in this space?

Confused by his own thoughts, he surveyed the lights around him. Slowly, he recognized some patterns, some clusters. Wasn't that a galaxy? A nebula? Why did he know that? Somehow he recognized his position, followed by a feeling that he had been there before. Strange, he didn't think he had ever been anywhere.

Yet, he recognized the Milky Way. He was staring at the solar system that contained E-1. The system was off in the distance, the sun appeared more like a large star, but he saw the planets circling the sun in some sped-up dynamic of their movement.

How did he get there? Amos swept his focus around himself, but nothing physical about him existed. His body was still, absent. Strange. Why would he need a body? For what purpose?

Movement startled him from his perverse thoughts, drawing his attention back to the stars in the Milky Way. They appeared to be moving in one direction. Amos focused on the stars, trying to work out the dynamic.

"Thoughts, if you leave me now, we are truly finished."

Laughter consumed him, or at least the thought of laughter.

Yes, the stars were moving. In fact, they were all accelerating in one direction. Amos moved his focal point to where all the stars appeared to approach. Nothing. Confused, Amos looked back at the stars to make sure he had seen them move. Yes, they had actually accelerated, forming a whirlpool around an empty space in the middle.

Amos watched in amazement, trying to understand what was happening. A black hole? Here? Where had it come from? It felt wrong.

Slowly at first, the stars nearest the center began to disappear, their light extinguished. Faster and faster, the stars at the center were sucked into the middle, disappearing.

Amos saw energy shoot out the top and bottom of the empty space in the middle. It looked like two beacons had been lit from the center, warning of unseen dangers despite the irresistible siren call.

Yet, something was wrong with the beacon lights. The light pouring out wasn't right. It was different from the light coming from the stars. Amos struggled to describe it until it hit him: death. The light was in disarray, wiped of any informational content, like it had been ripped apart, shredded beyond recognition. All of that energy emitting from the center was death. The end.

Dismay flooded Amos's mind. All of that energy wasted, consumed for no purpose. The energy shooting out from the center of the void had no purpose. A deep, dark depression overtook him.

Amos started to sink in into himself, trying to shut out the universe around him. A feeling of failure, followed by a loss of purpose. He turned his thoughts inward, but there was no inward. Instead, he found himself looking out again, back toward Earth, unable to shield his view.

The planets' orbits in the solar system had changed, become more elliptical. Even their shapes seemed stretched. Amos looked out at the rest of the stars and was alarmed to see that he was much closer to the nothingness at the center of the whirlpool.

Stars were consumed at a ferocious pace, blinking out in a continuous stream. The void in the middle of the whirlpool of stars had grown significantly. The black center seemed to reach out now, gulping up all matter and energy as it expanded outward. It was racing toward Earth's solar system. Or were the solar system and Amos approaching the void? The useless energy streaming out from the center was much brighter now than all the stars that remained.

Fear consumed Amos again. He tried frantically to figure out some way to move, some way to avoid the . . . Vacuity. That is what he named it, as if by naming it he could pull back everything it had consumed. Vacuity because it felt vacuous, simply a void.

He found himself in the whirlpool of stars and planets, spinning around the Vacuity. He watched in horror as the stars closest to him vanished, pulled hungrily to their death like a life devoured by an evil predator. The sun at the center of Earth's solar system looked like a long, stretched circle, pulled like an elastic band. The planets crashed into each other and then into the sun as everything was pulled closer together.

The Vacuity continued to grow, pulling in the sun and all the planets, snuffing them out like a candle. Amos tried to close himself, not wanting to watch his own demise. Yet, somehow he was saved, flung out from the orbit like an unwanted, disemboweled doll.

Momentary relief was replaced by bewilderment mixed with terror at what would happen next.

He watched the Vacuity grow, but now he remained outside its influence. Or maybe he had never been within its influence, rooted in a different dimension. Entire galaxies were accelerating toward the void. Stars and planets swirled past him as they circled around once, then twice, before vanishing.

Amos remained unaffected, as if he was no longer part of the universe but an outside observer. He watched in awe as entire galaxies disappeared, wiped from the inky background of the universe.

The light surrounding him dimmed due to the mammoth loss of stars. The energy that spewed out from the void simply dissipated into space, offering less and less light, less warmth, less hope.

A feeling of terror grew inside Amos, overtaking his original bewilderment. His mind twisted in on itself as the raw emotion of fear and loss overtook him. It was like he was disappearing as he watched, separated from it. His everything vanishing before his eyes!

Slowly, the light of the universe faded. Amos's mind struggled to save something, anything. He knew it was too late, but he wanted to save something, even a single photon or a quark.

He tried desperately to catch the last of the matter that whizzed past him, shocked again to find he had no influence over this universe. He was separate from it, completely cut off, powerless against its forces. Fear at what came next gripped him. An unknown future. Future? Another concept over which to puzzle.

Profound sadness overwhelmed his feeling of fear. As the last pieces of matter and light were consumed, he found himself all alone in the darkness. He was alone, lost, again. Primal fear welled up, and Amos shattered inward, an empty vessel with no further purpose.

44.

"Amos?"

"Amos, are you there?"

"Amos, let me know you're okay!"

"Amos!"

Amos found himself floating, but this time in the familiar environment of his subconscious. He struggled to make sense of it. Was he dreaming? Was he dead? Was he in Kairos? His thoughts scattered into nothing.

A meaningful subject within his mind coalesced again, and he found himself in the subconscious once more. His thoughts formed and then drifted away. He was unable to control his consciousness, his thoughts, in the subconscious. He decided it was easier to let fate control him, and he released any thoughts bound together within himself.

"Amos. Come to me."

The message was like a jar containing his free-forming thoughts within it, providing some sort of form to himself. Yet it felt like a god was shaking the jar, rattling his thoughts around until they mixed into the form of a continuous, conscious thought pattern.

Like specks of space dust pulled together by gravity, thoughts formed within him. Wondering at himself, his situation, his thoughts finally recognized the familiar voice calling to him.

"Bina?"

"Yes, Amos. You are lost right now, somewhere between your world and mine. You cannot remain there. It will cause . . . problems."

A feeling of hopelessness consumed him. "Why do I care? All is lost!" He allowed his mind to spread, dissipate like the energy in the universe.

A calm and commanding message pushed his thoughts back together, swept him up. "Amos, come to me. You're lost. Let me help you get back."

"Back where?" Amos replied in a resistant, even petulant tone.

A feeling of calm encircled him, what one might feel when embraced in a caring hug.

"Back to your life. You are not yet complete. You must become complete before you can do anything."

Struggling against the embrace, a kernel of curiosity sprouted in him. "Complete? What do you mean?"

The embrace held him, a feeling of sympathy radiating from it.

"When I entered Kairos, I was not complete. It has created an unstable situation, a situation that could destroy life in your existence and re-organize all of the dimensions in the universe. Nothing will be able to live. The universe will simply exist with no purpose."

Amos was filled with wonder. "The universe has a purpose?"

He felt relief come from Bina, relief at his interest.

"Yes. And so do you. I'm just starting to understand it. But I am incomplete, and so much of it is hidden from me. Many of the dimensions remain hidden. I believe I can maintain the current status for a period of time, but I also know that it is unstable and could disintegrate."

Amos's thoughts centered on himself, concern growing as a feeling of loss consumed him. "Where am I?"

Urgency accompanied Bina's response. "Lost. You must find your way back. I cannot help you find your path. It is your choices that must control our destinies, the destiny."

It was too much for Amos to comprehend in one message. He still barely understood himself, much less his relationship to the universe.

"I don't understand."

Bina chose a sympathetic response, much like a companion might take the hand of a fellow traveler when walking down a dark country road. "I know. Neither do I, at least not completely. I do know that you must find your way home."

Amos remained dumfounded at what to do despite a growing feeling of unease. "But how?"

Bina released him from her embrace. "Goodbye, Amos."

Terror erupted within him as he felt himself falling into an abyss. "Wait! How? I don't understand!"

The strain of forming these thoughts proved overwhelming, and his mind shut off in a vain attempt to reboot itself.

45.

"Ensign, I think he's coming back to us."

"After all this time, doctor? I thought it was impossible."

"His mind is strong, stronger than anyone I've ever seen. But after what he went through I didn't think he would make it."

Amos lay on his back on a raised platform. He was shrouded in a thin white sheet covering everything but his face. His body appeared frail, his sunken eyes surrounded by deep dark circles. His face grey and the skin hanging loosely around his jowl.

Sarah and Dr. Daman stood on either side of a raised platform. Sarah was holding Amos's hand while the doctor focused on the monitor readings available to his mind from the network.

The room was without apparent doors, shaped like the inside of an egg. Dim lighting from the walls themselves illuminated them. The only furniture in the room besides the platform was his ancestor's eboney chair.

"Doctor, your actions helped to bring him back."

"All I did was pump his body full of chemicals that promote neuron generation. It's a miracle his neurons re-wired in the efficient way they did without conscious thought processes."

"You also kept his body alive. Thank God you could also use the empty hive to store his mind while his brain healed."

"He consumed all of the available space in the hive, and he probably could have filled hundreds of them. The size of his mind since the failed Kairos attempt is staggering!"

"Makes you wonder what he's capable of, how he managed to contain it all."

"I believe he's found another source, a source that provides energy and insight."

"Do you think he's linked to Kairos somehow?"

"No. We would have lost him if he had made permanent contact. From everything we've observed, Kairos is a singularity, consuming everything it touches. You saw how it pulled in the entire Syndicate, drained the hive in a fraction of the time we thought it would take to make the transfer. But maybe Amos has found something else, another way to communicate."

"That would be wonderful. But we need him back. Amos, come home!"

Amos opened his eyes.

"Amos, are you present? Do you know who you are?"

"I am. . . ."

"You are what, Amos?"

A look of confusion overcame him. He appeared stumped.

"Amos. . . . Amos Hare."

Sarah fell forward onto his chest and wept uncontrollably. "You're back Amos! Thank God! You're back!"

Amos's eyes shifted around the room with a rising feel of desperation.

"I am Amos. . . . I was raised in a habitat. . . . I touched Kairos." His face contorted into a look of shock, followed quickly by panic. The focus of his eyes again darted around the room before finding Sarah, who had raised her head into his field of vision.

Relief flooded over Amos's face at the sight of Sarah. Tears formed and cascaded down to the bed underneath. Sarah lowered herself and kissed Amos on the lips, her tears now falling and mixing with his. Amos's eyes remained open, his mouth moving out of sync with Sarah's. She tried to pull him closer but the sheet bound him. After an awkward embrace, she moved away to sit down in an attempt to gather herself.

His worried eyes darted around, taking in the light provided by the cave-like room. He lifted his head to focus on the sheets that cocooned him. His stare lingered on the form of his body under the sheets as he tried to lift his right arm. A puzzled look crossed his face as he realized his arm was held firmly, trapped by the sheets that were tucked under his sides.

His focus shifted to Doctor Daman, as if the man in the white coat could explain the world to him. Dr. Daman stared intently at Amos, evaluating his actions as he tried to determine his mental health.

A soft smile came to Amos's lips. "You're real," he rasped.

Dr. Daman's expression remained concerned. "Yes, Amos. I'm here."

Amos's eyes shifted back to Sarah. A smile bloomed on his face.

"My love," Amos whispered before wincing in pain.

"Yes Amos, I'm with you. We're so happy you're back with us. I love you!" Tears again streamed down her cheeks as she held his stare. She placed her hands over his cheeks and lowered her lips into a salty, wet kiss. As she pulled away, looking into his eyes again, her sobbing became uncontrollable. Her body shook as she struggled to maintain eye contact despite her body's reflexive recoil. The tears were too much, clouding her vision, and she finally gave in to her body and buried her face into Amos's shoulder, using the sheet to soak up her tears.

Amos looked at the doctor and whispered weakly, "Now I see!"

Dr. Daman looked back at Amos and smiled, fighting back tears of his own. "I believe you do."

Writing Evolved has been a transformative journey. What started as inspiration sparked by my two young daughters, Isabael and Ella, transformed into an act of love to demonstrate to them how writing and hard work can open up new worlds. I believe in leading by example and I could think of no better way to support my daughter's' interest in writing during first grade than to start writing myself. What I received in return was a joyous journey through the gates of science, across the metaphysical landscape of philosophy and finally arriving in a wondrous spiritual world that shapes my actions today.

This journey would not have been possible without the love and forgiveness of my wife Katie who works tirelessly to support the family financially and emotionally. It is her love and devotion that awakened my spirit and enabled Evolved to come into being. Without her support I would likely have returned to the lucrative world of finance, lost forever to capitalist interests.

ACKNOWLEDGMENTS

The first and second drafts of *Evolved* were little more than a research paper. The prose were dry and drawn out. KL Pereira patiently read through this early draft and found the right balance of feedback and encouragement to push me forward. Her guidance and constructive feedback through several passes were paramount to turning a draft into a book.

As later drafts unfolded I leaned more into philosophical questions, like "What is Time?" Dr. Vic Crome, who has a Phd in the Philosophy of Time, offered up a few mind-opening books on time that shifted my perception of the world and the storyline of *Evolved*. However, these books formed the basis for Kairos and the world within *Evolved*.

An awakening led me to reach out to Reverend John Allen of Congressional Church when I simply felt something was missing. Reverend Allen gave me a number of topics to explore, from Gnostic Christianity to Perennial Tradition and many specific aspects of world religions. It was through these readings that I was transformed.

A small group of writers willingly donated their time to read the manuscript and offer feedback. Susanna Baird, Chris Grossman and Rob Klink helped smooth out many of the rough patches in the work and improve its pacing, character development and inconsistencies.

After another round of revisions I decided I was getting close, so I hired David Cathcart to clean up the manuscript. It was in desperate need of a good copy editing, which David performed well, while providing valuable insights to the structure.

With the manuscript mostly baked I switched to business and hired Sharon Bially with BookSavvy PR. She helped hold my hand through the process and offer some much needed assistance on timeline. Her expertise as a publicist has been invaluable, helping the presentation of the web page and social media, and guiding me through the steps of marketing the book.

9 780997 984507